NOWHERE TO RUN

When he entered the room, she was propped up with three pillows, her nostrils a little more flared than Clark remembered last, her lips a little bluer and trembling slightly.

"Clark, I think I need a little more oxygen. I have the strangest sensation right here—" she gestured to her throat. "It's like—like I'm choking."

Clark's eyes rounded at the word *choking*. It was the original meaning of the word *angina*.

"What's going on, Doctor?" the son demanded. "She did this before her last heart attack."

Clark stepped into the hallway and pulled a manual from his white coat pocket.

He glanced up half-embarrassed at the nurse who was looking at him expectantly. "What would you like me to do . . . Doctor?"

Clark blinked. "Let's get her some oxygen. One hundred percent face mask. STAT. Did you page the intern?"

"Three times. He's not answering."

Clark turned away. "I'll get him myself."

The nurse grabbed his shoulder. "I don't think you'd better go anywhere right now. You're needed in there."

He felt his feet move into the room toward the woman's tight, shallow breathing. In a surge of adrenaline and confidence and fear, the thought struck him that he could help this woman, that disaster might strike but he would react coolly and appropriately. At some point during the crisis, he began looking at himself not so much as a terrified medical student, but as a doctor.

By the same author

A MATTER OF TRUST

Available from HarperPaperbacks

Rites of PASSAGE

Mark Vakkur

HarperPaperbacks
A Division of HarperCollins*Publishers*

HarperPaperbacks *A Division of* HarperCollins*Publishers*
10 East 53rd Street, New York, N.Y. 10022

Cover illustration by Mitchell Hooks

First printing: October 1994

Printed in the United States of America

HarperPaperbacks and colophon are trademarks of HarperCollins*Publishers*

❖ 10 9 8 7 6 5 4 3 2 1

To Susan:
    my favorite
        pediatrician,
            internist,
                best friend, and
                  wife

ACKNOWLEDGMENTS

To Susan, for the inspiration, love, and encouragement, and for demonstrating again and again that competence does not have to come at the price of compassion. Your technical and editorial skills helped improve the quality of care delivered to my characters. I'm still your biggest fan!

To my father, a neurologist, for teaching me never to be satisfied with a half truth, but always to grapple with the larger questions, however painful, and for coaxing me, in your own way, to take the road less traveled.

To my mother, once a medical student yourself, for challenging me never to let my mind become stultified by the grind of medicine, and for passing on to me that bizarre Australian sense of humor.

To my editor, Jessica K. Lichtenstein, for once again demonstrating your keen insight and doing your editorial magic over a manuscript that was probably very rough at the edges when it reached your desk. Your encouragement, gentle criticism, and invaluable guidance are appreciated once again.

To my agent, Richard Curtis, for challenging me to pursue this deal, even though the idea of selling a book I had not yet written terrified me.

To Duke University School of Medicine and Medical Center, for providing me with some of the most unusual years of my life, giving me the opportunity to serve as a medical student, as an intern in internal medicine and pediatrics, and as a resident in psychiatry, and for showing me that I didn't really need all that much sleep anyway.

To the hundreds of patients who gave me the awesome privilege of entering your lives and helping you through some difficult times; the hope, courage, and nobility I observed remind me what is at stake in the training of today's physicians and why it is so crucial to infuse humanity and decency into medical school and residency training programs.

Rites of
PASSAGE

THE WORLD ACCORDING TO JEB

Mount Rosemont Medical Center rose from the center of the city like some alabaster monolith. Clark Wilson stared up at the very top, fourteen stories above the street, where the Life Flight helicopter was taking off. The turbine engine screamed and three rotary blades beat the air with an angry *wop wop*, then the white-and-red chopper lifted into the sky, dropped its nose, and swooped out of sight between two buildings.

It was a powerful feeling to watch it disappear. Clark quickened his step.

So this was it. After two years and forty thousand dollars of debt, after memorizing a thousand and one biochemical pathways, the name of every bone in the human body and the insertion and origin of every muscle, as well as the indications and side effects of several hundred medications, he was going to lay hands on a living patient.

Today.

He lugged twenty pounds of equipment and books in his rucksack, but was oblivious to the weight. He covered the quarter mile separating the parking garage from the hospital in three minutes, then walked into the cavernous lobby of the hospital.

Clark was of medium height, square all over, with a cleft chin and broad forehead. He looked taller than he really was because of his breadth. His white coat was starched, fully buttoned, and brimming with pens, ECG calibers, a code algorithm card, and his brand-new ID clipped to his breast pocket: CLARK WILSON, MEDICAL STUDENT.

He saw her from across the lobby. She was sitting with her legs crossed, her back to the base of a fountain someone had donated to the hospital years ago. When their eyes met, she rose. "Clark, I lost you."

"Sorry. I missed the exit."

Tracy McHugh was a thin girl, with light brown hair and sky-blue eyes that seemed especially large right now. She wore a pleated green-and-blue skirt and a blue, low-cut blouse under her white coat. The outfit was at once coquettish and professional. Clark knew she was as nervous as he was; he had watched her try on over ten different outfits before settling on this one.

"Nervous?" He squeezed her shoulder as they headed toward the elevators.

"I probably should be, but I'm not. How about you?"

"I've been through worse." He ran one hand through his hair. He felt the ridge of flesh under his fingers, all that was left of the surgical scar.

Tracy's eyes met his again. "You sure you're ready for this?"

"Of course."

"They would have given you six weeks of medical leave."

"To do what? Sit around and worry? That would just be worse." He grinned and punched her in the shoulder. "I'm okay."

He had been going out with Tracy since midway through first year and they had been a unit ever since. It was only natural therefore that when Tracy asked him that summer to move in, Clark said yes. The novelty of living together hadn't yet worn off. They had driven in separate cars, since neither of them knew what time the other would be coming home that evening.

Or even if they'd be coming home at all; there was a one-in-three possibility they would be on call that night and have to sleep in the hospital call room.

They were alone in the elevator. It was all glass and chrome and black quartz, like the rest of the hospital. They stepped out on the sixth floor.

The sunlight slanted in through the windows in the patients' rooms, glinting off the linoleum floors. One patient was standing up, shaving. He waved to them when they passed.

"This won't be so bad," Tracy said.

They passed another room. The door was open, but the curtain was drawn around the bed. Someone was groaning and a man was saying in a loud voice: "You have to hold still, Mr. Thompson. We're almost done. Just a little more." The air was thick with the smell of shit.

"It'll be fun," Clark said.

They reached a door marked PHYSICIANS' WORKROOM.

"This is where they said to meet, right?"

She nodded. Inside, a tall red-bearded man sat with his feet propped up on a table, a local newspaper held open before him. He wore khaki pants and beat-up tennis shoes. "So you must be the new studs." He didn't look up at first. He carefully folded the paper and stretched his hand toward them. "I'm Jeb Morris, your resident. You're nine minutes early, but that's okay. If it was my nine minutes, I'd be anywhere but here, but that's your choice. Take a seat." They sat at the long oak table half-covered with book bags, blood-drawing equipment, and patient charts. A printer made an electrical farting sound in the distance.

"The Department of Medicine will give you a formal orientation later today, but most of that will be useless information. The things you really need to know I'll teach you." The man blinked several times each time he spoke. He sipped from a large coffee mug stenciled with the words TRUST ME, I'M A DOCTOR.

"We round in half an hour, but since you're here, why don't you guys each adopt a patient? Clark, you take Mr. Lehman. He's pretty straightforward—a forty-six-year-old guy who's shot his lungs to shit with two packs of cigarettes a day every day for the past fifty years. Go see him and tell me what you think."

Clark set down his bag. "Right now?"

"No, sometime tomorrow." Jeb snorted into his mug. "Of course right now. Don't make any big deal of this—just talk to him."

Clark pulled from his bag everything he'd been trained to use: his stethoscope, an ophthalmoscope, three differently pitched tuning forks, a reflex hammer, a penlight, a tongue depressor, and two cotton swabs. He reached for more equipment, but Jeb stopped him.

"Clark, what are you going to do to that man, anyway?"

Clark felt his ears burn. This wasn't a good way to begin, not at all. Even Tracy looked amused. "A complete physical examination."

Jeb scratched at a spot under his beard and grinned. He pulled from Clark's pockets all his instruments except one: the stethoscope. "Take all that other stuff back to the medical center store and get a refund. You'll never use it again."

"But how can I examine him if I don't—"

"Just get his story. Then listen to his lungs, look him over, and come back to see me." Jeb looked at his watch. "It shouldn't take more than fifteen minutes."

As Clark stepped toward the door he was almost flattened by a blur of white carrying the scent of perspiration and fear. "Ohgodohgodohgodohgodohgod."

Jeb reached out his hand and stopped the blur. "What is it now, Bob?"

"I screwed up. I mean, really screwed up."

"You're an intern—that's your job. What did you do?"

Bob Graves peeled off two soiled latex gloves and tossed them in a trash can. He washed the talcum powder from his hands, then toyed with the buttons of his white coat and wiped a bead of sweat from his forehead. He was about Jeb's size, except stockier. He had long, wavy blond hair now matted down against his skull. He looked as though he were about to cry. Completely oblivious to Tracy and Clark, he said, "While I was disimpacting Mr. Thompson, it hit me—I wrote Mr. Johnson's orders in Mr. Person's chart."

"What did you write for?"

"Gentamicin and heparin."

Jeb thought about that a moment. "And I suppose you wrote Person's orders in Johnson's chart? I mean, that would only be fair."

The intern waved his hands through the air. "That's just it. I have no idea whose chart I wrote Person's orders in. But I know I wrote them."

"And what's Person to get?"

"A soapsuds enema."

Jeb smiled. "So someone in this hospital will have cleaner bowels than they're supposed to. That ain't so bad. The heparin stuff is, though. Did he actually get a dose?"

Bob shook his head. "Nope. The nurses caught it."

Jeb nodded. "Fine. Go hunt down Person's orders. But first I need a BP check."

Bob rolled his eyes. "Not now. I don't have time."

"You always have time. Toss me that blood pressure cuff, would you, Clark?"

Clark watched as the intern was commanded into a chair by the door. Bob pulled off his white coat and rolled up his shirtsleeve. Both armpits were wet with sweat. Jeb leaned over Bob and put the bell of his stethoscope against the crook of his arm as he inflated the blood pressure cuff. "Aha! That's a record." He ripped off the Velcro cuff and let the cuff deflate. Then he grabbed a piece of orange chalk from a tray at a blackboard, erased an old number, and scribbled: "185/85."

The intern had already pulled on his coat and was headed back out the door.

"He just set a record. Any day now he'll break two hundred systolic." Jeb plopped down in a chair and kicked his feet up on a table. "What are you looking at, Clark? I bet him at the beginning of internship that at least once his blood pressure would exceed two hundred systolic. If it does, he owes me fifty bucks."

"I see." Clark stepped into the hallway, wondering if he was working for a lunatic.

Whatever the case, Clark was finally going to see a patient. *His* patient. Someone he'd be responsible for, take care of, help bring back to health. He smiled at the thought.

Clark walked down the hall and into Mr. Lehman's room. The sunlight was blinding now and *The Price Is Right* blared on the television mounted on a mechanical arm over the bed. "Mr. Lehman?"

"That's me." He was a man with a swirl of black-gray hair running like a tornado down his chest. He sat at the edge of his bed, leaning forward to speak, and pursed his lips between sentences. The muscles of his neck flared with each breath. Tiny blue blood vessels crisscrossed the man's nose.

"My name is Clark Wilson, a third-year medical student. I'm here to interview you, to get your story."

"What the hell for? It's all in the chart."

"Just one more time, if you would, sir."

Lehman's neck muscles flared and relaxed, flared and relaxed. It made Clark aware of his own breathing. Somebody on television was trying to guess the price of a bottle of concentrated orange juice.

Clark sat in a visitor's chair and pulled out a notepad.

"So what brings you here?" He had been told to begin as broadly as possible, to give the patient unstructured questions, to let him expand as much as possible.

"My wife."

"What's that, sir?"

"My wife, she brought me here. It's what you asked."

"But more generally?"

Lehman leaned back in the bed. His pajamas were far too small for him; they bulged at his midsection. "I got the breathing disease."

A bell rang on the television set and the contestant jumped up and down. She was off by only five cents.

"What kind of breathing disease?"

"Jesus, boy, I don't know. I'm not the doctor. It's in my chart."

"I'd like to hear it from you."

"You just did. I got the breathing disease."

Clark nodded. Maybe he should start with something easier, more concrete. "Do you smoke?"

"No. I quit."

Clark scribbled that down. "And when did you quit?"

The patient looked at his watch. "About half an hour ago."

A buzzer went off on the TV and the woman who had guessed the concentrated-orange-juice price correctly had lost her chance at winning ten thousand dollars. But she won a year's supply of rice, or something like that.

Clark leaned forward. "Do you mind if I turn down the TV?"

"Turn it off, for all I care."

He did.

"Now tell me—do you have difficulty breathing now?"

"Hell, yes, after answering all these questions."

Clark hung his head. This was going nowhere. Well, there was always the physical exam. Something objective. Something he could report to Jeb. He rose, pulling his stethoscope from his pocket. "Let me take a listen to your lungs, sir."

Mr. Lehman said nothing as Clark touched the bell of his stethoscope to the man's chest. Wherever he listened, the medical student heard a singsong sound like gale-force winds through a ship's rigging.

"Thank you, sir. Is there anything we can get for you?"

"Yes. A woman. A succulent blond one, with big tits, if you wouldn't mind."

"I'll see if I can write an order for one."

"Please do."

In all that time Clark had learned nothing. He stepped out of the room with a growing sense of failure and frustration.

Jeb pulled down his feet and stared up at him when Clark entered the workroom. "So what should we do with your patient?"

"Shoot him."

"Not a therapeutic option. What did you learn?"

Clark told him. "He quit smoking half an hour ago and has 'breathing disease,' whatever that means. That's all."

"What about your physical exam?"

"He wheezes. You could hear that from across the room."

"No, even from the cafeteria downstairs. Excellent." The resident winked. "You just did your first workup. Flesh it out with a few thousand words and you're set."

"I didn't learn a thing."

"Of course not. Here, this is where you'll learn about him." Jeb tossed Clark a manila-bound tome.

"What's this?"

"His old medical chart. Remember this—the old chart is your friend."

Clark sat down and thumbed through the first few pages. "I'll never get through it."

"Of course not. Most of it's bullshit. Here." Jeb flipped through the chart.

"What are you looking for?"

"Something typed. Aha. His last discharge summary. Read that and skim the rest. Go on."

Clark ran his eyes over the text:

This is the fourteenth admission for Hugo Lehman over the past two years. Mr. Lehman is a forty-six-year-old white male with a 100 pack-year smoking history, COPD, CAD s/p CABG x 3, angina, hypothyroidism, hyperlipidemia, chronic noncompliance, Type II diabetes mellitus, alcohol abuse and PUD, who presents now for COPD flare.

"I don't understand half of this."
"You will. Just write it down for now."

He was in his usual state of poor health until two days prior to admission, when he became more short of breath than usual, developed a cough productive of green-yellow sputum, and was unable to complete his normal activities of daily living (Mr. Lehman has a bed-to-couch existence).

Once through the bog of acronyms, Clark could understand most of the rest. He looked up when he was done.
"Now flip to the emergency-room note. That's from today. Anything new?"
Clark read through the note:

46 y/o WM w/ CAD, COPD, s/p CABG, Type II DM, ETOH and TOB abuse. Patient was in his usual state of poor health until 24 hours prior to admission, when he developed SOB, cough → green-yellow sputum, and exercise intolerance.

"It's the same thing."
"Exactly. So what are you going to do for him?"
Clark pursed his lips. "Well, I suppose I could—"
Jeb stopped him with a wave of his hand. "You're thinking too much. What did they do for him last time?"

Clark scanned the discharge summary. "It looks like they gave him IV steroids, supplemental oxygen, and a bunch of breathing treatments."

"Excellent. Did it work?"

"I think so—he was discharged four days later."

"Then it will work again. Your assessment and plan are all there in the old chart. This is a true no-brainer. Next patient."

Clark plopped himself down into a chair and pushed the old chart away. "This seems too easy."

"Of course it is. That's why the attending will want to see a fifteen-page discussion of chronic obstructive pulmonary disease on your write-up tomorrow. Gives you something to do. Also, it'll take a couple hours to draw up his admit orders, write up all that we just discussed, and get his labwork drawn and flowed. But before you do any of that, our man's going to need an arterial blood gas." Jeb smiled. "This is a sentimental moment—your first procedure. Come on."

He rose, pulled on his white coat, grabbed a handful of supplies, and walked to Mr. Lehman's room. "Hello, again."

"Hey, Doc." Mr. Lehman put down a fishing magazine he was reading and stared up at them.

"Gotta play mosquito again, I'm afraid. We need more blood." The resident pulled on a pair of latex gloves.

Lehman shook his head. "Are you guys starting a blood bank in my name or something?"

Jeb rolled back the man's pajama sleeve, flipped over his hand so that his wrist was exposed, and felt for the radial artery pulse. "This is going to hurt, sir. I'm not going to lie to you. Take some deep breaths and think about something pleasant."

"Like getting laid."

"Not that pleasant." Jeb turned to Clark. "Once you got the pulse centered under your finger, go down straight. Plunge for the artery. You'll feel a lot of crunching and the patient probably will squirm, but just keep going deep and true until you get bright red blood pulsing back into your syringe." The resident paused a moment, concentrated on the wrist, then stabbed. Half the needle disappeared in the man's wrist, then a tiny pulse of blood appeared in the syringe.

"Thar she blows." He withdrew the needle after filling the syringe, then clamped a piece of gauze over the wound.

Clark followed Jeb into the hall and watched him sink the syringe into a cup of ice. "You went pretty deep."

"That's where the artery lives."

"He looked like he was in pain."

"He'll be in more pain when you do it because you're going to be mucking around in his wrist, ripping up all sorts of nerves and shit, but that's how you learn. You do the next one, then teach Tracy to do one, too. Monkey see, monkey do, monkey teach. Nothing to it, huh?"

When Clark reached the workroom, Tracy was reading over something she had written. She looked up at him and smiled.

"I have the sweetest patient," she said.

"Mine doesn't talk."

"Is he mute?"

"No, he just doesn't like me."

Tracy touched the back of his hand. "Well, you should meet mine. Mr. Thurgood's a regular charmer. Told me I looked just like his daughter, except twice as pretty."

"So maybe you can go out with him when he's discharged."

He closed the door and sat next to her. "What do you think of Jeb?"

She touched her pen to her lips. "He seems okay."

"Well I think he's a lunatic."

The door flew open and there was another sweep of white as Bob whooshed into the room, grabbed an instrument from a book bag, and whooshed out, trailed by a stream of "Ohgodohgodohgod."

The door opened again and Jeb stepped into the room. "Tracy, how's your patient? I haven't a had a chance to see him yet."

"Well, if you want my opinion, I don't think he should be in the hospital."

"That's your expert medical opinion, huh?"

Tracy studied his face for signs of sarcasm. Jeb was deadpan. "I've only been doing this for twenty minutes, but Mr. Thurgood looks good. He's feeling fine except for a little cough and some weight loss—twenty pounds over the last year."

Jeb rubbed his eyes. "So we must all be pretty stupid to have let him in this place. Good thing you came along—now I'll just let him know he can go."

Tracy pursed her lips. "Fine. It's my first day. It's easy to make me look stupid. So tell me what I'm missing."

Jeb smiled at her. "You tell me."

Tracy ran her index finger over her notes. "Well, they did find a four-centimeter mass on his chest X ray."

"Hmm. Do you have the film?"

Tracy nodded. "He brought it up with him from the emergency room." She pulled out the film and hung it on a light box on the wall. She hit a light switch, illuminating a shadow of the man's chest. "It's here," Tracy said. She pointed to an area marked off in grease pen with hash marks.

Jeb stroked his chin and scrunched up his eyes. "Uh oh. The old grease-pen sign."

Clark leaned forward to make out the ghostlike swirl of white. It looked like a tiny hurricane in one of those satellite pictures of earth taken from thousands of miles overhead.

"You kind of have to hallucinate to see that, don't you?" Jeb said. "But it's there." He turned to Tracy. "You left out the most important part of his history. Where's his old chart?"

"He doesn't have one. This is the first time the guy's ever been to the hospital for anything."

Jeb gulped at his coffee. "Then we have to pretend we're doctors and think. Let's see—how old is he?"

"Fifty-six."

"And has he been trying to lose weight?"

"Nope. He said he's been eating like a horse."

"Smoker?"

"He quit."

Clark smiled at her. "When?"

She looked through her notes. "He didn't say."

Jeb studied Clark. "What are you thinking?"

"That he quit this afternoon, just like my patient."

Jeb grinned. "You're catching on quick. We'll make a cynic of you yet there, Clark." He turned back to Tracy. "So what do you think is going on?"

Tracy cleared her throat. "He could have a viral bronchitis."

"Possible. And he could have a mole on his ass. What's making him lose this weight?"

Tracy puffed out her cheeks. "Well, I suppose there's a remote chance he has tuberculosis."

"Good. How bad is his cough?"

"Not so bad."

"Did he cough up any blood?"

"Yes."

"Hmm. Any night sweats, chills, exposure to anyone with TB?"

"No."

"Does he look real sick to you?"

"No."

"So TB's less likely. Possible, but less likely. I'm still waiting for you to tell me the next most important piece of information."

Tracy frowned. "I don't understand."

"That's okay. This is only your first day." He sat next to her and looked her in the eye. "Is he *nice*?"

She looked to Clark as though for explanation, then back at Jeb. "Yes, as a matter of fact, he's *very* nice."

Jeb threw back his head and groaned. "Oh, no!" He picked up a phone and punched a number.

Tracy was confused. "I don't get it."

"Of course not. They don't teach you this in medical

school." He spoke into the phone. "CT, please." While he waited, he covered the phone with his hand and looked at Tracy. "Nice guys get the worst diseases. Tracy, I think I know what your man has." Someone came on line. He uncovered the phone. "Hey, this is Dr. Morris calling again. I have a patient up here who needs a chest CT. What's your schedule look like today? Think you could squeeze him in? Great. We'll send him down."

He hung up the phone and stepped out of the room. They could hear him giving orders to the nurses.

Tracy leaned toward Clark and whispered, "I think you're right."

"How so?"

"I think he *is* a lunatic."

Jeb reentered the room and sat down.

"So what does he have?" Tracy demanded.

"A goomba."

"A what?" Clark searched through his notes, as though he might find the answer there.

"The world's greatest weight-loss program." Jeb had picked up the phone again and dialed another number. "And it's free."

Tracy seemed to understand what he was saying. Clark was at least three or four logical steps behind her. But then again, that was nothing new; Tracy was near the top of her class. Clark struggled to stay out of the bottom fifth. "Tracy, what is he talking about?" he whispered to her.

She was about to say something when Jeb spoke into the phone. "Yeah, may I have whoever's on call for pulmonary? Sure, I'll wait." He held his hand over the receiver. "Tumor's the rumor." The resident scribbled something onto a notecard. "Tissue's the issue." He winked. "Cancer's the answer."

Tracy looked chagrined. "Lung cancer was in my differential, of course, but I thought he'd look sicker."

"You thought wrong." The sunlight streaming in through a window was blotted out by a cloud. "We'll order some tests to confirm he's got lung cancer."

Tracy bit the inside of her lip. She looked worried. "How can you be so sure?"

"Experience."

Tracy found a textbook of medicine, a ten-pound, two-thousand-page monster chained to a corner of the workroom. She began leafing through it.

Jeb tapped his pen on the desk as he waited for someone to come on-line. "By the way, we're on call tonight." Then he cleared his throat and spoke into the phone. "Pulmonary? Hey, this is Jeb Morris. I think we got another goomba. That's right—number three this week. Are you guys still running that three-for-one special? Just add it to my tab. I'll leave a consult sheet on the front of the chart. The patient's name is Thurgood. Thanks." He hung up the phone and turned to them. "So, in about forty-eight hours we can tell him he's got cancer." He blinked at them. "Welcome to the wonderful world of modern medicine." When he pushed himself out of his chair, his knees made a popping sound. "Now we round."

Tracy sighed as she got up. Clark noted that she seemed to be taking this personally. When Jeb wasn't looking, Clark put a hand on her shoulder. "You okay?"

She brushed it off and frowned at him. "Of course."

They could feel rather than hear the entrance of the intern. Bob created a breeze wherever he went, he flew so fast. Like a nervous bird, he'd dart in one direction, then another, holding his hand over his forehead to help jolt some memory. "Now what am I forgetting?" he asked no one in particular.

"I don't know, but it has to wait," Jeb told him. "We're rounding."

They moved into the nursing station where all the patients' charts were kept in a circular rack. Jeb spun it round, stopping it four times to withdraw four charts. "Our census is low," he said. "And with any luck we'll diurese a few today." He turned to the intern. "Any progress on the nursing home front?"

"Nope. They sold Winfield's bed."

"Bastards. He was a dump in the first place." Jeb lugged the charts under his arm into the hallway. "Why don't you tell the studs about Mr. Winfield? He's our first stop anyway."

Bob consulted an index card. "Mr. Winfield is a seventy-two-year-old white male with chronic renal insufficiency, cancer of the—"

Jeb cut him off. "They don't need to hear all that." He turned to the students. "Winfield is a train wreck and a dumped train wreck at that. He's demented, has two metastatic cancers, and has at least fourteen different reasons he should be dead. But he's too sick and old to die, so the nursing home got tired of taking care of him. They shunted him here and now they sold his bed."

Clark thought Jeb was joking. "They can't do that."

"They did," Bob said. "I just spoke with them."

"But isn't that illegal?" Tracy asked.

"No, it's American medicine. Let's go see the man."

His room was empty. Jeb looked down the hall and smiled. "There he is."

Clark saw a withered old man strapped to a wheelchair with canvas restraints. His arms and legs were free so he could wheel himself around. On the back of the wheelchair was a sign that said in big black letters: HI. MY NAME IS MR. WINFIELD. PLEASE DO NOT LET ME GET ON THE ELEVATOR. IF YOU SEE ME UNESCORTED, PLEASE CALL WARD 6 WEST IMMEDIATELY. THANK YOU.

"Mr. Winfield, how are you today?" Jeb's voice boomed with friendliness. "Seen better days, huh?"

Mr. Winfield turned to them, searched Jeb's face with a blank expression, and opened his mouth a little wider. They surrounded the wheelchair and stared down at him.

"His potassium was a little low, so I supplemented him with forty by mouth," Bob said.

"Strong work. We can't do shit for this man, but by God we can tune his labs."

Winfield smiled for no reason, as though he understood and agreed with what Jeb had said. He reached up and tugged on Clark's sleeve. "Aru ruffa ru?"

Clark studied the fingernails resting on his sleeve—they were the color of rust, with black-purple specks under them.

"Answer the man," Jeb commanded.

Clark leaned toward the patient. "What's that, sir?"

Winfield now laughed, sagged forward, and let a glob of saliva dribble into his lap. "Aru ruffa ru, aru ruffa ru. Ru commy now."

Jeb tapped Winfield on the shoulder. "That's right, sir. Couldn't have said it better myself." He ran his stethoscope over the man's back, then took his pulse.

Clark watched him carefully. "What are you checking for?"

"Nothing. It just gives me something to do." Jeb winked at Tracy. "Next patient."

"That'd be Mr. Lehman," Bob said.

They walked into the patient's room to find him watching a talk show. Jeb knocked twice on the open door. "Mind if we visit for a minute?"

Clark was surprised to see Lehman smile when Jeb entered. "How did that blood gas turn out, Doc?"

"Not back yet. They'll page me with it in a minute. How you doing?" There was a cheerful, singsong quality to Jeb's voice when he spoke to patients.

"A lot better before my interrogation this morning." Mr. Lehman recognized Clark. "That man came in here asking a thousand and one questions, questions I already answered for you."

"Ah, now you know that's how we do business, Mr. Lehman. He's a doctor in training. It's his job."

"Well, have him train on someone else."

"Mr. Lehman, you don't really mean that, do you?"

Lehman crossed his arms. "No, I suppose I don't. But it gets so aggravating sometimes."

Jeb nodded. "A teaching hospital's a terrible place to come when you're sick, is what I always say."

"Ain't that the truth."

"So how's the breathing?"

"Fine."

"Any shortness of breath, difficulty breathing, nausea, vomiting, diarrhea, chest pain, sweating, swelling of your limbs and joints, anything bad?"

Lehman nodded. "Yes, yes, no, no, no, no, no, no, no. I think I got them all."

"Good." Jeb ran his stethoscope up and down the man's back, watched him breathe a minute, then patted him on the shoulder. "We'll have you tuned up and ready to go in a day or two, how's that sound?"

"Great."

A nurse entered the room, handed Jeb a slip of paper, then left. "Thanks, Maria," he called, then studied the computer printout. "This is your blood gas, Mr. Lehman. These numbers look all right. Not great, but all right. Let us know if you need anything."

When they were in the hall, Jeb said, "You're taking great care of him, Clark."

"But I haven't done anything."

"Exactly. Next patient. Mr. Thurgood, I believe." Jeb clucked his tongue. "Poor guy has cancer and he doesn't even know it yet."

"Neither do we," Tracy countered.

Jeb arched an eyebrow at her. "Perhaps not."

They could hear the sound of voices from outside Mr. Thurgood's door. There were at least three people in there, from the sound of it, and they all laughed at once.

They won't be laughing long, Clark thought.

Jeb knocked twice then stepped into the room. When Clark saw the patient, he could understand at a glance why Tracy thought the man didn't belong in the hospital. He looked young—in his fifties or so—dressed in a set of light blue pajamas that matched his eyes. His face was small and angular and now one big grin. He looked like someone who liked to be alive.

There were three women and a teenage girl in the

room. They were also grinning at something. The girl looked at Clark, then whispered something to the woman sitting next to her, who slapped her on the hand and told her to hush.

"What's this?" Jeb boomed. "A family reunion?"

The woman next to the teenage girl spoke first. "I suppose it is. We have three generations in here."

"I'm Dr. Morris."

"And I'm Anita Thurgood, Thomas's wife. This is my daughter, Emily, and my mother-in-law."

Jeb shook hands with all of them, then swept his arm toward the intern and medical students. "This is our fearless team. You've already met Dr. McHugh."

Tracy seemed a little jolted at being called Doctor, but didn't protest.

The patient said, "Yes, she is a very thoughtful young lady. She says I probably have a virus. Of course, I knew all along I didn't have anything, but just try telling that to *them*." He jerked his head toward his family.

"Now hush up, Thomas," his mother said. "We may be overreacting, but there's no harm in that. Better to drag you out here ten times than to miss a bad pneumonia or something." She didn't elaborate on that something. "Isn't that right, Doctor?" She addressed her question to Jeb.

"Absolutely, absolutely."

The woman seemed the unquestioned authority in the group. The smiles left the others' faces when she spoke and they remained silent. "You do agree, don't you, that this is all probably just some virus?"

Clark was glad that this was only his first day, that no one expected him to field questions like that. He watched Jeb, looked for some twitch in his face, some hesitation that would betray his worst thoughts. "Ma'am, it's too early to state definitively what is causing your son's symptoms." He sounded both cheerful and respectful.

"Understood." The woman elevated her chin a notch. "But what are the possibilities?"

"Well, there are several. He could have some sort of

infection—a viral bronchitis, a bacterial pneumonia, or even tuberculosis."

"Do people still get that?"

"Certainly. There are also some strange infections, such as a fungus, such as histoplasmosis."

"What else?"

Clark glanced over to see Emily staring up at him with big, round eyes. She grinned, exposing two rows of braces, and blushed.

"We must always entertain the possibility of cancer."

If the woman was shocked, she didn't show it. She nodded her head, looking almost satisfied. "That's what killed Harold, you know." Something in her daughter-in-law's expression made her say, "Now, don't be sentimental, dear. It was sentimentality and fear that kept me from taking *him* to the doctor and we all know how *he* turned out. God rest his soul." She smiled for some reason. "Stubborn old fool."

The patient was chuckling now, a throaty laugh that dissipated much of the tension. "Mom, he was ten years older than I am now when he first got sick. Besides, he smoked like a chimney—I quit."

"Only six months ago," his mother said. "And all my brothers got cancer before they were sixty. You're fifty-six. We have weak genes, son. You might as well face it."

He appealed to Jeb. "Do you see what I'm up against, Doc, living in a house full of women?"

"I'll keep my mouth shut, seeing as we're outnumbered." Then he grew serious. "I know you told Dr. McHugh your story, but why not give it to me again?"

Mr. Thurgood toyed with a button on his pajama top. "There's not much to tell, really. I was doing fine, never missed a day of work in my life. Then one morning about six months ago I got a little cough. Nothing to write home about, really, but there was blood in my tissue."

His wife looked worried. "You didn't tell me that."

"I didn't want to get you upset. Besides, it went away a day or two later."

"This went on for three days and you didn't tell me?"

The patient grinned at her. It was a sheepish, disarming grin that seemed to ask, "Now how can you be mad at me?" "The bottom line is it did go away. And I felt fine."

His wife stared at her hands. "You were not fine. You said you felt tired most of the time. Remember when we had to miss the hog roast in Martinsville because you said you weren't up to it?"

He laughed. "I had had a hard week."

"And you started losing weight. Your clothes began to sag on you."

The patient patted his abdomen, which was firm and taut, and looked up at Jeb, as though for support. "Some men would consider that a blessing, I would think."

His wife rearranged her handbag. Clark shifted his weight from one foot to the other. He was beginning to agree with Tracy; this man's wife seemed a worrywart.

"And his color's wrong," she said now. "I don't know how to describe it exactly, but he looks kind of gray in the face."

Jeb paused. "So what made you come in to see us?"

"He started coughing up blood again," his wife explained for him. "He tried to hide it from me, but I saw it on his shirt. Then I went through the laundry and saw little dabs of blood on a few others and realized something was up."

Jeb nodded. It was as though she were telling him something he had already heard, the plot to a movie he had seen countless times. "Well, we've scheduled you for a few tests. Don't eat breakfast tomorrow; we're going to pass a tube down your throat to look into your lungs. Dr. McHugh will explain all that to you later."

When they stepped back into the hallway, Jeb closed the door to the patient's room and said to Tracy, "Well, as his doctor, do you want to be the one who tells him he has cancer?"

Tracy narrowed her eyes. "We don't know that."

"We will in about a day or so. If you don't feel comfortable telling him, I will."

"No, if it comes to that, I'll do it."

Jeb nodded. He looked grim for a minute, then smiled again. "You were absolutely right—that man and his family are *nice*. The room stank of cancer. Next patient."

ORIENTATION

The seats were leather, deeply upholstered, and mahogany-colored. Clark looked around the room and watched his classmates greet each other for the first time since the two-month summer break began. "Two months too short," he heard someone say. "All I did was sleep and eat and lie in the sun."

They had bonded in the trenches of anatomy and biochemistry and pharmacology. They had studied through the night with each other, ordered midnight pizzas with each other, and tried to forget it all with each other on the weekends. And they had competed with each other, jealously watched each other's exam scores, and reassured each other time and again that they didn't care a hoot in hell what grade they got.

There were a half-dozen faces missing, faces of those who decided it wasn't for them after all or—rarely—had it decided for them by the deans. It was harder to stay out than to get in. There were three members of his current class who started a few years earlier, dropped out, then dropped back in.

Clark hadn't dropped out, had never fallen behind, but at one time it looked like he'd have to. He tried not to run his fingers over the patch of skin where the surgery had been, but knew the scar was still there. Those sitting behind him could see the tiny clearing in his forest of hair. The hair would never grow back, but if he combed it just right, you couldn't tell.

Everyone knew and that seemed to make them scared, subdued. A few friends asked Clark how his summer was, but they did it politely, almost apologetically. They knew. Everyone knew. If there was anyone who could start and sustain a good rumor, it was a medical student.

My summer was great, he wanted to tell them. I found out it was just scar tissue. They had to open me up to find out, but the pathology came back negative for malignancy.

Clark was an expert on tumors of the posterior fossa. His had been diagnosed, excised, and treated ten years before he entered medical school, eight years before he entered college. His childhood had been spent shuttling back and forth between clinics and hospitals and operating suites. He had grown up in a medical Disneyland, clutching his teddy bear as the huge white doughnut called a CAT scanner passed over his body. (He had always wanted to ask where the cat was, but had been too embarrassed to ask.) He had been told to hold still and relax while needles were shoved into his back and his arm and his wrist. It had taken three people to hold him down in the beginning as his mother looked on and let them do it to him. He could not understand that mute betrayal. But by the time he had completed his first course of radiation therapy, they had a deal: he would stay still in exchange for a toy of his choice.

His room at home was still cluttered with them.

His mother cried when they found out the tumor was killed, that it was gone, that the headaches and blurred vision and funny walk would never come back. "But we have to check every year or so," Clark remembered them saying. "Just to be sure."

So every summer he and his mother would drive the hour and a half to Mount Rosemont Medical Center for the CAT scan and physical exam. It had become a routine, something he had grown up with. He had known nothing else. It was hard to understand what life would be like without this friendly rhythm.

Clark had every reason to hate the smells and sights of the hospital, but he found himself looking forward to every visit. Even when he grew old enough to understand what was at stake, he found nothing more fascinating than sitting on the knee of the neurosurgeon who operated on him as the woman went over the CAT scan of his head.

There was no friendly chat that summer, though. Dr. Borowitz looked like an executioner as she marched into the room, addressing not Clark's mother, but Clark himself. "Clark, you always told me to be straightforward, so I'll be straightforward now. To be honest, I am worried. There's something—a high attenuation mass—on the medial surface of your cerebellum. I would like to go back in and look."

Clark, then a rising third-year medical student, knew enough to be scared. "Okay."

That wasn't supposed to happen. It was a rule. He would come back every summer, but they weren't supposed to really *find* anything. He had been through hell with the surgery and radiation therapy and it was supposed to be over. It was as though the cancer was something he outgrew, a bad memory of childhood, like chicken pox or acne.

It turned out to be nothing, a scar scare, as his mom put it, but it had jolted him back to the realization that he was different, that no matter how much he wanted to be like everyone else, he would be forever separated by that tiny bald spot, by the scar tissue underneath, by the tumor that one hundred years ago would have killed him for sure.

"Clark, I heard. I'm sorry." Clark looked to his right, annoyed that someone had violated the unspoken rule not to bring it up unless he did. And he didn't want to.

Even if it was Heather.

She had blond hair in a bobby cut. Her eyes, large, round, and green, made Clark think of the Caribbean, the way the surface of the ocean looked on those tourist posters. She had a deep tan now, despite the statistics drilled into their heads about skin cancer and ultraviolet rays.

"Hey, it was nothing."

"What do you mean? It must have been scary there for a while, not knowing and all."

"I've been through worse." It was nice, having her look at him that way, sucking in her sympathy. From anyone else it would have made him squirm, but from her, it was almost thrilling. His eyes rested on the peach fuzz on her arm, white against her bronze skin.

Heather looked around the room, then leaned toward him. "My brother had something like it. If you ever want to talk, let me know." Then she straightened, tore open the brown envelope containing her orientation materials, and said nothing more.

Clark was surprised by that exchange. He had rarely spoken to Heather before and now she seemed almost interested in him.

He wanted to say something to her, but saw she was now engrossed in a schedule, so he opened his envelope and pulled out his materials also.

The first document he pulled from the envelope was a one-page memo, one sentence long:

One of the essential qualities of the clinician is interest in humanity, for the secret of the care of the patient is in caring for the patient.

—FRANCES WELD PEABODY (1881–1927)

Clark put that aside and pulled a schedule and some miscellaneous forms out. *How to Report a Needle Stick. Dealing with the Combative Patient. Consent Forms and Confidentiality. "Do Not Resuscitate Orders" and Advanced Directives.*

The last handout was a four-page article entitled "Stress and Medical Training: Who Heals the Healers?" Clark skimmed the opening passages about the number of physicians each year who kill themselves or get divorced or abuse alcohol or drugs. He had heard the dreary statistics so often, they had become clichés.

Besides, things couldn't be that bad.

He sensed from the sudden hush in the room that someone had walked in. He looked up to see a tall, thin man stroll into the room. He wore no white coat and had already sweated through the armpits of his shirt. His face was damp with sweat. A black plastic beeper was clipped to his belt and a stethoscope was looped around his neck. "Good morning," he said. Before even sitting down, he looked at his watch, as though already anxious to move on to some other task. "I understand this is everyone's first rotation. Welcome aboard."

He looked at his watch again, then swept his gaze around the room. Twenty pairs of eyes stared back at him. "I'm Dr. Murdoch, the residency training director for the Department of Medicine and the head of your course. He pulled a handkerchief out of his pocket and wiped some sweat from his forehead. "Have you all met your house staff yet?"

Clark nodded with his classmates.

"Good. I think it's better this way, going to the wards first, then coming here for orientation afterward." He popped the tab off a diet Coke, then gulped down half its contents. "I apologize for being late. One of my residents decided to let a woman's potassium drift to seven, so her heart decided to stop beating. We coded her for thirty minutes." His beeper went off, a shrill, pulsating sound that made half the students in the room jump. He looked down at the plastic box, silenced it with one hand, then rose to his feet. "Excuse me a minute."

He grabbed a phone from the wall and punched several digits. "Murdoch here . . . That's right . . . I don't care what medical records wants. They can do the post without the chart. I told him to report by my office with the chart and all her records. We can take care of the death certificate later. This takes precedence . . . That's right." He hung up the phone and turned back to the group of students. He reminded Clark of an athlete, an athlete with a tie and button-down shirt. His movements were quick and darting, almost nervous. He gulped at his diet Coke again.

"I don't have time to say much and there's not much to say, really. You're going to work hard here, as hard as you've probably ever worked, but you should be having fun, too. If you're not having fun, you're probably doing something wrong." He didn't look like he was having too much fun, Clark noted. "But you're all big boys and girls now and you knew what you were getting into. Good luck."

He got up and left, just like that, leaving behind the scent of his perspiration and something else. Maybe that's what responsibility smells like, Clark thought.

The next person to come in was a white-haired physician in a long white coat. His name was embroidered over his left breast: Dr. Bertrand. He sat in the chair Murdoch had vacated and looked around at them all. He paused several seconds to study each face staring back at him, saying nothing for a full three minutes as his eyes made a lap around the room. By the time the psychiatrist spoke, Clark and a few others were shifting in their seats.

"I had a good friend," he began, without introduction. "A respected radiologist, an excellent clinician, a fine man. We went to medical school together. I was best man at his wedding. He had two sons and a wife. One day, about two years ago, he decided to park his car at a rest stop on the interstate and take about three hundred and fifty Imipramine tablets. To make sure he did the job right, he covered himself with gasoline and set himself on fire."

The group was absolutely silent. Clark could feel the hair on the back of his neck, brushing against the bald spot when he breathed.

"Why am I telling you this?" Dr. Bertrand removed his glasses and wiped them very methodically with a tissue in large, slow circles. "Because I am tired of losing friends. Every time I hear or read about a physician suicide, I lose a friend." He looked around the room again. "You've left the books behind now. The stresses on the wards are of a whole new flavor than you've ever known before. Most of you will cope just fine, and many of you will flourish. Each of you, however, will probably find yourself depressed at some point in your careers. If that happens, I'd like you to remember one thing and one thing only. Seven digits, far less than they'll expect you to know out there." He nodded to the hallway beyond the closed door, then rose and walked to the board. In bright green chalk, he wrote: 938-2626.

"That's all." He turned and left the room.

They were alone a minute, but no one wrote down the number. Clark looked around and his eyes met Heather's. She rolled her eyes and shook her head, her blond bob bouncing from side to side. It was nice to look at her, to dispel some of the gloom.

The students waited in silence for a few minutes. Then someone realized that that was it, that the orientation was over.

"My first patient and he's got lung cancer! Jesus." Tracy tore her sandwich in half and shoved one end in her mouth.

"We don't know that."

"Jeb seems to." She looked at Clark. "What do you think of him?"

Clark shrugged. "Well, he's an arrogant, flippant ass. Other than that, he's okay, I guess." He stirred his microwaved lasagna with his fork and waited for it to cool. "What do you think of him?"

"I don't know yet. I heard they didn't want him to have contact with medical students."

"Really? Why not?"

"There was an incident last year. I don't know all the details, but he's on some sort of probation right now. The only thing that saved him, from what I heard, was the fact that he's considered a brilliant clinician."

"Well, he's certainly an eccentric one."

They were sitting in the hospital cafeteria. It was a light, spacious room, with a glass ceiling arching high overhead, cathedrallike, and Mozart piping through the air.

The voice to Clark's right startled him. "Nice to see you guys weren't devoured by the Department of Medicine." Clark looked up to see a pair of blue eyes under a sweep of blond hair: Randolph Paisley, one of their classmates.

He was about ten years older than most of them. No one was entirely certain what he had done before medical school. Clark knew he had been a construction worker at one point, and that he had traveled through Pakistan and India alone, but otherwise Randy was a mystery.

During the first year, Randy developed a note-taking service so that only one person, who would take notes for everyone else, would have to go to class. Half the class participated. As a result, lecture attendance dwindled. The professors fought back with elaborate overheads and graphics that only those in attendance could see, then demanded reproduction of the diagrams and schematics on exams.

Randy failed two classes first year—microanatomy and biochemistry—and had to give up his summer to take them over.

Undaunted, he returned the next fall with an even better idea. He polled the third-year students for their memories of second year exams, and compiled pamphlets on each topic, such as: "110 Factoids You Must Know to Pass Pharmacology." His ultimate goal was to write a book entitled *Everything I Really Had to Know to Get Through Med School*, with a length of no more than twenty pages.

He was of medium height, with a small chin always covered with stubble. His hair was tied into a vestigial ponytail. His eyes were small and narrow, and always seemed pulled inward somehow, as though he were watching everyone else from a distance.

He wore no white coat, just a plain khaki shirt with his ID badge clipped to his collar, which was unbuttoned beneath his tie. His stethoscope hung around his neck like a pet snake.

"So how you doing, Randy?" Clark asked.

"All right. Neurology seems pretty doable. Every fourth night call and we don't have to come in on Sundays." He eased himself into a seat beside Tracy. "And it should be pretty easy; they assigned me three patients and not one of them can talk to me. Two in a coma, one demented. So I don't have to take a history."

Randy pulled out a grapefruit and carved it in halves, then fourths, then sixteenths. "So what are you guys up to tonight?"

"We're up to call."

"My condolences. But tomorrow night you're free, right?" Clark thought he caught Randy exchanging a furtive glance with Tracy.

"Yes," Tracy answered for them. "We're free."

Randy smiled at his grapefruit. "Good."

"Very good."

Clark thought he caught Tracy winking at Randy and felt a twinge of jealousy. He changed the topic. "Do they really keep us up all night?"

Tracy nodded. "If it's a busy night. That's what I heard."

"And expect us to work the next day?"

"Absolutely."

Clark puffed out his cheeks and exhaled. "Do you realize what we let ourselves in for? Call will define our lives. Every day we'll either be preparing for call, on call, or recovering from call."

Tracy nodded. "No one said it would be easy." She chewed a moment in silence, then looked at her watch. "We'd better get back to the fort."

Randy grinned at them as they headed back to the ward.

"So what was all that about tomorrow night?" Clark asked Tracy.

She arched an eyebrow. "Oh, you'll find out."

▲
HEAVY METAL
▼

Jeb was waiting for them with a coin in his hand. "The next admission is here. Who wants it?" He flipped the quarter, caught it in his palm, and slapped it onto the back of his hand. "Call it, Tracy."

"Heads."

"Tails. The patient's yours, Clark."

The patient was sitting up in bed when he came in. Clark's first thought was: Why is she in the hospital? She was dressed in a peach floral nightgown with a high ruffled neckline reading the *New Yorker*. She was a little thin, and slightly pale, but otherwise looked healthier than he was. And she was young: only twenty-three. Clark knew this from reading her bio sheet. She had never been in the hospital before, had no past medical history to speak of, and had never really even been ill until now.

A man sitting by the bedside rose when Clark entered. He was a tan, muscular guy about Clark's age, in a polo shirt and tennis shorts. When he stood up, he grinned, revealing a set of perfect incisors. "Hello, Dr. Wilson," he said cheerfully, reading Clark's name tag.

"Actually, I'm just a medical student."

"Oh, it's all the same. I'm Terrence Brooks and this is my wife, Angela."

Clark told them to sit, then pulled a notepad from one of his white coat pockets. "So what's been going on?"

"I don't know how to explain it really," the woman said. "It all started about a week ago. I had bad cramps and diarrhea, some nausea, and a headache. I thought it was just the flu, but my ears started ringing and I became very dizzy. The other thing that bothered me was this metal taste in my mouth."

"Do you have it now?"

"Yes. I can't get rid of it."

Oh, no, Clark thought. Not a hysteric.

Terrence leaned forward. "Tell the doctor about the burning in your hands."

"Oh, yes. I have this burning sensation in my hands and feet. It's awful. And I'm always weak."

Clark had been told to direct his history to focus on only the most relevant organ system involved. But here that seemed impossible: what organ system wasn't involved?

It took two hours to finish. He scribbled over three pages of notes. With a sense of panic, he realized that he had drawn no labs on this woman, had written none of her admission orders, and couldn't even read parts of what he had written.

Only focus on what's important. Well, how was he to know what was important? It was only his first day.

He decided to bag the history and move on to the physical exam. He set down his pen and approached the bedside.

It was an awesome privilege, this violation of every taboo with which he had been raised. He touched her, a perfect stranger, in places her husband probably never probed. He scanned her retinae, thrust a tongue depressor in her mouth and deliberately gagged her, pressed down hard on her abdomen until she moaned, feeling for a liver edge or a spleen tip, had her sit up, stand up, walk, and name the last ten presidents of the United States in reverse chronological order.

Then he asked Terrence to step out of the room.

When she was curled up and facing away from him, it wasn't so bad. Once the lubricant was on his gloved fingers and he was inside, he could detach himself and think about the task at hand. Normal rectal tone. No impacted feces. No lacerations or fistulae.

He withdrew his finger and smeared it on a chemically treated strip of paper, then touched a drop of solution to the substance. It turned black: positive.

This woman had trace blood in her stool.

"May I have a tissue?" She was still lying there, obediently, waiting for his command.

"Of course. I'm all done." As he handed her a tissue, avoiding her eyes, he said, "You have some blood in your stool."

"Is that bad?"

"I don't know really. I think so."

"You're just starting, aren't you?" She had wriggled onto her back, pulling her underwear on and scooching her nightgown back underneath her.

It was easier to tell her the truth, without Terrence present. "Yes."

"That was the first time you ever did that, wasn't it?"

"Yes. Could you tell?"

"No. But I can now."

Clark knew his face was red. He peeled off his gloves, rinsed the talcum off his hands, and called the husband back in.

"So what's wrong with me?"

Clark became very interested in drying his hands. "Well, it could be—that is, based on what I've seen—one must narrow down and can't overlook—it's a rather complicated picture because—um—"

"You mean you don't know?" she asked. It was a gentle question, but it hurt to admit it.

"No. Not at all."

"Well, what did the physical tell you, Doc?" Terrence asked.

"Um, it was essentially normal. Except for some decreased sensation to pinprick and vibration on her hands and feet."

"I could have told you that," she said.

"Your nails also look—well, not quite right."

Terrence gave him a funny look.

"It's his first day," she explained.

"What do you mean, not quite right?"

"These stripes, see?" He held her fingertips in the palm of his hand and pointed out a series of faint white stripes, almost imperceptible.

She scrunched up her face. "So what does that mean?" When she spoke, Clark noticed a funny odor on her breath, a kitchen smell, some sort of pungent herb maybe.

"I don't know." The veneer of authority was gone now. Clark was standing with them, an observer of her body, intrigued, but baffled.

When Clark was in the hall, he felt the same sense of failure he had experienced with Mr. Lehman. With Angela Brooks, it was a problem of too much information. He thought he knew every detail about her life from her birth to the moment she walked into the hospital. He had chronicled every pain, every itch, every cramp, but it didn't add up to anything, at least anything he could recognize.

He desperately needed someone to tell him what was important and what wasn't, what to disregard and what to focus on. With a sinking feeling, he understood that his entire medical training to that point, from his days of biology and organic chemistry in college, to his pharmacology and pathology classes in medical school, had been taught backward: he had understood how a certain disease produced certain symptoms. What no one had taught him was how to work from symptoms to disease.

He had no idea how he could function in the swirl of chest pains and belly pains and diarrheas and other complaints with which patients would assail him. How could he sort through the possibilities that could be causing this woman's illness, that could be eating away at her right now, while he waffled?

"Christ, Clark, I was starting to think you'd moved in with your patient. So what has she got?" Jeb asked, not looking up from his newspaper.

Clark closed the door to the conference room and pulled out his notes. "Too many symptoms."

Jeb folded up his paper. "What should your next question be?"

"What does the old chart show?"

"Excellent."

"But this is all we have." He handed Jeb a single sheet of paper. "That's it. A single emergency-room visit for a broken nose five years ago."

Jeb scanned the sheet, then tossed it aside. "So we're going to have to play doctor again. Tell me everything she told you, and everything you saw."

Clark did the best he could, searching his notes for anything unusual or pertinent. Jeb corrected him several times, told him how to be more systematic, less verbose. When he was finished, Jeb said nothing for several minutes, just stared at a spot on the wall over Clark's head. "Again, like Tracy, you left out a key piece of information."

Clark tried to remember what that was. "Oh. The family was nice. But I only met the husband—does that count?"

Jeb nodded, winking at him. "That's even better. Let's go visit them."

When they got in the room, Terrence was sitting by the bedside, stroking the patient's hair. He didn't seem embarrassed by that display of affection, but rose anyway, showing Jeb his perfect teeth. "I sure hope you can help us, Doc. This has been baffling us for I don't know how long."

"Well, there aren't any guarantees in this business, but we'll do the best we can." Jeb turned to the patient and asked many of the same questions Clark had, exploring some, just nodding at others. Again, there was a sense of purpose to his questioning, as though he knew where he was going, and half anticipated the answer. He reminded Clark of a lawyer.

"And how have you been eating?"

"Fine."

"Do you prepare your meals?"

"On Mondays and Thursdays. You see, Terrence and I have an agreement—I cook on those days, and he cooks on Tuesdays and Fridays. On Saturdays we go out and Wednesdays are sandwich nights."

"So Terrence cooks?"

"Better than I do."

"Is there any chance you ate any undercooked poultry?"

"Absolutely not. I had a girlfriend who got salmonella and I've been paranoid about it ever since."

"Any travel to a foreign country?"

"No. Unless you count New Jersey as a foreign country."

Jeb smiled, formed a tent with his hands, and rested his beard on the tips of his fingers. "Do you drink well water or city water?"

"Bottled water. We buy it from the store."

The resident turned to Terrence. "And you haven't been ill at all?"

"Not like this."

"Did you get any diarrhea, nausea, or vomiting?"

"Not since last summer, and that was just a virus."

Jeb nodded. He then pulled his stethoscope from his pocket and began a deliberate physical exam. It took over half an hour and ended with his studying her hands. "Dr. Wilson tells me you have interesting nails." Clark held his breath, sensing his credibility was on the line. "And they are very interesting indeed." Jeb drew out his words as he ran his eyes over her fingers. He then released her hand and smiled at her and Terrence.

"All right. We'll get some tests sent off, then get back with you."

When they were in the hall, Jeb asked, "So what do you think now?"

Clark was as clueless as before. "Giardia is a possibility."

"Does Giardia explain the numbness in her hands and feet?"

"Maybe she has two diseases."

Jeb jerked his head toward him. "Two diseases? *Two* diseases?" He gripped Clark's shoulder and shook his head. "Clark, my boy, I have so much to teach you. Patients aren't allowed to have two diseases. It's a rule—only one disease per patient per hospitalization."

Jeb released Clark's shoulder and walked on. "So does Giardia do all this?"

"I don't know."

"I'll give you a hint—it doesn't. Try again." They went to the nursing station, where Jeb flipped through and signed some charts. While he wrote he said, "I'll put you out of your misery. But not completely. I want you to think about this some more. While you're thinking I want you to do something. Here." Jeb pulled a specimen bag from a dispenser on a shelf. "Fill this with hair."

Clark was confused. "Whose?"

Jeb blinked up at him. "Well, I suppose you could put yours in there, but that wouldn't do us much good, would it?"

"No, I suppose not."

"Ask a nurse for some scissors and collect it from her head. The lab will need a good amount, so don't be timid." He rubbed his chin. "And get some pubic hair, too. Put it in a separate bag." He handed Clark another.

Clark stood there inert for a moment. "Can you tell me what this is for?"

"Yes, I could." Jeb opened another chart and started scribbling. "But you would learn more if you tried to figure it out on your own. I'll make up the labels and the specimen slips."

Terrence wasn't there when Clark returned to her room. "I need some hair," he explained.

"Oh."

"I have to take it from two sources."

She blinked twice. "Okay."

He could smell the scent of her shampoo as he held the strands of hair between his fingers. He snipped cautiously, as though he were cutting through nerves. "I'm sorry."

"Hey, if it's what you've got to do to make me better, take it all." When Clark continued to snip, she added, "You know that was just a joke, right?" Mingled with the scent of shampoo was the scent of that herb again. Clark recognized it now: garlic.

"Did you have Italian food recently?"

"No."

"Anything with garlic in it?"

"No. I hate garlic. Why? Is that the way you doctors tell your patients that their breath is bad?"

Clark shook his head. "No. It's just part of the history I forgot to ask." He filled the bag with about half a cup of hair. He figured it was enough. "Now I need a little pubic hair."

He let her pull down her panties just enough to show a little triangle of black. He wanted to finish this part quickly, so quickly that he pricked her with the head of his scissors.

"Ow!"

"I'm sorry." Then he had that bag filled, too, and it was over. "All done."

There were two knocks on the door and Terrence bounced into the room. "Hi, Doc! Honey, here's your orange juice."

"Thanks."

As he set down the cup Terrence noticed the two bags of hair. "What's that?"

"Hair samples."

"What for?"

Clark felt his ears turn red. "To be quite honest, I don't know myself. I was just sent in here to collect it."

"That sounds like the most ridiculous thing to me." Then the look of annoyance was gone, and his smile reappeared. "But you're the doctor."

When Clark tossed the two bags of hair onto the counter in front of Jeb, the resident grinned. "Strong work. You figured it out?"

"No."

Clark watched Jeb fill out the pathological specimen slips. In the blank for *Test Requested*, Jeb wrote: *Heavy metals and arsenic.*

Clark eased himself into a chair. "You think she's got some toxic exposure?"

"I ask again—was the family nice?"

"Yes."

"Well then, that's a strong prognostic factor for arsenic poisoning."

Clark shot to his feet. "I thought you said it meant she'd have a bad disease."

"That, too. These rules aren't rigid."

"Then they're not really rules, then, are they? I mean, how do you know when they apply and when they don't?"

Jeb held up a finger. "That's why medicine is an art and not a science." He finished filling out the slip and turned to Clark. "He cooks for her twice a week."

"But he brought her to the hospital! Why would he bring her here, only to have us find out he was poisoning her?"

Jeb shrugged. "Arrogance, maybe. Ignorance of what we can and can't detect. I've seen it before. Seen patients poisoned by their family members right within these hospital walls."

Clark ran his fingers through his hair. "And he just brought her an orange juice."

"I would strongly suggest that orange juice be confiscated. And write an order that the patient is to receive no further food from any family member or friend. Not Terrence, not her grandmother, no one."

Clark backed away and trotted down the hall. He tried to look casual as he strode into the room. The orange juice was half-gone. "I'll have to take that, I'm afraid."

Terrence frowned up at him. "Now really. This is getting ridiculous. What on earth for?"

"We have to test it."

"For what?"

Clark stared down at the orange juice. "For various things. Also, she's not to get any more food, except what we order for her. We need to control her environment as much as possible."

Clark held the cup of orange juice at arm's length, as though the poison might jump out and singe him, then stepped out of the room.

When Clark got to the nursing station, Jeb had made out a third slip. "Pour that juice into a specimen cup. I'll bet you ten to one it's got one hundred percent of your recommended daily allowance of arsenic."

ON CALL

t wasn't until midnight
that Clark realized what being on call really meant. Since
reporting to the hospital that morning at eight, he had
worked virtually nonstop for sixteen hours, but was less
than halfway through his workday. In eight hours, they
would begin work rounds and it would start all over
again. He would be expected to work the next day as
though he had slept all night. He would be forced to keep
moving, thinking, and working until five or so the following evening.

He was being introduced to one of the oldest, most
vehemently defended rituals in the training of a physician:
the thirty-six-hour day. Some states outlawed the practice—calling it cruel to the residents and hazardous to the
patients—but not Clark's.

He had spent all afternoon drawing blood, running
samples off to the lab, and writing up his history and physical. He was helping Bob, more out of pity than anything,
retrieving phlebotomy supplies, IV equipment, anything

that might make the intern's night a little less insane. The novelty of being part of the team, in however menial a role, kept him going.

But he could feel himself starting to sag. As he sat in the conference room, poring over his write-up, words he had written only ten minutes earlier made no sense to him. They swam on the page.

Jeb was working up a new admission. Tracy strained over an old chart, trying to understand a word some medical student had scrawled twenty years ago.

"Look at this signature," she said. "Emmanuel Gutlieb. He was a medical student then."

"So what?"

"So now he's chairman of the Department of Radiology. Just goes to show this doesn't last forever."

The hospital felt different at night. They had room and peace. The only sound in the corridor outside was that of an occasional IV machine beeping or of a patient shuffling by in his hospital-issue foam slippers. The nursing station was virtually deserted and the printer was silent.

It made it that much harder for Clark to stay awake. He found himself dozing off, then waking up again when his head slumped forward.

He woke up at one point with a start. A long string of drool connected him to his workup, forming a little pool. He wiped away the spit and glanced up to see Tracy smiling at him.

"Why not head up to the call room and get some sleep?"

"Because I've got too much to do. I haven't even read up on this guy's problems yet."

"Well, you won't be any good to anyone half-dead from exhaustion."

Jeb burst into the room, tossed three tubes of blood and an ECG printout on the table, and laughed. "Hogwash. One of the greatest myths of medicine is that exhaustion is bad. Contrary to popular belief, it enhances concentration, improves memory, and does wonders for your mood. Stay up all night every third night for three years and you'll become a machine—an efficient, non-sleep-dependent machine."

Tracy clucked her tongue. "Jeb, you know that's not true."

"Of course it isn't, but I figure if I say it enough times, I might start to believe it. Sleep is for wimps. Et cetera, et cetera." Jeb hummed as he scanned the ECG tracing. "Oh, the joys of call. You might not be able to sleep, but you'll probably get a chance to shower." He tapped on his lower lip with his pen. "A shower is worth an hour of sleep."

Tracy considered that. "So if I took eight showers, I should be completely rested."

"Something like that." Jeb continued to hum. As the night wore on he grew more animated. It was as though he thrived on sleep deprivation. "So how do you guys like medicine so far?"

Clark rubbed his eyes. "I just wish I had half a clue about what I'm doing."

Jeb chuckled. "So do I. Each year I advance to a more refined level of ignorance. I know in more detail exactly what it is I don't know. How are you holding up, Tracy?"

She nibbled on the tip of her pen. "Fine. I just wish I had some time to read."

"Read what?"

"You know. A textbook or journal article."

Jeb thumped a patient's chart. "This is your textbook. You'll learn infinitely more from studying your patients than from some book. Textbooks will only confuse you."

Clark's wristwatch alarm sounded. It was time to listen to Mr. Lehman's lungs to check if the man's wheezing had improved after another breathing treatment.

Clark got up and strolled down the hall. It wasn't so bad when he was on his feet. Life came back to him then, made it easier for him to blink the sleep away.

Mr. Lehman's room was at the end of the hall, a good fifty yards from the nursing station. Clark quickened his step when he heard the sound coming from the room.

It was a high-pitched, raspy breathing sound, quick and shallow, audible from twenty feet away. Clark burst into the room. "Mr. Lehman?"

The man was sitting up, hunched forward, staring at the floor. The great swirl of hair on his chest and back rose and fell. Lehman raised his eyes and Clark saw something in them that made him catch his own breath. There was stark, human, animal terror, and it was infectious.

This man's dying, Clark thought. He's dying right before me and I have no idea what to do.

"Sir, are you all right?"

Lehman shook his head, a trickle of saliva working its way loose from the corner of his mouth. Of course he wasn't all right.

Clark felt a million miles from the nursing station. He pushed the call button by the patient's bed and a crackly voice came over the intercom: "May I help you?"

"Yes, could you send Dr. Morris down here right away?"

There was a pause. "He's on his way."

Clark was paralyzed, confused, completely unable to think of anything rational or doctorlike to do. He knew there were a million things to check and do, but right now he couldn't think of one of them. So all he did was reach out his hand, touch Lehman's shoulder, which had the clammy feel of a dead fish, and say, "It's going to be all right, sir," which was a lie and he knew it sounded like one, but it seemed a lie Lehman wanted to believe, for the man looked up and the terror seemed to dissipate a little and the patient winked.

Watching Mr. Lehman struggling to breathe was like watching someone drowning in front of him.

Jeb trotted into the room. "Not doing so well are we, Mr. Lehman?" His voice exuded enthusiasm and infectious good cheer. Clark understood in an instant that the same tone of voice that normally sounded flippant, in a crisis sounded reassuring. The casualness reminded Clark of an airline pilot coming over the intercom during a bad storm: "Ladies and gentlemen, we seem to be experiencing a bit of turbulence up ahead. You just might want to find your way to your seats and fasten your seat belts."

The patient stared up at Jeb with enormous round eyes, then the eyelids sagged. "I can't breathe, Doc," he rasped.

"Well, that's no good." Jeb turned to a nurse who had trailed him into the room and began issuing orders in a calm, friendly voice. Clark was amazed that the man could be so unruffled. Maybe it was an act, put on for the patient. If so, it seemed to work. The man's breathing slowed perceptibly.

So did Clark's.

Bob sprinted into the room. "What's going on?" he demanded from Jeb, who turned to him and said, "Don't worry about it. It's taken care of."

Technically, managing little emergencies like this was the intern's job. The resident was just there to back him up. But Jeb took the intern by the arm and guided him to the door. "Go do whatever you were doing. I know you've got more than enough to keep your hands full without this."

"You sure?"

"Did I stutter?"

As Bob stepped out of the room a respiratory therapist came in, inserted nasal cannula into Mr. Lehman's nostrils, tuned some dials, then cranked it up.

"Three liters," Jeb said in that same calm tone.

"What do you want in your blount?"

"Albuterol point-five cc in four-point-five cc normal saline."

"Got it."

Clark was baffled by the numbers, the drugs, the doses, rattled off without hesitation or consultation.

"And let's get a STAT blood gas." Jeb turned to Clark and winked. "Do you feel up to it?"

Clark didn't, but nodded. He was now completely awake. A nurse thrust a syringe into his hand and he stepped forward. His hand trembled slightly as he prepped Lehman's wrist, which felt even clammier than the man's shoulders. It rose and fell with the man's breathing, a definite moving target.

He felt for the pulse, then lowered the needle until it contacted, then broke, the skin. He felt something crunch as he pushed deeper and deeper. Mr. Lehman held his arm as still as he could, but sucked in his breath sharply at one point. "That was bone!"

The patient was right. Clark had gone too deep. Jeb leaned over him, put a hand on his shoulder. "Steady now. You're doing fine. Just pull back, ever so slowly." Clark did and almost jumped when he saw a sudden vermilion spurt. The blood pulsed as it filled the syringe.

He pulled out, twisted off the needle, and stabbed the sample into a cup of ice. It was a little thing, but he had that same feeling of accomplishment he got when he caught a largemouth bass while fishing.

"I'll take that," the nurse said, grabbed the sample, and stepped out of the room.

Jeb issued some more orders, listened with his stethoscope to the man breathing, then backed up and watched for a minute. Clearly, the patient was doing better. The wheezing was noticeably less. Lehman even leaned back at one point and lay back on his pillows.

When the nurse returned with the values from the blood gas, Jeb looked down at them with his poker face. "Well, we'll tune you up, sir, and get you feeling better. You should start loosening up real soon."

He stepped out of the room. Clark followed him down the hall. "Is he going to be okay?"

"No, he's going to die. His lungs are shot to shit and there's not much we can do about it. But he won't die tonight." Jeb looked at him and winked. "So how does it feel to be a doctor, saving lives and all that?"

Clark rubbed the back of his neck. "You sounded so calm in there. Weren't you worried he was going to crump on us?"

"Sure I was. It's all an act, Clark. The guy had enough to be worried about without his doctor sounding worried, too."

"Am I supposed to know all those drugs and everything?"

"Not by tomorrow morning, but someday you will. Trust me."

"How?"

Jeb draped an arm around Clark's shoulder. "By not knowing them once when you're supposed to. Then you'll never forget them again. You'll never do anything wrong twice. Especially if you really screw up. It's against the rules." Jeb squeezed Clark's arm, then let go. "Maybe I should call the intensive-care unit resident and warn them they might have a new customer on the way."

Clark looked back toward Lehman's room. "Do you really think he's dying?"

Jeb looked at him and for a moment the resident seemed serious. "We're all circling the drain, Clark. Some of us are just a little closer than others." Then he looked ahead, down the hall. "Our job is to stabilize him so he can die in the unit. Having someone like him die on our service is embarrassing, know what I mean?"

It was impossible to tell if the man was joking or not.

Tracy looked up at them as they reached the nursing station. "Bob just got called away to see Mrs. Burton. She's having chest pain and shortness of breath."

Jeb nodded and sat down.

She continued to stare at him. "Aren't you going to do something?"

"Such as?" He blinked at her and waited for her response.

"I don't know. It doesn't seem Bob is very experienced. And he's flustered and overworked."

Jeb chuckled and shook his head. "And how do you expect him to gain experience?"

Tracy remained silent.

"I am supremely confident Bob can handle this beautifully," Jeb added. "Halfway through internship you should be able to handle chest pain in your sleep. And if he needs me, he'll page me." Jeb picked up a phone and punched a digit. "Operator, please page the MICU resident. I'll wait." He scratched at his armpit and addressed Clark and Tracy. "He's here tonight, boys and girls. I can feel his presence."

The students exchanged glances. "Who?"

"Mr. Death. The Grim Reaper."

Clark began to chuckle, but Jeb's face remained stony.

"He and I have spent many a night together in this hospital," Jeb said in a low voice. "I know the scent of him, how he moves, the trail he leaves."

Clark studied his face. "You're joking, right?"

Jeb said nothing.

There was the sound of footsteps behind him and a short, red-haired woman entered the room. "I'm from the intensive-care unit. What's the story here?"

Jeb told the story of Mr. Lehman. "Here's his first blood gas."

"Wow. Is this on room air?"

"Yep."

"Well, this bought him a unit bed. I'll need a brief transfer note in his chart. We'll take care of the other paperwork."

Five minutes later Mr. Lehman was being wheeled down the hallway. Jeb pulled out a stack of index cards, riffled through them, and removed one. "Good work. That's one less patient we have to follow."

Tracy frowned at him. "How can you keep doing this job if you're so cynical?"

Jeb smiled. "Cynical?" He listened to the sound of the word, as though he didn't understand its meaning. "You know, Tracy, I used to be like you."

"In what way?"

"I don't know. I was once idealistic and zealous. Eager to read and learn and save humanity."

Tracy smiled. "Is that the way I come across?"

"In a word, yes." Jeb's eyes looked tired for a moment.

"So what happened?" Tracy asked.

Jeb chuckled. "Medical school and residency. Somewhere along the line, I realized that we can't do squat for eight out of ten patients who come to us. Some we even make worse."

Clark looked up from his write-up. "So why'd you stay?"

Jeb sipped at his coffee. "The puzzle. This job is one never-ending puzzle. We're detectives, searching for clues at the scene of the crime." He paused. "And maybe the two out of ten patients we could help had something to do with it."

ROUNDS

Jeb was right about at least one thing: a shower was equal to an hour of sleep. Clark found it strange watching the sun rise above the city's jagged-tooth skyline as he toweled his body dry. It didn't feel like morning at all, just like one long night that didn't want to end. He tried to blink himself awake. But after he pulled on his clothes and strode out of the call room into the hall, he knew that for the rest of the world, another day had begun.

He resented them, the secretaries and nurses and even his classmates who had had the luxury of going home to sleep. They smelled of sleep, of fresh, warm sheets, of showers at home, of a long commute with the *New York Times* in their laps.

The hospital was starting to beep again, to pick up the pace that had slackened overnight. The nurses were gathered around the chart carousel, giving report. Phlebotomists roved from room to room looking for their next victims. And the other teams were rounding, passing from room to room and patient to patient, updating each other on what had passed the night before.

Clark's head hadn't touched a pillow. He was going on twenty-five hours without sleep and by the end of the day it would be over thirty-six. One thing after another had kept him up the night before until he found himself staring at a textbook of medicine as the eastern sky was turning pink, not remembering how or why he had turned to that particular page or what on earth he was reading.

"Get in the shower," commanded Jeb, who had seemed only a little slowed as the night wore on.

Clark now searched for Jeb, wondering how he would drag himself through this day. His feet seemed heavier and his steps seemed longer. Everywhere was uphill. It seemed he had been on a long, international flight through four time zones while the rest of the world stayed still.

He ran into Tracy by the elevators. "You look about as bad as I feel," he told her.

"I'm okay," she said, rubbing her eyes with the back of her hands. They walked toward the nursing station. "Do you think there's any way we can present our patients from memory to Dr. Murdoch during attending rounds?"

"We'll just have to wing it the best we can." Clark shook his head as the image of Tracy went blurry for an instant.

"Clark, are you okay?"

"I'm fine." He was tired of answering that question. Everyone, from his mother to his neurosurgeon to his worried classmates, always seemed to be asking him.

And he was always asking himself.

He ran his fingers over the ridge of scar tissue on the back of his head and wondered if his body could take this. He had had a seizure once, six months after the first operation, and had taken an anticonvulsant for a year afterward. The medicine was slowly stopped and the seizures never recurred. Still, he worried. He knew the things that lowered his seizure threshold: sleep deprivation and caffeine, among others. He was powerless over the sleep deprivation, and he couldn't imagine trying to focus on anything without the stimulation of some coffee.

He poured himself a cup from the communal pot by the nursing station. A second pot was always brewing.

Jeb strode into the room, filled his TRUST ME, I'M A DOCTOR mug with steaming coffee, and grinned at them both. "What a great day to be a doctor, huh?" He winked at them. "So this is what being postcall feels like. Ahh."

Tracy patted her cheeks to wake herself up. "I'm going to look stupid during attending rounds."

"Of course. You're a medical student. You're supposed to look stupid. Besides, attending rounds aren't what matters. Taking care of patients is."

Clark tried to think who he would present first. He had known Mr. Lehman the best, had read up on chronic obstructive pulmonary disease, could even give a three-minute talk on the treatment of an acute flare-up, complete with drugs and dosages. But all that was for naught, now that the patient had been transferred.

It was really very inconsiderate of the man to get sick.

His only choices were to present Angela Brooks or a little old lady named Abigail Foster with fever of unknown origin whom he had admitted during the night. They were both very complex cases that could lead him down murderous paths of questions, exposing his ignorance for the entire world to see.

"I'm going to get hammered," he groaned as he studied what he had written about Brooks. He realized he was getting pieces of her story mixed up with that of Foster.

Jeb pulled on a white coat that seemed to appear from nowhere. Clark didn't even realize the resident owned one. "You'll live. Which is more than we can say for some of our patients. Let's get the charts together and get moving. We're late."

They marched down a hall to the same conference room in which they had held orientation. Murdoch, the armpits of his shirt already beginning to show his trademark perspiration stains, sat at the head of the table, tapping his watch. "Where's your intern? Let's get this show on the road."

The other team was there, too, sitting at the table in the expansive, deeply cushioned seats. They had also been on call last night, admitting patients to a ward on the other side of the hospital.

There was Erich Boorman, looking as though he had gotten a full night of sleep, his white coat starched and fully buttoned, his wavy black hair looking perfectly combed, even blow-dried, his shirt without a wrinkle, his deep red power tie knotted tight against his throat. The crease in his slacks was as sharp as the day he picked them up from the dry cleaners, whereas Clark's were wrinkled and rumpled from his abortive attempt to get fifteen minutes of sleep in the call-room bed. Every time he began to drift off, he was paged for another admission. In Clark's eyes, Erich was unquestionably the most intelligent person in the entire medical-school class, perhaps in the entire medical school. Erich was humorless, stiff, and had few friends, but Clark had a deep respect for him that transcended the fact that the guy had the personality of a fish.

Clark took one look at them and knew he was going to fall asleep if he sat. "Do you mind if I stand, sir?" he asked Murdoch.

Murdoch gave him a wry smile. "You can stand on your head, for all I care, as long as your presentation is buffed." The attending turned to Jeb. "Where's Bob?"

"Probably taking care of patients." There was a hint of irritation, even accusation in Jeb's voice.

Murdoch obviously sensed it. "You know didactic conferences take priority over nonemergent clinical duties."

Jeb stared at his coffee mug. "Sure." He pushed his chair away from the table. "I'll page him."

Before Jeb reached the phone, though, Bob bolted into the room, panting. "Sorry I'm late." His hair was tousled and he was wearing last night's scrubs.

Murdoch grunted at him. "Rough night?"

The intern nodded. "The admissions weren't so bad, but I was getting killed by crosscover." Crosscover referred to crises that came up in the night with patients that weren't on the intern's team, but for whom he was responsible when on call.

"The best way to learn," Murdoch said. "On your feet. I learned more about medicine at two in the morning than I learned at any other time of day. So who's got the first patient?"

Erich lifted a finger. "Perhaps I should start. My patient's fairly straightforward."

Murdoch, who probably knew nothing of Erich except his composite picture and maybe a summary of his first two years' academic performance, shot him the same sarcastic half smile he had given Clark a little earlier. "Straightforward, huh? We'll see." He nodded. "Go ahead."

Erich cleared his throat, removed the three notecards he had neatly arrayed in front of him on the table, and tucked them into a pocket of his white coat. He didn't begin right away but studied a spot high over Murdoch's head. The silence continued to the point that Murdoch, as were the others in the room, was tempted to swivel around and see just what it was the medical student was looking at.

Clark had seen this before, the way Erich gathered his thoughts before speaking, could almost hear the neurons discharging as what he was about to say was taking shape in his head.

When Erich spoke it was in a quiet but authoritative, unhesitating voice. "Robert Lochman is a forty-five-year-old white male with a twenty-two-year history of alcohol abuse, averaging two fifths of whiskey a day over the past ten years at least, who now presents with a three-day history of nausea, vomiting, and abdominal pain."

"Stop right there," Murdoch commanded. He turned to Clark. "Differential diagnosis."

Oh, shit. "Sir?"

"What's your differential at this point?"

Clark cleared his throat. The quiet, rhythmic cadence of Erich's words had lulled him into semiconsciousness. "I suppose one must consider—um—gastritis."

Murdoch scratched at his ear, nodded, then looked over at Tracy. "What else?"

Tracy cleared her throat. "Well, there's also peptic ulcer disease, even pancreatitis."

"Not bad."

Tracy looked toward Clark and Clark winked at her. She had no intention of showing him up—peptic ulcer disease and pancreatitis were much more elegant than gastritis—but that's the way it had been over the past two years, struggling to maintain a relationship while at the same time struggling to pretend they weren't competing.

Once, during pharmacology, the tension had risen to the point that Clark suspected Tracy had deliberately sabotaged her own grade to bring her exam score down to Clark's level; she had gone out with some friends two nights in a row before the exam, something she never would have done, after they got in a fight about something unrelated, but triggered by a comment Tracy had made that hurt Clark to the quick: "You spend so much mental energy worrying about whether that tumor will grow back that you have nothing left to study with." It hurt for two reasons—it was true, and Clark hadn't realized it had shown.

But after that was out in the open, their relationship had changed and she became one of the few people Clark felt comfortable with talking about his past—the tests and the scans and the waiting.

Now Murdoch seemed delighted that Tracy was proving that not all medical students were as incapable of forming a thought. "So, Clark"—it was a bit unsettling knowing this man had obviously memorized their names and their pictures before ever meeting them—"we have a vomiting alcoholic with belly pain. What key piece of information would you like to know at this point?"

Clark thought for a moment. "Well, I'd like to know if there was blood in his vomit."

"Outstanding. So you ask the patient, and no, he hasn't seen any blood in his vomit. He's okay, right?"

Clark ran a forefinger over his eyebrow. "From the tone of your voice, no."

Murdoch liked that; his smile broadened. "Is that a question or a response?"

"Both, I suppose."

Tracy chuckled, as did everyone in the room except Murdoch, who no longer seemed amused. "Both, you suppose. Is that what you're going to say when you're an intern and a nurse asks you whether you really want to give three hundred joules of defibrillation to a patient whose heart just stopped, or if you're just asking her?"

Tracy pursed her lips together and answered for him. "Well, I hope that by that point in his training he'll have enough experience to—"

Murdoch turned to her. "Is that right? Well, Tracy, what would you want to do next? The patient hasn't noticed any blood, so there isn't any, right?"

"Of course not. There might only be microscopic amounts of blood present."

"Excellent. And, Clark, what is the big doctor word we use to describe bloody vomitus?"

Clark struggled, but it was as though his neurons refused to fire in synchrony. He knew the word in an earlier, less sleep-deprived time, but right now he was having difficulty just stringing a sentence together. "Sir, can I buy a vowel?"

Murdoch studied Clark silently a moment and Clark wondered whether he hadn't committed a major blunder. But humor seemed the only way he could make his ignorance feel a little less painful.

Then the other half of Murdoch's face twisted into a grin. "No, you may not. But you may have the whole word. It's *hematemesis*. Tomorrow, I want you to give us all a three-minute talk on hematemesis, starting with its Greek word roots, then moving on to the three most dangerous clinical entities that you must rule out if you admit a patient with hematemesis. Got it?"

Clark nodded, scribbling down the assignment on his clipboard. He knew that anything he attempted to commit to memory at this point would be lost forever within moments.

"And another thing," Murdoch said. "Give me *numbers*. If you can't quantify it, you don't know it. I want data, not just opinions or generalizations. Percentages, proportions, incidences. Know those and you know what you're talking about. Everything else is just bullshit." Murdoch turned to Erich. "Continue with your presentation."

Clark looked at a clock over Murdoch's head: only twenty minutes had elapsed and they were only on the second sentence of the first presentation. This could easily go on until noon.

Clark fought the overwhelming urge to sleep by tightening up the muscles in his legs, holding his breath, balling up his fists, even driving the tip of his pen into the palm of his hand to use pain to keep himself awake. Nevertheless, he drifted off to sleep for a moment, waking to find everyone staring at him.

"Clark, I believe you were sleeping," Murdoch said.

"I believe I was, too, sir."

"Well, don't. People will think you're weak."

Clark almost laughed, then realized the man was serious. "But I didn't sleep at all last night."

"Is that right? Maybe we should give you the day off."

Clark had no idea where this was leading, but knew it wasn't anywhere good. He remained silent.

Murdoch studied him. "This business you're in, as you're discovering, involves work, hard work, maybe the hardest work there is. Surprise. Patient care doesn't end at five. If you expect to be a physician, you will lose sleep. It's that simple. Somehow you must learn to deal with that fact. And if you can't, then the door is that way." He pointed toward the corridor, where an exit sign glowed orange red. "Sleep is for wimps."

Murdoch turned to Erich. "Sorry about the distraction. Continue your presentation."

There were no more questions now from the attending. The presentation was a masterpiece, delivered without hesitation, without stumbling, without a single filler word. It was rumored that Erich had a photographic memory and now Clark believed it. He listened with a sense of awe and terror; the awe from his innate respect for intelligence, and terror from the sinking realization that his own presentation was woefully inadequate. Erich concluded by rattling off the Librium taper he would start the patient on to prevent seizures and delirium tremens, complete with doses and timetable.

"Suppose your alcoholic's liver was shot to hell?" Murdoch asked. "What would you use then?"

"Ativan or Serax."

Murdoch looked surprised the student knew that. "And what alternative to benzodiazepines is there for tremulousness and autonomic hyperactivity?"

"A central-acting alpha adrenergic antagonist."

"Such as?"

"Clonidine would be my first choice."

Murdoch studied Erich in silence a moment. "What specialty are you interested in?"

"I'm not sure."

The attending grinned. "That's the first question of mine you couldn't answer without hesitation. I hope you consider internal medicine." He then turned to the rest of the group. "This presentation," he announced, "was a model one. If you want to achieve honors in this course, think of what you just heard. Now let's go see the patient."

As they stepped into the hallway Clark leaned toward Tracy and whispered, "I'm dead. I mean, I'm really, really dead."

"How so?"

"My presentation. There are times I really hate Erich Boorman and this is one of them."

Tracy tugged at her pleated skirt, the same one she had been wearing since the morning before. It was now covered with lint and was matted in places. "We'll survive."

"I hope so."

As Erich handed Murdoch his patient's chart the attending's beeper went off. "One minute," he said, and trotted off. While he was on the phone Clark walked over to the chart rack and pulled one out: Angela Brooks.

Tracy was on his heels, sitting down next to him.

Clark leaned forward and closed his eyes. He felt the world swirl around him, knew that if he didn't open them immediately, he would fall asleep right where he was. With the greatest of efforts, he pried his eyelids open.

Tracy nudged him awake. "Hey, I love you," she whispered out of the blue.

He grinned at her. "Even if I fail out of medical school and become a dishwasher?"

"Even then."

She placed a hand on the back of his wrist and Clark looked her in the eye.

"I love you, too." Clark felt strange saying it with another medical student standing only ten feet away.

He turned away from her, glanced down, and flipped open the chart. He read Jeb's admission note, scanned the plan section, then realized no one had checked the arsenic from the patient's hair samples.

He hopped over to a computer terminal. All lab results were accessible by punching in his user identification code and password, then pulling down a few menus. He found Brooks's file and scrolled through her labs. Most he had already seen. He yawned.

Nothing on the arsenic yet. Jeb had said it might take a week to get back.

But Jeb was wrong.

Clark scanned the backlit green capital letters:

SAMPLE: PUBIC HAIR, SPECIMEN #1 OF 3
UNIQUE IDENTIFIER: A34552
ARSENIC: ** POSITIVE **

"Clark, what is it?"

"One of my patients is being poisoned."

He pushed the pagedown key and another sample filled the screen, then another. All three pubic-hair samples were positive for arsenic. Then he reached her scalp hair.

The last screen made him start:

SAMPLE: UNKNOWN, PRESUMED ORANGE JUICE ??
UNIQUE IDENTIFIER: A34557
ARSENIC: ** POSITIVE **

Repeatedly, he encountered: ARSENIC: ** POSITIVE **

Clark looked at Tracy, then at the screen, then back at his classmate. "Jesus, he's really poisoning her."

"Who?"

"My patient's husband."

Tracy eased herself into a chair and looked over Clark's shoulder into the computer terminal screen.

Clark felt his head spin when he rose. He would have to do that more slowly next time. Sleeplessness was a new state of being, like a foreign land he had only visited briefly, once or twice in college while pulling out papers or cramming for an exam. But then it had always been to return, after a brief foray, to the safety of the land of the living. The thought that he wouldn't see a bed for another twelve hours or so made him woozy.

"Where are you going?" Tracy asked.

"To see Jeb. I've got to tell him about this." Clark trotted out of the nursing station and down the hall.

Everything felt a little out of proportion. There was a covey of white coats at the end of the hall; he recognized Jeb and Murdoch. The attending was off the phone now and scribbling something down.

"Try not to drift off during rounds," Murdoch said.

"Yes, sir. I just had to check a lab."

"You could have checked it before rounds."

He had; it wasn't back then. But Clark said nothing. He wasn't about to launch his clinical career with a confrontation. But he did want to get Jeb's attention, to tell him about the arsenic.

He never had a chance. The group filed into Erich's patient's room, shuffling into place around a man sound asleep, snoring loudly. A network of blue and green blood vessels crisscrossed his nose and cheeks. It wasn't until they were all in place and the door was closed that Erich shook the patient's shoulders.

The man bolted awake, saw all the faces around him, then looked to Erich for explanation.

"We're rounding, sir," Erich said. "I told you about this yesterday, remember?"

"Oh, yeah, right."

Murdoch stepped forward, introduced himself, then asked the man to unbutton his shirt. When the patient's belly was exposed, Murdoch tapped on it with his fingers, asked the patient to roll onto his side, then tapped again. He pressed, inspected, asked the patient to take several deep breaths, and pressed some more. Much of it was a mystery to Clark, but Murdoch seemed to know exactly what he was doing, working systematically. At one point he got out his ink pen and asked, "Sir, is it all right if I write on you?"

"All depends what you write."

Murdoch made a few marks, measured something, then listened to the man's heart and lungs. Then he had the man hold out his hands and nodded. "How do you feel right now, overall?"

"Hung over."

Erich said, "He has a little ascites and some voluntary guarding, but no rebound and only slight tenderness to deep palpation."

"Murphy's sign?" Murdoch asked.

"Negative."

Clark didn't even know what a Murphy's sign was. He had a spasm of guilt, though, knowing he had heard of it and that he probably *should* know what it was. He jotted it down on his clipboard to look up later, adding it to a list of things he didn't know that now spanned two pages.

Murdoch studied Erich, his half smile returning. "Negative, eh? Clark, why not step forward and show us how to test for a Murphy's sign?"

The patient and everyone else in the room looked expectantly at Clark. "Well, sir, to be quite honest, I'm not sure how to do that."

"Really? Don't they teach you guys physical diagnosis anymore? Step up here and I'll talk you through it. What's it test for, by the way?"

"Well, actually, I don't know that either."

"I see. Well, what organ system does it involve?"

"I don't know."

"What's its sensitivity?"

"I don't know."

"Its specificity?"

"I don't know."

"Its positive predictive value?"

"I don't know." Clark felt his ears turn a little redder with each *I don't know*. He had no idea why Murdoch was persisting in this line of questioning, since it was obvious from the outset that Clark couldn't answer any of these questions. He was certain that Erich, not to mention Tracy and the patient, were discovering him for the imbecile that he was certain he now must be. There was a cloak of anonymity during the first two years of basic science, where tests were taken in secret and grades returned anonymously, that was gone now. It was a little like being asked to strip naked in front of your classmates; they could see you for what you were, and there was no place to hide.

Clark vowed that no matter how tired he was, he would read everything that had ever been written about

Murphy's sign before going to sleep that night. This was too painful, even more painful than sleep deprivation. And, he began to realize, it was the genius of the system, the threat of humiliation in front of your peers and your patients whipping you into shape.

Murdoch took both of Clark's hands in his and directed them onto the patient's belly, so that his fingertips pressed deep, almost under the man's rib cage. "Now tell him to take a deep breath."

When the patient did, Murdoch forced Clark's fingers deeper than he thought they would go without the man screaming in agony. The patient looked uncomfortable, but seemed to be enduring things okay.

"Do you feel anything?" Murdoch asked.

"No."

"Well, that's where the gallbladder lives. If this man had caught his breath in agony, we would call that a positive Murphy's sign, and it would be a sign of what disease?"

Clark shook his head. If he didn't know a minute ago, how could he know now? But he was tired of hearing himself say he didn't know. "Cholecystitis?"

Murdoch released Clark's hands and smiled. "That's right. And is this a test for acute or chronic cholecystitis?" he asked, turning to Tracy.

She paused. "Chronic."

There was enough uncertainty in her voice to make Murdoch smile. "You don't know, do you?"

Tracy paused again. "No."

Murdoch picked a clinical handbook out of Jeb's coat pocket and threw it at her. It was a gentle, underhand, softball pitch, but either it caught her completely off guard or she decided she wasn't going to catch it. It struck her in her shoulder, bounced off, and hit the floor, pages sprawling over the linoleum. She didn't pick it up.

No one moved for a full minute as the attending and the student stared at each other. "Nice catch," Murdoch said.

"Please don't throw things at me," Tracy returned. She then stepped away from the patient, reached down, and scooped up the handbook. A few loose pages fell out, which she collected, straightened out, and put back into place.

"Now," Murdoch commanded, "turn to the index and look up cholecystitis. Do it."

Tracy flipped through the book and came to the appropriate section.

"What does it say about Murphy's sign?"

Tracy scanned the text. "It says it's a sign of *acute* cholecystitis."

"So you were wrong?"

"Yes."

"But you guessed?"

"Yes."

"And you guessed wrong. What did I tell you about guessing?"

Tracy said nothing.

Murdoch reached out and took his handbook back.

The patient, who had watched the exchange with fascination, broke some of the tension by asking, "Can I button up my shirt?"

"Sure, go ahead," Murdoch said. He slipped the handbook back into a pocket of Jeb's white coat and turned to the patient. "Well, sir, Dr. Boorman here has told me all about his plan for you and it sounds like an excellent one. The exam of your belly was entirely normal. We'll keep you on the Librium for a few days to make sure you don't go into withdrawal, then let you go. How's that sound?"

The patient nodded. He had a large, square head, flanked by unruly gray hair. "The sooner the better."

"And stay off the booze," Murdoch said, wagging a finger at him. "I know you've heard this a hundred times, but let me be number one hundred and one. The stuff will kill you."

The patient looked indignant. "Hey, Doc, I'm done with the stuff. I swear. Never a drop again. This time is different." There were almost tears in his eyes as he said this.

"Let's hope so," Murdoch said.

As they filed out of the room Murdoch turned to Jeb. "Twenty-four hours."

"Nope. He won't make it home sober."

Murdoch sighed and pulled out his wallet. Withdrawing a twenty-dollar bill, he handed it to Jeb. "This is for Mrs. Jones. You beat me then. But let's go double or nothing that this man lasts a full day after discharge without drinking."

Jeb paused. "All right. Deal." He took the money.

Jeb turned to Clark. "Now, what was this about the arsenic?"

It was becoming obvious to the medical student that this resident had a mind like a file cabinet; he seemed capable of opening one drawer, closing it, then immediately going back to where he was in the last case. Clark himself had forgotten about the arsenic during the past few minutes.

"Well, sir, the arsenic on Brooks is positive. I mean everything—her hair, her pubic hair, even the orange juice."

Jeb looked at him and smiled, a sardonic, knowing smile. "Was there ever any doubt?" He turned to Murdoch. "He's talking about Angela Brooks, the first admission I told you about."

Murdoch nodded, then scrutinized Clark. "So, Clark, how long must she have been exposed to the arsenic for it to have been deposited in her hair?"

Here we go again, Clark thought. But now at least he was prepared. Somewhere during that infinity of time that had elapsed since the previous afternoon, he had read a half chapter of an internal-medicine textbook about this. "Um, I believe it's two weeks."

"Two weeks is correct," Murdoch continued. "Now tell me the names of the lines you saw in the patient's nails."

"The name?"

"Yes, the eponym. And stalling won't help."

Clark felt pinned like an insect by Murdoch's questions. Now that he was reminded of it again, what Clark wanted more than anything was to get to Angela's room and make sure her husband hadn't snuck her an arsenic Danish for breakfast. "I knew those twelve hours ago. Um, Aldrich-Mees lines."

"Outstanding." Murdoch twisted his mouth into one of his half smiles. "You're going to be all right, Clark. A little rusty, but you're all right." He put a hand on Clark's shoulders and gave a fatherly squeeze. "So your first night was a little rough, huh?"

It was hell, but Clark heard himself blurting out, "It wasn't so bad."

Why did he say that? It was then that he realized how much he wanted to be accepted into this little white-coated brotherhood, how much he wanted to be trading quips and bets about patients who wouldn't make it while sipping coffee from a TRUST ME, I'M A DOCTOR mug.

No, it was even more primal than that. He just wanted them to like him, or at least not to think he was stupid.

The attending fixed his small eyes on Clark again, studying for a moment his name tag as though discerning some hidden meaning in Clark's picture. "You know, Clark, you *are* all right. When I first met you, though, I thought you were another Cheeton."

Clark frowned. "Who's Cheeton?"

Jeb and Murdoch exchanged glances. "Let's just say," Murdoch said, "that he was a former student who had some difficulties adjusting to life on the wards."

Jeb made a grunting sound and began walking toward the nursing station. Murdoch followed, saying, "Cheeton might be an excellent researcher, but clinical medicine was a mistake for him."

"Well, medical school was," Jeb said.

"Same thing. I think we helped him see that."

When Jeb turned around, his eyes were narrowed. "You mean you did."

Clark found this conversation unsettling. An unspoken but palpable threat hung in the air. Erich trailed Murdoch as they walked, listening to it all.

Murdoch's smile disappeared. "When I was a medical student, we worked hard."

"And when you were a medical student," Jeb said wryly, "blacks and whites drank from different water fountains. That doesn't make it right."

Murdoch didn't see the connection. He shot Jeb an annoyed glance and continued. "The students who've rotated through here lately have been a different breed. They have this expectation that they will get through this experience without *suffering*. That's not possible. Medicine involves work and work involves suffering. The reward is that you will find yourself part of the greatest and most challenging profession possible." He put a hand on Clark's shoulder. "It's a privilege, see, and in my day, which wasn't so long ago, we kept that in mind. Do you know what the guy on the assembly line at General Motors would do to have a job like this, to be able to come in each day and take care of patients? Students today have it backward; they focus not on the magnificence of this work, but on ways to avoid it."

Clark sighed. He realized he was no longer in the back of some darkened, hushed auditorium half-asleep, completing the crossword puzzle while some lecturer droned on. He had responsibility now. Patients, in some small way, depended on him.

Murdoch jerked his head toward Jeb. "Let's go see this Brooks woman."

Clark's mind focused again on the arsenic. "So what are we going to do?"

Jeb turned to him. "Nothing. We have our answer: stop the poison. We'll let it wash out of her system."

"Are we going to press charges against the husband?"

Jeb chuckled at that. "That's not our job. We'll pass this info on to the district attorney and let the cops and lawyers handle the rest. Don't meddle in attorneys' business."

Murdoch nodded. "I hate to say it, but Jeb's right. I once stopped on the way home from the hospital to help a kid who'd been hit by a truck. I made sure he had an airway, assessed him, and did some basic shock prevention, but I knew he was as good as dead. Turned out, he ruptured his spleen. When the ambulance arrived, I let them take over and didn't hear about him until that night on the six o'clock news. He died in the OR.

"Next morning I got the notice from his parents' lawyers—they were suing me for professional negligence. I've thought it over a hundred times since then and there was nothing, absolutely nothing, that I would have done differently." Murdoch paused for a minute. "Sometimes I think I shouldn't have stopped at all."

They strode down the hall at a good clip, Clark having to trot at one point to keep up. He understood in an instant why Murdoch soaked his armpits by midday. "Can't do much for most of our patients," Jeb told him when Murdoch stepped out of earshot to drink from a water fountain. "But we can sure as hell do it *fast*."

Clark pulled the patient's chart from the rack and handed it to Dr. Murdoch. The attending opened it to Clark's write-up. Clark held his breath, remembering the hours he had spent on it, the three separate drafts he had completed at two in the morning before finally deciding which one he would place in the chart.

But it was a masterpiece, just as Jeb had asked for, with six references and over three pages of discussion. He went into the history of arsenic poisoning, how it could be detected, the difference between acute and chronic toxicity, what organ systems are affected, and possible therapies. He even discussed other heavy metals and how their clinical presentation could be differentiated from arsenic. It was a polished work. He waited proudly for Murdoch's agreement, for the man's hard-earned approval.

The attending pulled the write-up from the chart and handed it to Clark. He didn't address the medical student, who accepted the write-up without question, but turned to Jeb and said, "In the future, don't let them put their first drafts in the chart. When he's buffed it up, have him resubmit it to me."

Murdoch walked away. Jeb turned to Clark and whispered, "It's all bluff. He does this to every group. I'll just submit the same draft in a day or two; he'll never know the difference."

Clark wasn't about to create another draft. He didn't even want to look at that history-and-physical form; he just wanted—what was it exactly? A word of approval? A single grunt, maybe, an affirmation that he was part of the team?

But he wasn't to get that, at least not today. What Clark felt was a heroic effort was, after all, just his job, no more no less, and every physician in the hospital was going through or had already survived the same ordeal he had.

Jeb and Murdoch paused at Brooks's door, which was closed, and turned to him. "Clark, are you ready?"

He felt his gut tighten. "Sure." He rode a wave of adrenaline. He wanted a chance to redeem himself, to prove to Murdoch that Clark Wilson was no dumb shit.

He knocked twice on the door, then pushed it open.

It took a moment for his eyes to adjust to the darkness. The venetian blinds in the room were twisted shut and the curtains were pulled together. Angela lay in her peach nightgown, her face looking pasty and damp. She squinted up at them, tried to rise from her pillow, then lay back down.

She was alone in the room.

"Hello, Doctors," she said, her voice groggy.

"Hello, hello," Murdoch said cheerfully. "Kind of dark in here, isn't it?"

"My eyes hurt," she said. "Everything's blurry and I keep throwing up."

Murdoch nodded. "That's to be expected. You're being poisoned." He turned to Jeb. "Has she been told?"

"Not really."

She managed to prop herself up on one elbow, coming to life at the word *poison.* "What do you mean?"

Murdoch pulled out a seat by her bed, the only chair in the room, and rested one foot on it. "You've got arsenic in your hair and there was arsenic in your orange juice. It probably didn't get there by accident."

She shook her head, sliding herself away from them both, as though they were the ones who were trying to kill her. "Why? Why would anyone want to poison me?"

"I don't know." Murdoch turned to Clark. "Go ahead."

Clark cleared his throat and looked down at her. A tear was welling up in her eye; then worked its way loose, coursing down her cheek.

Clark paused, waiting for her to get control of herself. He felt like touching her, like offering some words of reassurance, but would never dream of it in front of Murdoch and Jeb. Without having been told, he knew that would be unthinkable.

"Don't stall," Murdoch commanded.

"Yes, sir. Um, Mrs. Brooks is a twenty-three-year-old white female from Springfield who now presents with a one-week history of muscle cramps, headache, nausea, dizziness, malaise, and a metallic taste in her mouth."

Murdoch didn't look up as Clark presented, but buried his face in Angela's chart, reading sections here and there. He seemed particularly interested in her labwork. Clark didn't know if the attending was listening or not.

There was a format to the clinical presentation, just as there seemed to be a format to everything in medicine. Jeb had gone over it with Clark at least five times the night before: patient identification, chief complaint, history of the present illness, past medical history, social history, family history, review of systems, physical exam, labs, and finally assessment and plan. Medicine was nothing if not ritualized compulsiveness.

No, Clark decided, Murdoch definitely wasn't listening. The man was running his fingers over a series of numbers that represented certain serum electrolyte values. At one point, he even called Jeb over and whispered something in the resident's ear.

Throughout the presentation, which went pretty smoothly once Clark found his rhythm, Angela stared up at him, listening to him tell her story. Her eyes were dry now and she seemed caught up in the narrative, as though it were about someone else, as though she were listening to see how it would turn out.

Clark knew what it was like to sit in a bed hearing someone he had met the night before drone on about the most intimate and riveting moments of his life history.

He remembered the cancer, how it defined his childhood, which toy he had gotten with which doctor visit. But to the stranger in a white coat, they were a series of dates without meanings. Or the meaning was different, a clinical one, not one associated with a teddy bear or a toy castle or a set of army trucks.

"Clark, what did you do about her potassium?" The question didn't come from Murdoch, but from Erich, who was perusing Brooks's chart over Murdoch's shoulder.

Clark screeched to a halt somewhere in the middle of her family history. The question from his classmate was so unexpected he almost didn't comprehend it. "Um, I believe we supplemented her with forty millequivalents intravenously."

Jeb gave Clark a wink and a thumbs-up. The resident seemed to understand Clark's primal fear; after all, Jeb had been there himself, only a few years ago.

"Continue," Murdoch commanded.

Clark reached the summary. "Given the history, physical findings, and laboratory test results, I believe this represents a case of arsenic poisoning."

Murdoch nodded. He was still studying the chart. "You sound pretty confident of that."

Clark paused. "What else could it be?" They had laboratory proof that this was arsenic toxicity. He looked to Jeb for support.

"What else?" Murdoch looked up as he repeated the

question. "Clark, that was a fine presentation, and I'd bet you ten to one that this is arsenic toxicity, but it's the *what elses* that will get you burned in this business. Medicine, like life, is a probability cloud. Nothing is certain. Labs make errors. Samples get switched. And no test is one hundred percent specific or sensitive."

Clark nodded. "Of course not. But if you add in the clinical picture, the lines in her nails, the deposition in her hair, why—"

Murdoch smiled. "Fair enough. When you resubmit your write-up, I'd like at least ten other diseases that can give you virtually identical presentations. If medicine were simply a matter of matching textbook descriptions with what you're seeing, a trained monkey could do it."

Angela Brooks was silent during the presentation. Now she spoke again. "Am I dying?" Her voice didn't tremble as she addressed Murdoch, obviously the most senior person present.

Murdoch nodded toward Clark. "Why don't you ask our expert on arsenic? Dr. Wilson, what do you think?"

Clark felt his mouth go dry as her eyes fixed on him. Answering the queries of Murdoch was one thing; what the attending wanted was information, clinical, dry, sterile. He demanded precision and correctness, nothing more. What Angela was asking was something quite different, a response that was beyond the percentages and incidences he had committed to memory.

She wanted to know if everything was going to be all right.

And she didn't want to hear about any probability cloud.

"Well," Clark began, realizing for the first time that his write-up was still in his hands, that perhaps he could have referred to it during his presentation, that he had perspired through the first page where his hands grasped it. "I don't think you're dying. We'll watch you closely and support you until the arsenic is cleared from your system." He glanced at Murdoch's face to make sure he was doing okay. Murdoch nodded and crossed his arms. "And we'll make sure you don't get poisoned here."

At the word *poison*, Angela's chin crinkled up and it looked as though she were going to cry. Clark let go of his write-up with one hand and instinctively reached for and touched her shoulder, before he remembered that Murdoch, Jeb, and everyone else were watching. He let his fingertips rest there a minute, then withdrew them, his ears reddening.

"It was Terrence, wasn't it?" she demanded. "That's what you tested the orange juice for."

Clark remained silent.

"It had arsenic in it, didn't it?"

Clark nodded.

"I'm sorry," Murdoch said. "But the good news is you're going to get better."

They stepped out of the room and left her alone in the half darkness. Before they were completely out, though, Angela called to them. "Dr. Wilson," she said.

Clark turned, his hand on the doorknob. "Yes?"

"Will you be in to see me later?"

He nodded. "Sure."

In the hallway, Murdoch grunted at him. "Not bad for your first presentation, Clark. Jeb can show you ways you might have made it more smooth."

Clark felt his spirits soar. He sensed that from Murdoch this was glowing praise. It was strange the way a few words from this man could have such a profound effect on him.

That was when he first discovered how sharply his mood would swing during the postcall emotional roller coaster.

It was Tracy's turn next.

She led them down the hall, handed Murdoch the patient's chart, then directed them toward the patient's room.

It seemed the entire Thurgood clan was present. His mother, wife, and daughter were clustered around the bed, and three men Clark didn't recognize stood nearby.

The patient grinned up with his small, boyish face. "Well, look who just dropped by. Come in, Doctors, you might as well squeeze in here, too."

The three male visitors took a hint and stepped out of the room as the attending led the others in. "I'm Dr. Murdoch," he said. "If you don't mind, we're going to talk about you in front of you."

The patient laughed, a full-bellied, deep-throated laugh. "Go right ahead. Everyone else chooses to do it behind my back."

Tracy positioned herself at the head of the bed. She stole a final glance at her clipboard, then looked Murdoch in the eye. "Mr. Thurgood is a fifty-six-year-old gentleman with no significant past medical history who presents with cough, intermittent hemoptysis, malaise, and weight loss over the past year."

"Stop right there." Murdoch's index finger rose, swept the room, then stabbed in Clark's direction. "Differential diagnosis."

Clark was ready this time. Not only had he listened, but he had heard Jeb's discussion of the case. He was about to blurt out "cancer" when he noted the way the patient was looking at him. The man's small blue eyes had a twinkle in them, as though he found something enormously funny. He seemed to view this whole hospitalization as some gigantic joke, a humorous adventure prompted by an overzealous wife and worrying mother.

It was painfully obvious that this man had no clue that he was probably dying.

"Sir, the most likely diagnosis is—um—some—that is—" He couldn't signal to the attending that he didn't want to say it in front of the patient without probably worrying the patient just as much as if he out-and-out said it.

Murdoch saved him. "Some mitotic process, perhaps?"

Clark thought about that. What the hell was a mitotic process? He knew that mitosis was the division of one cell into two, but what did this have to do with—then it hit him: this was one of many cryptic bedside euphemisms, used as shorthand to hide painful information from patients. "Yes, sir, exactly. A mitotic process."

"And what piece of information did Tracy omit that is crucial to helping us decide what priority to give this diagnosis?"

"Whether the patient smokes."

"Exactly." Murdoch turned to Tracy. "Does he?"

"Well, he quit."

"When?"

"Two weeks ago."

"And before then?"

"He smoked a pack a day for forty years."

Murdoch nodded, giving the same self-satisfied look that Clark had seen on Jeb's face the day before, as though the man were hearing the plot of a movie he had seen before. His eyes came to rest on Clark again. "Next diagnosis."

"Tuberculosis."

"Excellent. What's his PPD status?"

"Unknown," Tracy answered. "We just placed one last night." The PPD, or Purified Protein Derivative, was a skin test for TB.

Murdoch was back on Clark again. "What else could he have?"

Clark struggled to think. "Blastomycosis."

Murdoch looked as though someone had dashed a glass of cold water in his face. "Possible, but it sure isn't the next thing that comes to my mind." He nodded to Jeb, who was standing close to the door. "Would you open that please and look out in the corridor?"

Jeb evidently knew what was coming. His mouth twisted into a half grin as he stuck his head out into the hallway. "No zebras in sight," he reported, rolling his eyes. Murdoch apparently had done this before.

Murdoch nodded, then turned back to Clark. "If you hear hoofbeats, think of horses before hunting for zebras."

The patient bellowed with laughter at that joke. He seemed to be enjoying the entire performance, swiveling his head to watch each speaker like a spectator at a tennis match.

He probably wouldn't find it so funny if he knew what a mitotic process was, Clark thought.

Murdoch turned to Tracy. "Continue."

She did and he didn't interrupt her once from then on. Clark was impressed with her delivery—it rivaled Erich's. He was experiencing that familiar sinking feeling he had known since his first days in medical school: he was living proof of the Peter Principle—he had been promoted to his level of incompetence. He had excelled in high school and done well in college, but medical school was a whole new ball game.

Murdoch nodded to her. "Good job." He then turned to the Thurgood women and asked if they had any questions.

"Yes, I do," the mother said. "Several, in fact." She referred to some notes she had taken on a notepad. "For one, what is a *mitotic process*?"

The room fell silent, deadly silent. Murdoch rested his eyes on Tracy. "Perhaps Dr. McHugh would like to explain what a mitotic process is."

If Murdoch's intent was to fluster her, he failed. Tracy looked the woman in the eye and said, "Lung cancer. As we discussed last night, it's a possibility being entertained by our team."

Clark watched the patient's expression out of the corner of his eye. The man didn't flinch, but his smile seemed to fade a bit and the mirth left his eye.

"I see. And it sounds as though you're entertaining that possibility pretty strongly."

Tracy worked her mouth for a second before any words came out. "Well—we always must consider the worst things."

"But is the worst thing the most likely thing in this case?"

Murdoch whispered something to Jeb.

Tracy shifted her weight and hugged her clipboard. "It could be."

"What do you think?"

The woman wasn't about to let this drop. Clark realized Murdoch had directed Tracy into a hornet's nest, allowing the patient's family to give her a grilling far worse than any he could dish out.

"What do I think?" Tracy echoed. "Well, I think blastomycosis isn't such a terribly remote guess."

The mother made a quick note to herself, then moved on to the next question. "And what is *blastoffmyosis*?"

"That's *blastomycosis* and it's a kind of fungus."

"Like the kind you get in your feet?" the patient asked.

"No, like the kind you get in your lung."

The mother patted her son's wrist as though to silence him, then asked her next question. "When will you know what my son has?"

"In a day or two," Murdoch answered. He turned to Jeb. "You might want to consider bronchoscopy."

"Already scheduled."

"Excellent." The attending looked at the mother. "We could have something more definitive then. What other questions do you have?"

"Just one." She took the patient's fork and stabbed it through something on his tray that must have once been a stack of pancakes. "What on earth is *that* supposed to be?"

Murdoch smiled and shrugged. "Well, ma'am, there are some things we have answers for, and others"—he gestured toward the breakfast tray—"others will always remain mysteries."

When they were in the hallway, Murdoch took Thurgood's chart, held it by its spine, and dangled it high overhead. "It must be in here somewhere," he said.

Tracy trotted to catch up with him. "What's that, sir?"

"Your patient's lab flow sheets."

"Oh." Tracy rummaged through the loose sheets on her clipboard, but couldn't find the missing documents. "I filled them out, I just must have forgotten to put them in there. Maybe they're in my book bag."

Murdoch tilted his head and studied her. "Well, they're not doing us any good in there, are they?"

"May I get them?"

"Please do." Tracy ran off, pulled her bag from a heap of others in the corner of the physician workroom, and looked through the contents for the lab flow sheets.

"They're not here either."

"Well, this is unacceptable," Murdoch said. "How can we take care of this man if we don't know his labs?"

"I also copied them on my write-up, if you'll look on the second page by the—" But he flipped open the chart to where her write-up was supposed to be and it, too, was gone.

She pulled the chart from him and studied it. "Are you sure this is the right patient?"

"Unless there is more than one Thurgood in that room. Jeb, why don't you go back and look? Maybe there was someone else in there, hiding under the bed or something. You know how the nurses like to sneak them in without telling us, just hide them from—"

"All right!" Tracy snapped. "I get the point. So where's my write-up? I know *that* was in there not five minutes ago."

"Oh, you mean this?" Murdoch held up the completed history-and-physical forms in his hand. "I don't know if I'd admit having written this if I were you."

"And why is that?"

"It's wordy, there are multiple scratch-outs, and it's completely disorganized. I could use as an excuse that you just didn't know what the hell you were doing, but your presentation made it obvious that you can do a hell of a lot better."

Tracy had chosen the wrong time to get angry. Her chest heaved and she pushed her sweat-soaked hair from in front of her eyes. "Fine."

Murdoch stepped toward her, leaned over her, and pushed her write-up into her hands. "Do it again."

Tracy gulped. Clark could tell she was fuming. "Fine," she said again, between gritted teeth. Her mouth twitched and Clark sensed that she yearned to say something. She could say it, and probably a whole lot more, but if she did, she would be crushed. In the intellectual ghetto of the hospital, she was entering a dark alley unarmed.

For a minute she stared into Murdoch's face, then slowly, ever so slowly, she broke eye contact and stepped away.

Clark felt something in him relax, some inner tension dissipate as, for now at least, Tracy backed down.

"Well, that's it for the medical students," Murdoch told them. "Not bad for your first day. Your presentations were all right. Your write-ups as a whole were lousy."

He turned around and walked away.

Jeb stretched an arm around each medical student. "Cheer up. He ripped an even bigger asshole through the last group."

"Charming, isn't he?" Tracy asked.

Jeb pulled the twenty-dollar bill from his pocket. "Oh, he's all right. But he is a lousy gambler."

▲ POSTCALL ▼

When Clark had imagined being a doctor, he had envisioned himself the same way he remembered the host of doctors who worked on him as a child: walking into a patient's room, listening sympathetically to a story of pain and suffering, then laying hands on the patient. What he never could have known before now was what happened when the doctors stepped out of the examining room and were alone.

Clark had always pictured the doctors retreating to some large, oak-paneled study, the walls lined with tomes and journals, where they would study Clark's case and formulate a diagnosis and plan. Somewhere in there Clark imagined consultation with some council of sages, the members' hair as white as their long coats, squinting over bifocals, their faces wrinkled from years of awesome responsibility and wisdom.

What Clark had never figured on was a Jeb Morris or a Dr. Murdoch.

There was something about Murdoch Clark admired—

his murderous efficiency, his no-bullshit approach to patient care and student evaluation, his obviously high standards (this was, after all, a Mecca of medicine)—and even Jeb had a method to his apparent madness. But something essential was missing, something Clark thought would or should be present in a physician.

And then, as he chewed on it a while, it hit him: as a patient, he had always imagined that his physicians were, if nothing else, compassionate, caring human beings, sincerely concerned with his welfare not just as a patient, but as a person. It was the human element of medicine that seemed lost on these wards.

Jeb and Murdoch were technicians, apparently good ones, who operated with technical skills that Clark yearned to acquire. The idea of being able to step into a patient's room where a man couldn't breathe and rattle off a series of orders that would get the patient breathing again—well, *that* was being a doctor.

But it wasn't all and Clark was beginning to wonder if there were certain things about physicians that he didn't want to know after all. Part of him wished to be left with his boyish, idealistic fantasies intact.

Or maybe it was already too late. Even as he scribbled a progress note in Angela Brooks's chart, he wondered if his neurosurgeons hadn't bet twenty dollars on whether the CT abnormality that summer had been malignant or not.

No, probably not.

Maybe he would ask them.

The chart blurred before him again. He dropped his pen and rubbed his eyes as hard as he could, but the blurriness remained. He stood up and the room heaved up at him, as though the hospital floor was the deck of a ship caught in a massive swell. He gripped the table and did not fall and in a moment the dizziness passed.

Sleep deprivation, he told himself. It's just sleep deprivation.

A team of neurologists stood in a corner of the physicians' workroom, discussing a case. One looked over at Clark, but then quickly looked away. Clark realized they had probably seen this before. Bizarre behavior came with the territory. It was apparently part of the job.

His eyes focused again, but Clark was scared. They had said they got all of it, but as Murdoch said, life was a probability cloud.

Clark sat again and finished his note. He signed it, closed the chart, and picked up the phone.

Jeb had given him a "to-do list" half an hour after attending rounds. "Doling out scut," the resident called it, and ordered the students to check in with him every hour or so to see if there wasn't more stuff that had to be done. There always would be.

This was another part of patient care that amazed Clark: Only a tiny fraction of time was actually spent thinking up what might be wrong with a patient and doing something about it. Most of what he did was clerical: filling out forms, making phone calls, making second or third phone calls to make sure things got done. And most of the plans they generated were cookbook ones, copied straight out of a clinical handbook with a few minor modifications here and there. In fact, Clark had so much work to do, he realized that the only time he would see his patients would be five minutes during work rounds in the morning.

So this is what being a doctor was all about.

Still, it thrilled him to be part of it, to be picking up the phone and ordering an endocrinology consult, or trying to convince a radiologist that a certain patient needed an intravenous pyelogram (ten minutes ago, Clark didn't even know what one was, much less when one would be ordered), checking the computer periodically for lab results that could change patients' hospital treatments and prognoses.

Or sometimes their lives.

Clark's stomach told him it was early afternoon. He checked his watch, and sure enough, the hours had rushed by. The thought hit him that he'd be commuting home soon, that his head and his pillow would become one, that he would slip into the deepest sleep he had probably ever known.

"Do you mind if I grab something to eat?" he asked Jeb, who had entered the workroom and was reading a journal article.

"Is your work done?"

"Most of it."

"It's your time. The sooner you get done, the sooner you get out of here."

When Clark reached the cafeteria, it was closed, so his only means of sustenance would have to come from a set of vending machines. As he pushed the button for a factory-made sandwich, he was aware of someone standing behind him.

He grabbed his sandwich and a diet Coke, then turned around to see Heather. She looked a little startled to see him, a little worried even as she ran her eyes over him. His classmate looked fresh and pert and alive and Clark knew in an instant that she hadn't been on call the previous night.

"Clark, was it *that* bad?" she asked, running her eyes over him.

"Do I look it?"

She nodded. "Tracy said it was hell."

Clark smiled. "For once, Tracy didn't exaggerate."

"I'm on call tonight."

"Good luck."

"I'm scared, to tell you the truth. Do you have any words of wisdom?"

"Just flow your labs."

"What's that mean?"

Clark patted her on the shoulder. "You'll find out soon enough."

She selected a candy bar from a machine. "You want to join me for lunch?"

"I really should eat this upstairs."

"C'mon, Clark, just take it easy for a minute. Here, we'll sit over by the window. We have the whole cafeteria to ourselves." She swept her arm over the dining facility, which was empty except for a sanitation worker.

Clark nodded, although he felt uneasy with her. For one thing, he had had the most agonizing crush on her throughout the first year of medical school and still found her attractive. For another, as Jeb had alluded to, Clark knew that every minute he spent with her would be a minute later he got out of the hospital, which would mean a minute less of sleep he got that night.

But he found himself nodding. "Okay." They sat at a table by the window.

When her green eyes caught and held the sunlight as she stared outside, Clark found himself catching his breath. Christ, she was pretty. "What do you think will happen to our class now?" she asked.

He followed her gaze out to the hospital courtyard. A pajama-clad patient sat on a bench under a sycamore tree. He was holding his IV pole with one hand and smoking with the other. "What do you mean?"

"I mean, we're all scattered out now on different rotations. Our schedule sounds pretty brutal. It changes people."

Clark frowned at her. "It's not so bad."

She turned to him, fixing him with those eyes. "Not so bad? Clark, I added it up—I won't have a free weekend for six months. I won't get to sleep in one morning for the next eight weeks. Seven days a week, one hundred and twenty hours a week, did you realize that? And that doesn't include time spent reading or studying, which for me will be significant." She leaned toward him. "Clark, I don't know *anything*. Those first two years didn't prepare us for this."

Clark realized she was right. But he didn't like to get bogged down in negativism. "We learned the Krebs cycle, didn't we?"

Heather laughed. The Krebs cycle was the central biochemical pathway involved in generating adenosine triphosphate, or ATP, the fuel of life. Countless hours had been spent memorizing each intermediate, its name and structure, how many units of ATP were generated at each step, what would happen if a deficiency of one intermediate occurred. "You know," Heather said, "I'm really glad we learned it. If someone comes in the emergency room tonight, I can say, 'Sir, you obviously have an alpha-ketoglutarate deficiency and aren't generating enough ATP.'"

Clark looked out the window. "I haven't been out of the hospital since yesterday morning. What's it like out there?"

"Beautiful. I got out around four yesterday and headed straight to the quarry. The water was aquamarine—you know how it gets in the late summer—and the granite slabs were so warm you could just lie on them without a towel and go to sleep."

The abandoned granite quarry was a favorite medical-student retreat twenty minutes out of the city. They would go there to swim or hold group study sessions or get terrifically drunk—or all three at once. Clark called it the world's largest bathtub, with a rim of sheer granite walls plunging into a pool of rainwater. Clark had never swum there, just watched, out of a promise he had made to his mother years ago about not swimming in water over six feet deep, since he always had a theoretical risk of having a seizure.

And there were no sections of the quarry less than two hundred feet deep.

There was a rumor that a medical student had drowned there once, that his body had never been found, and that sometimes when the water was clear enough and the sky a little overcast, you could stare straight down and see his skeleton on the bottom. It was nonsense, of course, but it gave everyone a little thrill before they plunged over the precipice into the water.

"Who did you go with?" Clark asked.

Heather grinned at him, her front teeth coated in chocolate. "No one."

Clark clucked his tongue. "That's dangerous, you know. We're always supposed to take someone else along."

"Actually we're not supposed to go at all. It's trespassing, you know." She bit into her chocolate bar again, her blond hair jostling as she tore off a piece like a shark, with exaggerated gusto. "Besides," she said, the candy garbling her words, "it was the only way I could go skinny dipping and lie out naked."

Clark felt a gulp of his tasteless sandwich catch in his throat. His eyes watered as he said, "Heather, that place is pretty isolated. How did you know some weirdo wouldn't wander along and molest you?"

She laughed. "Oh, come on. I was safer there than I am in this city."

Clark had an image of her naked, her body shimmering in the sun as the beads of water dripped off her one by one. He tried to shake the image, but couldn't, despite a twinge of disloyalty toward Tracy.

Tracy would never skinny-dip and she would never lie out naked. At least he couldn't imagine her doing it.

Heather smiled at him. "What are you thinking about?"

"You. Naked. Lying on warm granite."

She averted her eyes. Clark thought he detected the beginning of a blush. "So, Clark," she said, changing the subject, "it's that bad, huh?"

"Yeah. It's bad. But you work so hard, you hardly notice the time go by. And it's interesting." He finished off his sandwich.

She swept her eyes over his face, as though looking for something. At first he thought it was more words of encouragement and he got ready to say something, but then she asked, "Clark, is it hard doing this after what happened this summer?"

He didn't know what she was talking about for a moment.

"You know, the tumor?"

Clark looked out at the courtyard, at the enormous sycamore tree that seemed to be dying in places. The patient was gone. "Sometimes, but overall I'm fine." He looked her in the eye. "Really."

She reached across the table and touched the back of his hand. It was a little thing, but it made Clark almost jump. "You know, Clark, when we first heard about the relapse, all of us—I mean the whole class—well, we've been through a lot and we were all pulling for you. You should have told us yourself, but that's okay. I can understand why you might not want to. I just want to tell you that if you ever need anything, someone to talk to, let me know, okay? Things are going to get crazy up there"—she nodded toward the door, in the direction of the wards— "and we've all got to support each other." She squeezed his hand, then pulled back, maybe looking a little embarrassed.

Clark knew his ears were turning red. "Thanks."

She smiled at him, brushing the chocolate from her teeth with little darting movements from her tongue, then asked, "Back to the sweatshop?"

Clark nodded.

As they got up Clark tried to blink away an image that kept popping back in his head.

He tried to stop thinking of Heather lying there on that outcropping of granite, naked in the sun.

FREE AT LAST

The phone calls were made, the labs were checked and flowed, all the orders were written and cosigned. Clark wrote a progress note in every patient's chart. His scut list was done.

Now, at last, after thirty-seven hours without sleep, Clark was heading home.

Or almost. Before he left, he went by to check on Angela Brooks. He debated not going, but he remembered his promise to visit her after rounds.

She looked worse than she had that morning, sleeping fitfully, a scowl on her face as she tossed from side to side. A woman in her forties sat at the bedside in a dark blue business suit. She rose when Clark entered and, without introducing herself, said, "What is this I hear about my daughter being poisoned?"

Clark wasn't ready for this, had not intended on placating a family member, especially one who seemed intent on a fight.

"Ma'am, all the tests we've run so far have shown that—"

"All the tests you've run so far don't mean a damn to me, young man, not a damn. My daughter is *distraught,* do you understand me, I mean, *delirious* with the idea that Terrence is trying to kill her. When I first heard it, I thought it must be her illness, that she must be fevered, but I asked a nurse, who told me it was true—you had found arsenic in her *pubic* hair, of all places."

Clark took a deep breath before continuing. "That is correct."

"So who is poisoning her?"

"That's a matter for the police to decide."

"The police? The *police?* Young man, as Angela's mother, I can assure you there will be no police investigation. This is the most ludicrous thing I've ever heard."

"I'm sorry, ma'am, but one has already been launched." One of his calls that day had been to the hospital attorneys, to relay the results of their tests. They said they had notified the district attorney, who would investigate the case.

The mother sat, not using her chair back, just staring up at Clark. "How do you know this test is right? How often does it give false positives?"

"I don't know, to tell you the truth."

"You don't even know if your test could be wrong, but that didn't stop you from reporting this to the police, I imagine? How long have you been a doctor?"

"Well, actually, I'm not a doctor. I'm a medical student."

The woman looked horrified. "What? Well, as a medical student, how many patients have you seen like Angela?"

Clark cleared his throat. "Um, actually she's the second patient I've ever taken care of."

For some reason, this seemed to pacify the mother. Maybe she realized that it was a waste of energy venting at Clark, that he was such a neophyte he couldn't have been doing anything more than following orders.

Which was exactly the case.

She hung her head and sighed. "Terrence is a friend of the family, you see," she said, in a different tone of voice. "He and Angela used to play together as children. They grew up together. We trusted him completely." She jerked her head up and looked Clark in the eye. "You think it was him?"

"There was arsenic in the orange juice he brought her."

The mother held a hand up to her mouth and looked away. Even in the murky light, Clark could see the tears. "Why would he do this to us?"

Clark had no idea. "I suppose you could ask him." At this point, he just wanted to make sure Angela was doing all right, then head home. He ran his eye over the door chart, checking her vital signs, her urine output, her IV flow rate. It took him a while to translate the numbers into something meaningful, even into the simplest of terms: good, bad, or okay. Well, she was okay, as far as Clark could tell.

"I can't contact him. I've called him three times and each time I get his answering machine. He said he would visit her this afternoon, but he hasn't shown. Oh, God." As the meaning of her words hit her she crinkled up her face and leaned forward.

Clark moved toward her and touched her arm. "I'm sorry." He then looked at Angela, who seemed to watch them with half-open eyes.

"You look awful," the mother said, and Clark thought she was addressing her daughter.

"Well, ma'am, she's doing all right from a fluids standpoint and—" But when Clark turned to the mother, he realized she was talking about him.

"How long has it been since you've slept?" she asked.

Clark added it up. "Almost thirty-eight hours now."

The woman let out a long, slow whistle. "Why do they do that to you?" She asked it in the same tone she used when asking why Terrence would poison her daughter.

For a moment Clark couldn't think of anything. Then

he remembered something he had overheard once justifying the thirty-six-hour day. "Continuity of care."

The woman looked confused. "And what does that mean?"

Clark's ears turned scarlet. "Um, I really don't know myself, to tell you the truth."

The woman smiled at him, brushing away her tears with a Kleenex she produced from her purse. "Well, go home and get some sleep. I'll see you tomorrow, I suppose?"

Clark nodded. "Yes, ma'am." He wanted to say something to comfort her, but could think of nothing. "Good night."

As he stepped from the room he almost collided with Bob. The intern blinked at him. "How's she doing?" he asked.

"The same."

"Ins and outs?"

"Twenty-five hundred cc in, two thousand cc out over the last twenty-four hours."

The intern nodded, jerking his head up and down like a nervous bird. He stank, perspiration drenching his shirt, a layer of oil and sweat covering his face. The top button of his shirt was undone and his tie was loose. Now he smiled for the first time that Clark remembered. "Good job, Clark. Go home."

He didn't have to be told twice.

Tracy was waiting for him in the physicians' workroom. "You ready to get out of here?" he asked her.

"Do we really get to leave?"

It was a strange feeling, stepping out of the hospital lobby through the automatic doors into the bright August sunshine. Clark inhaled deeply as the first gust of humid air hit him. It was laden with diesel fuel and the scent of a pretzel vendor, but it couldn't have smelled better than if it were the sweetest perfume of Arabia.

It was the smell of freedom.

"That was one hell of a day," Clark said.

"It was two, actually."

Clark stood there on the dirty, cracked, blazing sidewalk a moment, turned, and grinned up at the hospital. "Suppose I don't show up tomorrow?"

Tracy grabbed his arm and tugged him toward the parking lot. "You will."

Clark shrugged. "Not necessarily."

Tracy stopped at her car, pulled the keys from her purse. "You sure you can drive home safely?"

"No. But neither are you. We'll get there somehow." Clark had felt more confident in his driving skills after drinking a six-pack of beer than he did now. But he had no choice. "See you at home."

He fell asleep three times on the way there. The first two times, he was stopped at red lights and the horns behind him woke him up. The third time, however, he was cruising along at sixty-five miles per hour and woke up to find his car careening across two lanes into an embankment. His tires screeching, he managed to regain control of the vehicle and blink himself awake.

He and Tracy rented a small house forty minutes out of the city, just beyond the beltway. It was something they had agreed on last fall, when they had made the decision to move in together. They could either live in a two-room efficiency and watch eighty percent of their loan and grant money go toward paying the rent, or they could commute half an hour and get a real place of their own, a little piece of suburbia, complete with fresh air, a yard, and the drone of lawn mowers in the distance.

The house was a ten-year-old ranch house, with fading yellow siding and red shutters. Clark had wanted something a little bigger, but Tracy showed him they could never afford it. At least she couldn't, and she wouldn't feel comfortable making Clark pay more than half.

Money was always a sticky issue with her. Tracy refused to talk about it much, being very secretive about account balances and how much debt she was accumulating. The average medical student would graduate with almost $100,000 in debt. Clark knew Tracy's money was in short supply, that she had done almost anything for a little extra cash during their first two years of medical school. When oocyte donors were needed, she was the first to volunteer, and was given $1,200 for allowing someone to take an egg from her ovary for the in vitro fertility program. When they needed bone marrow, she had endured the agony of having someone drill a corkscrew-like needle into her hip and suck out a sample. And of course she was there at every drug trial, from Valium to new narcotics to one drug that just made her puke all the next day (but for thirty-five dollars, she said, it was worth it). She had taken two part-time jobs, even during their most critical exam crunch times, as a phlebotomist and as a lab tech. During the summers, when most of the class was trekking across Europe or lounging around with their parents, Tracy stayed in the area and worked full-time.

And somehow she still managed to outperform Clark academically. If there was one thing Tracy was not, it was lazy.

The owner of their home was an obstetrician in Houston who had purchased the house when he was doing his residency training and now rented it out. The yard was run-down and bare in spots, there were cracks in the sidewalk, and the kitchen and bathrooms were cramped, but it was theirs. It was home.

Clark pulled off the highway, the traffic thinned, and the neat little lots and homes came into view. He smiled to himself with the smug self-satisfaction of a new home-owner.

Even if they were just renting.

So this is how Dad must have felt, he told himself, trying to imagine the man he never really knew coming home from work. Then he saw his own house, the lot now overgrown because he and Tracy hadn't figured out a way to finance a lawn mower.

Tracy's car was already in the driveway. It was a sixth-hand, fourteen-year-old tank whose rear chassis the last owner had jacked up two feet. At traffic lights, high-school kids would rev up their engines and challenge her to races. Once, when she was angry about a pharmacology exam, she had taken them on, and almost got pulled over as a result. Clark made Tracy promise she would never do that again.

The gas-guzzling monster of a car was so patched up with mismatched paint and toner that from a distance it looked as if it were a green dinosaur with a horrible skin condition.

"Honey, I'm home!" he called out with exaggerated enthusiasm, stepping across the threshold.

But she wasn't in the living room, the kitchen, or out beyond on the patio. He walked through the house, coming to the small bedroom.

The door was locked.

"Tracy?"

There was some shuffling inside, the sound of—could it be voices?—then she came out, a smile on her face. "Yes?"

"What are you doing in there?"

"Nothing."

He looked over her shoulder, but everything was in order: his things were on one side of the room, including his alarm clock and nightstand; her things were on the other. "Don't worry about what's in there. Now come on," she said.

She led him by the hand toward the kitchen, where she turned on the stove and pointed to the sink. "Rinse out that pot, fill it halfway with water, and put it on the stove. And remember to wipe off the bottom this time." She was cheerful, almost playful as he obeyed.

"Tracy, what's going on?"

"I told you. Nothing. Now start peeling these." She tossed a couple onions on a cutting board and grabbed some items out of the refrigerator. "I'm famished. How 'bout you?"

"I ate a sandwich just a couple hours ago, but it's all I had all day."

Tracy nodded. "Wash these tomatoes, rinse off the lettuce, and make us a salad. Don't add so much oil and vinegar this time. Oh, and the noodles shouldn't go in until the water's boiling."

She trotted back to the bedroom.

"Tracy, would you like me to scrub the kitchen floor, too, while I'm at it? And where are you off to again?"

"Never mind. I gave you more than enough to keep you occupied for the next fifteen minutes."

Clark's mouth began to water as the kitchen was filled with the various smells of dinner. He hummed as he worked, looking every now and then toward the bedroom door, behind which Tracy had disappeared.

When she came out, she had a mischievous little smile on her face. "Done yet?"

"No. I don't know how to peel these onions exactly, but I tried my best."

She laughed when she saw the way he had butchered them, then took over herself.

"What's the main course?" Clark asked.

"I'm not entirely sure, to tell you the truth."

Clark opened the oven, but it was empty. "Do you want me to start on a chicken or something?"

"That won't be necessary." She turned to him before he could demand explanation and asked, "So what took you so long?"

"The laws of this state." It was a little joke between them. Tracy seemed to think that the speed limit on every road was seventy-five miles per hour, especially after buying her monster. The jacked-up chassis seemed to bring out something demonic in her. She darted her way through rush-hour traffic as though it were some Nintendo game.

Clark looked around the tiny kitchen, at the trim in bad need of a paint job and peeling wallpaper, and the light overhead with one dead bulb and three good ones, with the dead family of spiders silhouetted against them, at the grimy window that Tracy had been begging him to clean. He put an arm around her and pulled her little body toward his. She was still wearing her pleated skirt, still had the scent of perfume and sweat and fear and a night without sleep. He kissed the top of her head. Tracy's hair was damp with perspiration under his lips.

He found it terrifically sexy.

Clark walked to the refrigerator and grabbed a beer. "Do you mind if I shower?"

"I do actually," she said. Before Clark could ask why, she added, "By the way, your mother called."

"Oh. What did she say?"

"Just wanted to know how your first day of medicine went."

"Anything else?"

Tracy looked him in the eye silently for a moment. "No."

Clark nodded. His mother had been worried about him, worried and proud and delighted all at once. She knew this was what he wanted, that Clark had always talked of being a doctor, but was also afraid of him starting his rotations so soon after the surgery. It had been eight weeks, actually, but she wanted him to take a semester off. "No, Mom," he had told her. "I don't want to get behind. I want to graduate with my class."

Tracy squeezed one hand while he stirred the noodles with the other. "You should try to call her tonight."

Clark nodded. "I will." He nodded toward the bedroom. "What do you have hiding for me back there?"

She smiled. "I don't know what you're talking about."

Then Clark heard it: it was a bump, like the sound of something heavy falling, coming from the bedroom. He looked at his housemate, who seemed not to have heard it. "Tracy—"

"Yes?"

There was another bump and the sound of someone murmuring, maybe two voices answering. They were definitely voices. There were at least three people in his bedroom.

Clark picked up a frying pan and stepped toward the bedroom. "I think someone's broken in."

Tracy grabbed his free wrist and tried to swing him around. "What on earth do you think you're doing?"

"I'm going to defend my home."

"It's *our* home and I don't know what you're talking about."

Now something heavy fell again and the distinct sound of someone swearing, then laughter, made its way to Clark's ears. He pulled his wrist loose and walked out of the kitchen.

"What are you going to do with that frying pan?"

"I'm going to clump whoever is in there over the head with it!"

Clark marched back to the bedroom. He tried the handle, but it was locked.

He looked to Tracy for explanation. "This can only be locked from the inside, right?"

Tracy nodded. "I think so."

"Then someone's in there, and they locked me out of my own bedroom." He pounded on the door. "*Open up! Open the goddamn door!*"

He reached for the handle again, but it swung out of his reach. As the door opened he looked into the room and at least three dozen faces stared out at him.

They looked half-guilty, half-amused. Someone was being helped into the room through an open window. The screen lay propped against the door.

The faces were those of his classmates.

"Surprise," someone said weakly.

Then the others echoed, like a horribly out of tune chorus: "*Surprise!*"

Clark looked at his watch, ascertained the date; no, it definitely wasn't his birthday. "You're damn right it's a surprise. Now, what are all you people doing in my bedroom?"

Randy Cribshaw stepped forward, his little mustache twitching as he did. "Welcome back, man." Before Clark could step back, Randy swept him into a quick bear hug. "And welcome into this little love shack. We couldn't think of a better place for the first class party of the year."

"I thought you were on call in neurology," Clark said.

"Oh, I told my resident my migraines were flaring."

"But you don't have migraines."

"No, but he doesn't need to know that."

The others spilled out of the room, gave Clark a quick slap on the back, then hurried out toward the living room. Someone threw open the front door and shouted, "He's blown our cover—come on in!"

Amazed, Clark watched as almost every member of the class trekked through his living room, shook his hand or slapped him on the back, then headed toward the sliding door and piled out on his deck. The smell of something barbecuing met his nostrils.

"We don't have a grill," he said to Tracy, who was giggling, pinned against a wall by three medical students forming a beer-can chain gang from the refrigerator to the others outside.

"You do now," Randy said. "And it's a beauty. Come look."

Clark stepped into his yard and saw a monster of a barbecuing machine with three racks that were fully loaded with steaks and chicken. Black smoke poured out of its belly.

"But here's the real surprise," Randy said, nodding to Erich Boorman, whom Clark recognized in the crowd. Erich disappeared around the corner and came back with a lawn mower. A red ribbon was wrapped around its motor. As Clark inspected it closer he noticed the lawn mower was rusted on the bottom and deeply stained by grass and spilled oil.

"Where did you guys get this?"

"My landlord gave it to me," Erich said. "Vintage 1968 technology. He had it in his basement, unused for at least a decade."

"Does it still work?" Clark demanded, inspecting the engine block.

"Hell if we know," Randy said.

"There is a small but finite possibility the thing will explode," Erich warned. The crowd stepped back several feet.

Clark looked around, searching for one face in particular, half-ashamed of himself as he did. Tracy worked her way to his side. "Who are you looking for?"

"No one," he lied.

Then he remembered that she was on call; of course Heather wouldn't be here.

Erich rolled up his shirtsleeves and bent over the lawn mower, the same way he might over a gravely ill patient. Everyone grew quiet as they watched him. He reached forward, checked the oil level, adjusted something out of Clark's sight, then rose. Inhaling deeply, he gave the starter cord a terrific yank. It sputtered to life, belching blue-gray smoke into the yard. There was a smattering of applause.

"It works," Erich announced, reaching down and turning off the lawn mower.

Someone handed Clark a beer. He gulped at it and felt the familiar, cozy wooziness that came from alcohol and the company of his classmates. They hadn't all been together in one place since spring. It didn't matter that he hadn't slept all night; all the fatigue was stripped away as he looked at the familiar smiling faces that he had gone through so much with, and would now go through so much more with. It seemed he had known them all his life.

They were looking at him expectantly and he realized they wanted him to say something. "Well," he began, "I don't know how to thank you for this lovely grass-devouring beast. How'd you finance it?"

Erich turned over his wristwatch calculator and hit a few buttons. "We passed around a hat, dipped into the class fund, stole a little from the dean while he wasn't looking, and charged the rest to Tracy's VISA. That was okay, wasn't it?"

Clark nodded. "Fine with me." Tracy punched him in the ribs. "But thanks, really. My neighbors thank you, too, I'm sure."

He wondered if this was more than a housewarming party. Maybe it was as much a thank-God-you-didn't-die-from-your-brain-tumor party as anything. They all must have heard about the relapse. Being back with his class had more than one meaning.

There had been a time that summer when he wondered if he would ever get back to them. That's all he wanted, more than anything. Even if it was benign, even if he could continue with medical school, it wouldn't be the same if it wasn't with the same group of men and women he had started with. They were his classmates, and although they never talked about it, never said it out loud, they loved him and he loved them as much as he had ever loved anyone in his life. And during that long dark summer of waiting, of being aware of every breath, every flower, every bird, of never feeling more aware of the blood coursing through his veins, he wondered if he would lose them.

Then the initial pathology: benign, glial scar. Two days later his neurosurgeon marched into his room, telling him the final path was negative for recurrence of tumor, speaking the language of medicine without translation, going through the markers and stains and microscopy without hesitation, knowing Clark would want to know everything. He remembered wanting to hug this white-coated woman, to reach out through the pain and the Demerol fog and touch her and tell her that that day she was more than an angel, she was godlike, something he wanted to be himself one day. He remembered gripping her hand as she patted his shoulder, and the way he let go of it just as quickly when he realized he had embarrassed her. The rules of the game had changed; they were both professionals now and that altered things in a way he understood without understanding.

For the rest of his life Clark would never play the role

of patient so easily and naturally again. There would always be something stiff and forced and unnatural about sitting on the other side of that white coat.

Clark wanted to go up to each of his classmates and hug them, but knew he would do no such thing. He had thought of them often during that long, hard summer, certainly much more than they must have thought of him. Being in a hospital bed, waiting and wondering and, as he never admitted it to himself then but could see now, preparing himself for the worst, for his own death, had given him time to think.

He searched the faces he had seen so often in his mind.

There was the Grunt, so named because he had been an officer in the marine corps for three years before coming to medical school. He was suntanned and muscle-bound and peppered his speech with militarisms, such as "say again" instead of "excuse me" or "latrine" instead of "bathroom." He had a scar on his back, a ten-inch-by-one-inch swath of rough white flesh, that Clark first saw during a shirts versus skins basketball game. "Beirut," he said without comment, and that was as elaborate as he got. Why he made the switch from the profession of killing to the profession of healing no one was quite certain (he said he had nothing better to do with the rest of his life), but it might have had something to do with the two kids pulling at his legs; the little girls had his same blond hair and blue eyes. The Grunt (no one called him anything else) was the only one of the first-year class to order meat when the second-year medical students took them out on a traditional steakhouse dinner after their first day carving cadavers in gross anatomy.

And there was Alicia in a calico summer dress. She was the last woman Clark had slept with before going out with Tracy. Alicia had black hair and an olive complexion and a body that had grown hungrier for sex as midterm exams of the first year approached. She was quiet and avoided most parties, but Clark knew she had a wild side. Alicia had a Harley-Davidson in her apartment and liked to ride it late at night through the streets of the city. "It clears the mind," she said.

And then there was Erich and Randy and Tracy and a score of others, every face with a story attached.

As they filled their bellies with chicken, noodles, and beer, the medical students found themselves talking of nothing but the hospital. They exchanged war stories of their first two days on the wards. They competed to see who worked the hardest or was the most miserable, who saw the most body fluids or the worst gore over the past forty-eight hours. They talked with gusto of vomit and blood and pus and urine while chomping into barbecued chicken breasts and slurping down beers.

Clark looked around with awe at classmates who only a year ago had turned gray at the sight of a cadaver. GAV's they called them, or *Gross Anatomy Vegetarians*—students so repulsed by their graying cadavers that they refused to eat meat, sometimes for the rest of their lives, but usually just for a semester. Now even the most militant of the Vegetarians was talking about lancing a boil the size of his fist, the way the blood and pus spurted from here to that fence back there, the way a nurse didn't get out of the way in time. Mmmm. This is great chicken; was there another piece?

Randy came up to him, grinning. "Hey, Clark, I'm glad you're back. We all are."

"I didn't know I had left."

"You know what I mean."

Clark winked at him. "Listen. I'm not going to leave you guys. I play a very important function. The class needs someone at the bottom of the bell curve."

Randy remained serious. "They got it all, right?"

"Yeah. That's what they think."

"They had clean margins?"

Clark nodded. "They didn't need clean margins. There was no tumor. Pathology came back negative for malignancy; it was just scar tissue from the first operation."

Randy whistled. "That's great. That's just wonderful."
He sounded relieved.

Clark put an arm around his shoulder as they walked
into the house. "You know what I don't get—why is
everyone else more worried than I am? I'm the one that's
supposed to be doing the worrying, and I'm not. I had a
team of neurosurgeons poking around in my brain this
summer to make sure it was free of tumor. That's more
than you guys can say. How do you know *you* don't have
a grapefruit growing in there, huh?"

Randy smiled. "You're absolutely right. I'm going to
report to neurosurgery clinic tomorrow and demand they
do a screening craniotomy. Just to be on the safe side.
And while they're at it, they can do a laparotomy and a
thoracotomy and any other otomy they happen to think
of."

"There you go."

It wasn't until midnight that the last person left. By
normal standards, this might have been considered a reasonable time for a party to break up. But when the host
and hostess hadn't slept for two days and had to be up in
six hours, it was very late indeed.

"Sorry about ruining your surprise," Clark told Tracy
through the bedroom door as they got ready for bed.

"That's okay. I should have planned it better, maybe
sent you out for groceries or something." An enormous
yawn drowned out her last words. She flipped out the
light and slipped into bed.

Clark did not understand how he could grow so horny
so quickly. But the feel of her leg against his made him
want her.

He wrapped his arms around her, pulled her hard
against his chest, then buried his face in her neck.

Tracy had taken a quick shower before coming to bed,
but her body still had the faint scent of two days in the
hospital. It was an indefinable something, maybe the anti-
septic used in the soap. It was enough to distract him.

"What's the matter?" she asked.

"Nothing. Nothing at all." He rolled away, his erection wilting. This had never happened before. He thought of something to say, but before he could, he heard the sound of Tracy snoring. He closed his eyes, telling himself he was just too tired, and within a few minutes he was sound asleep.

He dreamed about Heather lying naked on a sun-warmed slab of granite.

THE GRIND

Clark slept only ten minutes when the alarm went off. Swearing, he reached up to reset it when he looked at the time: 6:15. Christ, somehow he had reset the time also. His whole body ached for sleep, but he had to get out of bed to correct the damn thing.

Tracy was snoring beside him, murmuring something as he jostled the bed. He would have to be careful not to wake her.

Clark felt cold and naked as he huddled by the clock. He hit the light button on his watch to see what the correct time was: 6:16.

He stood there in the darkness staring at the green-glowing LED numbers staring back at him. It couldn't be, it just couldn't already be time to get up.

But it was. And he hadn't slept ten minutes; he had slept six hours.

Jesus. Clark leaned over the bed and shook Tracy. She didn't wake up right away but required another shake, a flipping on of the lights, and a pulling away of the sheets.

Even then she squinted up at him, tried to cover her body with her hands, and said something about flowing her labs later.

"Tracy, c'mon. It's time to get up."

Then she sat straight up and stared at him. "You're kidding."

"I wish I were. I'll get some coffee brewing; you can take the first shower."

He returned to the bedroom to find the lights out and the sheets pulled back over her head. She was snoring away as peacefully as ever.

"*Tracy!*"

He gave up on her and went to take a shower himself. He'd let her sleep another ten minutes or so.

As the water cascaded over his body he realized that this was just the beginning, that what stretched before him was two more years of this, then internship, which would be worse, then a couple of years of residency. It seemed like an infinity.

Using Jeb's rule, the shower brought his effective total sleep to seven hours.

Jeb didn't factor in alcohol, though; the three beers Clark drank the night before gave him a dull, aching feeling behind his eyes.

Then he remembered: he had forgotten to call his mother. He'd call her later that day.

Clark was fully dressed when Tracy finally stumbled out of bed and into the bathroom. He opened the front door and snatched up the paper. Before he reached the table, he saw the headline:

TERRENCE BROOKS ARRESTED FOR ATTEMPTED MURDER

It took him a minute to remember where he had heard the name. Then he scanned the article:

At approximately 8:00 P.M. yesterday evening, the district attorney announced that Terrence Brooks had been arrested in the attempted murder of Angela Brooks.

Mr. Brooks is charged with poisoning Mrs. Brooks with arsenic. Mrs. Brooks is now hospitalized at Mount Rosemont Medical Center, where she is in stable condition. Mr. Brooks, the husband of the victim, was unavailable for comment; he is being held without bail.

The crucial piece of evidence linking Mr. Brooks to the crime was provided when the district attorney's office was contacted by Mount Rosemont Hospital officials, who had detected high levels of arsenic not only in the patient's hair, but in a cup of orange juice given to Mrs. Brooks by her husband.

Clark stood in the middle of the room and stared at the paper. "Oh, my God."

Tracy almost bumped into him. "What is it?"

"My patient made the front page of the newspaper."

Tracy looked over his shoulder and read the article also. "Oh, my God. That's the woman whose urine came back positive for arsenic." She read further. "They didn't mention you."

"Why should they? It was Jeb's idea to check the juice."

Tracy walked to the refrigerator and pulled out a carton of orange juice. She poured herself a glass and took a swig.

But a sudden thought made her stop gulping. She held the glass away from her and studied it, then looked at Clark. "Do you think she trusted him?"

"Probably. He seemed like such a nice guy." Clark's eyes met hers and he realized what she was thinking. "Go ahead and drink the OJ, Tracy. You're too late; I poisoned the barbecue last night."

"Very funny."

Fifteen minutes later they stared at each other over the dining-room table. With her wet hair plastered to her head and sticking up in places, her bloodshot eyes, and the drained expression on her face, she looked like a hunted animal, chased by bloodhounds through a cold stream.

"I'm more tired today than I was yesterday," she said.

He slid an egg onto her plate and one onto his. "Eat quick; the radio says traffic's backed up on the beltway."

Tracy wolfed down her food, staring ahead unblinking. Clark drank two cups of black coffee and began to feel life seep back into his body. "Tracy, can you promise me something?"

"What?"

"That you won't mouth off to Murdoch." She remained silent. Clark studied her. "It makes it harder for the rest of us if we have to work in an antagonistic atmosphere."

"It's already antagonistic. It was antagonistic from the beginning."

Clark turned off the coffeemaker and packed his medical gear and clipboard. "But why make it more antagonistic?"

"I don't see why they have to be so sarcastic."

"There's not much we can do about that."

Tracy was incredulous. "Nothing we can do about it? We're paying almost twenty thousand dollars a year for this experience; is it so crazy to suggest that we should have some input into it? I don't remember signing any waiver of my First Amendment rights when I started med school."

"Oh, no. Tracy, whenever you mention the First Amendment, it's a prelude to something bad."

Tracy was silent a moment. "Clark, forget how they treat us. Just consider this—would you like to be taken care of by a doctor who makes bets about whether you'll have cancer?"

Clark puffed out his cheeks. "I was asking myself that exact same question yesterday."

Tracy ran a comb through her wet hair. "Clark, it isn't a matter of being opposed to people like Murdoch—he's already set in his ways. And Jeb is strange, but he has some spine. But they're not who I'm afraid for."

Clark thought about it. "Who then?"

"I'm afraid for me. I'm afraid for us. This year is going to change us. Maybe in ways we won't even know." She looked at Clark. "Do you realize what they've done to us? They've plunged us into a strange new environment, put us into a uniform"—Tracy tugged on her white coat—"and thrown in a little sleep deprivation."

Clark smiled. "Or a lot of sleep deprivation."

"Well, you've got all the elements of a powerful socialization experience."

"Also known as brainwashing."

"Exactly. We can't go through this and be the same. I'm afraid that if I don't at least hear myself fighting it, if I don't show myself in some way that I'm struggling against the system, well"—she looked at Clark and her eyes were large and sad—"something inside me, some essential part of me, will die."

Clark sensed a desperation in Tracy's voice that concerned him. He wanted to say something, but she suddenly glanced down at her watch and swore. "We're going to be late, Clark."

As they headed out the door and locked up the house, Clark said, "Tracy, write all this down. Record it. Like you said once, be a witness. Then, if you still feel this strong two or three years from now, do something about it. But not now. Right now survive medical school."

Tracy nodded. "All right. I'll try to keep my mouth shut."

Clark felt some tension slip from his body. He placed his hand over Tracy's, gave it a quick squeeze, then rose and headed for the door. He believed in simple solutions to complex problems, which was one reason why he never completely understood Tracy. His book bag was markedly lighter than it had been the day before, after Jeb removed half its contents.

"Let's just take one car today, okay?"

Tracy nodded. "Yours. I'm sleeping."

The sun was dipping over the horizon as Clark nosed his Pinto toward the skyline of the city. He thought he could make out the silhouette of Mount Rosemont Medical Center as he pulled into the morning traffic.

Tracy slept as Clark drove. He promised himself he would sleep that night and the next night he would—

Then it hit him: the next night he would be on call again. Thirty-six hours, no sleep.

He had a moment of panic; he didn't see how he could do it. He felt like a runner in a marathon who was developing a cramp during the first fifty yards. He wasn't expecting this.

Well, he would sleep that night. He vowed to himself as God was his witness that he would sleep that night. At least eight hours.

But something else bothered him as he drove and he couldn't identify it. Then he remembered the dream, the one he had during what seemed only ten minutes of sleep.

It was a still life, devoid of action or movement, an image of Heather, naked in the sun, the light glistening off the beads of water as they trickled down her body. He remembered the emotion associated with the dream: longing, but not just an animal, sexual longing. It was something more, something deeper, a yearning for something Tracy might never be able to give him.

He looked over at her, curled up, her mouth open and her wet hair tousled. He told himself that he loved her, that he was ready to spend the rest of his life with her— they had been talking obliquely of that—but couldn't blink away the image of Heather.

Clark felt a stab of terrible loneliness for a moment, but it passed just as quickly, replaced by a sense of fear and anticipation. The hospital loomed into view.

He shook Tracy awake and they hustled into the hospital. At the nursing station, Clark grabbed Angela's chart and read over the nursing note from the night before. Vital signs stable, no complaints.

Then he rose and walked down the hall to her room. After examining her door chart, he knocked twice and stepped into her room.

He was stunned at the change in her. She sat up in bed, brushing her hair and watching TV. "Good morning, Dr. Wilson."

He nodded to her. "You know I'm not a doctor. How are you this morning?"

"My feet feel numb and my stomach is in turmoil. But overall I feel much better." A smile appeared then disappeared on her face, like the sun poking through the clouds on a stormy day. "I heard they arrested Terrence."

Clark remembered the newspaper article. "I'm sorry."

"So am I. But you know, we were fighting a lot. I didn't want to tell my parents, but I was thinking about filing for divorce. He would have been crushed, said he didn't know what he'd do without me." She ran the brush through her hair one last time and set it on a nightstand. "I knew exactly what he'd have to do without me—work. I just had no idea my money was so important to him that he'd kill me for it."

When Clark returned to the physician workroom, a nurse approached him. "Call on line two."

"Thanks." Clark lifted the receiver and punched the blinking yellow button. "Clark Wilson, may I help you?"

"Yes, Dr. Wilson, are you the physician taking care of Angela Brooks?"

Clark cleared his throat. "I'm not a physician—I'm a medical student, but I am taking care of her. How may I help you?" He felt himself brimming with importance. Clark was feeling the first seductive tug of being a physician in American society, even in the days of malpractice and Donahue.

"My name is Sydney Johnson of Network Twelve News. Can you confirm the story that Angela Brooks was being poisoned for her money?"

Clark looked over at Tracy, who was studying him from across the room. "It's a reporter," he whispered to her, covering the mouthpiece.

He uncovered the mouthpiece. "Sir, I don't think it would be appropriate—"

"Oh, we all know the story already. We just need confirmation. It is true, isn't it?"

"Even if it was, I couldn't—"

"Oh, c'mon, Dr. Wilson."

"I told you, I'm just a medical student."

"*Just* a medical student? Aren't you the one who solved this puzzle, who ran the arsenic tests and notified the DA?"

Clark felt the tug again, the desire to be important, needed, helpful. But he also sensed the reporter was trying to exchange flattery for information. "I ran the tests, but it was only because—"

"So you are the one who discovered that Mrs. Brooks was being poisoned?"

"Well, in the sense that I took the samples to the lab, yes. But—"

"Thank you, Dr. Wilson." The reporter hung up. Clark stared at the phone a moment before hanging it up himself. "Uh-oh."

Jeb burst into the room. "Who'd you kill now, Clark?"

Clark stood up. "No one."

"Then what's the problem?" He threw down his bag, pulled out his stethoscope, and scratched at his beard. "Let's rack the charts and get rolling. We got a long day ahead of us." Jeb was sipping from a mug that said DON'T TAKE YOUR ORGANS WITH YOU WHEN YOU DIE. HEAVEN KNOWS WE NEED THEM HERE.

As the students gathered the charts Jeb pinned a clipping from the *New York Times* to the bulletin board. "We're all heroes," Jeb said. "Saving lives and all that shit. Read it after rounds."

Clark ran his eye over the headline of the article as he strode out of the room:

TOXIC LOVE: MAN POISONS WIFE; BETRAYED BY
ORANGE JUICE AND PUBIC HAIR

"Where's Bob?" Jeb asked Tracy.

"Haven't seen him," she said.

"There's never an intern when you need one!"

"I heard that!" Bob walked in with a grin on his face. He was all movement, but looked crisp, clean, and well rested.

Jeb winked at him. "Did you hear about yourself on the news today?"

The intern looked confused. "No."

"That's probably because they didn't mention us by name. The medical center likes to control those things, to make sure the proper people get the credit."

Clark smiled. "You mean, they know about you figuring it out?"

"Hell, no. They know about Murdoch figuring it out."

Clark was confused. "But Dr. Murdoch wasn't even there. By the time he met the patient, the arsenic had already come back positive. There was no mystery at all then."

Jeb took Clark aside, draped an arm around his shoulder, and said, "My boy, I want to let you in on a little secret—we don't exist."

Clark frowned. "What do you mean?"

Jeb's eyes seemed to dance with merriment. "We're not here. We seem to be, but we're not. We are the invisible workers, the oompa loompas in the chocolate factory of medicine, the waiters in the restaurant of disease. We are faithful servants and apprentices." Jeb leaned forward and whispered in Clark's ear, "Murdoch saved your patient's life."

Clark was completely confused. "So you get absolutely no credit for what you did?"

"No. I get a paycheck every month that almost equals minimum wage when you factor in my hours, allowance for overtime, et cetera, and I get the training I need to be a pretending myself someday."

"A what?"

"Oh, I slipped. An attending."

Clark tried to read Jeb's expression for bitterness or mirth or seriousness, but couldn't discern what was real and what wasn't.

"So the official Rosemont Medical Center line," Jeb continued, "is that Murdoch was all over this arsenic thing from the start. It's going to be great for business. In fact, they're making Murdoch hold a live press conference at noon. Until then, the word is out—don't speak to any reporters about this business. All information is going through Murdoch and the public-relations office."

Clark thought about the reporter he spoke with on the phone. "Suppose we were to—um—leak something out?"

Jeb laughed, a deep, throaty laugh that Clark thought had a sadistic tinge to it for some reason. "Oh, Clark, woe unto him who incites the wrath of Murdoch. If you would like to see him rip off your head and shit down your neck, I would do just that." When Clark wasn't laughing, Jeb asked, "You didn't talk to a reporter, did you?"

"Well, yes, but it was before—"

Jeb covered his eyes as though protecting himself from witnessing some atrocity. "Oh, Clark. Poor, poor Clark. And how long have you wanted to be a doctor?"

Clark felt his heart thudding. He exchanged looks with Tracy, who rolled her eyes and thumbed her nose at Jeb behind his back.

"I saw that, young lady," the resident said, turning to her and flashing her one of his most lopsided, sardonic half grins.

Tracy shrugged. "Dr. Murdoch is a prototypical pompous ass."

Clark tried to make eye contact with her, to remind her of the promise she made that morning over breakfast, but her eyes were locked on Jeb's.

"Prototypical pompous ass, eh?" Jeb asked, enunciating each word. "You get five points for the alliteration and ten for the pentasyllabic word, giving you a grand total of fifteen points." He looked over his shoulder, leaned toward Tracy, and winked. "Can't say I disagree with you, though." He straightened up. "Let's round."

"No change on Winfield," Bob reported, referring to an index card. "I called the nursing home yesterday and tried to get his bed back, but they kept transferring me from one office to another, putting me on hold, sometimes just cutting me off. Then I called back and pretended I was a lawyer for his estate. They were very polite to me, but said they gave his bed away because he was a management problem."

Clark looked down at Mr. Winfield as they approached. The man smiled up at them, strapped in his wheelchair, half his breakfast clinging to the front of his pajama top.

"Mr. Winfield, are you a management problem?" Jeb boomed.

The man's smile widened. "Aru aru," he said.

"That's what I thought." Jeb turned back to Bob. "You get his potassium back up?"

"Yep. From a lab standpoint, this man is completely normal."

"You hear that, Mr. Winfield?" Jeb asked. "You're a regular miracle of modern medicine."

"Aru ruffa ru."

"That's right."

The innocence of Winfield's expression and the way his eyes searched their faces reminded Clark of a baby. In fact, there were many aspects of this man's existence, from his diapers to his drooling, that were infantile. It was as though the last days of this patient's life came to resemble his first.

Jeb listened to the man's heart and lungs carefully.

Clark could see the back of Winfield's wheelchair, the sign saying in big black letters: HI. MY NAME IS MR. WINFIELD. PLEASE DO NOT LET ME GET ON THE ELEVATOR. IF YOU SEE ME UNESCORTED, PLEASE CALL WARD 6 WEST IMMEDIATELY. THANK YOU. Over the man's shoulders was another sign: MR. WINFIELD YOU LIVE HERE ➔.

The resident turned to Bob. "Next customer."

BRONCHOSCOPY

The tube was about the diameter of a golf-club handle, long, sleek, black, and flexible. The pulmonary attending, her face hidden by her surgical mask, her body draped in an aqua surgical gown, coated the snake with a thick petroleum lubricant.

Tracy adjusted her surgical mask and watched every movement of the attending's gloved hands.

From his position on the examining table, so did Mr. Thurgood. When Tracy glanced down at him, the patient smiled up at her and gave her a wink, as though she were the one who needed the reassuring.

Maybe she did.

"You sure you don't mind my watching?" Tracy asked the attending.

"Absolutely not," the attending said. "When I was a medical student I tried to make it to as many of my patients' procedures as I could. By the way, my name's Dr. Rosencrantz."

"Tracy McHugh."

"Pleased to meet you." Dr. Rosencrantz was a pretty woman in her early forties, Tracy guessed, with light brown hair that was streaked with gray and large brown eyes. She addressed the patient: "This is going to feel unpleasant. We're going to pass this tube into your windpipe, then into your bronchus, which is a branch of your windpipe, okay?"

Mr. Thurgood nodded. "Personally, I'd rather spend the morning golfing, but if this is what it takes to get my wife and mother off my back, so be it." He yawned. "What was that shot you gave me earlier?"

"A little sedative to help calm you through the procedure."

"Oh, I'm calm."

"Well, you might not be if this tube makes you gag."

Thurgood thought about that. "No, I imagine not." He looked up at the pulmonologist. "You've done these before, I hope?"

"Yes. Quite a few."

"And nothing has ever gone wrong, right?"

"Every procedure has its complications. As I explained, there is the chance, a small chance, that we might collapse a lung from this. But we can insert a chest tube to correct that if it happens. There's also the chance of a bleed and—"

Mr. Thurgood held up a hand. "Just tell me you're good at this."

Rosencrantz smiled. "All right. I'm good."

"That's all I want to hear. Go ahead."

She spritzed the back of his throat with a topical numbing solution, then advanced the snake into his mouth and down his throat. He gagged once, tears formed at the edge of his eyes, then it was in.

Tracy watched the snake, whole feet of it, disappear into the man's mouth. She didn't think there would be that much room.

"Tracy, look up there," the attending directed, nodding toward a television monitor. "We're passing his vocal cords right now."

Tracy watched the view from the head of the fiber-optic bronchoscope, magnified and transmitted to the television. "And that's his trachea, huh?"

Though the patient was within inches, it was surprisingly easy to lapse into referring to him in third person. "That's right."

The television showed a long tunnel with pink, moist, glistening walls. The tunnel disappeared in the distance, fading to black. It gave Tracy a lonely feeling somehow; although she had been studying the body for two years, it never struck her until now just how completely dark the interior of her body was. All the cellular, glandular, and organ functions she had learned about occurred in total blackness.

The tiny search beam of the fiber-optic scope advanced. "It all looks beautiful so far," the attending said, winking to the patient. "You have a nice trachea. Bet you've never had a woman tell you that before, have you?"

The attending turned to Tracy. "It's somewhat disorienting, I know, but do you have any sense of where we are now?"

Tracy looked at the screen, estimated how many inches of the snake had disappeared, tried to gauge where that should be on the body. She was about to hazard a guess when she saw something glistening in the distance down the tunnel. "Oh, that must be the bifurcation of the trachea into the left and right main-stem bronchi—the carina, right?"

"Excellent." The attending turned to her and smiled. Tracy couldn't see the woman's mouth, but knew she was smiling from the way the crinkles formed at the corners of her eyes. "I've had pulmonary fellows that couldn't figure that out. What branch of medicine are you interested in, Tracy?"

"I'm just interested in surviving this rotation right now," she said.

"I remember that feeling well. Don't worry—you'll do fine, I'm sure."

Tracy smiled back and wondered why she couldn't have had this woman as her ward attending instead of Dr. Murdoch. But maybe she was like Murdoch on the wards. Maybe they were all like him.

God, she hoped not. "So should we turn left or right at the carina?"

"You tell me. There's his chest X ray hanging over there. Where's the lesion?"

"I'd go left."

"Outstanding. It's left we go." The attending guided the head of the snake past the brilliant, glistening, mucus-covered piece of cartilage representing the fork in the road of the man's windpipe.

Then Tracy saw it.

Evidently, so did Dr. Rosencrantz. The snake froze, and the attending became very interested in the video monitor. She rotated the scope, pulled it back a few inches, then advanced it again.

It was huge, an enormous fungating mass the color and size of a small tomato. It almost blocked the tunnel. It was impossible to see beyond it.

"Is that—" Tracy began, and stopped when the attending slowly nodded.

The attending pushed a button and what looked like a sword appeared in the foreground of the monitor display. Rosencrantz edged the sword toward the tomato, then buried the blade in the mass.

Tracy almost jumped back as the display turned a lurid, liquid scarlet, then went black. The gush of blood looked hopelessly out of control, but Tracy reminded herself it was probably just the magnification and illumination.

The attending hit another button, there was the sound of suction, and the tomato reappeared for an instant before another wave of scarlet coated the probe.

"We hit a little vessel," she said, her voice betraying no emotion whatsoever.

"I see." Tracy wondered how the attending could stay

so calm. The thought of all the things that could go wrong, the possibility the vessel was an artery, the possibility they couldn't stop it, was terrifying. This man could drown in his own blood before they could get him to the operating room. Tracy had read enough about the procedure the night before to know that it had happened before. The medical student's body tensed. She wanted to look at the patient's face, to see if he was in pain, but the man was hidden from her by a surgical drape.

The second set of probes advanced. They touched the tomato, about where the bleeding seemed to originate, then Rosencrantz depressed a button. There was a spark and a buzz, then smoke filled the tunnel. The lazy black curls were sucked away just as quickly as they appeared. The tomato had a gray-blue scar where the cauterizer had branded it, but the bleeding had stopped. The attending watched for a minute before withdrawing the probe.

Tracy tried to see past the mass, but it blocked most of the bronchus. Rosencrantz backed out to the carina, then pushed the tube down the other bronchus, scanning the ribbed, pink walls. They looked normal at first. Maybe the cancer, or whatever it was, was just one little bleb they could remove through surgery.

But then Tracy saw them: hundreds of little blebs of bright purple tissue the same consistency as the tomato they had biopsied. The blebs coated the walls of the bronchus, forming ugly, gnarled little swirls.

It's everywhere, Tracy thought. The man's lungs are riddled with cancer.

She couldn't get the thought out of her head. "Is there any way that could be—blastomycosis?" she asked.

The attending didn't laugh as Jeb might have, but slowly turned to Tracy and shook her head.

Mr. Thurgood coughed and gagged as the snake was pulled free. "You see anything interesting?" he asked between coughs.

The attending gave him some water to sip. "You have a mass, in your left main-stem bronchus," she said. "It's about the size of a marble, maybe a little bigger. You also have some abnormal tissue in your right main-stem bronchus. I took a little biopsy of what I saw in the left. We won't know for sure what it is until the pathology comes back."

Thurgood considered that as he managed to get his coughing under control. He nursed his throat. "So there is something there?"

The attending nodded. "Afraid so."

"Is it cancer?"

"Like I said, we can't say until—"

"But does it *look* like cancer?"

"Again, Mr. Thurgood, we can't say—"

"So it does."

The attending removed her surgical mask and indicated that Tracy could do the same. "I'm sorry, Mr. Thurgood. I wish I could be more definitive."

He stared at her, at the snake in her hand that still glistened with his lung's secretions, then nodded and smiled. When he spoke, it was as though he were trying to imitate the man he had been a minute earlier, before he found out there was something to be afraid of. It was as though he wanted to be cheerful and glib, but had forgotten how. "Well, I still say the women in my family are going to have to eat their words." He crossed his arms and coughed into a Kleenex. "Getting me all worked up like that, can you believe it?" Then he looked down at the tissue and noticed the flecks of blood.

After all the equipment was put away and the patient was being wheeled back to the ward, Tracy lingered with Dr. Rosencrantz a moment. "That was cancer, wasn't it?"

The attending smiled at her. "You're as bad as the patient."

"But he's a smoker with weight loss, hemoptysis, and fatigue. He's the right age for it. And he's got a mass on chest X ray that we now know is bigger than we originally thought, right? So what are the odds it's *not* cancer?"

Dr. Rosencrantz realized that for Tracy this was far

more than an intellectual question. "How long have you been on the wards, Tracy?"

"I just started the day before yesterday." Tracy looked away.

"And how do you like it?"

Tracy paused. "The truth?"

"If you care to give it to me."

"It's depressing. I can't remember being so miserable in my life."

Dr. Rosencrantz nodded, reached into the pocket of her scrubs, and pulled out a business card. "Here," she said, handing it to Tracy. "You remind me of me when I started out. It gets better, you have to believe that. If you find things getting out of hand, give me a call."

Tracy looked at the attending, then down at the card, then back at the attending. It was the first time anyone had asked her how she was dealing with things, she realized, the first time anyone cared about how she felt about things.

"We have a Women in Medicine meeting the first Tuesday of every month," the attending continued. "I didn't know about the group until I was a resident, but I could have used it when I was a medical student."

"What do you do there?"

"We vent, support each other, remind ourselves we're still human." Dr. Rosencrantz chuckled. "It's easy to forget that around here sometimes."

As a nurse wheeled the next patient into the room, the attending pulled her surgical mask back on and said, "Hang in there, Tracy. I mean that about calling me. Anytime."

"Thanks." Tracy clipped the card to the top of her clipboard and walked back to the ward.

▲
FAME
▼

They crowded into the resident dayroom and stared up at the television screen. "It's about to begin," Jeb announced. "Everybody listen up."

As Clark looked around at the roomful of residents, interns, medical students, nurses, respiratory therapists, physical therapists, and even attendings, he wondered who was minding the patients on the ward. All activity must have been put on hold so that the staff could watch Murdoch's live press conference.

A local newscaster stared out of the screen, microphone in hand. She said something that Clark couldn't understand because of the noise in the room, then motioned over her shoulder. Clark recognized the backdrop as the entrance to the Hyatt-Regency ballroom, where his mother had once taken him for dinner.

Then the camera panned right and there was Murdoch, looking somehow small and pale in the harsh television lights. This wasn't his turf. He probably realized he couldn't intimidate the journalists arrayed before him the same way he could cow his medical students and house staff into submission.

"Be quiet!" Jeb shouted, swatting through the air with his hands.

"Yesterday morning," Murdoch began, "as I'm sure you're aware, our staff at Rosemont Medical Center discovered that a patient entrusted to our care had an illness that did not fit into any known syndrome." His voice had a softness to it that didn't seem to fit the man Clark knew. As Murdoch canted his head and stared into the lights, it was as though the attending were imitating the kind, compassionate physician one of the Rosemont public-relations men had coached him to portray. For Clark at least, it wasn't working; Murdoch came off stiff and awkward, like a politician speaking at a rival's funeral. "As I've indicated in the handout distributed before this news conference, we ran the usual diagnostic tests, but nothing made any sense. At another hospital, her true malady might have gone unnoticed or unknown, but at Rosemont, our standards are higher. During the exceedingly thorough medical exam performed by our able house staff—"

"That's us!" Jeb shouted, thrusting a hand Napoleon-like into his white coat.

"—we were able to detect characteristic lines on her hand that clued us in to the possibility that she was being poisoned. That, and the faint scent of garlic on her breath, prompted us to order the test that very well might have saved her life and put a potential murderer behind bars."

Clark was growing annoyed by the use of the imperial *we*. Murdoch's account made it sound as if the attending himself had been in the room with the patient, discovering all this for himself.

Murdoch elevated his chin a notch and blinked into the lights. He looked a bit more himself now, a little less the Marcus Welby look-alike he seemed to have been attempting to impersonate. "At this time," he said, "I would be happy to entertain any questions. Yes?"

The camera panned to a short chubby man with a five o'clock shadow and a pencil on his ear. When he spoke, Clark thought his voice sounded familiar for some reason. "Is it true, Dr. Murdoch, that it was Clark Wilson, a medical student on the case with only one day of experience, who was the first to unravel this arsenic mystery?"

Clark felt the world spin as every eye in the room swiveled and fixed on his face. Yes, that was his name that journalist had said on television, and yes, he now realized why the voice of the journalist sounded familiar. He must have been the man on the phone that morning.

"Way to go, Clark," Tracy said, patting him on the knee. "You're famous."

"No, I'm dead."

"What are you talking about?"

Clark nodded toward the television screen. "Look up there."

Murdoch didn't seem prepared for the question. He looked at his notes, then out at the questioner, then down at his notes again. Probably the name Clark Wilson rang no bells for him whatsoever. He sounded annoyed as he answered the question. "I'm sorry, but I'm not aware of the identity of the exact person who made the first discovery that led to our detecting arsenic in Mrs. Brooks's hair and orange juice. We work as a team, you see, and—"

The journalist cut him off. "But, Dr. Murdoch, this morning I spoke directly with Mr. Wilson, who told me not only that he was the one who notified the lab and DA's office, but that he smelled garlic on the woman's breath and notified his resident of the strange lines on her fingernails."

Murdoch, arms crossed, seemed unable to suppress a crooked half smile. "Oh, he did, did he?"

Clark scowled into the television monitor. "No! No, I didn't! It's not true, Dr. Murdoch!"

Every eye in the room was on him again. Jeb, standing two feet away, leaned forward, patted Clark on the shoulder, and whispered, "Nice knowing you, kid. Murdoch's going to eat you for breakfast for that."

Clark didn't understand a single word of the rest of the conference, which was an obvious pitch for the greatness of Rosemont's care and expertise. Murdoch even prepared a graphic, showing a pie chart of money spent on acquiring the latest technology, tying it in somehow with the fact that if the hospital had not been able to test for arsenic themselves, they would not have had a six-hour turnaround, and the sample might very well be sitting in some state lab, while the patient might very well have died.

But all Clark could think about was that he was most assuredly going to die now, that Murdoch would want to know why the hell a punk of a third-year medical student, on the ward his second day, was telling a reporter that he was some kind of goddamn hero.

Then something on the screen caught his eye. There was a cutaway to a cemetery somewhere, and someone was being buried in reverse. At least that's how it seemed; ugly piles of mud surrounded a hole, out of which a casket was being lifted. There were no mourners, though, just three workers and a man in a long white coat.

The voiceover was spoken by the journalist who had introduced the press conference: "And Terrence Brooks may well have another charge against him, besides that of the attempted murder of his wife; the charge of murder of another woman. When the district attorney's office was notified that Mr. Brooks had attempted to poison his wife, investigators immediately probed the young man's past, to determine if any other friends, relatives, or lovers had died mysteriously. Sure enough, a woman whom police identified as his former girlfriend through questioning of the suspect and his neighbors, died two years ago of an insidious disease process that was never fully understood. She has since been exhumed and her hair and nails tested strongly positive for arsenic. At the request of the woman's family, her name is being withheld to protect her anonymity."

Clark shuddered. He wondered if there were other victims out there, and other Brookses.

And he seemed so nice.

Clark recalled Jeb's rule about nice people. Maybe there was something to it.

The medical student looked up at the screen, unable to blink away for a moment the image of the casket being pulled out of the ground.

Neither, apparently, could Jeb. As they walked out of the conference room after the briefing ended, the resident gathered him and Tracy and said, "Rather awesome business we're in, don't you think? By examining a patient and ordering a few tests, we broke up a marriage, put a man in prison, and exhumed a corpse." He winked at them, tugging on his red beard. "You won't do that working for IBM, now, would you?"

Jeb's beeper went off. The resident grinned as he recognized the number scrolling across his LCD window. He picked up a phone, punched four digits, and waited. He only spoke a few minutes—"What was the exact time he came in?" and "When did he start drinking?"—then hung up.

The resident turned to Clark with a triumphant grin. "That was an old compadre of mine from medical school who's now doing his psychiatry residency over at Riverside."

"So why did he call?" Clark asked.

"Just to let me know that I'm twenty dollars richer."

"How so?"

"Well, do you remember Mr. Lochman? Of course you do—he's the alcoholic gentleman your classmate presented at attending rounds the other day. Well, Lochman was just admitted to Riverside with a blood alcohol level of four hundred and thirty-two. He arrived home drunk, which means Murdoch owes me twenty dollars." Jeb withdrew his three-by-five cards and jotted something down. "Twenty-four hours, indeed! Murdoch's faith in humanity is going to be his downfall, I'm afraid."

Tracy exchanged a quick glance with Clark, but said nothing.

Clark could only think of one thing—how many minutes he had until Murdoch made it back to the hospital.

THE SUMMONS

Clark was pulled out of Angela's room by Jeb. "He wants you."

So this is how it would be. Clark nodded, straightened his tie, made sure his cowlick was as flat as it could be under the circumstances, then marched down the hall.

"Do you know where it is?"

Clark nodded. He had had enough time to figure that out.

He knocked twice, heard a gruff "Come in," then stepped into a small, dimly lit office. It screamed chaos and work, with journals forming haphazard little stacks around the room, on the floor, spilling out of his file cabinet, tilting in piles on his desk, not a square inch of which was visible. It didn't look like Murdoch ever sat there, and he probably didn't. Even now, the man was crouched over a stack of reprints, his back to the door. "Step in here and close the door," the attending said, tearing three pages from a journal and stapling them together. Then he scribbled something on the header and tossed it into his out box, which was full of similarly clipped and flagged articles.

"For the residents," Murdoch explained with a nod. "I try to guide their readings a little. Christ knows, no one can read all this crap." He swept his arm around the room, then stood there looking at Clark a moment, arms akimbo. "So what did you say?"

"It was a mistake, sir," Clark began, having rehearsed his defense since before the press conference had even ended. "I didn't even know he was a reporter until—"

Murdoch cut him off. "You don't need to apologize, Clark. Lesson learned—there are two species of humans you should never talk to, lawyers and reporters. Got it? Never. Not while you're working at this hospital. Need I say more?"

"But I didn't say I was the one who found out that—"

"You didn't? Why not? I would have."

"You would?"

"Of course. If you don't look out for yourself in this business, no one else will."

Clark nodded. "I see."

"Now the real reason I called you here."

Clark gulped. *That was it?* All that worrying and his ass was still intact, not chewed to shreds. "Yes, sir?"

"Oh, stop calling me sir, for Christ's sake. Only Jeb does that and that's because he thinks it impresses me." Murdoch smiled. "He's wrong, but I do owe him this." The attending pulled out his wallet and fished out a twenty-dollar bill, then tucked it in the pocket of Clark's white coat. "Do see that he gets that, would you, and tell him I'll take him double or nothing on Thurgood's final path—squam."

"Squam?"

"Yes, squamous cell cancer of the lung. I'll bet that's his diagnosis. Ask if he accepts."

Clark didn't even finger the bill, just nodded and smiled, though he didn't find guessing what kind of tumor someone had particularly funny. Murdoch tilted his head and sat at the edge of his desk, almost knocking over two piles of magazines. "Tell me this, and be honest with me."

"Okay."

"How are you enjoying this rotation so far?"

Clark tried to think of some way of answering that, of summing up all he had experienced and felt and thought over the past few days, days that seemed longer than weeks. "It's very—challenging."

"And intellectually stimulating, I would hope?"

"Definitely."

"Good, those are the right responses, Clark. You pass."

Clark was relieved that Murdoch wasn't chewing him a new asshole.

Murdoch crossed his arms and studied the medical student a moment. "Let me tell you this because you seem a sensible young man. Not brilliant, just sensible."

Murdoch reached between two stacks of journals and grabbed a long set of clear tubing that branched off into three separate heads. "Do you know what this is, Clark?"

Clark studied the object. "I believe that's a triple lumen catheter."

Murdoch nodded. "That it is. You drop this into someone's femoral vein and snake it up through their heart into their pulmonary artery. Amazing. When someone's crashing on you, this will give you a wealth of data that will help fine-tune them, keep them alive indefinitely, but only a few decades ago, no one had thought to do this, do you know why not?"

Clark shook his head.

"Because no one wanted to *hurt* anyone. *Primum non nocere.*" Murdoch twisted the plastic snake through the air and winked at Clark. "'First, do no harm.' Well, Clark, sometimes we can do a hell of a lot more harm by doing no harm, do you follow?"

Clark paused. "In a way."

"Don't bullshit me, Clark. I can tell you have no idea what I'm talking about. Look at this." Murdoch set down the triple lumen and flipped open a journal to an illustration of what looked like a bloody cavity. "That's a man's chest, Clark, filleted open, the flaps of skin pulled back, the ribs cracked and sawed open, the muscles torn, the heart put on ice and bathed in potassium, until it doesn't beat anymore, so that the heart, too, the metaphor of every poet, the object of Aztec worship, the central pump, is cut open and sewed back up again. You can't do this," Murdoch said, thumbing the picture. "You can't do any of this, if you don't understand that this business we're in involves *pain*. You might say that we are in the business of pain, that without suffering, we would all go broke."

"I never looked at it that way."

Murdoch tossed the journal back into its pile and walked to the window. It was then that Clark noticed the plaques on the wall: the Gothic-lettered doctor of medicine from Harvard Medical School, the certificate for board certification in internal medicine, his medical license, an award he won with someone's name Clark didn't recognize, a picture of a much-younger, almost boyish Murdoch above the caption *Chief Resident, Massachusetts General Hospital*. There were others, many others—plaques and awards and miscellaneous degrees— but what struck Clark most was the absence of any pictures of this man's family. The office could have been a monk's or a revolutionary's; it was dark, cold, ascetic, yet Clark could tell by the band on Murdoch's hand that the attending was married.

"Clark, if you don't understand what I'm talking about now, you will soon. We are surrounded by suffering and pain. To avoid it is absurd. Unlike the engineer or the lawyer or the banker, we cannot go to bed each night safe with the illusion of our own immortality. We understand that the world is a hard, nasty place. Even you, over the past few days, have probably seen more misery than most people see all their lives." Clark thought about that and imagined it might be true. Murdoch turned and stood so that he was silhouetted against the brilliant blue sky outside. "So understanding the misery inherent in life, we have one of two choices," the attending continued. "We can run from it or we can accept it. The third option—pretending it isn't there—is only an option for the layman." Murdoch paused. "And the radiologist."

Clark smiled at the quip. It was flattering, in a way, to be considered enough of an insider to be joked with. "I still don't see how—"

"Suffering is as important to your medical training as is learning what to do when Mr. Smith's heart stops. If you do not stay up all night, if you do not work like slaves, if you do not spend every waking minute of every day devoting yourself to your new religion, you will be condemned to mediocrity. I sense that you already understand this. Just make sure your classmates do."

Clark nodded, wondering why he still was in the ranks of the mediocre; he had certainly done his share of suffering during the first two years of medical school.

"Enough soapbox." The attending stooped down suddenly, his back to Clark, in the same position he had been in when the medical student entered his office.

Clark stepped into the hallway and found the light almost painful. He felt there was something not quite right about this department, something maybe that permeated the entire medical center, but he hadn't been here long enough to say exactly what it was. He thought that as a patient he had come to know this hospital, having been in every clinic and on half its wards at least once, but now he was on the other side of the white coat and there was something very unsettling about it, completely different from what he had expected.

Medicine, he had thought, would be the last bastion of compassion, the one profession where kindness and the gentle art of being with the sick and dying is passed on from master to apprentice. But the only message he seemed to be learning was that technical competence and the ability to go many hours without sleep was the hallmark of a good physician. In fact, no one had yet mentioned the word *compassion*.

But Clark didn't have time to think about that. If that's the way it was, so be it. Maybe that lesson was waiting for him up ahead. Maybe this was just the way they were broken in, then over time they would be told that it was just a test, a rite of passage, a hoop to jump through. Maybe examining the hoop itself, as Tracy seemed intent on doing, was wrong.

Something more was at stake, though. He sensed it was something that Tracy could articulate and oppose far better than he. For some reason, Clark found his fingers drifting toward the bald spot on the back of his head, where they brushed across his surgical scar.

FINAL PATHOLOGY

Tracy was beginning to take this personally. The phone rang twelve times before someone picked up. It was as though they knew it was her calling again and didn't want to speak to her, to give her the final word.

The voice that answered was curt to the point of rudeness. "Pathology lab, may I help you?"

"Yes," Tracy began, "this is—"

"I know. Tracy McHugh, right? The medical student who's called ten times during the past hour?"

"Nine."

"Whatever. Listen, I've told you before and I'll tell you again—we don't have the final path on Thurgood yet. The pathology attending is reading it as we speak, and we'll get back with you or your intern as soon as it's available. 'Bye."

Before Tracy could say anything, the line clicked dead. The preliminary, unofficial pathology report from a microscopic examination of the biopsies of Thurgood's lung mass obtained at bronchoscopy had sent her scurrying to the library to read everything she could on lung cancer. The malignancy was highly undifferentiated, the pathology resident had told her, which was bad.

Generally, the more primitive or undifferentiated the cells of a tissue appeared microscopically, the more aggressive the tumor, and the less responsive it would be to treatment.

But Mr. Thurgood seemed so healthy. It couldn't be cancer, but that's what it probably was.

A nurse was waving to her from across the nursing station. "Are you Tracy McHugh?"

"That's right."

"Pathology's on line one."

Tracy frowned down at the blinking yellow light. *That was quick.* "Hello?"

"Tracy, my attending just signed off and I knew if I didn't call you, you'd sure as hell be calling us, so listen up. Your man has small cell."

"Small cell?"

"Cancer."

Tracy was silent a moment.

"Hello, are you there?"

"Yes." Tracy let the phone dangle a moment. She knew enough to know this was bad. Very bad.

The pathologist continued. "It's a fascinating mitotic pattern. Cells dividing like crazy down there. It's a very aggressive tumor pattern. Very poorly differentiated. You might want to come down and check it out."

"That's okay." Tracy gently hung up, then stared at the phone a minute.

Jeb walked into the room. He had an uncanny ability to know everything before the medical students did. Nothing was news to him. He followed all the patients—the students only followed two or three apiece—but Jeb knew them all better than anyone. It was as though he were part of a hospital grapevine that transmitted information faster than the computer or the telephone.

"Sorry about our man Thurgood," Jeb said, flopping down in a chair, kicking up his feet, and riffling through a pile of mail. "Look at all these articles Murdoch put in my box. The man is a journal freak. By the time I get around to breaking the plastic on my *New England Journal of Medicine*, he's already fired off two letters to the editor." He noticed something about her expression. "Tracy, you look kind of gray."

"I feel kind of gray. Why couldn't he have blastomycosis?"

"I don't know. Why couldn't I have a census of zero?" Then he noticed that she was really crushed and he was silent a moment. He scratched at his beard. It made a sound like a Brillo pad against a countertop.

He leaned forward and said, "I suppose this is my cue for a 'sensitivity moment,' where I'm supposed to take you aside, put an arm around your shoulder, and ease you through the psychic trauma of losing your first patient."

"He's not dead," Tracy snapped.

"But I wouldn't advise him to buy any green bananas."

Tracy clamped her mouth shut to keep herself from saying anything. She knew she couldn't hold herself back if she started.

"What was the final path?" he asked.

"Small cell."

Jeb winced, as though Tracy had hit him. "Ouch! That's bad news." Then he considered something, paused, and arched an eyebrow. "There's a bright side to all this, though."

Tracy looked at him as if he were insane. "The man has cancer. How could there possibly be a bright side?"

Jeb waved her question off like an errant fly. "I knew he had cancer from day one. The histology is what I care about."

"You mean because of treatment and prognosis?"

"No, I mean because of the forty bucks Murdoch now owes me."

"You're twisted."

Jeb didn't say anything, just went through the rest of his mail, tossing most of it in the trash. "You would not believe the junk you get when people actually start to think you'll be on the market soon. Drug companies, group practices, other training programs. They all want to buy me. Me." He laughed at that, throwing back his head and spreading his arms.

Tracy opened a textbook of medicine without having to use the index; she had read this section at least five times already. Page 1096:

Small Cell Lung Cancer: The average survival time of any patient with small cell cancer of the lung is approximately three months from the time of diagnosis. Only 1 percent in the most optimistic of series survive five years. Since most cases are metastasized at the time of diagnosis, surgical resection is generally not indicated. Therefore, radiation and chemotherapy are the only means of treatment. Radiation therapy has been shown to statistically significantly improve survival (283 days versus 189 days), but the benefit is marginal.

The phrase *statistically significant* stuck in her mind. What did that mean in the context of a patient, a Thurgood, someone with a family, hopes, dreams, and aspirations? You could tell him that his probability of dying in three months might be a little less if he took a medicine that would rip out his stomach lining, shed him of hair, maybe fatally suppress his bone marrow from making the cells it had to make to sustain life. You could tell him that and mention the *p* value of the study, the probability that the results were due to chance, and say that probability was less than five in one hundred, but in the end that didn't mean squat.

The man would be just as dead.

She got up just as Jeb said, "Christmas."

"What's that?"

"I'll give him until Christmas. Order a bone scan, head CT, chest CT, abdominal CT, give him the full metastatic flog to see where this thing has spread to, but my hunch is he won't make it until Christmas."

"Why not? No, let me guess—he's too nice."

A wide grin spread across Jeb's face. His teeth were bared under his beard. "There's hope for you yet, Tracy."

She paused. "Suppose it's metastatic?"

"It will be. Small cells usually are."

Tracy was about to leave when Jeb touched her lightly on the wrist. "Hey, you're taking this way too seriously."

She slapped her hand against her forehead, as though suddenly remembering something. "Well, hell, I just found out my first patient has cancer. I suppose I should giggle."

Jeb studied her. "He's the one with the disease, not you. Remember that."

Tracy thought about that a moment. "It's just that—" She looked outside to where some bruised, sullen storm clouds were gathering on the horizon. "Who's going to tell him?"

"You can if you want to."

Tracy nodded. A bolt of lightning knifed through the clouds. The skyline of the city was obscured in a gray haze.

"But you don't have to if you don't feel comfortable with it. It's a hard thing telling someone they're going to die."

"He might not die."

For once, Jeb didn't quip, just let her words hang there. She knew how ridiculous they sounded—less than 1 percent in five years was about as certain as anything got in medicine.

When Jeb did speak, it was in a tone of voice she had never heard him use. He sounded almost gentle. "Tracy, you probably can't understand this, but one day you will—shit happens. You have to learn to deal with it."

"Like you have?" Tracy thought it had already started

to rain, but it was a tear that distorted her view. "Let me order those tests later. I'd like to go to the library right now."

Jeb didn't stop her as she walked away.

She managed to get enough control of herself to make it to the elevator before breaking down. She huddled in a corner alone and sobbed for ten seconds, then regained control of herself before the doors opened again. It was the first time she had cried since she could remember, maybe since the night Clark came home and told her in as cheerful a voice as he could muster that he thought he might be having a relapse and that they would have to do another craniotomy.

But now it was for a stranger or for whatever class of relationship a patient fell into. Tracy had no analogy in her past for that strange blend of intimacy and professionalism. On one hand, she knew more about Mr. Thurgood, from his bowel habits (he was constipated unless he had three bowls of Raisin Bran every day) to his sexual difficulties (his wife was urging him to see a urologist about getting a penile implant) to his childhood history (his biological mother had given him up for adoption and he was raised in a warm, loving family, but always wondered who his real mother was). On the other hand, she couldn't call him a friend and certainly not a lover, but what was he then? He was a human being, someone she had made the mistake of getting close to, someone with a terrible illness that was going to kill him.

The medical-school library was halfway around the block once you stepped out of Rosemont Medical Center. It was part of an enormous complex of shimmering white buildings that reminded Tracy of the monuments in Washington, D.C., the first time she saw them. When she first looked up at the massive Doric columns supporting the limestone slabs and the sweeping stairs of the administrative buildings that had taken four years to build, she knew this was where she was going to become a doctor.

She turned down Harvard and Columbia for Rosemont and didn't regret her decision once.

Until this week.

She climbed the same white stairs that had impressed her so much the first day she visited the campus. Now her feet were sore from standing up and running around for most of the past four days. Her steps were heavy and weary.

When she reached the front of the library, she felt something akin to peace. The smell of the old books and journals and whatever disinfectant it was they used to clean the floor brought back a flood of memories. Already, those first two years, grueling as they were, seemed to belong to another time, a time when cancer was something you read about in a book, not connected to a face or a man or a family. It was an age when you commanded your own time more or less, and if you were exhausted from studying all night or just needed some extra time, you would blow off lecture, catch the subway home, and sleep during the day. There seemed so much more to do now, so many more things to order and check and document in patient charts.

But for a few minutes at least, she was going to get away from all that.

She found her old study booth on the second floor and was half-surprised to see it was occupied. Of course they had been reassigned, but until Tracy saw a stranger in there, it never hit her that the ten-foot-by-ten-foot sound-proofed square of space that had been where she had sweated through biochemistry and anatomy and pharmacology would no longer be hers to return to.

Tracy wandered through the library now, not really certain where she was headed. She hadn't been there ten minutes when she felt a twinge of guilt for not being on the wards.

She ran her fingers absentmindedly over the spines of some archived journals running down either stack. They were arranged in alphabetical order and they stretched the length of a football field down either side of her and ten feet overhead. There were probably fifty such rows on this floor, and two floors of journals above her. If she read one journal a minute, her life wouldn't last long enough to read half the wealth of information in this library.

Much of it was pulp, she knew, arguments and counterarguments about obscure points that she couldn't imagine would ever make much difference either in her life or in the lives of the patients she would care for. There were entire journals so hyperspecialized she wondered how they maintained their circulation: *Journal of British Military Orthopedic Surgeons*.

It was too much, she realized, too much noise, and never before in any field had there been such an explosion of information. No one really knew what to do with it all, or how to winnow it out and ask what was important and what wasn't.

The result was the modern medical-school experience, in which Tracy and her classmates had been asked to memorize information in as much detail as those who had preceded her twenty years earlier, even though since then the number of diagnoses and therapies had probably quadrupled.

She wandered through the stacks, wondering if she would ever know enough to keep even one patient alive.

Then she saw it: *Cancer*. It was a simple enough journal name. She traced through the years of bound articles until she came to the most current one. With both arms, she lugged the book to a table and pulled it open. She didn't have to flip long before coming to an article on lung cancer. One sentence in particular caught her eye: *Promising work on small cell chemotherapy is under way at Sloan-Kettering. The results of the latest trial of—* her eyes glazed over a series of drugs she only remotely remembered from pharmacology *—show a remission rate of almost 5 percent, with five-year survival roughly doubled*. That sounded great, she thought, until she told herself that two times a small number is still a small number—in this case, roughly 2 percent. She read on, found the name of the principal investigator of the study—Jonathan H. Blumenthal—then put the journal away.

Within two minutes, she was sitting before a computer terminal linked to several million journal articles written over the past twenty years. With a few key strokes, she had every article Jonathan H. Blumenthal had ever published. She scrolled through the abstracts, then scribbled down some citations.

It was a thin hope, but it seemed the only one Mr. Thurgood had right now. Her tears had dried now and Tracy had one consuming thought: she was going to find the combination of drugs that might save this man. Not because she was smarter, but because she was the only one who seemed to have the time to lug the dusty journals over to the copy machine and xerox the articles she needed.

She lost herself in the task, forgetting about her conflict with the staff, forgetting about the misery of the hospital, forgetting about the long hours and her sore feet.

Her enemy had a name now, a name and a face. And she would win. Jeb could sneer all he wanted, but by God, she, Tracy McHugh, third-year medical student at Rosemont Medical Center, was going to save Thurgood's life.

COLLAPSE

Clark wanted to throw the phone across the room. He had made at least ten phone calls for his new admission, a fifty-two-year-old diabetic with weeping, pus-filled ulcers on his feet—but had made absolutely no progress. The man needed a surgical consult for evaluation for below-the-knee amputation. But the general surgeons wanted to know why the orthopods hadn't been called. Clark said he didn't know, then called the orthopedic surgeon on call, who didn't answer his pages. Clark then called his boss, the orthopedic chief resident, who wanted to know why the hell a medical student was paging him out of a case and why hadn't they called the general surgeons? When Clark explained that they had, the chief resident said he should stick to his guns—call them again. Clark did, but this time the resident just said to schedule the patient for the next available surgery clinic appointment. Clark called the surgery clinic, they told him to call scheduling, who in turn told him he would need the general-surgery chief resident to approve any appointments. When Clark finally got hold of the chief resident, he was asked why the hell he hadn't called the orthopods, and Clark was back to square one. That telephonic runaround had consumed one hour of his day, an hour he didn't have.

As Clark contemplated trying to get in touch with the orthopedic surgeon and start all over, Jeb came barreling through the door, followed closely by Bob, who was chanting "Ohgodohgodohgodohgod," as though it were some mantra. Bob tried to shoot through the conference room, but Jeb halted him and forced him into a chair.

"The cuff."

"Not *now*. I don't have time *now*, Jeb!"

"The cuff!" Jeb commanded, his voice a low grumble.

The intern almost threw the blood pressure cuff at his resident as he slumped into the chair by the door and rolled up his sleeve. Jeb strapped it on, placed the bell of his stethoscope against the crook of Bob's arm, and listened carefully for a minute. "Aha! One eighty-five over ninety. That's a new diastolic record; this must be pretty serious." The resident scratched out the old number and wrote "90" on the board.

"It is, Jeb, God help me it really is this time."

If Jeb were frightened or angry or concerned, it didn't show in his face as he nodded. "Go on."

"I screwed up the IV orders on Mr. Winfield by a magnitude of ten. The nurse caught it, but not until after she had given it."

"Then I guess she didn't really catch it, now, did she?"

"No." Bob bit his lower lip. "Jeb, in anyone else, this would have been a lethal dose. I was convinced I had killed the man."

"Did you?"

"No. Not yet, that is."

"What did you do after you found out about the error?"

The intern canted his head back and ran his fingers through his hair. "I rushed to the bedside to see how Mr.

Winfield was doing. He hadn't turned blue, he was drooling happily, with stable vital signs."

"Then what?"

"I got an ECG."

"Excellent."

"No change since his admission tracing."

"You've done fine so far. Just like a doctor on TV."

The intern rubbed his eyes. "Then I ordered a whopping dose of Kayexelate to flush the potassium out of his system, drew a STAT potassium level, and ran it off to the lab myself. It's still cooking."

Jeb looked at Clark. "Can you think of anything to add, Clark?"

The medical student smiled. "No, not a thing."

"Either can I." Jeb turned to the intern. "Just relax." Then, over his shoulder to Clark: "Tell him why he can relax, Clark."

"Because Winfield's too sick and old to die?"

"Exactly. Christ, Clark, with a learning curve like yours, you're due for a Nobel Prize in Medicine in about six weeks."

Bob looked visibly relieved. "So I shouldn't file an incident report?"

"Only if you like reading about yourself. I know about it and that's all that matters. Now go in peace and don't sin again. And work on that blood pressure; I got some hard-earned dollars riding on you."

Bob grinned as he shuffled off.

Jeb clapped a hand on Clark's shoulder. "Any progress on the surgery front?"

The medical student explained what had happened.

"I see. Let me try." Jeb broke into a singsong Tennessee drawl when he got the chief resident on the line: "Hey, Mike, how ya doing? Yeah, fine, fine. Listen, my stud tells me you guys couldn't fit my patient into your busy schedule . . . Uh-huh . . . uh-huh . . . Well, that's a shame, Mike, but it leaves me no choice. Here's what I'm gonna have to do—after I get off the phone with you, my next call will be to the chairman of your department. I'm gonna have to let her know that she's gonna have to hire more surgeons because there aren't enough of you guys to come by and do consults on our patients. What's that? No, I never make threats, Mike—you know me better than that. This is a logistical thing. I'll just tell her that you said you couldn't come by—and I'm sure you have good reason—and—oh, by the way, how do you spell your last name again? . . . Now, now, Mike, these phones are monitored, I wouldn't use that kind of language . . . Oh, you could? Well, what time, then? So I should be expecting a note in his chart by this afternoon? Excellent. It was a *pleasure* doing business with you, a real *pleasure*."

Clark stared at the resident as he hung up the phone. "You can't expect me to do that."

"Of course not, not yet. But I can guarantee you this— next time you call, if you tell them you're Jeb Morris's student, they won't jerk you around so much. They'll still jerk you around, but what would be the fun of being a medical student if you didn't get jerked around?"

"Of course." Clark found there was a harmless rhythm to Jeb's banter, that if you just didn't take it seriously, he was actually fun to be around.

"Where is Tracy?" Jeb asked.

"In the library."

"Again?"

"She said she'd be there only an hour this time."

"Hmm."

Clark was on his feet before Jeb had to say it. "I'll get her."

Clark was grateful to get off the ward, if only for a few minutes. It was refreshing somehow to walk away from the illness and beeping machines and charts and patients' families, all calling for his attention, and journey back in time to that place where he had felt relatively safe.

For Clark, the first two years of medical school had been a brain-numbing memorization marathon. The grind of basic science had sapped him of his idealism. It had been like staring at the bark of a thousand different trees without ever once being allowed to step back and catch a glimpse of the beauty of the forest.

Clark never thought he would welcome the humid September air laden with all the scents of the city. He closed his eyes, buried his hands deep in the pockets of his white coat, and inhaled deeply as he walked. A stream of patients and their families walked into and out of the hospital, and already he felt different in their eyes, as though they were looking at him as a different species of man now.

For he was. He wore the white coat.

They would never know how low he groveled at the base of the totem pole or how high and greased it was; all they knew was that he wore white and a Rosemont Medical Center ID tag, and that meant he represented all that American medicine had to offer.

Clark found his steps growing a little brisker at that thought, found himself slipping into the role, into their hungry expectations of what he should be, as easily as if he had been training for it all his life. He felt himself grow an inch taller and his chest thrust out a little farther when he heard a woman tell her husband to get out of the way to let the doctor pass when she saw Clark coming toward her.

It was intoxicating.

The crowd thinned as he strode around the block to the library. The people he saw making their way to the subway stations and bus stands were a different breed now, carrying book bags slung over one shoulder, most in jeans and khakis, some of whom he recognized from medical-school parties. Half were brand-new faces—the new first-year medical students, who were going through their orientation that week. Clark looked at them with the same curiosity and amusement with which he had looked at freshmen when he had been an upperclassman in college. Had he really looked that young and carefree once?

"Clark, what's it like?"

He turned to face a tall, overweight second-year named Danny Flannery. Clark had spent half of his second year trying to figure out what endocrinological disorder Danny had. Or maybe he just liked to eat. "It's not so bad," Clark found himself saying automatically.

"You look beat. They keeping you up all night?"

"Most of it."

"Do you have time to study?"

"Since when have you been interested in studying?"

"I'm not, but I figured if you had time for that, I'd have time to sleep while all the gunners caught up on the *New England Journal of Medicine*."

Clark winked at him, feeling like an old vet now. "Don't count on sleeping, that's all I can say. Gotta run to catch my favorite gunner, who *is* studying right now."

"Hang in there."

Clark liked the sound of his heels against the cool, cavernous library interior. Within three minutes he found Tracy.

"Hey, Jeb's been looking for you," he whispered.

"I told him I'd be here," Tracy said without looking up.

"I know, but he wants you on the ward."

"Why?"

"Why—because it doesn't look too good to be off the ward so much."

Tracy shrugged. She was hunched over a textbook of hematology oncology. Around her were scattered half a dozen articles, most of which were highlighted and scratched up in her four-color ink pen. "Tell Jeb that I've ordered a bone scan on Thurgood, scheduled him for a full-body CT, and did everything else that he asked me to do. If he has more scut for me to do, tell him to leave a list and I'll knock it out when I get back."

"When will that be?"

"I don't know. Another hour or two."

Clark looked around. Clusters of medical students studied at each table, hunched over notes and textbooks. He could almost hear them think. He could remember exactly how it felt to be where they were. The first-years hadn't really gotten started yet and they hadn't gotten the shock of their first exams back. All hotshots in college, they would wilt when they realized an hour or two of studying a day wouldn't hurtle them to the top of the class at Rosemont—hell, wouldn't even let them pass.

But the second-years were halfway through the basic science grind and they knew they were in for another twelve months of memorization before they'd see a living patient. In a way, Clark thought, staring at a guy he'd seen drunk off his ass at a medical-student party last spring, the wards were better. Given a choice between that mindless studying versus staying up all night, even dealing with people like Murdoch and Jeb, Clark would take clinical medicine any day.

He looked down at Tracy, but she was lost in thought, her forehead furrowed as she stared at the text in front of her. He watched her eyes make little darting movements over the page. She was oblivious to him.

"How much time are you putting into this?" Clark asked.

"As much as I need to. Clark, they're doing some incredible work up at Sloan-Kettering, I mean fascinating. The numbers aren't final yet, but the initial results are promising. I think Thurgood deserves a shot at this protocol."

Clark looked over her shoulder. "You mean getting him enrolled in a clinical trial?"

"Why not? It's an open trial and he meets all their research criteria. I even called Memorial Sloan-Kettering on the hospital Watts line and managed to page the principal investigator, who said I was welcome to send Thurgood down."

Clark sat down in the chair next to her. He had to displace a volume of *Cancer* to do it. "Let me see if I got this straight. You're talking about getting your patient involved in a trial of a new chemotherapy protocol?"

"No one else is."

"But wouldn't Murdoch have brought this up already if this had been a possibility?"

"Not if he hadn't thought of it." Tracy pulled off her glasses, rimless oval spectacles that she only wore when reading for more than fifteen minutes or so, and looked at him. Her eyes were red and she had to blink several times to bring Clark in focus. "There is so much out there," she said, sweeping her hand over the table. "So much untapped knowledge, so many resources, how could anyone possibly keep on top of them? Of course he hadn't thought about it."

Clark found that hard to believe. "Tracy, isn't that a bit presumptuous of you, a third-year medical student, to assume you know more than an attending?"

"About this tiny segment of medicine right now I just might." She rummaged through her pile of Xeroxed articles and handed one to Clark. "That's the trial I want to get Thurgood enrolled in," she said. "It's randomized, double-blind, and placebo-controlled. That's the only catch."

Clark looked at her. "You mean he could get sugar water?"

"Right."

"And never know it?"

"Exactly."

"And die even quicker than if we gave him some chemotherapeutic agents that we know do some good?"

"That's the rub." She grabbed his hand and held it in hers. "But, Clark, don't you see? If he gets this research protocol, it might prolong his life."

"Or shorten it. Did you read this about the bone-marrow suppression?"

"Of course, every procedure has its risks."

Clark got up, rubbing the back of his neck. "Well, Madame Curie, while you're working on the next Nobel Prize, I'm going to go draw some blood and stick my finger in someone's rectum to make sure his prostate isn't enlarged."

"Have fun."

Clark was about to walk off when a thought made him falter. "Tracy, did you stop to ask what Mr. Thurgood thinks of all this?"

Tracy blinked up at him. "No. I just assumed—"

Clark smiled at her. "He should have a little say in this. It is his life, after all."

"Sure. But if I gather all the facts first, then present them with the odds of success, the side effects, all that, he'll be much more likely to come around."

"You're starting to sound as though you've already made up your mind for him. This isn't a car you're trying to sell him, you know."

Tracy narrowed her eyes. "Clark, you're starting to sound like Jeb.

"God forbid."

The medical student who had raised her head when Clark walked in now stared at them.

"How are you getting home?" Clark whispered. "I imagine all this will keep you here late."

"The subway will carry me out to the L terminus. That's only twenty minutes from our house. I can catch a bus from there."

"Good luck." Clark turned and walked away.

He looked back after walking off ten feet. Normally, even during exam hell week second year, when they would cram for one final, then have to turn around and cram for the next, four times within as many days, Tracy would have looked up at him, smiled, maybe waved as Clark walked off. Now, however, she was already buried in her work, her nose only inches from the textbook.

He was clutched by a sudden, lonely feeling, as though he were losing her. He wanted to go back to her, to be reassured that it wasn't over, but of course he didn't do that.

He was a third-year medical student. He had work to do.

Clark forced himself to go back to the hospital and that's when it happened.

Half the room disappeared for a second, half the books were enshrouded in a black curtain. The floor seemed to come up to him, to hit him in the knee. It hurt, but it was pain that let him know that he wasn't completely losing it, that he was still conscious. He heard himself say "Shit" as though from far away, then staggered into a wall, which he clutched like a drunken sailor in a gale at sea.

He thought it was Tracy who came up behind him, who touched his shoulder and demanded to know if he was all right. He turned to her, tried to smile, but it wasn't Tracy. Tracy hadn't even noticed, she was so absorbed by whatever she was reading.

Clark found himself staring into the eyes of Heather. He had dropped to his knees, so he had to look up to see her.

"Yeah," he managed. "Yeah, I'm fine." His head pounded but the room came back into focus and he managed to find his footing.

Heather was good, didn't make a scene, just ushered Clark to his feet, pulled an arm around her shoulders, then helped him to a chair. She took his pulse and timed his respirations.

"What are you doing?" he asked.

"The only thing I know how to do right now. Are you having any chest pain, shortness of breath, nausea, vomiting, diaphoresis, jaw pain, arm pain, or—"

"For God's sake, Heather, I'm not having a heart attack."

"Then what are you having? You're tachycardic," she said. "Your heart is racing."

"I could have told you that."

There was something about her that didn't look as fresh as usual, something mussed up about her. Nevertheless, Clark found her stunning, a delight to look at. Her fingertips felt cold on his wrist, but he liked to look at them, to imagine her skin on his.

"Let me get you to the emergency room," she said. "Do you feel well enough to walk?"

"Of course I'm well enough to walk."

"Then let's go."

Clark half expected the room to spin around as he got to his feet, but everything stayed still.

"Has anything like this happened to you before?" Heather asked.

"Never."

"Do you think it's related to the—"

"I don't know." The quickness of Clark's response must have made her realize he had been thinking it, too, but didn't want to say it out loud.

They walked quietly toward the hospital. "Thanks," Clark said.

"For taking your pulse and telling you something you already knew?"

"No. For being with me." He looked at her. "I was scared and it was nice having someone there. Not doing anything necessarily, just being there. I guess that's what this job is supposed to be all about."

Heather frowned. When she did, her thin, fine eyebrows disappeared. Clark felt a stab of guilt as he remembered the image of her that had haunted him for the past few nights, the thought of her lying naked on a sun-warmed slab of granite.

They entered the lobby and walked back toward the Emergency Department. Clark wondered what they would do for him; it was almost certain they would want to observe him overnight in the hospital. That meant a night of call missed, but it also meant that Clark would have to make it up somehow. He had so much to do already, and knew there probably would be an admission waiting for him when he got back to the ward.

He couldn't do this. The idea of taking a day off was somehow unthinkable. "Actually, Heather, I feel one hundred percent better. I don't think I need to have anyone look at me." His head pounded, but he didn't need to tell her that.

"Clark, you collapsed in there. You should have seen yourself. Now come on and get it evaluated."

Clark pulled away from her. She froze in the middle of the hallway, crossing her arms. "What is it?"

"If I walk in there, they'll be obligated to keep me overnight, even if nothing is wrong. They'll get a head CT, maybe a spinal tap, give me the full flog."

"You need it."

"But it will make me lose at least a day on this rotation."

"Clark, listen to yourself. How can you compare missing a day or two on this rotation to your health?"

He shook his head, moved off toward the elevators. Clark punched the up button. "Look. Let me run this by someone I trust, okay? Someone who can tell me honestly what he thinks is wrong with me, but who doesn't have a medicolegal responsibility to do anything about it."

"You're not making any sense."

"No, Heather, I'm making perfect sense." The elevator doors opened and Clark stepped inside. Heather had no choice but to step in after him. As they rode up Clark said, "If they hospitalize me again, I might have to repeat the rotation. If I have to repeat the rotation, I'll fall behind. If I fall behind, I won't graduate with our class."

"You've got the summer."

"No, Heather, I've used up my last summer. The only way I can begin internship on time is by cramming two rotations into June, July, and August, then working up to graduation day. Don't you see? If I can just hold on a little while, maybe get some treatment as an outpatient, then I'll graduate with you guys."

Her eyes searched his. She seemed to understand without further argument how important this was to him. She nodded. "Okay. But you will run this by your friend?"

"Definitely."

"Promise?"

"Trust me."

The doors opened and they stepped out. Before she walked off, he caught her by the elbow. "Heather?"

"Yes."

"Thanks again."

"No problem." Was it his imagination, or had she winked at him before turning to walk away?

REVELATION

▲

▼

"**H**e doesn't know yet, does he?" Jeb asked.

Tracy dumped her book bag in a corner and pulled out her clipboard and two manila files bulging with articles. "Not unless you told him."

"I didn't. You said you wanted to."

Tracy nodded. "I do."

Jeb stretched his long arms overhead and stared at her as she straightened her white coat and patted her hair. "You really want to do this. Usually the medical student watches the first couple times. It's a tough thing, telling a man he's going to die."

"Who said he's going to die?"

"We're all going to die, Tracy. Life's a terminal process." When she didn't say anything, Jeb added, "I could come into the room with you if you want, for moral support."

"No, that's fine."

Tracy couldn't imagine having Jeb in the room when she did it. She could picture the resident making some

159

quip or dismissing Mr. Thurgood's grief with a sarcastic truism. No, she wanted to be alone with the patient, to do this right, if for no other reason than to prove to herself that she was better than Jeb Morris.

A chorus of women answered when she knocked on the door. Tracy hadn't been expecting this; she had thought she would be alone with Mr. Thurgood. Well, she would just have to politely dismiss them.

"May I be alone with the patient?" she asked, striding into the room.

The patient's mother lifted her chin a notch and looked Tracy squarely in the eye. "You've come to tell us about the cancer, haven't you?"

Tracy froze like a deer caught in someone's headlights. "I'm sorry?" Jeb couldn't have told them already.

"Mother!" Mr. Thurgood chided. Turning to Tracy, he said, "She's asked that of everyone who walked in the room, expecting them to slip up and confirm her worst fears. She's always like this, assuming the worst. She's convinced I have cancer, although I know it's nothing like that at all. What would *you* do, Doctor, if you had to live with women like these? It's enough to make a hypochondriac out of anyone." He grinned.

When Tracy didn't grin back, his smile faded. "It isn't cancer, is it, Doctor?"

Tracy's mouth was too dry to swallow. "As I asked before," she said, "may I please be alone with the patient?"

Mr. Thurgood blinked at her now, an almost hateful look on his face. "Whatever you have to tell me, they can hear, too."

His wife had already begun to cry, sobbing into her hands. Tracy didn't think to slide her a box of tissues; her mother-in-law, dry-eyed and collected, reached over and handed them to her. It was as though she had been through this before, and remembering the story of how her husband passed away, she evidently had been.

"The final pathology did come back," Tracy finally

managed, as she had rehearsed in her mind. "And I have some good news and some bad news."

"The bad news is I have cancer, right?" Mr. Thurgood crossed his arms and gave her a look that seemed to demand that she contradict him.

Tracy nodded. Christ, this wasn't how she wanted it to be at all. She felt she was completely botching this. "But the good news is there is treatment available."

The mother and son stared at her. The teenage daughter, who had been hiding behind the mother-in-law, now stared up at her mother and began to cry, too. This was awful.

On the walk back from the library, Tracy had imagined sitting by the bedside, perhaps holding Thurgood's hand, then looking him in the eye and breaking it to him. But this—this was a mess.

"Look," Tracy added, when no one spoke, "I can get you in this clinical trial where—"

She was interrupted by the patient's mother, who demanded, "How long?"

"What's that?"

"How long does my son have to live?"

The patient rolled his eyes. "Oh, for God's sake, Mama."

"It's a reasonable question. I think I have a right to know the answer."

Tracy nodded. "We can't say for sure. Some people live as long as five years."

"How many people live as long as five years? One half, one third?"

Tracy bit her lip. She felt she had been caught out in a lie and in a way she had. "One percent."

The mother looked as though she were going to throw Tracy out of the room. "One *percent*. You mean the odds are ninety-nine to one that my son will—"

Tracy nodded and at this piece of information the mother lost it, too. She shot a hand to her mouth, which had formed a red little O, then stepped back toward the window, where she stared out into the street. She made a high-pitched soughing sound and Tracy realized she was the only one in the room not crying. For even Mr. Thurgood, staring down at his hands now, let a tear work its way down his cheek.

Why didn't I go into research? Tracy asked herself, not for the first time since the rotation had started. In a lab, she would never have to face the human side of this. Cancer would be an abstraction, an intellectual enemy, as it was while she was reading about it in the library. Now it was something else, a man and his family and the virtual certainty that he would be dead before Christmas.

"Maybe you should talk to the attending more about prognosis," Tracy offered. "He could give you some more exact numbers."

No one listened to her now, but she continued anyway. "I have some good news. A glimmer maybe, a ray of hope, but it is good news." She had practiced those phrases and now they sounded stilted and false.

She tried to believe them herself. "There are some drugs available that can prolong your life significantly, Mr. Thurgood. But they still add only months. There may be others that can double your chances of living. I want you to know about a trial going on up in—"

The mother blinked at her. "A trial?"

"A clinical trial."

"You mean an experiment? You mean using my boy as a guinea pig?"

"Oh, Mama, let her be." Mr. Thurgood scowled back at his mother, then nodded to Tracy. Gone was his playful, enthusiastic grin. Tracy thought for a moment that she liked him better this way. He seemed more original. Fear of death had made him what he was, simpler and more direct somehow. "Go on, Dr. McHugh."

Tracy sensed the hope in his voice and hoped she wasn't raising it prematurely. "The study would involve the chance that you would be getting a placebo, that is, that you would be getting no chemotherapy at all.

Though if you got the drugs in this new protocol, you might have a chance of doing much better than anyone with your disease has ever done."

"Really?"

Tracy nodded, egged on now by the hope in his voice. She wanted to believe it herself. She moved toward him, touched the back of his hand, and he grabbed her arm, pulling her toward him as a drowning man might. He was a surprisingly strong man. "I'll do whatever you say, Doctor," he said, his face two inches from hers. "You tell me to eat a live toad at midnight and I'll be out there rooting around for the biggest toad this side of the Mississippi and I'll eat him and ten others, just for good measure. You got it, Doctor? I want to live. I'll do anything to kill this cancer. Anything!"

She found her arm hurting where he gripped it, but Tracy didn't pull away. She nodded and stared at him a minute in silence. She could see the tiny blood vessels on his cornea, the darting movements of his eyes as his pupils searched hers.

He let her go at the sound of his mother's voice. "What sort of cancer is it?"

"Small cell lung cancer."

Clearly, that meant absolutely nothing to the mother. "But that's bad, eh?"

"I hope not." She pulled an article from her clipboard. "I copied this for all of you. These are the preliminary findings from Sloan-Kettering, where the clinical trial I was talking about is going on. The first page is about small cell. You might find this helpful."

The mother took the article and nodded at Tracy. "Thank you," she said. "This is the first time I think that a doctor has ever assumed that I wasn't too stupid to understand a medical article."

Tracy smiled. She remembered what they had taught her about today's patient being an increasingly informed consumer, about giving them all the information they could. "You don't have to make any decision today. Read it over, think it over, and if you have any questions, ask for me, the intern, or my resident." She paused. "Or Dr. Murdoch."

The mother nodded, stroked her son's hair. "I remember, and it wasn't so long ago, when I would see you off to school, Thomas."

He didn't silence her, just stared at the floor as she spoke.

"I was so scared that something would happen to you, that when you walked out of the house, you weren't safe anymore. Well, that, I suppose, was a dress rehearsal for this." She was silent a moment. "And now you have this cancer and there's not a damn thing I can do to stop it."

"Maybe there is," Tracy said, tapping the article. "Maybe there is."

Then she turned and walked out of the room, feeling she had salvaged the exchange. It was the first time since reporting to medical school that she really felt she was a doctor. This was as close as it got. This was life on the edge. Cancer, death, a family in grief.

She tried to feel sad, but couldn't help experiencing an exhilarating rush at the idea of what she had just been through. This was it. This was doctoring.

And somehow, she told herself, this man was going to live. Maybe it was just inexperience and maybe it was just naïveté, but she really believed he was going to make it.

She was going to do everything she could to improve his odds.

FIELD CUT

Clark waited until a lull in his work before slipping away to the other ward. His team was up next for an admission, but there were none scheduled and there was nothing brewing in the emergency room. With a little luck, it would be a quiet night. With a little luck, Clark just might sleep.

He found Erich tapping away at his computer keyboard. Clark grabbed the surge protector connecting the computer's AC adaptor to the wall and acted as though he were going to give it a yank. "Don't even think about it," Erich warned.

Clark grinned at him. "How much is all that data worth to you?"

"It's backed up," Erich said. "And this notebook runs on batteries, but I'd have to kick the shit out of you, just on principle." He grinned up at Clark. "So what's up, amigo?"

"Nothing right now." Clark tried to sound casual as he peered over Erich's shoulder. "You know, you make me look bad, doing your write-ups on the computer like that."

"No, Clark. You would look bad even if I did my write-ups with a broken crayon." Erich hit a couple keys, then something started printing out. He inspected the text as it came humming out of the printer. "How's the lawn mower, by the way?"

"Haven't had a chance to use it."

"You mean you can't mow at night?"

"I could, but I don't know if my neighbors would mind." Clark tried to sound casual. "Hey, listen, Erich."

"Uh-oh."

"What?"

"Your tone of voice. You must want something from me."

"I do."

Erich looked up and shook his head. "I'm as broke as you. Just because I'm on scholarship doesn't mean my cash flow is any better than yours."

Clark acted wounded, although he did owe Erich at least forty dollars from various small loans his classmate had advanced him. It was to Erich's credit that he never brought them up, although Clark was at least one year overdue in repayment. Whenever Clark managed to gather enough cash in one place, it always seemed someone less forgiving would snatch it away first. Such as the power company, for example. "I don't want money."

"Well, I don't have another lawn mower."

Clark chuckled. "Not that either."

"Well, what then?"

Clark looked around to ensure that no one was listening. They were alone in Erich's physician workroom, which was a mirror image of Clark's. "I want an exam."

Erich scowled up at him. "A *what?*"

"A physical exam, especially a neurological one. I want you to look me over and make sure I don't have an expanding intracranial mass."

Erich rolled his eyes. "Oh, for God's sake, Clark, how

often do we have to go through this? My clinical experience is as extensive as yours—it can be measured in hours."

"But you're good."

"Flattery will get you nowhere."

"You are. I remember in physical diagnosis, the way you examined that woman with the Bell's palsy in front of the entire class."

Erich laughed. "Clark, any first-year medical student could have diagnosed that woman; half her face drooped. It looked like it was going to slide off into her lap."

"Yes, but you put it all together and explained which cranial nerves had to be involved and which branches of—"

Erich held up his hand. "All right, all right. The flattery is working a little. If you want me to, I'll look you over. But why not go to a real doctor?"

Clark looked down at his hands. "Because they'd have to admit me if they found anything."

"So would I."

Clark shook his head. "No, you wouldn't. And I wouldn't go."

"Then why do you want me to examine you?"

"Just because." Clark looked out the window at a woman crossing an intersection far below. She had to hustle because the light changed as she was halfway across. "Because I want to know, that's all."

"You mean if you're having a relapse?"

Clark nodded.

Erich didn't hesitate anymore. He hit a button to put his computer in sleep mode, folded it and locked it up, then tugged on the sleeve of Clark's white coat. "C'mon."

"Where are we headed?"

"To the treatment room. I'll look you over in there. You don't expect me to stick my finger up your ass, do you?"

"Not unless you want to." Clark punched his classmate in the shoulder.

"Don't tempt me."

They entered the treatment room, cold, sterile, utilitarian. There was a tissue-paper-covered aluminum examining table, a stool, an eye chart, and an entire wall devoted to supplies. It reminded Clark of a thousand such rooms he had visited in a thousand clinics. He hopped up on the table and watched as his classmate stood two feet away and studied him.

"Feel free to start the exam anytime," Clark said.

"I already have. I'm studying your face and your body for any obvious asymmetries. We can skip the mental-status exam, I suppose?"

Clark nodded. "This rotation is one long mental-status exam." He loosened his tie and unbuttoned his white coat and shirt. "This could look really strange if anyone walked in on us."

"We'll just tell them we're practicing on each other." Erich removed his stethoscope from a pocket—Clark recognized it as an expensive cardiology model—warmed up the bell by blowing on it, then placed it on Clark's chest. "Which isn't so far from the truth."

Erich looked deadpan as he ran his stethoscope over Clark's lung fields and his heart. "I don't have pneumonia, for God's sake!" Clark said.

"If I'm going to examine you, it's got to be on my terms. I insist on being thorough. Do you know you have a faint systolic ejection murmur?"

Clark arched his eyebrows. "Yes, as a matter of fact. I always did, but only half the doctors who examined me ever picked it up. You're good."

Erich grunted. "No, half the doctors who examined you just don't know what the hell they're doing. Either that or it's a transient murmur. You can button up your shirt. Let me examine your eyes now."

Erich then grabbed an ophthalmoscope, mounted on the wall by the bed, and shined it in Clark's eye, bouncing the light off one retina, then the other. He then went back and forth, spending what Clark thought was an inordinate amount of time.

"What is it?"

"You have some papilledema, my friend."

"Really?" Papilledema meant that his fundi were bulging forward, presumably from increased pressure from behind. It was a sign of some mass expanding inside Clark's skull.

Next, Erich asked Clark to squeeze his fingers, shrug his shoulders and straighten his arms against resistance, lift both his legs off the table, kick out, and dorsiflex his foot. He then tapped out Clark's reflexes with a tomahawk hammer, so called because the red triangle of rubber made it resemble the Native American weapon. "Everything else is normal so far."

Erich then produced a red-tipped match and told Clark to stare at his nose as Erich held the match out to Clark's side, then slowly brought it in. He repeated this from every direction, asking Clark to cover one eye, then the other.

Erich paused again.

"What now?"

"Clark, see your neurosurgeon."

"Why?"

"I shouldn't say. It will only get you worried, and I could be dead wrong."

"Oh, for God's sake, Erich, you've already gotten me worried. Say it."

Erich leaned back against a sink and crossed his legs and arms. "I think you have a bit of a bilateral temporal hemianopsia."

Clark swallowed. "Really?"

"It's subtle, but I think it's there."

Clark remained silent a moment. "So I have a lesion in my pituitary? At my optic chiasm?"

Erich held up his hands. "If you trust the exam of a third-year medical student, probably."

Clark blinked twice. "I've never had any involvement there." The pituitary was a small, but crucial gland, located on the front surface of the brain, deep behind the nose. He looked at Erich. "Thanks."

"If you call now, you might be able to see someone this afternoon. Otherwise, it'll be a long wait in the ER." When Clark didn't say anything, Erich added, "You are going to schedule an appointment to have this worked up, aren't you?"

"I'll think about it," Clark said. "After all, like you said, you are just a third-year medical student."

Erich followed him out into the hall. "True, but you probably do have papilledema and a bilateral temporal hemianopsia. At least have someone tell you you *don't* have it."

Clark waved him away. "Look, I just need—just need some time." Maybe Erich was wrong, Clark told himself. He should never have asked his classmate's opinion. They even had a name for this: medical studentitis, the syndrome where you become convinced you're afflicted with half the illnesses you're studying. This could all be explained by sleep deprivation and fatigue with a little hypoglycemia thrown in for good measure.

Clark could find out later. He could find out when internal medicine was over.

Clark started to walk away, but Erich grabbed him. "Don't sit on this, Clark."

"I won't," Clark said. "I'll get an appointment in the heme onc clinic tomorrow."

"Today."

"Okay. Today then." Clark had no intention of doing any such thing.

He wasn't going to fall behind his class. In fact, he didn't want to spend another minute thinking about this business at all. He could see someone down the hall being wheeled onto his ward: an admission.

TOO SICK AND OLD TO DIE

Beatrice Campbell led a full life. She had never seen a doctor until the age of sixty-five. After four days of shaking chills, she decided it might be a good idea to find out if something was terribly wrong with her.

There was. She had bacterial endocarditis, a serious infection of her heart valve. By the time she was treated with broad spectrum antibiotics, it was too late; the diseased valve had to be surgically removed.

Since then, she had done remarkably well. She saw her local doctor once a month and he tinkered with her blood pressure medicine, listened to her heart, and adjusted her Coumadin, a medicine they gave her to thin her blood and prevent a clot formation on her artificial heart valve.

It wasn't her heart that brought her in now. When waking up that morning, she felt a sharp, annoying pain in her foot. When she examined her sole, she discovered a marble-sized, pus-filled abscess surrounded by a halo of red. It hurt like the dickens. She thought of sticking a pin

171

in it herself, but decided to have her husband drive her in to the hospital, just to be on the safe side. After a six-hour wait in the emergency room, during which the boil began to throb, she was called back and the emergency-room staff discovered her complicated past medical history.

In anyone else, they would have incised and drained the boil and put the patient on a ten-day course of oral antibiotics. But no one wanted to take a chance on a patient with an artificial heart valve on blood-thinning medication.

At least the screening resident, whose job it was to decide who was to be admitted and who was to be sent home from the emergency room, didn't.

"So we're admitting her, just to be on the safe side," he told Jeb a minute after paging him.

The resident nodded, got some more information, then hung up the phone and went by the call room to nudge Tracy awake.

"You got a hit. Stop dreaming about oncology and admit this woman."

Tracy rolled out of the top bunk, pulled her white coat on over her scrubs, and squinted at the information Jeb had scribbled down. She jotted a few notes for herself.

"This time let me do the whole workup, start to finish," she told him. "Admitting orders, blood work, history and physical, assessment and plan."

Jeb studied her. "You sure you're ready for this?"

"No, but Bob can help me."

Jeb winked at her. "If crosscover doesn't keep murdering him."

"The patient sounds pretty straightforward to me," Tracy said.

"That's because this is your first week. She worries the hell out of me."

"Why?"

"Because she's too healthy. It's the healthy ones who get it. If anyone's going to do anything bad on us, it's her."

"And if she's nice," Tracy added, "I suppose she's really had it?"

Jeb stroked his chin and considered that a moment. "Yes, I believe these negative prognostic factors are additive." He clapped a large, freckled hand on her shoulder. "Perhaps multiplicative."

She didn't smile back at him. "I suppose I have to switch her from Coumadin to heparin for the procedure."

"Good. Do you know why?"

Tracy nodded. "If she starts to bleed while on heparin, we can give an antidote to stop the bleeding immediately. Coumadin takes a few days. She could die by then."

"You stayed awake in pharmacology, I see. Make sure you page me or Bob to look over your orders."

"Right." Tracy grabbed her clipboard and a pen and headed for the ward.

When she arrived, they were wheeling Mrs. Campbell into her room. "My lands, this is the silliest thing I ever heard," the patient said as a nurse helped slide her from the gurney to the bed. "First they tell me I have to stay overnight for this little boil, then they tell me that they can't lance it until day after tomorrow at the earliest. Should have just popped the sucker myself and been done with it."

Tracy walked in and extended a hand. "Hello, ma'am, I'm Tracy McHugh and I'll be taking care of you while you're here."

"You will, will you?" The woman pulled a pair of bifocals from a purse and tilted her head back to read Tracy's ID tag. "Until I got here, I didn't know I needed all that much taking care of, but if you say so . . . I suppose you have a lot of ridiculous questions to ask."

"I hope they're not too ridiculous."

"They are and it's late and I'm tired, so be done with it." The woman tucked the sheets under herself, slapping away the nurse's hand as she tried to help her. "I might be old, but I'm not infirm. And get one thing straight from the outset—I refuse to use a bedpan. Refuse, understand me?"

As the nurse left the room she whispered in Tracy's ear, "Good luck."

Tracy settled herself into a chair and supported her clipboard on her crossed legs. "So, why not tell me what brings you to the hospital, in your words?"

The woman rolled her eyes. "I refuse to go through this with my nurse. Get me my doctor and I'll tell him."

Tracy sucked at the inside of her cheek. "Actually, ma'am, I'm not a nurse."

"Well, what are you, then? Don't tell me a doctor, because there's no MD after your name."

"I'm a medical student."

"Oh, Lord have mercy! Get me my doctor!"

Tracy tucked her pen into the pocket of her scrubs and looked at the patient silently for a moment. "Ma'am, I am a doctor in training. No, I don't have my MD yet, but I spent two long years studying to prepare me to be in this room tonight. I feel I've earned the right to take your history, so if you would please, I'd like your story."

The patient looked a little taken aback at that. She seemed to be scrutinizing Tracy's name tag again. Then she gave a little grunt, nodded her head, and said, "I like you, *Doctor* McHugh." Then she told the story of the boil.

Tracy thought through every question she would be asked tomorrow at rounds. Was there any associated fever or chills? Any red streaking up her leg? Any hard cords in her leg? Any swelling of her leg or foot?

No. No. No.

Tracy then asked a series of rapid-fire questions about family history, past medical history, endocarditis, the prosthetic valve, then a directed review of systems. As she asked the questions she could envision how she would write up and present this patient. When she was finished, forty-five minutes had elapsed.

"Well, thank you, ma'am. Now I need to examine you." When she came to the rectal exam, Mrs. Campbell crinkled up her chin and gaped, horrified. "You can't be serious. What on earth for?"

"I need to see if there's blood in your stool."

"How about if I just look tomorrow morning and tell you?"

"It might be microscopic."

Mrs. Campbell rolled over and hiked up her dress. Tracy was quick, but thorough. There was no blood, nothing abnormal.

Tracy then walked out to the nursing station and paged Bob. "Hey, Bob, did Jeb tell you about this new patient?"

"Of course. Oh, God, wait—no—yes, he did. She's the boil, right?"

"She's the *woman* with the boil. Yes."

"Whatever. Listen, I'm getting killed down here. Can you scratch out some admission orders? I'll be by to cosign them in about twenty minutes."

"I've got you covered," Tracy said. "They're already written."

"How much heparin did you write for?"

"I bolused her with sixty units per kilogram, then ordered a fifteen-unit-per-kilogram-per-hour drip. And I ordered a PT/PTT to be drawn in six hours."

Bob paused. "Christ, I really should be up there to write those myself, but all that sounds good."

"Are we shooting for one-point-five-to-two-times control?" Tracy asked.

"Yeah, yeah. Oh, I better come up there myself. I'll be there in five minutes." Any order Tracy wrote would be ignored by the nurses until cosigned by an MD.

When Bob arrived, he was coated in sweat. "This is unbelievable. I have three chest pains and two fevers to work up, as well as two admissions."

Tracy whistled. "How many patients are you covering?"

Bob did some calculations in his head. "Forty-nine, not including the new ones."

"That's ridiculous."

"Tell me about it." He bowed his head forward and rubbed his eyes. "I am so goddamn tired."

She studied him, a worried expression on her face. "So I'm going to be going through what you're going through in a couple of years?"

Bob nodded.

"But you're learning a lot, I suppose?"

"In theory." Then he looked up at her. "All right. Let's see those orders."

Tracy opened the chart to the orders section. Bob scratched in a few corrections here and there, but overall he seemed pleased. "I know I should go over these more closely, but I just don't have time. Do you feel pretty comfortable with her?"

"Jeb said he's worried about her."

"Why? She's wasting a hospital bed, if you ask me."

"Jeb says she's too healthy."

Bob made a face. "Another of Jeb's worthless truisms. They're true about fifty percent of the time. Same as a coin flip. Thanks for all the work, Tracy. Flag the orders and the nurses will take them off. Gotta run."

Before she could stop him, the intern was gone.

A NEEDLE IN EVERY BODY CAVITY

Clark had been sleeping in the bunk below Tracy. His last conscious thought before drifting off to sleep after she was summoned by Jeb was that he was grateful it wasn't his turn, that maybe with luck he might get a few more hours of sleep before a patient came in for him to admit. During the first night on call, he hadn't even seen a bed, didn't even know where it was.

His luck ran out about twenty minutes after Jeb nudged Tracy awake. The door flew open and Jeb stood there in the crack of light, the harbinger of a hit, of an admission, of the end of sleep.

"Wake up," the resident said. "Clark, we got a train wreck in the emergency room."

A train wreck? Clark shot to his feet, almost staggering against a wall with dizziness.

"You okay?"

"I'm fine. How many people were hurt?"

"Huh?"

"In the train wreck—how many people were hurt?"

Jeb's laugh was gentle at first, then grew so loud a surgery resident sleeping next door pounded on the door and asked him to keep it down. Jeb stopped laughing, put an arm around Clark's shoulders as he led him into the brightly lit hall. "A train wreck, my friend, is a metaphor for someone who is so sick they should be dead by all rights. To be a true train wreck, at least three organs, preferably five to seven, must be diseased or dying."

Clark nodded. There was the strong smell of coffee on Jeb's breath. "I see."

"And Terry Johnson qualifies as a prototypical train wreck. Listen. A fifty-four-year-old black male with congestive heart failure, renal failure, fever, mental-status changes, and vomiting after a weeklong alcoholic binge." Jeb stopped and turned to Clark. "Oh, and he's HIV positive."

Clark arched an eyebrow. "Are we going to be drawing blood on this man?"

"Are we ever! There isn't a cavity in this man's body we're not going to stick a needle into."

Clark shuddered. "He sounds pretty sick. Is he conscious?"

"I don't know. All I know is we have to stick lots of needles into him. Come on." Jeb led Clark into a treatment room and directed the medical student to hold out his hands. Then Jeb began handing him a wide array of brightly packaged plastic instruments and kits. "We are going to flog this man, Clark. I mean flog him like you've never seen anyone flogged since you've been here. By the time the sun rises, you will have done your first thoracentesis, paracentesis, and lumbar puncture, and have sucked off about a half liter of this man's various bodily fluids."

The patient was sitting on a gurney in the emergency room. He was about the age of Clark's father, but looked as old as his grandfather. The man's shirt was off and his ribs flared every time he breathed. His ebony body was coated in sweat, which glistened in the harsh emergency-room lights.

The man eyed them from behind drooping lids. "I'm Dr. Morris," Jeb announced. "No, no, no—don't get up." The man hadn't moved, hadn't made any sign of recognition whatsoever. "He's gorked, Clark," Jeb said over his shoulder. "So say what you want. You know what these are?" The resident tapped the man's arm with a bare finger. There were a series of scarred-over puncture wounds.

"Needle tracks."

"Exactly. And look here and here and here." Jeb pointed to the man's other arm, the back of his hands, his feet, even his neck. "He's a genius for finding veins, that's for sure. Anywhere you could possibly get a needle, he has." Jeb looked under the sheet covering the patient's midsection. "Anywhere."

"Shouldn't you wear gloves when touching him?"

Jeb clucked his tongue. "What are they teaching you in medical school these days? Watch this, Clark." The resident pressed both his hands against the patient's shoulders, then ran them down his arm. "See any little viruses jumping out at me?"

"No."

"You never worked with an AIDS patient before, have you?"

"No."

"Oh, Clark, you're in for a treat. HIV isn't very infectious; you really have to go out of your way to get it. Now don't look so gray. Step up. Come on. Touch him. Go ahead. He won't bite."

The man's eyes, yellow and brown, opened a little wider when Clark laid a fingertip on his belly. The muscles rippled under Clark's fingers. For a moment the patient's pupils seemed to focus on Clark and the medical student realized how far away the patient must feel from them. He was in another world, a condemned man with no hope of pardon, and they were examining him, trying to stave off his sentence, if only for a day or two. For no matter what Clark and Jeb did that night, one thing seemed certain: this man would die, and probably soon. "How long does he have?" Clark asked.

"To what?"

"To live."

Jeb shook his head. "He's not the one we should be worried about. Not tonight anyway. Do you know why?"

"No."

"Because he's too sick and old to die." Jeb pulled back the sheet covering the man's torso. "I am intimately familiar with this patient, and do you know why, Clark?"

"No."

"Because he has very graciously taught at least five classes of residents by experimenting to see how badly the human body can be abused without dying. I could tell you his story without looking at his chart—he went out on a binge, smoked some crack, maybe shot some cocaine up with a dirty needle for good measure, then he comes in here for detox. Only tonight he's brought some friends with him. Some bacterial friends that have made a home of his lungs and his belly. And he probably vomited up some blood, so we have to give him some, tank him up, so he can safely go out and abuse again." Jeb grinned at him. "When they got nowhere else to go, they come to us."

A male nurse entered the room and took the patient's vitals. "You'll want to drop an NG tube, I suppose?"

Jeb stepped back and gestured to Clark. "Here's the doctor. Ask him."

Clark looked to Jeb with an expression of panic as the nurse looked impatiently from resident to medical student. "What'll it be? I haven't got all night."

He sounds like a bartender around closing time, Clark thought. "What's an NG tube?"

"A nasogastric tube," Jeb said. "And the answer is yes, we are going to drop one."

"I'll help hold him, then," the nurse said with a sigh.

Clark was completely confused. He watched Jeb rip

open a plastic package containing a long, plastic snake, and smeared lubricant over the tip.

"We're going to get an aspirate from his stomach," Jeb explained. "Then test it for blood. Here." He handed the end of the snake to Clark. "We'll hold the head. Just choose a nostril and pass it down his nose into his stomach."

Clark moved toward the patient, who was now a bit more alert. He seemed to anticipate that Clark was about to do something unpleasant. It was a strange feeling, sliding the NG tube into the man's nostril. The man's head reared up off the bed, but Jeb and the nurse pulled it back into position.

"Keep going, Clark. Don't hesitate. It's the most merciful thing to go quick and get it over with."

He did and the patient began to cough. "You're in his trachea, I think," Jeb said calmly. "Back out a few inches and try again. We'll get the patient to swallow for you this time."

When the patient began to gag, they had him sip some water. He was able to comply enough to take a couple of gulps. "Now push!" Jeb ordered.

Clark rammed the NG tube home and felt a sudden absence of resistance. The man was neither gagging nor coughing anymore.

"Home free," Jeb said. He attached a mammoth syringe to the end of the tube and pulled back. It filled with yellow, frothy fluid, in which swirled purple-black flecks. "Coffee grounds," Clark. "This man is bleeding into his gut. What are you going to do?"

Clark looked around the emergency room, as though the answer was on the walls somewhere. "We could start some IV Zantac and give him NG lavage."

Jeb smiled. "Very good. What else?"

Clark blinked three times, as though to jar the correct thought out of his brain. "He needs fluids, maybe blood."

"Excellent. But he has an IV, so he's okay, right?"

Clark noticed the hep-lock, a heparin-filled IV

catheter, taped to the back of the man's wrist. "No. He needs a second large-bore IV."

"Why?"

"Because if he crashes, he may crash so fast that one IV won't be enough."

Jeb seemed impressed. "Christ, you're learning, Clark. What labs do we need?"

"A complete blood count would be nice."

"Sure. That's already drawn and back. His hematocrit is twenty-four."

Clark thought about that. "What's his baseline crit?"

"Another good question. He usually runs around thirty-five."

"Then he's pretty low. I think he meets transfusion criteria."

"I think so, too. Let's give him fluids first." Jeb issued some orders to the nurse, who nodded, disappeared, then returned with a bag of normal saline, which he hung on an IV pole, then connected to the patient's IV.

"We need the fluids in there fast, don't we, Clark?"

Clark nodded. "From the tone of your voice, I'd say yes."

"Sure. So how do we get them from that bag to his body quick?"

Clark looked at the nurse, who was smiling faintly. He must have seen this before, a hundred medical students just like Clark bumbling at the bedside for the very first time. It was a game, but it felt like a deadly serious game, one involving a live human being, his heart beating, his lungs sucking in air not two feet in front of them. Clark sensed that Jeb wouldn't let him kill this man through his inexperience, but the tiny taste of authority, of being in command of all these resources, of being the one to make the decisions that would kill or save this man was both terrifying and exhilarating.

It was what he had come to medical school for.

Then Clark spotted the blood pressure cuff. He wrapped the Velcro-fastened armband around the bag of

IV fluid, pumped several times to inflate the armband, driving the fluid into the patient's vein.

Within a minute the bag was half-empty. The patient's eyelids fluttered, his eyes opened fully, and his lips began to move. "Wha' happened, man? Wha' happened?" the patient demanded, his chest muscles rippling as he struggled against the canvas restraints that Clark noticed for the first time.

The resident winked at Clark, who was staggered by the transformation. "Amazing what a little intravenous fluid will do, isn't it, Clark?" Jeb turned to the patient. "You're in the hospital, sir. You've been vomiting up some blood."

"How'd that happen?"

"It probably had something to do with the half gallon of vodka you've been drinking every day. And that crack cocaine doesn't help either."

The man looked offended. It was ludicrous, Clark thought, with the man strapped down to a bed, needle tracks all over his body, half-dead from abuse of drugs and alcohol, but he really looked offended. "I jes' a social drinker. Jes' had a few with the fellas, that's all."

Jeb leaned over the man. "That kind of social drinking will get you killed, sir." He turned to Clark. "Now let's get some of the labs we need."

At that point Bob rushed in. "I just got Williams transferred to the unit. Let me take over." Jeb gave the intern an update. "He sounds pretty unstable."

"He is," Jeb said. "But I wouldn't worry too much. As I told Clark, this man's too sick and old to die."

Holding a needle over the flesh of an AIDS patient was only frightening if Clark thought about it. He found he could focus on the task, tell himself slowly, step-by-step, where he was going to put the needle, how he was going to advance it, what he was going to do with the tourniquet. By keeping one gloved hand out of the way of the other, he figured he wouldn't get hurt.

Bob stepped in when Clark couldn't get blood from the

man's hardened veins. The intern seemed fearless here, fast and efficient. He moved quickly and got blood return with his first stick.

Clark watched the blood fill the syringe. The fluid was a loaded gun. As he took over he tried not to think that pricking his fingers at this point could be fatal. The glove offered no protection against sharpened steel.

But Clark managed to withdraw the needle, then stab it six times into six different Vacutainers, without coming close to stabbing himself. When he had disposed of the needle in a biohazard container, he was surprised to find his shirt damp; he had perspired completely through it.

He smiled at Bob, who gave him a pat on the back. "Good job, but you do realize, I hope, that we aren't even half-finished?"

The next three hours were a blur of procedures. Clark did as Bob directed, carefully poking and withdrawing needles on command. He performed a thoracentesis, plunging a needle deep into the patient's pleural space that lined his lungs and withdrawing fluid that dripped back after a frightening little pop. Clark couldn't watch the patient's face as he advanced the needle between the man's ribs; if he went even a half inch too far, the patient's lungs could collapse, and he could die. But once he was in position and had been given another liter of fluids, Johnson didn't complain once, didn't even flinch. The fluid looked like iced tea. Out of sight of the patient, Bob shook his head.

"Is this bad?" Clark whispered, hoping the patient couldn't hear.

Bob reached forward and adjusted Clark's wrist. Out of sight of the patient, he nodded.

The paracentesis, where Clark stuck a needle into the man's belly, wasn't as bad. The stainless-steel probe seemed to take forever before fluid came back. It looked like there was pus in it and it smelled. Clark had to hold his nose away as he squirted the syringe of putrid fluid into the sample vials and squirted some into culture tubes. Each time he handled the needle with as much gentle respect as he would a live cobra.

When all the labs were sent off, the man transported up to the ward, and everything apparently stabilizing, the sun was beginning to pinken the eastern sky. Clark could see it out of the hospital window, could watch office lights begin to come on in a few buildings. The rest of the world was just getting out of bed; Clark was hoping to crawl back into his, if only for half an hour.

He wasn't so lucky.

As he and Bob headed to the call room, the intern's beeper went off. Before Bob had taken even three steps back, it went off again. He started to run. "It's Mr. Johnson, I'll bet you ten to one."

And it was.

The first thing Clark noticed when he entered the room was the blood. It looked like someone had been murdered. If he was too squeamish for this business, he would find out now, but nothing happened as he looked at the blood on the walls, blood on the floor, blood soaking the sheets. Somewhere in all that scarlet was the patient, his eyes huge and white in a face now almost as pale as Clark's. He tried to say something to them, but his face was contorted and he vomited again. A gush of red streamed forth.

Clark jumped back instinctively, but Bob moved forward, dodging the blood. He looked toward the nurse standing by the bedside.

"How long has this been going on?"

"Two minutes, if that."

"It just came on suddenly?"

"That's right."

"Blood pressure?"

"Just took it—ninety over fifty."

"What was it an hour ago?"

"One ten over eighty."

"Shit." Bob turned to the patient. "Sir, everything is going to be all right. I just want you to relax, turn your head to the side, and let us take care of you."

Clark didn't know if that was bullshit or not, but it was apparently what the patient wanted to hear. His eyes seemed a little less wide as he rolled onto his side.

Clark couldn't take his eyes off the pool of blood at his feet. He wondered if his leather shoes were absorbing any and if he had open sores or cuts on his feet. A blister right now could kill him.

He was aware of Bob pushing something into his hands. It was a package containing a gown, mask, shoe covers, and a pair of gloves. Clark had them all on when the patient vomited again. He could hear it splash against the far wall.

"Let's give him twenty-five of Phenergan I.M. And order up two units of packed red blood cells STAT," Bob said, his voice surprisingly calm. "Meanwhile, let's get some Ringer's lactate going in both his IVs."

"Flow rate?" the nurse asked.

"Wide-open."

"You got it."

"And put him on his head."

The nurse hit a button and the patient was tilted so that his head was down and his legs were up in the air, allowing his blood to pool in his head and vital organs.

The two units of packed red blood cells arrived at the bedside. They were wrapped in clear plastic and held together by a rubber band. "Could you take that, Clark?"

"Sure." It felt cold under his gloves, two units of blood that someone had donated during a Red Cross drive, stored in a refrigerator until now, to be transfused into a vomiting, HIV-positive cocaine addict.

Bob was fiddling with the IV. He then grabbed one bag from Clark and flipped it over so the label was showing. The nurse seemed to anticipate his move. She clutched the patient's wrist and turned it over, exposing his ID bracelet. "I read, Terry H. Johnson, history number B962B3."

Bob nodded. "Check. Blood type A positive?"

"Check."

"Okay, let's hang it." The tubing turned red as the blood flowed down and into the patient. Clark found himself holding his breath as he watched the drip-drip-drip of the blood into the clear plastic Y-shaped IV tubing. The man must have vomited one fifth of his total blood volume over the floor and walls and sheets; how could a slow dripping of blood make up for that loss?

The patient vomited again.

Clark found himself so caught up in the technical aspects of what he was doing that he lost his fear. He stepped up to the bedside. "Is there anything I can do?"

"Yeah. Connect his NG tube up to suction. Show him how, would you, Tammy?"

The nurse, a slightly overweight, gray-haired woman, directed Clark to a vacuum suction device, which she turned on, then talked Clark through the connections and tubings needed to get some frothy red fluid sucked out of the patient's stomach.

"Do you want some Zantac?" the nurse asked.

"Yeah, it's already written for, but give him another fifty milligrams IV push. Where's that other unit of blood?"

Clark grabbed it. "I'll hang it."

"Do you know how?"

"I just watched you, didn't I?" Clark fiddled with the tubing, checked the bag's label against the patient's identification bracelet, then adjusted the flow rate.

"Let's send off a STAT complete blood count," the intern said. "Clark, can you draw it off?"

Clark nodded. He handled the needle with even more care now, knowing that when he was rushed he was more likely to make a mistake. The blood came back on his second stick and he had it safely in the Vacutainer.

"Label it, date and initial it, and get it off to the lab," Bob commanded.

"I'll take it," someone said from over Clark's shoulder. He turned to see Tracy standing there, reaching for the bag. "I finished with my patient, so thought I'd help out."

"Put some gloves on first," Clark said. "He's HIV positive."

Tracy's eyes widened a notch as she yanked on some gloves, grabbed the bag, and disappeared from the room. She was back in five minutes with Jeb, who sauntered in, coffee mug in hand. This one said, "FIRST, KILL ALL THE LAWYERS." —WILLIAM SHAKESPEARE.

Jeb surveyed the blood-filled room like a detective at a homicide scene. He and Tracy looked very clean compared to Bob and Clark, whose gowns and gloves were now smeared with blood. Bob filled the resident in on what he had done so far.

"Looks like you're handling this situation with consummate skill, Bob." Jeb said. "Only thing I can add is to call GI. We might want to scope this man to see where the hell all this blood is coming from. We'll follow his bleeding by serial crits and blood pressure."

Clark unhooked the negative pressure hosing and pulled back on the NG tube. It slid out, long and slippery and covered with blood.

Bob's beeper went off. His hands were too bloody to silence it, so Tracy reached around under his gown and turned it off. "Do you want me to call that number?" she asked.

"Please."

She picked up a phone by the bedside and punched the digits. "This is Tracy McHugh returning a page for Dr. Graves . . . Yes . . . How low? . . . Thanks." She hung up and turned to Bob. "That was the lab calling with an alert value hematocrit. It's twenty."

Bob nodded. "That's no surprise, though. Let's get another couple units from the blood bank. What's his pressure?"

"Seventy over forty-five."

"He's dropping out on us. Let's call the intensive-care unit." Bob looked at Jeb, who set down his mug of coffee and donned gown, mask, and gloves. "Maybe we better get the crash cart."

The resident disappeared, then came back in a minute wheeling a green metal cart. Known as a crash cart, it contained everything needed in case a patient went south on you or "crashed." Jeb pulled out some leads, plugged the cart into the wall, and attached the leads to the patient's chest, after first toweling off the blood and sweat. The man was panting like a dog now, staring up at them in wild-eyed wonder, his face hungry for reassurance or hope.

"You're going to be okay, sir," Tracy said, stepping forward. Clark noticed as he felt the warmth of her elbow against his that she was fully gloved and gowned also.

"She's right," Jeb said, staring at a green tracing on the crash cart monitor that reminded Clark of a submarine's sonar screen. "Do you like Ativan, sir?"

"Huh?" The patient managed to rasp.

"I said, do you like Ativan?"

"You mean the little white nerve pills?"

"The very ones."

"Oh, yes, sir."

"Well, if you don't do anything bad on us right now, I'll give you all the Ativan you want, okay?"

Despite all his misery, the patient smiled, and Clark understood that, bizarre as it seemed, Jeb's humorous bedside manner worked. The patient was distracted, if only for a moment, from his pain.

"We got sinus tachycardia," Jeb announced. "Pressure?"

The nurse inflated, then deflated the cuff around the patient's arm. "Eighty over fifty-five."

Jeb reached up and squeezed a bag of packed red blood cells with his hands. Clark grabbed an extra blood pressure cuff and wrapped it around the blood.

The resident tore off the Y-tubing and linked the IV directly to the bag of blood.

"Just for the record," the nurse said. "You're violating hospital regulations by running blood products in directly."

"Yeah, well, killing this man would violate hospital

regulations, too." Jeb squeezed the cuff and the blood rushed into the patient's vein.

The tendons in his neck flared as he tried to sit upright. "Ouch. That's cold, man."

"Sorry," Jeb said. "You need the blood, my man. How you feeling?"

The man collapsed back on the bed. "Like someone rolled over my body, man."

Jeb's eyes scanned the tracing. The machine on the crash cart beeped. "We're getting a few runs of V tach." Jeb looked toward the door. "Any sign of the ICU resident?"

Tracy stuck her head out into the hallway. "No."

Then the phone in the room rang. Clark, after hesitating a moment, picked it up.

"Hello?"

"Terry?"

"No, my name is Clark Wilson, a medical student."

"Well, is Terry there? This is his brother. I want to talk to him."

Clark looked at the patient, who looked as though he were struggling not to vomit. "He's tied up right now. Can I have him call you back?"

Bob yelled something to Jeb, the machine beeped loudly, and then Jeb yelled something back. The patient vomited. Clark was sure the splash of blood could be heard by whoever was on the other end of the line.

"What the hell's going on there? He's all right, ain't he?"

Jeb grabbed the phone from his hand. "We're going to need this line free, sir . . . He'll get back to you as soon as he can . . . Thank you very much." He turned to Clark. "Let's get a blood gas."

"Yes, sir." Clark held the man's wrist, which now felt cold and clammy under his gloves.

"I can't get a diastolic," the nurse said. "His pressure is sixty over nothing."

Bob felt for the man's carotid artery. "Shit. No pulse."

Clark looked at the patient and the man's eyes had

rolled back in his head. He looked almost as white as his sheet.

"Call a code," Jeb said, calm as ever, looking at the tracing. "He's in pulseless V tach."

"What's that?" Tracy asked.

"Ventricular tachycardia, but this is not a teaching moment," Jeb told her. To the nurse: "Call a code."

The nurse punched an emergency intercom button and called out, "We have a code in here!"

"Begin CPR while I get the defibrillators ready," Jeb said, his voice flat and emotionless. He sounded so casual, Clark almost thought the man would reach back and sip from his coffee mug. But he didn't, instead getting what looked like two irons from the top of the crash cart. He held one in each hand and depressed a button with his thumb.

Bob hopped up on the patient's bed, pivoting on his knees, felt for the man's xiphoid process at the end of his sternum, placed his palms firmly against the man's chest, and began doing chest compressions.

The nurse pulled out a mask with a big plastic bulb attached and formed a seal over the patient's mask and nose, then began squeezing the bulb.

"Stand back," Jeb said. "Someone wipe that blood away from the patient's chest or I'll shock myself."

Clark grabbed a bloodied towel and ran it over the man's ribs.

"Stand back!" In one smooth motion, Jeb laid the paddles in place, looked over both shoulders, and depressed a button on each paddle. The patient's body jolted and his back arched off the bed.

Clark's eyes darted from the patient, who sank back onto the bed with a groan, to the rhythm strip. There was a series of psychedelic green squiggles, then nothing, then what Clark recognized as a normal sinus rhythm.

"Do we get a pulse?" Jeb asked.

The nurse stopped bagging the patient and felt for his carotid. "Yes. Strong."

"Excellent. Stop bagging him and see how he does."

She did and his chest rose and fell, slower and deeper this time.

Emboldened by a surge of adrenaline, Clark plunged the needle into the patient's wrist. Blood pulsed back on his first stick.

He didn't take his eye off the tip of the needle, dripping with HIV-contaminated blood, as he twisted it off and dropped it into a biohazard disposal box.

"Blood pressure?" Jeb asked the nurse.

"One hundred over ninety."

The tension in the room, which had been palpable, now eased.

There was the sound of someone running out in the hall, then the intensive-care-unit resident ran into the room. "Sorry, but there was a respiratory arrest on neurology. What's going on here?"

Jeb winked at him. "Never an ICU resident when you need one, is what I say. We got the situation stabilized, but this man is going to need a unit bed." Jeb rattled off the story in about thirty seconds. To Clark, it was like listening to a native babble in a foreign tongue. There were words and phrases he knew, but most of the acronyms and slang formed an exotic new language, a language he was trying desperately to learn.

His eyes drifted to the window, where a bright orange light poured in. It was surprising that the sun had risen. The night had flown by in such a rush of adrenaline, sweat, and fear, that Clark had lost all sense of time.

"We'll take him," the ICU resident said, pulling on some gloves after jotting some notes onto a three-by-five card. He looked around the bloodied room. "Jesus, looks like a slaughterhouse in here."

As the patient was being wheeled off, Clark felt a strange sense of exhilaration. He didn't feel tired, just buzzing with something he hadn't felt since arriving at medical school. As he peeled off his surgical mask and tossed his shoe covers in a trash can, he had the self-satisfied sensation that a fighter pilot must have after a successful mission. No, the man they had saved was no pillar of society, and yes, he would die eventually of AIDS, but they had held him through the night. Another human being, who unquestionably would have died if they had done nothing, had survived.

He looked at Tracy, who seemed to be thinking the same thing. Her face was flushed as she pulled off her blood-smeared gown. Then he looked at Bob, who for once didn't seem flustered, but somehow bolstered and self-assured, if just for the next few moments. He was filling out some form on his clipboard as he walked.

Jeb pulled up the rear. He had reacquired his coffee mug, which dangled empty from his index finger, like a revolver found by a detective at a crime scene. "Ah, the joys of medicine. We just pumped a few thousand dollars' worth of medical technology into this man so he can safely go out and get high again. Kind of brings a tear to your eye, doesn't it?"

The nurse punched him in the arm and said, "He might sober up; you never know."

"Yes, and I might become hospital director tomorrow."

"You weren't so cynical when you were an intern."

Bob looked at her and grinned. "Tammy, you knew Jeb as an intern?"

"Oh, yeah. Jeb was as scared and clumsy as they come. Worse."

Jeb rubbed his beard with his free hand. "Yes, hard as it is to believe, I was flustered once or twice. I spent twenty minutes once agonizing whether to give someone Mylanta or not. Mylanta!"

Bob studied Jeb as though seeing him for the first time. "Then what happened?"

"The same thing that happens to all you young interns," the nurse answered for him. "You get cocky, forget you were ever bumbling and foolish once. But we nurses remember. Believe me, we do."

"Ha!" Jeb sipped at his coffee. "No one can call me cocky!"

"You redefine the word *cocky*," the nurse said.

Clark felt a sudden rush of happiness, a feeling that this was what medicine was about, being part of this team. And for all his quirks and caustic wit, Jeb was nothing if not competent, coolly competent with a grace under pressure that had ensured they all functioned as a team and not as a handful of panicked individuals.

"Do you think he's going to be okay?" Clark asked.

"Oh, he won't die, if that's what you mean. And you can tell me why."

Clark thought about it a moment. "Because he's too sick and old to die?"

"Exactly."

Tracy grinned at Clark. "That's the stupidest thing I've ever heard."

"Well, Jeb told it to me."

"Figures." She looked at the resident. "Where do you come up with these little maxims?"

"Experience, my dear. Many long nights like this worth of experience."

Tracy didn't get angry at that, didn't even flinch. She seemed in too good a mood for rancor. For the moment they all seemed to forget their differences and bask in the warm afterglow of a job well done.

"To the cafeteria," Bob suggested. "I think we all earned a chocolate-covered doughnut. My treat."

Jeb didn't seem too enthusiastic about that, but nodded his assent. "All right, but only for a few minutes. I'm still worried about the other patient."

"Mrs. Campbell?" Bob tilted his head back and laughed. "Jeb, you say *I* worry too much. We've had our quota of bad luck for the night."

Jeb arched an eyebrow. "Oh, you've jinxed it now. There is no such thing as too much bad luck in a teaching hospital."

He was right. They were in the stairwell, taking the stairs two at a time on their way to the cafeteria, when

Bob's beeper went off. He looked down at the number scrolling across the screen. "It's the floor. Someone's probably got a stupid question about an order I wrote." He stepped out of the stairwell into the first-floor lobby and picked up a phone on the wall.

It was cruel, Clark thought, how short-lived the confidence of an intern can be. Bob hadn't been on the phone ten seconds when his face was transformed by its usual mask of worry and fear. "I'll be there in thirty seconds." He slammed down the receiver and ran back into the stairwell. "Ohgodohgodohgodohgod."

Jeb ran after him. "What was that about bad-luck quotas?" he asked.

Tracy and Clark sprinted to keep up. The tail of Jeb's coat flew as the long-limbed resident leaped up the stairs.

"It's Mrs. Campbell," Bob said. "She collapsed and the nurses can't wake her up."

"An LOL FOF, huh?" Jeb said.

"What's that?" Clark asked.

"Little Old Lady Found on Floor."

Tracy looked sick, as though she were about to vomit. At first Clark thought it was because of the six flights of stairs they ran up, but even after they burst out of the stairwell and into the hallway leading to the ward, she still looked sick. She scanned her clipboard as she ran.

"Is Mrs. Campbell your patient?" Clark asked her.

She nodded. "Or she was."

They reached the room. The sun had now completely risen and the light was blinding. Clark had to squint to see a thin elderly woman lying in the bed.

"*Mrs. Campbell!*" Bob yelled. "*Mrs. Campbell, are you okay?*"

She was leaning over the side of the bed staring up at them. Half her face sagged. "I can't feel anything in my left face or arm."

Jeb heaved in huge gulps of air as he looked her over. "I told you she was the one to worry about. Tracy, where's the lesion?"

Tracy blinked at him. "I don't know."

"What about you, Clark? Where's the lesion that's causing this pathology?"

If there was one thing Clark knew, it was neuropathology. "I'd say the right middle cerebral artery." He felt sick, watching this woman drool on her pillow, trying to talk to them, while Jeb talked openly about her as some intellectual puzzle.

"Bingo. This dear old woman is having a transient ischemic attack." Jeb slammed his mug down on a sink by the door. It made a loud bang. For the first time since Clark had known the resident, Jeb was showing signs of anger. The resident's lips were pressed together and trembling as he snatched the patient's chart from a nurse and opened it to the orders section. "Who wrote these?"

Tracy stopped flipping through her notes and held her clipboard at her side. Clark took one look at her and assessed what must have happened. "I did," she said.

"And you cosigned them?" Jeb thrust the orders in Bob's face.

Bob blinked four times hard. "Yes." He and Tracy had identical expressions, like coconspirators whose cabal had been discovered.

Jeb pursed his lips together. "I see." All that could be heard in the ensuing silence was the sound of the patient making a mumbling sigh.

Jeb snapped his head to the nurse. "Bolus her with three thousand units of heparin then put her on a seven-hundred-and-fifty-unit-an-hour drip."

The nurse nodded. She trotted out of the room.

Jeb rubbed his eyes and took the patient's hand. "Ma'am, we understand what's happening and we're going to take care of it right away. Luckily, your nurse was on the ball and made sure we were called." He turned to Bob. "Get a STAT ECG and call radiology and get this woman an emergent head CT."

Bob shot from the room and it was apparent in an instant why the man was a nervous wreck. The intern had stayed up all night keeping a man from bleeding to death, performing marvelously as far as Clark could tell, but something had happened, some slip in judgment too subtle for Clark to understand, and now this woman was in serious trouble. There was no E for Effort in medicine. It didn't matter if you were right ninety-nine percent of the time if the one percent of the time you were wrong got people killed.

Or worse.

"Tracy, don't just stand there staring, draw off a STAT PT/PTT."

Tracy already had produced a tourniquet, which she wrapped around the woman's arm. The patient's flesh sank like soft dough under the rubber.

Bob returned. "The family's in the visiting area," he said. "Visiting hours start in five minutes."

Jeb grunted. "Well, let's not let her stroke out on us."

Tracy sank a needle into the woman's vein. "It's not his fault," she said, drawing back on her syringe. "It's mine. I wrote the orders. She wasn't adequately anticoagulated."

Jeb didn't say anything.

Bob puffed out his cheeks and exhaled forcefully. A bead of sweat formed and worked its way down his forehead. "No, Tracy, I'm responsible for everything that happens or doesn't happen to this patient. I cosigned those orders."

There was a knock on the door. It opened and Murdoch's face appeared. "I'd like to round early this morning, if that's okay. I have a meeting at ten and—what's going on in here?"

"We've got the situation under control," Jeb said.

Murdoch threw open the door and strode into the room. "Holy shit, that looks like Beatrice Campbell."

"It *is* Beatrice Campbell."

"I've been following her as an outpatient for years. She called me last night saying she had a little boil on her foot. I recommended she come to the emergency room. What the hell happened to her?"

No one spoke for a minute. Clark had the same feeling he had when his father came home to discover an expensive vase his brother had broken with a baseball and tried to Super Glue back together. They were all in deep shit.

"Looks like she had a TIA," Jeb said.

"It was my fault," Tracy said, squirting the blood into a Vacutainer with a light blue rubber top. "I screwed up her heparin orders, stopped her Coumadin, and—"

Jeb slowly stooped down and picked up the chart, which was still lying on the floor, open to the orders section. He handed it to Dr. Murdoch, who frowned at it, looked at the patient, then back at the orders. "Why wasn't my patient anticoagulated?"

"I told you—" Tracy said, but Bob cut her off.

"It was my fault. I screwed up and there's no excuse. I don't know what to say."

Murdoch approached the bedside. "What the hell do you expect me to do, come in in the middle of the night and do intern work?" He turned to Jeb. "Is that what I have to do?"

Jeb stared straight ahead. "No, sir."

"You don't deserve your MD," Murdoch spat at Bob, whose ears were crimson.

"I know."

"You're dangerous."

"I know."

"Shut the hell up and let me castigate you without your agreeing with everything I say." Murdoch looked at the patient and swore. She stared up at him with terror in her eyes. Then the attending took the chart and threw it at Bob. The three-ring binder holding it together burst open and progress notes, flowed labs, ECGs, nursing notes, and insurance information spilled out onto the floor. Bob immediately stooped to pick it up. Tracy helped him. Both their hands shook.

Murdoch looked dangerous, ready to kill. "Who wants to tell the family, huh? Who wants to walk out there and tell them, 'So sorry, but we fucked up. Your mother has a new facial droop and—'"

Jeb cut him off. "I chewed them out before you got here. They don't need to hear it again."

Murdoch blinked at him. "What did you say?"

But it was Tracy who answered for him. "You heard him. It's not Bob's fault this woman is lying here like this. This woman is a victim of your goddamn system. It's insane what you expect from your house staff—insane!"

She lunged for the door, brushing past Murdoch. "Where are you going?" he demanded.

"To tell the family. Someone has to. To tell the family that I screwed up."

"You will do nothing of the kind." Murdoch's voice made her freeze. It was cold and determined.

Tracy turned around, crossed her arms, and stared at the attending. There were tears in her eyes now, and when she blinked one coursed down her cheek. "Why not?"

"Because this is now a medicolegal matter. Whatever you say at this point can be used as evidence."

Tracy's forehead crinkled. "Evidence?"

"In a malpractice suit. If we handle this correctly, this will never go to court." He looked toward the door. No one spoke, not even the nurse who had begun the heparin drip. In the silence, they could hear the patient's breathing.

Murdoch placed a hand on the patient's ankles, looked at her silently a moment, then turned and stepped from the room. "Get her transferred to the stroke unit," he said over his shoulder.

Jeb turned to Bob and Tracy. "These things happen," he said. Then he grabbed his mug and walked from the room. Clark got a glimpse of the words KILL and LAWYERS.

Clark walked up to Tracy. "You okay?"

She didn't say anything.

"Hey, let's get out of here a minute."

Tracy remained silent as Clark led her out into the corridor, then away from the nursing station, away from the family waiting at the end of the hall, toward a far stairwell that led directly off the ward. He could feel her shaking.

Clark looked over his shoulder and saw the family around Murdoch, who was nodding and speaking, nodding and speaking. Clark didn't want to see or hear any more than that.

He put an arm around her when they reached the stairwell and her shoulders shook under his hand. She leaned her head against him and he could feel her cheek wet against his.

"Hey, it's all right," Clark said, but he knew it wasn't. This was a new territory for him. He had no analogy, no experience to guide him. There were no words of comfort he could offer.

"I could have killed her," Tracy said.

"But you didn't. No one can expect you to be responsible. This is your first week."

"Bob trusted me. He asked me if I had any questions and I could have—"

"Don't torture yourself like that." Clark brushed the hair from her forehead. "She'll probably be okay. We caught it in time."

She nodded, wiping the tears from her face with the back of her hand. "This is just too much."

"We had a bad night."

Somehow that struck her as funny, and she found herself laughing, laughing and crying at the same time as Clark held her.

Then she pulled herself away, blinked her eyes dry, and straightened her white coat. "Do you have a tissue?"

Clark handed her one.

"I must look like shit."

"You look fine. Let's get some coffee before attending rounds."

▲
AFTERMATH
▼

No one mentioned Mrs. Campbell during attending rounds. Murdoch sat at the head of the table, nothing in his expression or voice betraying that anything abnormal had happened that morning. Jeb sat to his left, sipping from a new mug, this one with a Norman Rockwell painting of a little boy in a doctor's office. Bob sat at the end of the table, near Tracy, who sniffled occasionally and whose eyes were bloodshot, but who otherwise looked fairly well composed. Clark sat across from her and winked at her and smiled whenever their eyes met. She didn't smile back.

Erich was sitting to Murdoch's right. He rattled off the presentation of a man he had admitted with peptic ulcer disease for endoscopy. It was a straightforward case. Afterward, without prompting, Erich gave a five-minute talk on ulcers.

"This rotation is giving me one," Clark whispered to Tracy, but she ignored him.

Murdoch didn't interrupt the presentation once. When

he spoke, it was obvious he hadn't been paying much attention, for he asked a couple of questions that had been covered in great detail by Erich. Then it was Clark's turn.

Clark then knew what a Christian felt like before being fed to the lions. This was not a good situation: Murdoch was furious, his patient was a train wreck, and Clark had had no time to prepare. Still, he managed to rattle it off all right, and—to his amazement—Murdoch didn't interrupt at all, even when Clark gave the family history before completing the history of the present illness.

Murdoch stared blankly at Clark when he was done.

There was an awkward silence. "And that's the end of my presentation," Clark repeated.

Murdoch seemed to come out of a trance. "And now he's in the unit?"

"Yes."

"Then there's no reason to see him either, is there?"

"No."

Murdoch nodded. "Tracy, I had the pleasure of knowing your patient for almost twenty years, so there's no reason to present her." He didn't look at her when he said that, just stared down at his hands, folded on the table in front of him. "I checked in with her right before attending rounds." He looked up. "Her facial droop is gone, her numbness is resolved, and she's almost entirely back to normal."

Tracy closed her eyes and bowed her head forward.

"We were lucky," Murdoch said. "It could have been much worse."

Tracy stared down at her hands. Clark noticed her knuckles were white.

"So, Tracy," Murdoch continued in a different tone of voice. "Give us an update on Thurgood."

"The pathology came back small cell." Her voice shook slightly.

He nodded. "So I heard. More bad news. We could have done something with a squamous. All right. Has he been told?"

"Yes."

"Who told him?"

"I did."

Murdoch turned to Jeb. "In the future, I don't want the medical students telling my patients their major diagnoses. Ulcers, yes. Cancers, no."

Jeb nodded. "All right."

Murdoch looked back at Tracy. He eyed her slowly. She looked back at him, her reddened eyes defiant and unblinking. "We have no reason to keep Thurgood now. When the metastatic workup comes back, we'll know how far the cancer's spread. Then we can give him some numbers. After that, we can send him home to die."

Tracy stared at the attending. "What about chemotherapy?"

Murdoch cupped his ear. "You're kidding, right?"

She bit her lower lip. "Not at all. There's an ongoing study right now at Sloan-Kettering that's showing a high response rate for his subtype of tumor after three courses of—"

Murdoch cut her off. "I'm sure if you look hard enough, you can find a study somewhere showing that tapioca pudding will cause spontaneous remission of male pattern baldness. That doesn't mean it's real. We're discharging Thurgood."

"But he's interested in the study."

Murdoch stared at her. "You mean you *told* him?"

"Of course I did. He has a right to know about everything to do with his disease."

"Not until you clear it with me, he doesn't." Murdoch slapped his forehead with an open palm. "You have no right to get his hopes up like that. You don't know what you're talking about."

Tracy balled one hand into a fist. "But I do. I was studying about this for the past few days and I say we try."

Murdoch sat back and cocked his head. "Okay. Let's tell the man that he has six months to live. Then tell him that during those six months, we're going to make him lose his hair, feel sick as a dog, and throw up half his intestinal tract. If he doesn't die of overwhelming sepsis, then he *might* live another week or so."

"Actually, the follow-up on some of these studies was over two years. The Sloan-Kettering study is showing roughly double the number of survivors."

Murdoch studied her a moment, just leaned back and stared at her. Then he turned to Jeb. "What do you think?"

Jeb shrugged. "She has a point. The Blumenthal group in Sloan-Kettering does good work. Maybe Thurgood deserves a chance."

Murdoch toyed with the stethoscope curled around his neck. "Fine. Get a heme onc consult, and if they agree, we'll go for it."

"I called Sloan-Kettering yesterday," Tracy said. "I faxed them Thurgood's chart so they can review it for enrollment in their trial."

Murdoch smiled at her. "And if I had said no?"

Tracy considered that a moment. "I would have given the patient the fax number and a Release of Information form and told him how to do it himself."

Murdoch stared at her in silence a moment. Then half his mouth twisted into a smile. "You really are something else, Tracy McHugh."

THE QUARRY

▲
▼

When Clark pulled his
car into the worst city traffic Friday had to offer, his entire
body hummed with a satisfaction he hadn't known for
years. He had survived his first week of internal medicine
and it looked like he would survive the one after that. It
wasn't so bad, not if you just kept your mouth shut,
worked like a mule, and didn't think about things too
much.

Clark found the best and worst thing about being a
medical student was that he had no ultimate responsibility for anything. Everything he did had to be countersigned, double-checked, supervised. He couldn't sneeze
in a patient's room, it seemed, without asking the attending permission first.

But at the same time the lack of responsibility was frus-
trating, since it made him wonder why the hell he was
there at all sometimes. When Mr. Lehman wanted to
know why he was asking all those goddamn questions,
Clark really didn't have a good answer. It was to train

Clark, he knew, but the awesome privilege of stepping into strangers' room, violating their bodies and their minds only for training, didn't seem quite right in his mind.

Then again, how else could he learn?

Clark tapped out the percussion to a song on his car stereo as he pulled into the outbound lane of the interstate that would take him home. He thought about the thousand little tasks he had performed over the past thirty-six hours, and was amazed. Two days merged into one; what he had done that morning didn't seem to belong to what he had done that afternoon. Sleep deprivation and the novelty of his work environment combined to distort his sense of space and time, blanket everything in a surrealistic haze.

It was a beautiful, balmy September day. He wished Tracy were with him. He loosened his tie, turned up the stereo, and looked around at the cars crawling past him; no matter how he tried, he always seemed to be in the wrong lane.

Something was worrying him, though, and he couldn't put his finger on it. It wasn't passing out in the library, or even the abnormalities Erich said he found on physical exam. Clark knew he should be, but he wasn't worried about a relapse.

No, it was Tracy.

Jeb had let them go early, had practically shooed them off the ward, but she had headed straight for the library. She said she was going to read some more about small cell cancer. What else more was there to know? It was as though she believed that if she just read enough, knew enough, studied enough, Mr. Thurgood would be okay.

Clark felt a twinge of guilt; maybe he should be studying, too. But, Christ, he had spent a hundred hours that week in the hospital already, and they would have to go in the next day and be on call Sunday.

Maybe that's what it was, the thing that was pulsing through his body, exhilarating him so. Maybe it was the exquisite sense of every moment of freedom having a shape and feel and texture that he had taken for granted before. "Work makes life sweet," his mother had told him, and this must be what she meant.

So what did he want to do? Whatever it was, he'd have to do it alone. Randy was on call. The Grunt was taking his wife out to dinner. Alicia was doing internal medicine at another hospital and was on call that night.

Clark found himself driving past his exit, speeding up as the traffic thinned, watching the white, cottony clouds scud past overhead. He turned onto a gravel road, drove a quarter mile, and came to a Cyclone fence gate, chained shut and marked with the words WARNING: TRESPASSERS WILL BE PROSECUTED. Another sign warned BEWARE OF DOGS but everyone knew that was a lie. Clark parked the car and killed the engine.

It was strange being here alone, he thought; he had usually come with Tracy. He remembered the way she would walk alongside him, stopping every now and then to remove a small stone from between her toes, the way he would tell her to hurry up and act annoyed but really wasn't annoyed at all, just wanted to let her know that he loved the little things she did that made her her. Her absence was almost palpable.

He got out of the car and walked to the spot in the fence where it was torn open. Who made the hole and why it was never repaired was as mysterious to Clark as why he had never seen or heard a dog anywhere near the site.

The path to the quarry was overgrown with vegetation, huge ferns that in places formed a canopy overhead. He remembered the way it was when Tracy walked ten feet ahead of him here; she would disappear completely and all he would see of her was the ripple where she had been. Sometimes he would stop, cut off the path, and wait until she realized he wasn't there. When she came back, he would ambush her, surprising her completely. The ferns were that thick.

Then they broke and there was a granite ledge, completely bare of any vegetation except for an occasional weed twisting its way out of a crack in the rock. The ledge always made Clark's heart stop when he first saw it, the way he knew the quarry lay just on the other side, thirty feet below.

He never dove in, just liked to sit and drop rocks into the water. Sometimes he would take another trail around to the side where the drop-off was gradual, and he could wade into the water.

Clark debated with himself whether it was worth dry-cleaning his trousers for a little dip in the warm, green water when he saw her.

She was completely naked, the sun shimmering off her back. Beads of sweat or oil or sunscreen covered the curve of her shoulders, her buttocks, her thighs. She was lying on a huge white towel, her head on her hands, one foot flexed and kicking lazily into the air.

In contrast to all the old, disease-racked bodies he had laid eyes on that week, Heather was a goddess, something not of this world. She was different from how he imagined her, thicker in places, thinner in others, but she was a work of art. She was a reminder that flesh can be beautiful.

Clark froze where he stood, then turned and slowly walked away.

"Clark, is that you?"

He debated his options. One was that he could walk on and ignore her, pretending not to be himself. From a distance she might not have recognized him. Another was to turn toward her and act shocked, pretending to see her for the first time. A final option was just to run.

He chose option number two, covering his mouth with his hand as he turned around. "Heather?"

She was smiling at him, but made no effort to cover herself with the neat pile of clothes lying at her side. "You ought to join me—the sun is so soothing. It's enough to make me forget about that goddamn hospital."

Clark didn't know quite what to do. "Speaking of that goddamn hospital, I thought you were on call today."

"I am. My resident said I could take off to the library; he'd call me if an admission came in."

"Heather, I hate to tell you this, but this isn't the library." Clark tried to imagine Jeb letting him go like that. "But I don't see a phone around here."

"Of course not. Randy and I rented a cellular one. It's in my canvas bag. For fifty bucks a month, it's worth it."

Clark tried hard not to look at her. "Well, this is one hell of a way to pull call."

"I'll say. It was Randy's idea; he was out here earlier, but got called in." She rummaged inside her bag and pulled something out. It glinted in the sun. "Here. Have one."

"What is it?"

"A beer."

As she tossed it to him she flipped the towel over her bottom. "You're embarrassed, aren't you?"

"Why do you ask that?"

"Because you haven't looked at me once since you came out here."

"Well, it is somewhat—disconcerting—to see a class-mate completely naked in the middle of nowhere." Clark looked around at the vegetation encroaching on the lip of granite surrounding the quarry. "Is this completely safe? I mean, what if some gang of roaming, horny youths gets sight of you?"

Heather tossed back her head and laughed. When she did, a bead of sweat coursed down her neck, disappearing in the shadow between her breasts. "I have protection."

Clark squinted at her. "What do you mean?"

She reached into the bag again and pulled out another, smaller bag. It had a purse string, which she untied. Then she removed a black revolver.

Clark's eyes bulged. "You're packing a pistol?"

"A thirty-eight. The Grunt said I could have gone for a smaller model, but then I might have to fire twice."

"The Grunt gave you that?"

"No, but he helped me buy it and took me out to the range to show me how to use it. Hey, get that look off your face—it's legal, and I'm a single female, and I'm tired of feeling like a hostage in my own city."

"When did you buy it?"

"After that nurse got raped last semester."

Clark popped the tab off the beer and squatted down next to her. "You amaze me."

Heather buried her face in the crook of her elbow. Only her eyes were visible as she stared at him. "Where's Tracy?"

"In the library."

"You're kidding. She's always in the library, isn't she?"

Clark nodded. "Lately anyway."

Heather pulled on a T-shirt and some bikini bottoms. "You can look at me now, Clark. I'm decent, so I won't have to keep talking to your profile. You really ought to loosen up. In Europe, everyone lies out naked." She paused. "Now, tell me," Heather continued, "is it true Tracy got some woman sent to the stroke unit?"

"Almost. Where did you hear that?"

"The rumor mill. There are no secrets among medical students—you know that. What do you mean, almost?"

"The patient had a transient ischemic attack. She's better now, but it scared the shit out of us." Clark stared down at the water shimmering up at them.

"So let me guess," Heather said. "Tracy assumed it was all her fault?"

"You got it. Since then, she's made a second home of the library. She doesn't think about anything except her patients. All I hear about is small cell cancer and Coumadin and randomized, double-blind controlled trials for this and that." Clark picked up a small stone and tossed it over the ledge. It always made him a little queasy to think about how long the rock fell before the splash. "She's driving me nuts."

"What about you?" Heather asked.

"What do you mean?"

"Do you think about your patients when you leave the hospital?"

Clark tossed another rock over the side. "Every now and then. Some of them are real characters. But they don't haunt me the way they do Tracy." He looked at Heather. "I'm worried about her. She's going to burn out if she keeps this up."

Heather shrugged. "Or make an excellent Rosemont Marine."

Clark studied her. "A what?"

"You know—the few, the proud, the Rosemont Marines. The residents and attendings who you see running around with worried looks on their faces, always citing studies and telling you to order more labs. The ones who somewhere along the line forgot how to be human."

Clark laughed, imagining Murdoch. "Is your attending like that?"

"Worse. She walks into a room and *I* get worried. She exudes fear, makes you want to double-check everything four times." Heather rolled over and pulled her hair back in a ponytail.

"But who would you rather have take care of you?" Clark asked. "Her or someone who spent half her time out here?"

Heather wiped the sweat from her eyes with a towel. "I think my mom is a pretty good doctor, and she hasn't forgotten how to have a good time. This hospital we're working at is an aberration. It's the sphincter factor."

Clark squinted at her. "The what?"

"You know." Heather made an O with her index finger and thumb, then curled her finger until the opening disappeared. "The anal sphincter. Mount Rosemont is so anally retentive, it's laughable."

Clark laughed. "Do you really think it's different in other teaching hospitals?"

"No. But my mom's life is pretty good. All we have to

do is sweat through two more years of med school, grind through internship and three years of residency, then we're home free. It's nothing more than a rite of passage, a vestige of the good-old-boy system that medicine once was. Then we're members of the club, see?"

Clark studied her. The way she sat, with her legs tucked up under her chin, made her bikini bottom disappear. It looked as though she had nothing on under her T-shirt. In some ways, it was more enticing than when she was naked. "So you've got it all figured out."

"Yep. Mom tells me life after this is so much easier. This is just an elaborate test."

"Of what?"

"Hell if I know. To see if we can stay up all night, for one thing. God knows you can't be a doctor if you can't do that, right?" She turned to Clark and smiled. "Have you heard how anyone else is doing?"

Clark shook his head. "I've been so caught up in just surviving this that I haven't had time for rumors."

"Well, I have. Or, more specifically, Randy has, and he filled me in. Alicia isn't weathering this too well."

Clark tried to imagine Alicia under the tutelage of someone like Murdoch. Alicia, mercurial and flighty, famous throughout the school for her midnight motorcycle rides. "What's she on?"

"Medicine, like us, but she's at Barrymore." Barrymore was a public hospital four blocks from Rosemont, where most of the patients without insurance were sent. And it was also where half the medical students were randomly assigned.

"So what's wrong with Alicia?"

"She's flipping out, or that's the rumor. They say she disappeared for a day."

"You're kidding."

"But she came back with a sunburn and a hangover. They would have failed her, but she's needed too badly. At Barrymore, students do all the scut work, I mean everything."

Clark could imagine Alicia walking away, just leaving all the misery behind for a day. "What other rumors are circulating?"

Heather eyed Clark suspiciously. "They say you're having a relapse."

"Who started that rumor?"

"I did. And Erich confirmed it. He says you had papilledema and a field cut."

Clark looked out over the water. "Yeah, well, that was Erich's opinion."

"Clark, I saw you, remember? You collapsed in the library." She touched the back of his hand.

"It's nothing."

"What did your neurosurgeon say? Was Erich right?"

Clark was silent a moment. "She didn't say anything."

"What do you mean?"

"I didn't see her yet."

Heather rose to her feet, standing over him, arms akimbo. "You're kidding."

"Heather, if they do think I'm having a relapse, they'll hold me back. If they don't know about it, that won't happen."

"And if this cancer kills you, that won't happen either. Did you ever think of that?"

Clark picked up a baseball-sized piece of granite and lobbed it over the edge into the water.

"I'm sorry," Heather said. "I shouldn't have said that."

He listened to the splash from below. "I'll see someone next week, all right? Stop looking at me like that. Now sit and tell me some more rumors. But not about me."

She plopped down on the towel. "I only have one more."

"Tell me."

"The Grunt might be getting a divorce."

Clark jerked his head toward her. "You're kidding."

"I wish I were. I always liked his wife. She was a little pipsqueak of a woman, but she was pretty nice." Heather slapped the back of Clark's head. "Now, don't pass that one on; it's unconfirmed."

"What's your source?"

"Randy."

Clark laughed. "Then I'm not going to give it another thought; it's obviously not true." He rose and walked to the edge of the granite bluff. The sun was low enough now that only a fraction of the green water below was in light. It looked like the world's largest bathtub. The rest of the water looked a deep brown, almost black. But where the sun was shining, the water seemed clear, almost translucent. He thought he could see the bottom, but knew that was ridiculous; it was over two hundred feet deep.

"Oh, Heather, I have never felt so alive. Being around all that illness and decay makes me so grateful for my health, for the simple joy of being able to draw each breath. Know what I mean?"

She apparently didn't. Heather looked at him with a worried expression at first, then her face broke into a smile. Her teeth were white against her sunburned face. "Sort of."

Clark began unbuttoning his shirt. "You dive in first, don't look back, and I'll join you."

"You're going in?"

"If I don't think about it too much."

She didn't move as he pulled off his shirt and kicked off his shoes. He had to be careful not to hurtle them over the precipice. "Go!"

He tried not to look at her as she peeled off her shirt. Her leg muscles flexed as she stood with her curled toes gripping the side. Then she stepped into the abyss.

Clark watched her fall, her body now pale against the water, now dark as she entered the area of shadow. She made a little circular movement with her arms to stabilize her body as she fell, as though attempting to backpedal against the current of air rushing up at her. Then she struck the water. The last thing he saw was a patch of blond hair swallowed by a giant splash.

Clark was completely naked by the time she disappeared. He held his breath, moved to the edge of the granite, and tried to imitate her. His body froze a moment and he would remember this always, this moment of rebellion against everything he had promised his mother, his doctors, the whole medical care system that had been trying so hard to keep him alive and was now letting him struggle through one of its most grueling rites of passage.

The air was cold against his flesh as he fell and the fall was like nothing he had ever experienced. His stomach was somewhere in his mouth and the water seemed to take an awfully long time to reach him. When it did, it was much colder than the air, much colder then he expected, and he wondered for a moment if he would drown.

It wasn't green now, it was black, and his feet stung from where they had broken the surface. He sank deep, deep, letting the water enter his nose, his mouth, his ears, sting his eyes. He opened them and saw nothing, a fuzzy murkiness.

Then he kicked his way to the surface and looked around.

Something brushed against his leg. It was large and slippery and strong, wrapping itself around him, pulling him down. His head was almost below the surface when she let him go, giggling and spitting water in his face.

"What'd you think I was, the Loch Ness monster or something?" Heather pushed away from him.

Clark formed a cup with his hands and splashed at her. She ducked and disappeared again, coming up behind him. He anticipated her this time, fending off her attack with a forearm. "You look like a seal when you're wet," he told her.

"You have a way of charming women," she responded.

"You have a way of scaring the shit out of me."

She cocked her head back and laughed and he could identify every anatomical feature in her throat. "You have a nice uvula," he told her, grinning like an idiot, feeling ten years old.

"And you have a nice ass."

"You can't see it."

"No, I saw it coming down."

He splashed her again. "Did not."

"Did too."

He followed her to where a slab of granite was tilted into the water, forming a shallow wading area. She sat back against the slab, only her neck and head visible. "Are you going to marry Tracy?"

"Where did that come from?"

"I don't know." Heather looked around at the place they had jumped from. "It's fun taking chances, isn't it?"

Clark nodded, swimming up behind her, not entirely certain what he was going to do to her. He thought he might dunk her, but when his hands gripped her shoulders, she leaned back into him and he felt her flesh against his.

It was then that it happened and it would be one of those moments Clark would replay for the rest of his life, trying to understand how it might have turned out if he had made a different decision.

It started when Heather turned to him and smiled, a warm, inviting smile, and then, his hands still on her shoulders, he knew what would happen.

He leaned forward to kiss her, his lips meeting her cheek, somehow salty and warm and cold at the same time. She didn't move at first, just continued to smile at him as he pulled back, then her smile disappeared and she placed her fingertips over the back of his neck as though to pull him toward her. She froze a moment and Clark knew she had found the bald spot, the craniotomy scar. It had scared more than one woman away, but had attracted others. He remembered a girlfriend in college who used to like to trace her fingertips up and down the length of it, as though it were some erogenous zone.

"Does it hurt?" she asked for some reason.

Clark shook his head and leaned down to kiss her. He had to sink down in the water to avoid embarrassing himself as his lips met hers. They parted and their teeth clinked for a second. She was so warm compared with the water.

Clark didn't think of Tracy, not at all. It was as though what he was doing had nothing to do with Tracy, an act in the world's largest bathtub so remote from anything out there in that world beyond that it had no bearing whatsoever. Heather's tongue flicked over his and he found himself growing completely aroused. Her hands explored his body as he shifted so that he was pressing her into the granite slab. "Is this uncomfortable?" he asked.

"It all depends what you have in mind."

Their heads slipped underwater for a minute as their movements grew more frantic and the water didn't seem so cold anymore. She was tight and muscular and positioned herself with the ease of an experienced dancer or gymnast. He clutched her to him and she clutched him. He could feel the rippling muscles of her back, her buttocks. His knuckles grazed against the granite and he knew they bled but he didn't care. It was regressive, a sinking back into a primordial, amphibious state.

But before he could lose himself completely, he realized what he was doing. It was only with a tremendous force of will that he managed to pull away. "I can't."

She smoothed the hair from his forehead. "I have protection, you know."

"It's not that."

She smiled at him and kissed his earlobe. "What then?"

"Tracy."

"Oh." She pulled away and splashed some water into his face. "You didn't answer my question before."

"About Tracy, you mean?"

She nodded, her head again reminding him of a seal.

"We're not engaged. But we've talked about it. It was always sort of expected."

"Is that what you want?"

Clark splashed her back. "Yes," he heard himself saying with a certainty he hadn't realized he felt. "Yes, it is."

Heather stared at her hands, just beneath the surface of the green water. "Then it's a good thing we didn't make love."

"Yes. Good thing."

Clark thought he saw movement high above them, but it was probably just a branch blowing in the breeze. "We should get our clothes before someone steals them."

Heather laughed at that. "We'd have much explaining to do then, wouldn't we?"

Clark covered himself as they climbed the path leading up the bluff. It was a two-second drop, but a five-minute walk in bare feet with broken glass glinting just off the path. She walked in front and he watched her legs and buttocks tighten, bunch up, then relax again. He couldn't help naming the muscles in his mind: quadriceps, hamstring, gastrocnemius. He knew their origin, insertion, innervation, what they looked like on a cadaver.

But he wasn't going to think of cadavers right now. He wasn't going to think of Tracy, or what he would do if their clothes had been stolen, or what he would say when he got home after sunset. For the sun was kissing the horizon now, an orange, hazy orb, distorted at the edges by the refraction of the atmosphere. There were moments, Clark felt, when everything seemed to come together in aesthetic perfection and this was one of them, as his pile of clothes came into sight and the light was orange and somehow unreal and he was completely awake and happy and wanted nothing more than to get home to Tracy, realizing now what he hadn't realized before, realizing something that it took lying naked in another woman's arms to discover.

She pulled on her shorts without underwear and a

T-shirt without a bra. It was only against the whiteness of her T-shirt that Clark noticed how much sun she had gotten.

"I'm sorry," he said.

"About what?"

Their eyes met a moment and Clark searched hers for some hint of anger or regret. "Nothing."

She turned away, pulled the strap of her bag over her shoulder, and walked away.

He knew this was the moment when he had to decide. He could let her go and she would let it drop. But if he later changed his mind, he sensed she would be gone forever. He found himself trotting after her, his untied shoes slapping against the gravel path. "Heather, wait." She disappeared into the ferns, and when he followed, he almost ran into her. She had pulled up short and faced him. To see her in the thick foliage and gathering darkness, he had to stand with his lips practically on hers.

"Heather, I want to be your friend."

"Don't be silly, Clark. We're always friends."

"Even after what happened down there?" He canted his head toward the lip of the quarry.

She smiled. "Especially after what *didn't* happen down there. I have more respect for you now. It would have been a mistake."

"It would have?"

"Sure."

Clark wasn't so sure, but couldn't say why.

"I suppose you have plans with Tracy tonight."

"No, I think she's closing the library." Clark suddenly felt very lonely and tired. It had been a long week and he wasn't looking forward to going home to an empty house. "Are you doing anything tonight?" he asked.

She flashed a smile at him. "You're not asking me out, are you, Clark?"

He thought about that. "I don't think so."

Heather's hand brushed against his. He didn't know if it was entirely accidental. "Are you hungry?"

"I'm famished."

"Greek or Italian?"

"I was thinking more Chinese."

"Sounds good. But no MSG."

"Deal."

They walked deeper into the ferns and the gravel path disappeared under their feet in the darkness.

▲ ATONEMENT ▼

Tracy didn't leave the library until midnight. Rosemont Medical Center had been built in what had been a bustling, manufacturing section of the city. But shifts in crime and urban rot were beyond anyone's powers to discern. Now an urban wasteland surrounded the hospital. It was relatively safe during the day, but at night it had the surrealistic feel of an evacuated war zone.

Tracy was oblivious to any danger tonight. Her thoughts flitted back and forth between two topics as she negotiated the shadows cast by the neon streetlights.

The first thought concerned the swirl of events in the hospital over the past few days. She felt she was riding the edge of things, a surfer negotiating the dangerous breakers of Murdoch's rage. Through a terrible blunder that she didn't completely understand but that Jeb and Murdoch apparently did, she had almost caused a woman to have a stroke. It didn't matter that the patient was better now; what mattered was that Tracy almost killed her. She couldn't get that thought out of her head. She felt sick with the knowledge of what she had done. It was her pen that had scratched the orders.

In atonement, Tracy had crammed into her head all that had been written about Coumadin and heparin and vitamin K since the dawn of medicine. It helped ease the sting to do everything in her power to ensure that it would never happen again.

The second thought concerned Clark. She had called home four times, the last time not ten minutes ago, but he didn't pick up. Was he in such a heavy sleep that he didn't hear the phone ring? Or had he gotten into some sort of accident? Maybe he had a seizure on the way home, maybe he needed her right now. She had promised him she wouldn't worry about things like that, but right now the darkest thoughts entered her head. There was a simpler explanation, that he had gone out with Randy or some friends and they had stayed out late, but he had seemed too tired for that.

Tracy hated the parking garage. There were so many blind spots, so many places for a rapist or murderer to lurk. The university had installed red emergency phones at two-hundred-foot intervals, but what good was a phone if someone had a gun to your head?

She reached her car without incident, though, started the jacked-up monster with a roar of blue-gray smoke, and squealed out of her spot. There was no traffic as she raced toward the interstate.

Tracy felt guilty for not doing anything with Clark that night; she had more or less promised to, but that had been before Monday, in that different world that was growing more distant as they plunged deeper into their new one.

It had taken forty minutes in rush-hour traffic to get into the hospital; at midnight it took less than ten to get home.

She pulled into the driveway; it was empty and the house was dark. Tracy felt something twist inside her, a feeling of panic, as though there was something waiting for her inside that she couldn't stand, the absence of Clark.

Where the hell was he?

She pulled out her book bag, which was stuffed with articles and notes she had taken, as well as all her medical gear and her white coat. Then she slammed the door of her car and entered the house.

She didn't turn on any lights at first, just stared at the answering machine and counted the number of times the light blinked—one more than the number of times she had called.

She listened to her voice on the recording, listened to the toll fatigue and uncertainty took as the evening wore on: "Hi, Clark, it's about six-thirty and I just wanted to let you know that I grabbed a sandwich in the library vending machine, so feel free to make yourself some dinner or go out. Don't worry about me. I'll see you in a few hours. Love you. Bye." Then, two messages later: "Clark, it's me again. I was hoping you were there, but oh, well, you're probably just out having a good time. Hope you don't have too good a time; we have to round at eight tomorrow morning, remember? Talk to you soon."

Then, before her final message, she heard his voice: "Tracy, it's Clark. Um, it's about eleven or so and I'm not sure if I'll be back at a decent hour. I wanted to call earlier and let you know I hadn't been kidnapped by Gypsies or anything, but figured you probably wouldn't be back from the library until after midnight. I guess I was right. I'll explain everything later. Take care."

He didn't say "I love you," she thought. Maybe he was in public and too embarrassed to say it out loud. There was music in the background; he might have been at a bar or something. Tracy tossed her head forward and rubbed her eyes. "Why am I working so hard for him? I'm sure he's fine," she told herself.

She tossed her book bag on the table, grabbed a piece of leftover chicken from the fridge, and munched on it as she tossed off her clothes, leaving a trail leading to the shower. After she scrubbed a day of hospital grime from her body, she powdered herself down, brushed her teeth, and grabbed a handful of articles. She slipped into bed and looked over the abstracts. Within half a minute she had forgotten about Clark, about the day, about everything except the study she was reading.

It was another clinical trial of chemotherapy for small cell cancer. She was lost in it, her eyes absorbing the figures and tables and percentages and p values. There was so much to learn and so little time, and in only five hours she would have to get up and go into the hospital again.

Her eyelids drooped and she woke up half an hour later drooling over the article.

She wiped off the spittle, tossed the article onto the floor, and turned out the light.

Clark still hadn't come home.

CONFRONTATION

Tracy stepped onto the ward. She felt as though she hadn't slept more than two hours total.

She had woken up at two, then at three, then every fifteen minutes or so, reaching for Clark's side of the bed, feeling the emptiness, the coldness of the sheets, trying not to imagine where he might be. She was half-angry and half-worried. If he had walked in, she didn't know if she would yell at him or run to him and take him in her arms.

Probably both.

She found the team huddled around Winfield. He was smiling up at them, drooling and making some unintelligible sounds. Jeb spotted her from ten feet away. "Well, well. Thought it was optional rounds day, huh?"

"Sorry I'm late."

"Sorry? Sorry is fine if you're a plumber. Luckily, Clark here covered for you."

She studied Clark, who seemed to be avoiding her eyes. He scrutinized his clipboard, jotted something

225

down. Was it her imagination, or were there bags under his eyes? What had he been doing all night? More importantly, who had he been doing it with?

"Kidnapped by Gypsies?" she asked, under her breath.

"Not here," he whispered. "I'll explain, but not here."

But Tracy didn't know if she wanted to hear. Not yet.

There was no time after rounds to confront Clark. Jeb handed her an index card with twenty things that had to be done. She snatched it from him and looked it over, ticking off those things that could wait until after attending rounds. She picked up the phone and called three consults, learning already the masterful art of bluffing her way through a patient's presentation. Getting a consultant, who was an overworked, harassed resident no different from Jeb or Bob, to come by to see one of her patients was a form of salesmanship; what she left out and what she stressed in the patients' presentations would determine success or failure.

She then checked the computer for all her patients' lab results, neatly transcribing the numbers onto a grid in the chart, then scribbled a few progress notes, documenting what was done or needed to be done. It was mostly mind-numbing routine, an exercise in compulsiveness, tracking a thousand pieces of data, following protocols established long ago for every conceivable contingency: anemia workups, hematuria workups, bacteriuria workups.

Tracy didn't argue with Murdoch during attending rounds. She had decided she wouldn't waste the energy. There were battles to fight and battles to avoid.

Murdoch asked for an update on Thurgood. "Hematology oncology said they'd work on the paperwork to get him enrolled in the Sloan-Kettering study. And they could do the protocol here, since we're an authorized study site. He'll start chemotherapy Monday."

Murdoch arched an eyebrow. "So we actually did some good for this gentleman. I'm impressed." He nodded to her and it was as close as he would ever come to telling her she did a good job and she knew it.

There wasn't much to do after attending rounds, but she found some additional work because she didn't want to face what came next. By noon, though, everything was done and there was no avoiding it. She and Clark were alone in the workroom and she had to know.

"So what's her name?"

He looked at her, rubbed his eyes, and said, "That's not important. All that matters is that I fell asleep."

Tracy scrutinized his face. "Where?"

"In a friend's apartment."

"Whose? Randy's?"

"What difference does it make what her name was?"

"*Her* name? It makes a hell of a difference." She crossed her arms. "Was it Alicia?"

"No. That ended over a year ago."

"Who, then? Jennifer?"

"No." He obviously wasn't going to tell her.

She glared at him in silence.

"Please, Tracy, it's not what you think. We talked late into the night about her brother—he has a brain tumor, too, you see—and I fell asleep on her living-room floor."

Tracy blew a strand of hair from in front of her eyes. "And you expect me to believe that?"

"It's the truth."

She continued to drill her eyes into him.

"Forget it. If you don't trust me, you don't trust me."

Tracy sank back into a chair. She had never felt so unattractive, so unwanted, as she sat there, absorbing the information. "Clark, you should have explained that in your call."

"You're right. But, Tracy, I was half-comatose from sleep deprivation. I was out cold on her living-room floor halfway through my second beer. I had no idea how much this rotation was taking out of me." He had a chart open before him, but she sensed he hadn't read or written a word in it for the past fifteen minutes. He closed it. "You don't believe me."

"Did you sleep with her?"

"Oh, Tracy, for God's sake, I—"

"Did you sleep with her? Just tell me that."

Clark turned to her. "No."

She wasn't going to cry. No, by God, she wasn't going to let Clark see her cry. "I stuck with you through the worst of things, through your tumor, through the relapse, through—" She had to stop herself. She wasn't going to cause a scene, and knew that her voice carried into the hall.

Clark stood up and shut the door. "Tracy, listen to me—I didn't sleep with her."

Tracy's eyes welled with tears, but with great effort she blinked them away. Bob came in, shuffled through some papers, then hustled off. "Why are you guys still here?" he asked. "Go home!"

Clark got to his feet, returned his patient's chart to the rack, and began gathering his things, packing them into his book bag. "It's pointless to continue this conversation," he whispered to her. "You don't want to believe me."

Tracy stepped into the hallway, began striding toward the elevator. It was the first time since the rotation started that they were getting out of the hospital before five, but they would have to come in the next day and stay for thirty-six hours.

Clark was behind her, trotting to keep up. He found himself getting mad. "You weren't even home," he said. "You said you wouldn't be home until midnight."

Out of the corner of her eye, she could see him growing more animated. His face was turning red. It gave her a secret thrill.

"Jesus, Tracy, what do you *expect?* You spend so much time in that goddamn library these days that I don't see what difference it makes to you if I *did* sleep with her."

She punched the down button to the elevator. "I know if you'll think about that a minute, you'll realize how stupid it sounds. We're medical students. We have a hell of a lot to learn and only two more years to learn it."

"You spend a hundred and twenty hours a week in the hospital. Isn't that enough?"

"No. Even if I studied twenty-four hours a day, it wouldn't be enough."

"Tracy, listen to yourself. That's both grandiose and neurotic."

She spun on him. "Look, Clark, I almost put a woman in the stroke unit because I wasn't prepared enough and my intern wasn't prepared enough. Is that neurotic?"

"Tracy, would you forget about that?"

"No, Clark, that's the difference between you and me. I can't just forget about my patients."

"Well, excuse me, Mother Teresa, but bad things happen to people. Even at the Mecca of Medicine. You better get used to it."

Tracy didn't say anything.

The elevator doors opened on the third floor and she stepped out.

"Where are you going?" Clark asked.

"The library."

"Oh, for God's sake, Tracy." He trotted after her. "Why don't we take the afternoon off, spend it together, try to make some sense of where we stand? Let's take in dinner, a show, maybe hit a comedy club. How about—"

She cut him off. "Look. I don't know where we stand now. I need some time alone."

Clark stopped, staring after her. "Tracy."

She whirled. "What?"

"When can I expect you home?"

"I don't know. I have a lot of work to do." She marched away.

CHEMOTHERAPY

▲

▼

Tracy stared at Thurgood's bone scan. It looked like a crudely drawn, fuzzy, glowing Halloween sketch of a skeleton, drawn by a six-year-old. The radioactive dye had been injected into his bloodstream, absorbed by his bone, then an image was obtained based on the concentration of the dye. Parts of Thurgood's skeleton were clearly recognizable, such as his skull and the long bones of his legs, but the rest of his body was one fuzzy smear. How the radiologist standing beside her could make any sense of it was a mystery to her.

"So he's got at least six areas of metastasis?" Tracy asked.

"That's right. Your man has hits to his ribs, his pelvis, and his right tibia. No surprise, though. Small cell is almost always spread by the time of diagnosis." The radiologist was a nervous little woman who kept leaning back on her heels and looking at her watch. Although she had sounded friendly and welcoming on the phone when

230

Tracy asked if she could look over the bone scan herself, the radiologist now seemed irritated. Maybe she hadn't counted on so many questions.

"But how do you know this is a hit?" Tracy asked, pointing to one area. "I mean, he broke that leg right about there when he jumped off his tractor three years ago. Isn't there the chance that—"

The radiologist shook her head. "No. Not this far out. That's too much tracer activity to be explained by a simple fracture."

"But suppose he has osteomyelitis? I know a bone infection can do this also."

"Does he have any clinical evidence of osteo? Any fever, tenderness over his leg?"

Tracy shook her head, struggling to find some reason why the radiologist might be wrong, why Thurgood might not be a condemned man with widely spread cancer.

The computerized tomography scans at least were negative for any obvious metastasis, but that didn't mean much, since small cell usually spread microscopically. There didn't seem much good news in Tracy's life right now.

She almost cried when she saw Mr. Thurgood. After three courses of chemotherapy, what was left of the man's hair was thin and wispy, like the fine down covering a baby's scalp. The medicines that had been infused into his body were selective poisons, designed to kill the cancer, but toxic to his body as well. Every day Tracy checked his white blood cell count, graphing out the slow suppression of the man's bone marrow. Every day she flowed his labs, double- and triple-checking them, making sure his potassium didn't drop too low from vomiting, or his creatinine drift too high from renal toxicity.

Three times a week she would help Bob hang the mysterious concoction—they didn't know what it contained exactly, since they were blind to the trial—that arrived from the pharmacy refrigerated and wrapped in bright orange plastic. She would meticulously copy and cross-reference the numbers on the bags, making sure they corresponded to the master schedule Sloan-Kettering had sent them.

Thurgood said the medicine burned when it went in and his IV had to be changed after every treatment because the chemotherapy was sclerosing his veins, turning them into rock-hard little pipelines.

Now he stared up at her, smiling as bright as ever, but his hair changed his entire appearance. That and the extra weight loss made his face seem longer and thinner, his cheeks hollow. "We're beating this thing, aren't we?" he asked her, when she closed the door behind her.

"Let's hope so," she said. She checked the chemotherapy bag: half-empty. It would be completely empty in half an hour, then Mr. Thurgood would start vomiting. It was a routine she knew well.

So did the family, gathered around the bed. Thurgood's mother pulled some papers from her purse and consulted them. Tracy recognized them as the article she had given the family about small cell cancer.

"Have any of the tests come back yet?" she asked. "In here it mentions that my son's prognosis is much worse if the tumor is widely spread, but that it usually is when the cancer is diagnosed."

Tracy gripped her clipboard with both hands. "That's correct. The bone scan actually did show metastasis, but that doesn't mean the end of the world."

Thurgood looked offended. "Where?"

Tracy didn't know what he was talking about a moment. "You mean, where is the tumor spread to?"

"Yes, where are those little buggers?" He looked over his body, as though he would claw them out if she only told her where they were.

Tracy pointed to his ribs and his left leg.

"That's ridiculous," Thurgood said, grinning. "I don't feel a thing."

"This is no time for levity," his mother warned. "You

know they are microscopic. You read that article same as the rest of us."

He waved her away. "If this isn't a time for levity, I don't know that there ever was one. I don't know if I ever laughed so much as I have over the past three weeks. My sides ache, Doc, I been laughing so hard."

Tracy was confused. She looked to the mother for explanation. "He got into his mind this crackhead idea he heard on some talk show that if he exposed himself to a nonstop barrage of jokes, he would bolster his immune system and fight off the cancer."

Tracy smiled at that. "That might not be such a crackhead idea."

"Well, I say it's foolishness."

"And I say," the patient said, winking at Tracy, "that it's no less scientific than this." He tapped the bright orange bag hanging on his IV pole. "Now, if you two don't mind, I'm twenty minutes overdue on my next joke." He then picked up a book entitled *The 500 Dirtiest Jokes of All Time*, opened it, and began to read. Within thirty seconds, he was fighting for air.

Tracy rushed to him, thinking he was short of breath, clicking through her mind all the things it could be—a myocardial infarction, pulmonary embolism, dissecting abdominal aorta—and all the things she would have to do—call Bob, order some oxygen, get an ABG—when he grinned up at her and laughed. "I'm telling you, Doc, I can't hardly stand no more of these here jokes."

If all this was a facade, she didn't care. She was just glad there were no scenes when she walked in the room, that he was dealing with this with a good dose of stiff-upper-lip humor. The thought crossed her mind that he was working so hard to laugh to keep himself from crying.

"Thanks for stopping by, Doc," Mr. Thurgood said.

"I'll be back in a few hours."

Thurgood's mother followed Tracy into the hall. "It's bad, isn't it?"

"There's always hope."

"Don't answer me with clichés. Even with this medicine, his chances are slim, aren't they?"

Tracy knew that this woman didn't want to be bull-shitted. She nodded.

Thurgood's mother didn't look crushed; she looked grateful. "I like you, Dr. McHugh."

When Tracy was alone again, she wondered if she weren't putting this family through hell for nothing, if all this wasn't a complete waste of time. She tried to imagine what she would do if she were given a diagnosis like Thurgood's. Would she sail around the world, try to read all the novels she never had time to read in medical school, maybe find some mountain to climb? None of that would be possible if she were tethered to an IV pole, puking her guts out and losing her hair because of some chemotherapy. Was she robbing this man of his last days on this planet? For what? To satisfy her own ego? To refuse to accept this man's mortality and, perhaps with it, her own?

Until she started work on the wards, death had been an abstraction, something remote and unreal, to be feared at the end of a full life. Now she was confronted with it every day. It now had a name and a family and even a smell.

Clark was frowning over a chart when she stepped into the workroom. "Why would my patient have had a chole-cystectomy in 1978?" he asked.

"Oh, for God's sake, Clark, how would I know?" She had hardly spoken to him during the past two weeks, except to try to hurt him. It was better than nothing, better than letting the anger build without some taste of revenge.

She had found out the name. There were no secrets among medical students and the Monday after Clark went skinny-dipping with her, Heather's name was passed among them with whispered zeal. Tracy tried not to hear all the sordid details—were they really naked in the quarry?—but couldn't help listening.

Tracy grabbed Thurgood's chart and opened it to the lab section. She noted that his white blood cell count was dangerously low and falling. They would have to stop the chemotherapy soon unless it drifted back up. "Maybe if you spent a little more time studying and a little less time skinny-dipping with our classmates, you could figure these things out."

He ignored her.

Tracy opened the chart to the progress-notes section and began writing a quick update.

"I told you I was sorry. I haven't seen her since that day," Clark said.

"How virtuous of you. But disloyalty isn't something you can turn on and off." She continued to write in the chart. Her handwriting had already degenerated from a neat, controlled, deliberate cursive into a scrawl that even she couldn't always recognize. She was beginning to understand why doctors had a reputation for such poor handwriting; to write several progress notes and a dozen orders every day, as well as personal notes and transcription of labs from the computer to the chart's flow sheets, she had to write fast, scratching her pen over the surface of the paper at a frantic pace.

She finished her note in seven minutes, slammed the chart shut, and returned it to the rack.

"Tracy, how long are you going to sulk?"

"I haven't decided yet."

"Well, when you do, let me know."

"I'll think about it." She walked away, leaving him with a scowl plastered to his face.

THE LIAISON

She was waiting for him in the parking deck. Her car was parked three spaces from his. He didn't notice the cherry-red Porsche until Heather flashed her lights at him and gestured for him to get in the passenger side.

Clark paused a minute, looked around, then slid into the car. "I thought we had agreed. I can't see you again. You know how much trouble I got in the first time."

"I know, but I had to." She looked straight ahead, her eyes hidden by a pair of black glasses. "Where do you want to go?" She started the engine and was moving forward before he could say anything.

"Heather, I can't just leave my car behind."

"I'll drop you off later. Right now we have to talk."

Clark had no choice but to pull his seat belt across his body and click it into place. He looked out the windshield and saw Tracy walking in their general direction. "Oh, Jesus, I promised her."

She was fifty yards away, making her way toward her

car, and seemed to be looking right at them. Instinctively, Clark unfastened his belt and crouched down behind the dashboard.

Heather waved and shot Tracy a friendly smile. "She hates me, doesn't she?"

"No, she hates me."

"But I'm the evil seductress. Isn't that how it works? And I didn't even seduce you. Even today it's the woman who's to blame."

The car shot out of the garage and Clark looked up to see streetlamps and the silhouettes of buildings. He hopped back into his seat and realized they were heading deeper into the city, toward the Riverdale district where Heather lived. "Are you kidnapping me?"

"Maybe. I realized it's the only way I could talk to you. Hanging up on someone isn't very polite, you know."

"Tracy was in the next room."

"You could have called me back later."

Clark puffed out his cheeks. Heather was right, but he was always too embarrassed, afraid rumors of any phone call would get back to Tracy. And all he wanted right now was to forget about what Tracy was convinced had happened between him and Heather and patch things up with Tracy the best he could.

"Look at you," Heather said. "You're terrified of that woman. You treat her better than any guy I've gone out with has ever treated me."

Clark straightened up and looked over his shoulder. The hospital was brightly lit with floodlights at its base and a searchlight swept the sky from the helipad. "So what did you want to ask me?"

"I wanted to know if it's worth it."

Clark was confused. "Huh?"

"I wanted to know if Tracy's worth the effort. I mean, nothing happened between us, Clark—"

"I kissed you."

"And that's all—but Tracy won't believe that, will she?"

"No."

"How can you be so willing to devote yourself to someone who is so possessive?"

For the past two weeks Clark's struggles on the ward had taken a backseat to regaining Tracy's trust. Now he sat here and realized Heather had a point. "You're right."

"You didn't do anything wrong."

"But she treats me as though I did."

"Exactly." Heather pulled the car to a halt at a red light. "Clark, I like Tracy. Until all this, I considered her a friend, and I still do. But I'm willing to risk all that to tell you this—I think you deserve better."

"And by better, do you mean you?"

Heather nodded. "Are you offended?"

Clark didn't know exactly how to feel. "To tell the truth, I guess I feel flattered. And tempted. And confused."

"So what do you want, Clark? Just say the word and we could have it all. I think there's something between us and—"

Clark reached over and gently laid his fingertips on her lips. "Please. Don't. I don't have much experience with women throwing themselves at me, and I'm not sure I could handle it gracefully."

Heather paused. When she spoke, her voice was so soft, Clark almost couldn't hear it over the roar of her engine. "Maybe you'll change your mind."

"I don't think so."

"You're not angry, are you?"

"Of course not." He reached toward her, but she batted his hand away. Also, at that point, he realized she was still wearing the glasses.

"Take off the shades at least. You'll get us both killed."

"Sorry. I guess I'm not very good at throwing myself at men." She pulled off the glasses and threw them on the floor at Clark's feet. She licked at her upper lip and the sight of the tip of her tongue brought back a flood of memories. He remembered the way she swam before him, the way she licked the cascading water from her lip. He remembered the way she arched her back, her body glistening in the sun.

He leaned across the stick shift and put an arm around her. "Heather, thanks for telling me about your brother."

"Thanks for listening."

Clark realized they had circled the block and returned to the parking deck.

She stopped along a curb, reached over, and unlocked the door. "See you on the wards."

"Still friends?" Clark held out his hand.

"Still friends." She shook it, then pulled him into her arms.

And that was it.

As he stared at her taillights, feeling the cool night air on his cheeks, he had a single, nagging thought: was he making the wrong choice?

He would probably never know.

LABOR DAY

Sickness doesn't observe holidays, but a hospital generally does. On Labor Day weekend, Rosemont Medical Center was run by a skeleton crew, the bare minimum needed to keep things running. Ancillary services, such as blood drawing, laboratory technicians, and radiology personnel, were scarce. Administrative offices were closed.

But for Tracy, Clark, and Bob, it was business as usual: they were on call and looked like they were going to get killed.

Clark's first admission rolled onto the floor around nine in the morning. She was a scheduled admission of Dr. Scroffo, a private physician who had admitting privileges to the hospital.

Leona Matravelli was going to be quite an experience, indeed. Before Jeb left—the residents could take call from home that weekend and the interns were promoted to residents for a day—he rolled his eyes at the name. "Oh, my God. A bona fide Scroffo patient."

Clark, who had never heard of the attending before, asked, "What does that mean?"

"You'll see. I want nothing to do with her. I beg of you, Bob. Deal directly with Scroffo, okay? I don't even want to hear about her."

Clark watched the resident walk away, then turned to Bob.

The intern sneezed into a tissue, then tossed it into a trash can. The can was already half-full of them. The intern's eyes watered and his voice sounded like it was coming from underwater. He clutched his head every now and then and made a little groaning sound. It was a hell of a time to be sick.

"You should take the day off," Clark said.

Bob laughed at him. "You just don't get it, do you, Clark? If I did that, some other poor intern would have to cover for me. So we never call in sick. It just doesn't happen."

Clark shook his head. "Well, what was all that about Scroffo?"

"He has a reputation for admitting people who aren't really sick, but who have a lot of money or really good insurance. Then he does questionable workups, on the fringe of accepted medical practice. He's brilliant and his patients love him—I mean, this woman's flown in from Germany of all places—but all the house staff dread working with him."

Leona Matravelli had a beauty that Clark recognized even in illness. She smiled warmly up at him when he entered the room, and took both his hands in hers. "Doke-tore Scrow-foe," she began, drawing out each rehearsed word. "I so long to see you have waited. You are so young to appear."

"Actually," Clark began, enunciating each word, "I'm not Dr. Scroffo. I'm Clark Wilson, a medical student."

Leona blinked up at him, still smiling, obviously not comprehending. "You cure me of all that has me sick *gemacht, nicht wahr?*"

"Sure." Clark just smiled back at her. "Now, what exactly brings you to the hospital?"

"Oh, so many things. So many things." The woman reached into a finely embroidered leather bag by her bed. She pulled out a pair of tortoise-shell reading glasses, which she put on, and a sheaf of papers held together with a rubber band. She handed the papers to Clark.

The papers were entitled: "The Story of Leona Matravelli and All That Hurts Me." Clark flipped through them: twenty-three single-spaced, typewritten pages documenting in exquisite detail every complaint and problem she could recall since birth, organized by developmental period and organ system. It was in excruciatingly bad English.

He excused himself and sat down with the document in the physicians' workroom. "I am the thirdest daughter of Ricole Matravelli, a restaurantes owner who moved his family to Berlin when I was three. Since then my complaints follow. . . ."

And they did. Sneezing, headaches, backaches, menstrual cramps, hot flashes, fainting, weakness, sensations of flashing lights (but only in August).

It was too much. Clark opened a textbook of medicine, not to read it, but to bang his head against it.

Bob entered the room. "That bad, huh? Let me see." The intern's eyes widened as he flipped through the pages. "Is there no note from Scroffo, no explanation of why she's here?"

Clark shook his head. "None that I could see."

Then they both heard something they had never heard on the ward before: the clinging of a little bell. It reminded Clark of Christmas for some reason. Bob and Clark stepped into the hall, but the ringing had stopped. Then it began again, more insistent, louder.

It was coming from Leona's room. "I'm not in the mood for this," Bob said, covering his bloodshot eyes and sneezing again.

When they stepped into her room, the patient was ringing a dinner bell with a great swing of her arms. "You must *schneller kommen!*" she said, clutching her hand to her chest. "A woman could have died in here. I had a—a—" She opened a German-English dictionary in her lap, then pointed to the word: "attack."

"Are you having any chest pain?" Bob demanded. His voice was muffled by his congested sinuses.

"No, no."

"Any shortness of breath?"

"No, nothing of the kind."

The intern shot Clark a confused look then turned to the patient. "What then?"

"I itch."

"You itch?"

"Yes," she said, throwing her hands in the air. "I always itch before the flashes. I think it is the sheets. I have special soap I need to do sheets with and they touch my skin. I also need lotion and the nurse say you none ordered have. If I do not have my soap and my lotion, I will have more attacks."

Bob puffed out his cheeks. "Ma'am, what type of soap do you need?"

She looked at him as if he were stupid. "It is in there—" She pointed to the document of "All That Hurts Me."

Bob and Clark turned to the last page and saw a list of at least forty medications, soaps, lotions, creams, ointments. Only two or three were recognizable. "I don't know if the hospital formulary stocks any of these," the intern said to her.

"*Kein* problem," she said. "I bring them myself." And the patient reached to her side and opened a small suitcase that Clark thought contained clothes.

It didn't. It was chock-full of medicines and potions, none of which Clark ever remembered encountering in pharmacology. "Now at six in the morning I take this and this and this. Then, at six-thirty, I wash off this and eat three of these with grapefruit juice. It must be grapefuit juice. Then, no pills until eight. At eight, with a breakfast, I eat four pills—these ones—and lie on my back until gas passes. Then—"

"All right," Bob told her. "Dr. Wilson here will take all that down in a few minutes."

Clark turned to him. "I will?"

"Do your best." At that moment Bob sneezed.

"You are sick," the patient said. "Where does the doke-tore go when the doke-tore is sick?"

"If he's an intern, he goes to work."

"But you must be in bed."

"I'd like to be, believe me." Bob smiled at her.

"So what will you do about these sheets? And my soap? You see my skin is already breaking out. You see how horrible it looks."

They didn't. They turned on every light in the room and examined every spot she pointed to, but there was nothing to be seen.

"Well, we'll have to do something about that right away," Bob assured her. "Let me take Dr. Wilson into the hallway to discuss your case."

"Oh, thank you, Doke-tore."

Bob sneezed as he closed the woman's door. As he blew his nose he looked as if he were going to cry. "She is going to hurt us, Clark."

"I know."

"I mean, really hurt us. And Dr. Scroffo will help her hurt us." He leaned back against the wall and stared up at the ceiling. "Here's what we have to do. We have to fight back."

Clark looked down at the typed list of complaints. "But how?"

"For one thing, we play along. We wash her goddamn sheets in her own goddamn soap. That's easy. Then we order every lab test known to man. Thyroid profiles, cortrosin stimulation test, whatever you can think of. It will give Scroffo a hard-on in the morning if he sees all that on your workup." Bob walked away. "And who knows? This woman just might have something. She looked a little hypothyroid. Even hysterics get sick." He sneezed. "Just like interns."

THE CRASH

Half an hour later Clark saw what looked like a surgeon in gloves and mask coming down the hall toward him. The eyes were weepy and the person's gait was somewhat unsteady.

Bob pulled back his mask just long enough to pop a couple of Tylenol and some cold medicine. He had developed a cough now, and had to wait half a minute to catch his breath. "Clark, there's work to do; we have a transfer from the CCU."

The CCU was the cardiac-care unit. Anyone thought to be suffering a heart attack or who had to be ruled out for one, had it done in the CCU. "Came in yesterday with chest pain and some ECG changes. Thelma White. Nice woman, only forty-eight."

The woman, as seemed the rule with half their patients, was accompanied by a half-dozen family members. Clark watched her being wheeled into her room, trailed by four men and a couple of women. She was on oxygen, had two IV's in, and looked like hell. There was a grayness to her face and a blue tint to her lips that gave her a hungry appearance whenever she took a breath.

"Clark. Such a nice name," she said as the medical student introduced himself.

The rest of the family stared at him. Her husband, a bear of a man who looked like he should have been a football coach, if he wasn't, and who kept patting his breast pocket as though in search of some phantom cigarette pack, gave Clark an unfriendly stare. "You going to be her doctor?" he demanded without introducing himself.

"No, I'm just a medical student."

"A student, huh? Well, where's the doctor?"

Just as he spoke Bob stepped into the room.

The husband didn't take the intern's offered hand. "Are you a real doctor or an intern?"

Bob paused, lowered his hand, and answered, "Both, I hope."

The workup was straightforward enough to allow them to get a quick history and physical and get out of the room. That was the advantage of transfers over admissions: most of your work was already done for you.

"Nice family," Clark said.

"I've seen worse, believe me." Bob began scribbling a transfer accept note.

"You ought to go to sleep," Tracy offered, stepping forward from the corner of the room where she had been working on a progress note. "Let us play intern tonight."

"A scary thought," Bob said. He doubled over with a bout of coughing that turned his face a mottled blue, then sat down. "I'll be okay."

The day drifted on, a series of things to be checked and double-checked, nurses' questions to answer, little fires to put out. Clark found himself helping Tracy to take over for Bob. It was a nice sensation, the closest he had come to feeling like a real physician since beginning the rotation. The nicest part was working side by side with Tracy, maybe catching her almost smiling at him once sideways as she was glancing up over a chart. Or maybe it was at something she read; the smile disappeared when they made eye contact.

"You can't keep ignoring me like this," he told her once as they took some stool samples on a woman with gastroenteritis down to the lab.

"I'm not ignoring you, Clark; we have a professional relationship now."

"Professional, my ass. You can't sulk forever."

"Is that a challenge?"

They dropped off the stool samples and walked back to the ward. When they returned, Bob had fallen asleep in a corner of the room, his feet propped up on the table, his mouth open, snoring loudly.

"Bob!" Tracy shook him awake. "Bob, go to the call room. You need some rest."

"I thought I was getting some." He shook his head, as though trying to clear it of something. "That Benadryl really knocked me out." He looked around, glanced at his scut list, then nodded. "All right. We've done everything, it's quiet, and I know you two are responsible enough to call me if anything comes up, right?"

"If we don't," Tracy said, "the nurses will."

When Bob was gone, Clark tried to engage her again. "I said I was sorry about Heather."

Tracy studied him, folding her skirt underneath her and easing herself into a chair. "I really believe you are."

"Then why don't you forgive me?"

"Because I'm not sure I want to. I think things have changed between us."

Clark walked up to her, touched her cheek with his fingertip. "Tracy, we've been through so much together."

She nodded and he knew from the look on her face that she was quiet because she couldn't trust her voice. "Then why did you do that to me?"

"Because—because—" He pulled up a chair next to hers and tried to form the words. "Because I felt I was losing you. Because I felt everything closing in and I was never so aware of time slipping away and I just wanted to live, and when I reached out for someone to taste life with, you weren't there."

"But Heather was."

He paused. "Yes. Yes, she was." He stood up, thrust his hands deep in his khaki pants, and stared out the window. He knew she could see the scar from where she sat. "Erich says I have a field cut."

"What—what are you talking about?"

He turned to her, his nostrils flaring. "I had him examine me after I collapsed in the library. He also says I have papilledema."

Tracy pushed a strand of hair behind her ear. "Back up to the beginning. What's this about collapsing in the library?"

Clark told her the story as best he could, leaving out a few details that he knew would worry her.

"Why didn't you tell me any of this?" she demanded.

"We weren't exactly on speaking terms."

"Clark, we're talking about your *health*. Maybe your life. And why didn't you see someone other than Erich?"

"Because I don't want to fall behind."

"Well, you'll fall awfully damned behind if you're dead."

Neither one spoke for a minute. There was the sound of traffic far below, a car honking, an ambulance siren wailing in the distance. After only a few weeks in the city, Clark had learned to distinguish an ambulance siren from a fire truck from a police car.

"That's what Heather said."

"Well, for once I agree with her." Tracy was about to say something else when a nurse walked in. "Mrs. White wants to see you," she said to Clark.

"Me?"

The nurse rolled her eyes. "You're the medical student taking care of her, right?"

Clark nodded.

"Well, I think you'd better come."

As Clark stepped into the hallway he was discovering one of the best, least-known fringe benefits of medicine; it forced you to pull yourself away, if only for a few minutes or hours at a time, to think about someone other than yourself. His own problems receded as he ran through his mind all the possible reasons Mrs. White would want to see him: chest pain, shortness of breath, constipation, loneliness, a question about the gray-brown gelatinous mass the cafeteria was attempting to pass off as turkey with stuffing.

"How may I help you?"

When he entered the room, she was propped up with three pillows, her nostrils a little more flared than Clark remembered last, her lips a little bluer and trembling slightly.

"Clark, I think I need a little more oxygen. I have the strangest sensation right here——" She gestured to her throat. "It's like—like I'm choking."

Clark's eyes rounded at the word *choking*. It was the original meaning of the word *angina*.

"You look ill," the woman observed.

Mustn't worry her, Clark thought, and attempted to put on his best Marcus Welby smile. It was a forced, fake expression, and probably came out looking more like a grimace than anything. "Ma'am, everything is going to be okay." He had heard Jeb say that to Mr. Lumbar and it seemed to work then.

Mrs. White smiled. "Of course it is. I figured if you could just up my oxygen a little, this choking would go away."

"What's going on, Doctor?" the son demanded. "She did this before her last heart attack."

"Is that right? Well, um. Hang on a minute, okay?" Clark stepped into the hallway and pulled a manual from the pocket of his white coat. He looked up *angina* in the index and flipped to page 72. A step-by-step discussion followed the heading of *Workup of Chest Pain*.

He glanced up half-embarrassed at the nurse who was

looking at him expectantly. "What would you like me to do . . . Doctor?"

Clark blinked. "Let's get her some oxygen. One-hundred-percent face mask. STAT."

"And maybe a STAT ECG?" The corner of the nurse's mouth was twisted into a half smile. She had been through this many times, Clark thought, the struggling of an acolyte in the temple of medicine, the asking of questions in such a way that the interns or medical students could act as though the thought were their own.

Clark nodded. "Yes, please. Did you page the intern?"

"Three times. He's not answering."

Clark felt his mouth go dry. "What do you mean?"

"I mean just what I said."

"He's in the call room. Did you call?"

"Of course. He's not answering the phone there either."

Clark turned away. "I'll get him myself."

The nurse grabbed his shoulder. "I don't think you'd better go anywhere right now. You're needed in there."

Clark was torn. He stared from her to the corridor stretching down to where he knew Bob slept. Bob would be able to handle this; Clark wasn't.

He felt his feet move into the room, toward the woman's tight, shallow breathing. The son's eyes bored into him, making him feel naked somehow as he positioned himself at the end of the bed and looked down at this woman struggling not to die.

"Feeling any better?" he asked, hoping she might have a spontaneous reversion to full health.

She shook her head.

"Everything's going to be all right," he told her, although he didn't believe it himself.

The nurse was at the other end of the bed, pulling off the nasal cannula and slapping on an oxygen face mask. He offered the only thing he really knew how to do. "I'll draw off a blood gas."

Clark looked toward the door, hoping to see Bob appear, but it remained empty. He pulled a syringe from his pocket, swabbed the woman's wrist with alcohol, then plunged deep. He got her artery with the first stick.

That was when it happened. In a surge of adrenaline and confidence and fear, the thought struck him that he could help this woman, that disaster might strike but he would react coolly and appropriately. At some point during the crisis he began looking at himself not so much as a terrified medical student, but as a doctor. He began to recall lines from his handbook. "Page respiratory therapy STAT. And have someone bring the chart to the bedside. Also, let's get a STAT portable chest X ray. Is the ECG on the way?"

The nurse nodded. "Called." She picked up a phone by the bedside and followed the rest of Clark's orders. Medicolegally, she shouldn't have, but there was no time to stand on protocol.

Another nurse entered the room, gave Clark the chart, and took the blood gas from him, saying she'd run it off to the lab.

A respiratory tech entered the room. "What's the story?"

"Forty-eight-year-old white female transferred from the CCU, where she was admitted to rule out for MI."

"Did she?"

"Yes. She was negative by enzymes and ECG changes."

The therapist nodded, clipped a monitor to the patient's finger. It measured the saturation of her hemoglobin with oxygen: eighty-eight percent. "A blood gas is cooking," Clark said.

The ECG technician rolled the cart into the room, hooked up the electrodes, and in a minute a tracing was printed out and handed to Clark. He frowned at it, praying if anything bad was happening, he could recognize it. Then he remembered the teaching of Jeb: the old chart is your friend.

"Let me see the old chart." He grabbed it and flipped it open until he came to an old ECG tracing, taken two months before admission. There was a definite difference in the ECG he was holding in his hand and the one they had taken then.

"Get the CCU resident on the phone, please," he said to the nurse.

She nodded, punched a few digits, and hung up. "I just paged him to this number."

"What's going on?" a new voice asked.

It was Tracy, her hand on his shoulder. "Mrs. White is going bad on us," he whispered.

Tracy scowled down at the bedside. "Is that her ECG?"

Clark nodded.

"I think she's got ST segment depression in her antero-lateral leads." He lifted the woman's wrist and felt for a moment. "One twenty. Let's get a blood pressure."

The nurse pumped up the BP cuff and let it slowly deflate. "One eighty over one-oh-five," she said.

Clark nodded. "Then she has some room. Slap on two inches of nitropaste now."

"And have her chew an aspirin," Tracy added.

The nurse hesitated a moment. "I really shouldn't take orders from you two, you know."

"I know, but it doesn't look like we have much choice right now, does it?" Clark asked.

The nurse looked from Tracy to Clark to the patient and the patient's son, who was standing in the back-ground, looking around at everyone anxiously. "I'll get some nitropaste," she said.

Clark turned to Tracy. "Any signs of Bob?"

At that moment the intern burst into the room, his shoes untied, his hair matted against his head, creases from the sheets having indented one side of his face.

But there was nothing for him to do. By then, Mrs. White had regained her color and was saying something to Tracy that was muffled through her oxygen mask. The woman's cheeks were flushed and she laughed at some-thing her son said.

"What's going on?" Bob asked, turning back to Clark. "I thought you said she was crashing."

"I wasn't doing too good a minute ago," Mrs. White said. "But the pain is gone away completely now."

The CCU resident also came running into the room. "What's up?"

"That's what I'm trying to figure out," Bob said.

The CCU resident picked up the ECG with the ST segment changes and whistled. "Is this her tracing?"

Clark nodded. "She had nine-out-of-ten chest pain with this tracing."

The resident studied the ECG and whistled. "Let's get another ECG to see if she normalized and how about another blood pressure, too?" He turned to the nurse and issued some orders, then grabbed the chart and scribbled a quick note.

"So is she going to be transferred?" Clark asked.

"What for? You guys handled her fine up here." He turned to Bob, assuming that the intern must have been behind her care. "Good job."

Tracy exchanged a quick look with Clark and he could tell from the glint in her eye that she was smiling inside.

Bob looked over the CCU resident's note, countersigned the medical students' orders, and took them aside. "Why didn't you guys get me?" he asked.

"We did. You didn't answer our pages."

The intern removed his beeper and depressed a button. "I must have slept through them." His face turned purple as he doubled over with a violent cough.

"You look like hell," Tracy said.

"Thanks, but it's obvious I can't go to sleep. Not if my beeper doesn't wake me up. That goddamn cold medicine."

The intern propped himself up against a wall in the corner of the physicians' workroom. Tracy and Clark continued to work on their write-ups until they heard the sound of the intern's snores; he had fallen asleep standing up.

They eased him out of a standing position and laid him out on the table, then Tracy ran for a couple of blankets and a pillow. Finally they pulled off his shoes and loosened his tie, then turned out the lights and left the room.

"That guy ought to see a doctor," Clark said as they walked toward the call room.

Clark tried to sleep, but felt too exhilarated, too pumped up about what he had just participated in. For the first time since hitting the wards he really felt like a doctor. That was what it was all about, he thought: the oxygen and the nitropaste had probably staved off a heart attack.

There was still so much to learn, but Clark knew he could function, alone and in the middle of the night, and somehow stumble through to the right decision.

Tracy was in the bunk above him. "Are you asleep?" he whispered.

"No, I can't sleep."

"Me neither." He could see the outline of her body above him against the mattress. "I was so scared in there."

"So was I."

"Really? You couldn't tell it." There was something in her voice when she spoke, maybe a trace of the old affection she once felt for him.

He rolled out of bed and stood up so that he could look her in the eye. She rolled toward him in the darkness. She was fully clothed in shoes and scrubs, lying over her sheets. Like a well-trained intern, she slept in perpetual preparation for disaster.

"Tracy, I'm so sorry about what happened between me and—though nothing really did and—"

"Clark."

"No, you listen to me, Tracy. I am so tired of enduring your cold stares and silent treatment and . . ." It might have been his imagination—it was hard to tell in the dark—but she might have been smiling at him.

He found himself leaning toward her, feeling the coldness of her sheets against his chin as he bent to kiss her.

She didn't push him away, but murmured softly and pulled him toward her. He was surprised to find her lips part and to feel the flick of her tongue.

"Oh, Clark," she murmured, pulling back, using the same mixture of affection and scolding that she might to an errant boy. "Clark, Clark, Clark."

He grinned at her, ran his fingers through her hair, which was damp with perspiration and fear. "I kind of love this, don't you?"

She nodded. "Yes. I don't know why, but I really do."

Then he pulled her into his arms, holding half her body suspended over the edge of the bed, and felt himself swelling to life as he kissed her. She didn't resist at first, just managed to pull back long enough to ask, "Suppose Bob comes in?"

"He won't—he's crashed on the table."

"What about a nurse or something."

"I'll lock the door."

"Suppose someone crashes?"

"Then we'll get dressed faster than we've ever dressed before in our lives."

It took Clark several minutes to overcome his self-consciousness at being naked with Tracy in the top bunk of the call room. He had read about this in novels and seen it in movies, but actually making love on a hospital ward, with the sound of a beeping IV drifting in through the door, was both thrilling and inhibiting.

After a few minutes, however, he became oblivious to where he was and Tracy had to cover his mouth to quiet him. When he rolled onto his back and panted, staring up at the ceiling, Tracy tickled his belly. She pulled on her scrubs again.

"I suppose this means I'm forgiven," he said.

"Don't press your luck."

There was a knock on the door. In one motion that made the bunk rock violently, he yanked up his pants, rolled over the sides, and shot into the lower bunk. "Yes?" Tracy asked.

It was the voice of a ward nurse. "I think one of you should come quick."

Not again, Clark thought. "Which patient is it now?"

"It's no patient; it's your intern. He doesn't look good at all."

Clark was still buttoning his shirt as he stepped into the hall. He felt a mix of guilt and euphoria and a profound sense of relaxation and peace as he watched Tracy march along beside him. He winked at her, but she just smiled and shook her head.

Bob was on the table where they had left him. He had kicked the blanket away and his scrubs were permeated with sweat. He was chilling so hard the table shook.

Clark grabbed an electronic thermometer from a slot on the wall. "How do you work these things?"

The nurse snatched it away and inserted the probe under Bob's tongue. "We better culture him up," Clark said.

Tracy looked confused. "He's our *intern*."

"That doesn't make him immune to bacteremia."

He gathered a handful of yellow-top culture tubes, then swabbed some Betadine in the crook of the intern's elbow. He inserted a needle and drew back about forty milliliters of blood.

Bob woke up at the stick and stared at him. "What the hell are you doing?"

"Culturing you up," Clark said.

Tracy looked at the thermometer and whistled. "One-oh-three-point-five."

Bob turned to the nurse, clutching himself to stop the chilling. "Just give me six hundred and fifty of Tylenol, if you have any extra lying around the ward. I'll be fine."

"Let's see what your white blood cell count is first," Clark said. A high white blood cell count could indicate a serious infection.

"You guys are nuts. I'm not a patient."

"You should be," Tracy said.

Bob rubbed his eyes, looked at his watch, and groaned.

"You shouldn't have let me sleep so long. I don't know if I'll get all this scut done by morning."

Clark frowned at him. "What do you need to do?"

"I have three progress notes and an admission history and physical to do."

"We already wrote progress notes on all the patients; you can just cosign those. And we can crank out a history and physical for you, can't we, Tracy?"

Tracy wasn't so certain. "I think Bob should examine the patient first."

"I already have," Bob said.

"Good," Clark said. "Then all we have to do is write it down while you dictate." He grabbed a blank history form, pulled out his pen, and sat down. "Now, let's see. 'Patient is a forty-eight-year-old white female with a past medical history significant for—'" He looked up. "Continue."

Bob slumped into a chair. "'—significant for two myocardial infarctions two years prior to admission, two-vessel coronary artery disease as documented by cath, and . . .'"

As Bob droned on Clark scribbled, slowing him down every now and then and asking him to spell a word, or whether a particular set of letters formed an acceptable acronym.

Tracy, meanwhile, was searching for labels for Bob's blood work. There was a problem, though; since Bob wasn't a patient, he had no history number and hence couldn't be entered into the computer.

She approached a nurse and told her the problem. The nurse thought about it a moment, then smiled mischievously back at her. "I have an idea that just might work. We can make him Mr. Frankworth."

Tracy was confused. "Frankworth—isn't he the man who died two days ago of renal failure?"

"Exactly, but I think his file is still active. We can use his history number." She sat at a computer keyboard and typed out a few commands. "Yep, it works. Here—write this down. . . ." She read out the history number and Tracy scribbled it onto the labels.

Before she put them into a transport bag, she asked, "Won't this become part of Frankworth's permanent medical record? Won't this screw up some vital statistics somewhere?"

The nurse laughed. "Honey, if they can't figure out that a man shouldn't be developing positive blood cultures and a white blood count two days after he dies, they should hire someone else to keep those vital statistics, now, shouldn't they?"

"I suppose so. Can we also get a urinalysis on—um—Mr. Frankworth."

She made a few more key strokes, grabbed a specimen cup, and winked at Tracy. "Coming right up."

When Tracy dropped the samples off at the lab window, she told the tech, "Please run these STAT."

The tech, who must have seen thousands of samples a day, frowned at the labels she had made. She held her breath as she waited for her fraud to be discovered. She wondered if it would be grounds for dismissing her from medical school.

"Mr. Frankworth—I seem to remember this name. We must have run a hundred samples on him." He turned to Tracy. "How's he doing, anyway?"

She sighed. "He'll be dead if we don't get these run right away."

The tech nodded. "All right, all right. I'll page you with the results."

Tracy, who didn't carry a beeper, had to give Bob's number. It was a weird twist, she realized, having to page an intern with his own lab values, but it couldn't be helped.

Twenty minutes later Bob's beeper went off. He was almost finished dictating the admission history and physical to Clark, who wrote as fast as he could. Bob picked up the phone and frowned. "It's the lab. Wonder what the hell they're paging me for."

Tracy had forgotten to pass on that she had given them Bob's beeper number. She tried to catch the intern's attention now, but someone had already come on-line. Bob whistled. "Whew. That's one hell of a white count. What's the patient's name again? Frankworth? Oh, I'm sorry, you must have the wrong intern. I'm not taking care of any Frankworth. What's that? Yes, that's my beeper number, but—"

Tracy finally caught the intern's attention. When Bob realized what had happened, he hung up the phone. His face looked a little gray. "What's going on?"

"Mr. Frankworth is dead." She explained what she had done.

"So this is my white blood cell count?"

Tracy nodded.

Clark looked over at the slip of paper on which he had written the value. "You should be on IV antibiotics."

Bob crumpled up the paper and threw it in the trash can. "I'll be fine. I have to be."

Clark picked up the phone, called the lab, and asked them to Gram stain the blood he had sent down. They told him they didn't have the manpower to do it; he'd have to come do it himself.

So he went back to the lab, pulled a smear of Bob's blood, mixed it with gentian violet and iodine, then passed it over a Bunsen burner a few times to fix it. When the slide cooled, he looked at it under a microscope, dabbing the slide with a drop of oil and zooming down with high power.

What he saw made him catch his breath: the field was chock-full of dark blue-black blobs, some in pairs, a few in chains. He turned off the microscope and ran back upstairs. Pulling Tracy aside, he whispered, "He's got gram-positive cocci in his blood. Maybe diplococci, I'm not sure."

"You did the stain right?" Tracy asked.

Clark nodded, explaining exactly what he did.

Tracy bit her inner lip. "Well, we could be purists and cover him with penicillin."

"I opt for something with broader coverage, just in case."

Clark was the one who told the intern what they would do. Bob rolled his eyes. "You're overreacting."

"Hey, you saw your white count." He blew two veins before he managed to get the IV started.

"This is absurd," Bob said, nursing the puncture sites where Clark had missed. "You're making a pincushion of me."

"We have no choice," Clark said.

The intern said nothing. The nurse was ready with the antibiotic, which she hung on a pole by Bob's side.

"Who am I going to order this for?" Bob said, pointing up at the antibiotic.

The nurse waved the question away. "Don't worry about it. The intensive-care-unit charge nurse is a friend of mine; she snagged an extra bag for me."

Bob nodded, dabbed at his forehead with a cold wash-cloth, then turned to the medical students. "I guess I owe you guys one, huh?"

Tracy nodded. "A large pepperoni pizza would do."

"With anchovies," Clark added.

"Your urinalysis is negative, by the way," Tracy added, staring into the computer monitor. "No white cells and no bacteria. Stone-cold normal."

The intern smiled at them. "Pretty thorough flog, there, studs. Pretty thorough flog, indeed."

Clark gave Tracy a wink. For the first time in weeks she winked back at him.

HYPOVOLEMIA

Murdoch was in top form during attending rounds. Bob stood in a corner, propping himself up against the wall to keep from falling asleep. He still had the heparin-locked IV catheter taped in place in his forearm, hidden under the sleeve of his white coat. His chills would come and go, but with great effort he could suppress them.

Tracy sat next to Clark and would turn and smile at him from time to time. Once he thought she blushed.

Jeb spent much time staring off into space, apparently daydreaming. Clark thought the resident hadn't absorbed a word of his presentation of Mrs. White, which included a blow-by-blow account of her crisis in the middle of the night. He had to blur over the fact that Bob wasn't in the room until it was already resolved.

Murdoch's mouth was twisted into its characteristic half smile. "Well. Not a bad presentation, Clark. I think you might be learning something on this rotation."

The attending turned to Bob, who was nodding off in

the corner. "Bob, you find attending rounds a little som-
niferous this morning?"

The intern snapped his eyes open. "No, sir. I'm just
feeling a little under the weather."

"Good thing you didn't wimp out and call in sick,"
Murdoch said. "You know, in my day, we never called in
sick."

Jeb chuckled. "Has the human immune system degenerated that much since then?"

Murdoch ignored that. "If we didn't do our work, who
else could? We depended on each other."

"I'm not calling in sick, sir," Bob said. He sounded so
congested that his voice was almost impossible to understand.

"I certainly hope not. Mrs. White was your only admission last night, right?"

Clark was surprised to hear the intern say no. Mrs.
White *was* the only admission Clark remembered and she
had already been presented.

Murdoch was as confused as Clark. "There's no other
patient on the census."

"He came in late, sir," Bob said.

"Well, let me get a blank card, then. Okay." He looked
up, his pen poised over the card.

"The patient's name is Frankworth. Jason Frankworth.
He is a sixty-four-year-old white male who presented with
stage-four prostatic cancer."

"The name sounds familiar," Murdoch said. "Go on."

Clark gripped Tracy's wrist under the table, and scribbled on the corner of his write-up: *What the hell is he
doing?*

Tracy shrugged.

"Frankworth was admitted for reasons unrelated to his
cancer, however," Bob continued. "He had developed
what began as an upper-respiratory-tract infection that
progressed to a cough productive of rust-colored sputum.
He also had fever and shaking chills. His differential was
significant for—"

Murdoch looked up and scowled. "Now, Bob, you know better than to present lab values in the middle of your history."

"—a white blood cell count of—"

"Bob, did you hear me?"

"—twenty-two-point-four, with a left shift. Gram's stain of his sputum revealed gram positive diplococci. He was begun on IV cefuroxime, without defervescence. His blood and urine were—"

"Bob!"

"—cultured; results are pending. Urinalysis was negative." Bob's head nodded back and forth.

Jeb seemed to remember something. He pulled an old, folded-up census out of his pocket and ran his index finger down it. Then he looked up at the intern. "Bob, Mr. Frankworth is dead."

The intern shook his head. "The cefuroxime didn't do the trick, huh?"

"He died last week."

The intern nodded, clutching himself. His teeth began to chatter, making a sound like ice cubes in a cocktail glass. All eyes followed Bob as he swayed, tossed his head back, then fell face forward.

His forehead slammed into the table, bounced off, and he slid to the floor with a groan. For an instant no one moved. Then Clark hopped around Tracy's chair and knelt down by him. "Bob! Bob!"

The intern rubbed his forehead, stared up at him, and smiled. "Oops."

"Bob, this is idiotic. We have to get you to the emergency room."

"I'll be fine."

Murdoch stared down at them both. "In my day we didn't collapse during attending rounds." He might have meant it as a joke, but no one laughed.

Jeb's jaw rested on his chest. "What am I going to do without an intern?" he asked himself. Then he seemed to realize what was going on and got down on the floor by

Bob. "Bob, old buddy, you experiencing any chest pain, headache, nausea, vomiting, abdominal pain, or shortness of breath?"

Bob shook his head. "Just headache."

"Any visual changes?"

"None." As Jeb spoke he got a pulse and directed Clark to take Bob's blood pressure. Tracy thrust a thermometer in the intern's mouth.

"Ninety over fifty-five," Clark reported.

Jeb nodded. "Well, let's get him tanked up with some IV fluids. You're running on empty, Bob." He rolled back the intern's sleeve and spotted the hep-lock. "What's this?"

"The medical students gave me a couple doses of cefuroxime," Bob's words were muffled by the thermometer probe.

"What? What on—" Jeb looked around, then grinned. "You old dog, you. Love work so much, you just couldn't tear yourself away, huh?" He turned to a nurse. "Let's get some normal saline going at one fifty cc's an hour."

Tracy pulled the probe from his mouth. "A hundred and four," she reported. As the nurse got a bag hoisted on an IV pole, the others helped Bob onto a gurney. "We need to get him to the emergency room," Jeb said.

CHANGE OF
COMMAND

▲

▼

The new intern was everything Bob wasn't: confident to the point of cocky, laconic to the point of rudeness. She had a habit of twirling a tourniquet until it completely wrapped her ring finger, then twirling it back the other way. She would do this repeatedly until Clark grew dizzy watching.

He knew that he wouldn't like her.

She was short and pretty, with red-brown, tightly curled hair. Her white pants were just a tad too tight, as though she were trying to convince herself that she was one size smaller than she actually was. She had a small, upturned nose and little gray-blue eyes.

Her name was Monica Stellar and the first thing she said was that every patient was on at least one wrong drug and why hadn't the students written progress notes in the correct format? She said this loudly and in the presence of Jeb, to whom she addressed every question and statement as though the students weren't there. She said she wanted the students to stay on the ward during lunch and formally present each patient.

"How do you know it's not porphyria?" she had asked Clark after he presented Angela Brooks, who was ready for discharge the next day.

Clark frowned. "*Porphyria?*"

"If you don't look for it, you won't find it." She looked to Jeb for support, but he only gave her a polite smile. "It's not worth keeping her here, but I think we should draw some more labs on her before she goes. And speaking of labs, why hasn't Winfield had any ordered for the past week?"

"Because—" Clark knew damn well why, but wasn't about to tell her. Jeb told them that every time they drew a lab, there was a chance of some abnormality coming up, and any abnormality could make it that much harder for Winfield to be placed in a nursing home. "Because we didn't feel it was indicated."

"Hospitalization," Monica said, "is the only indication you need for drawing labs. And how do we know Mr. Winfield isn't in atrial fibrillation? I say we get an electrocardiogram on him STAT, and maybe order an echocardiogram if it shows anything abnormal. We can Doppler his carotids and maybe put him on the board for a carotid angiogram."

Jeb looked toward the chalkboard where he had recorded Bob's blood pressure readings—the numbers were still there. To Clark, the resident looked like he really missed Bob.

When the intern stepped from the room to answer a nurse's question, Clark turned to Tracy. "She's pretty intense."

Tracy frowned at him. "You mean she's thorough. I think she's exactly right—we have let things slide around here." Jeb looked at her and arched an eyebrow. "Nothing personal, but it's true. Bob always seemed somehow flustered. I like her."

"But she wants to flog Winfield."

"Maybe he needs it."

"The guy's a million years old."

"If he were your grandfather, you wouldn't care how old he is. You'd want everything possible done."

Clark looked down at the list of things Monica had given him to do. "Life as we know it has just ended."

Bob's face looked the color of his pillow. He stared up at the medical students and grinned. "So they pulled Monica to replace me, huh?"

Clark stared around the hospital room, at the collection of cards and balloons. The intern followed his eyes. "Never knew I had so many friends. Hell of a way to find out, though."

They had tanked Bob up with two liters of intravenous fluid in the emergency room and given him IV antibiotics.

"What do you know about Monica?" Tracy asked.

"Only that medicine is her life. I'd love to have her as my doctor, but would hate to work with her."

Clark examined the bags of IV fluid hanging from the pole by Bob's bed. "How long before you think you'll be back with us?"

"I have no idea. My hunch is they won't let me work for another week or so."

Clark frowned at that. "Won't let you? I thought originally they wouldn't let you *not* work."

Bob spread his hands. "That was before word of this got out. The ER attending noticed how dehydrated I was and got really pissed off. Said I wasn't the first resident he had seen worked into this state, but if he could help it, I'd be the last." He smiled weakly. "If I miss too much time, they won't give me credit for this rotation."

Tracy smiled back at him. "It always comes back to haunt you in some way, doesn't it?"

◆   ◆   ◆

They came during attending rounds next day. Clark was giving an update on Angela Brooks when he heard the knock at the door.

"Tell them to go away, would you, Tracy?" Murdoch asked.

She hopped up and opened the door. Clark looked beyond her to a congregation of long white coats and whiter hair. He recognized the face of the hospital director. "Is Dr. Murdoch around?"

"Yes, sir," Tracy responded. "But we're rounding now. If you—"

"I think this takes precedence over rounds."

Clark looked over at Murdoch, who blinked toward the door. "What is it, Tom?"

"We need to talk, Peter."

"Now?"

"Now."

Murdoch rose and lumbered toward the door. "You do realize this is the only time all day I spend with my medical students?"

"I am fully aware of that fact. That is indirectly the purpose of my visit." They stepped into the hall and closed the door behind them. The students were left to stare at each other as the words *incident* and *embarrassment* and *allegations of abuse* drifted through the door.

Twenty minutes passed. The students pulled some charts from the rack and began their daily progress notes. When Murdoch finally stepped back into the room, his cheeks were a mottled scarlet. His lips were pressed firmly together and he seemed very distracted. It was obvious he didn't hear a word about Angela Brooks as Clark continued.

Then Murdoch did something he never did; he ended rounds early. Without grilling the students and without bidding them farewell, he walked out of the room.

The next morning they had a new attending. The rumor was that Murdoch had been laterally promoted, that he had been forced to give up his position as training director and instead had been put in charge of hospital quality assurance.

The next time the students visited Bob, they found him sitting up in bed, bouncing a tennis ball off the wall. "So when you coming back to us?" Clark asked.

"I'm not."

The students examined his chart, looked him over, and frowned at each other. "What do you mean?" Tracy asked. "You've been afebrile for forty-eight hours on p.o. antibiotics."

"And your labs look great," Clark added. "Surely you're ready for discharge."

"I'm ready," Bob agreed, "but they're sending me back to the outpatient clinic for a month." He slammed the ball hard enough into the wall to cause the patient in the next room to pound on the wall twice with his fist.

"So they won't give you credit for the weeks of hell you spent with us?" Tracy asked.

Bob smiled. "Doesn't look like it."

"And you'll have to do it all over?"

"Right."

"But I heard," Tracy said, "that things are going to improve around here. There's talk of easing up on the call schedule and instituting a night float system."

Bob smiled. "Rumors like that have been flying around this place for years. I wouldn't hold my breath."

"Well, I'm going to miss you," Tracy said, holding out her hand.

Bob shook it and winked at her. "We had some fun, didn't we?"

When the students reached the elevators, both had the same thought: they were stuck with Monica. But it was only for a few more weeks.

"We can do anything for a few weeks, right?"

Clark wasn't so sure. He was puzzled to see Tracy push the third-floor button. "Where are you going?"

"To see Winfield's carotid arteriogram."

Monica had talked the ultrasonographer into doing a Doppler of the blood vessels in the patient's neck. The ultrasound showed some stenosis, or narrowing, of Winfield's left carotid. The only way to determine if the lesion could be surgically removed via carotid endarterectomy was to perform an arteriogram that would outline the blood vessel with a radiopaque dye.

The patient was strapped to the table when Tracy entered the radiology suite. Poor Mr. Winfield, she thought; he was drooling, terrified at all the machinery hovering over his head, machinery he could never hope to understand.

His daughter, his legal guardian, had signed consent for the procedure, after Monica explained that a stroke, the most serious complication, occurred less than one out of a thousand times. The daughter had taken a week to think it over before signing.

Tracy had to don a gown, face mask, and gloves before entering the room. She barely recognized Winfield, who was quieting down now, after seeing there wasn't much use in fighting the inevitable.

His right groin had been exposed and shaved and was now being swabbed with Betadine, a copper-colored, lathery disinfectant. The procedure consisted of passing a catheter through a blood vessel in his leg up to his aorta, then squirting the dye while snapping X rays of his neck and head. The dye would outline the vessels and the X-ray camera would swivel around the patient's head to capture it in as many dimensions as possible.

The catheter appeared and disappeared in the man's leg. There was only a little blood as the radiologist punctured the man's skin and drove the sharp catheter tip into the femoral vein.

Tracy wasn't quite clear why the procedure was being done. She had argued against it, telling Monica she thought the risks outweighed the benefits. Monica had blinked at her and said that of course Tracy didn't understand; she was only a third-year medical student—if there was time, they would talk about it later.

They never did.

That was when Tracy began to agree with Clark about his assessment of their new intern.

Tracy stood over Winfield and winked down at him. "How you doing today, sir?"

The man's lids drooped as he stared up at her—they had sedated him for the procedure. She couldn't help thinking as she looked at him that it would be the last time she would see him this way.

But maybe Monica was right. Maybe the intern knew something that Tracy, with only a few weeks of experience, didn't.

Someone handed Tracy a lead apron, which she strapped into place. It weighed less than she expected, reminding her of the bulletproof vests she'd seen cops wear in movies.

"Stand back," the radiologist commanded as he pushed a button.

Tracy looked up at a television monitor that showed a real-time X ray of Winfield's heart, chest, and neck. A swirl of dye, appearing black on the monitor, pulsed through his arch, up his neck, and into the blood vessels in his brain. She tried to name them all before the dye disappeared. It would enter his venous system, then be filtered out of his body by his kidneys.

"Did we get a good shot of the arch?"

"Yep. Let's shoot one more, just in case." The tech changed the plate of film, then nodded to the radiologist that he was ready.

It was a little like a movie, with the radiologist directing. Tracy watched Winfield, who seemed to tolerate the procedure all right. So maybe all her fears were unfounded. It was completely painless except for the catheter stick.

The second time Tracy knew exactly where to look. She followed the dye carefully in the second or so that it took for it to disappear in the man's head. She thought she could see the stenosis—a narrowing in the channel like a sandbar in a river.

Then it happened. Winfield made a sound like a dog kicked in the stomach, his eyes rolled back in his head, and the radiologist swore. It happened in a fraction of a second.

Three nurses and a doctor rushed into the room. Tracy was elbowed out of the way and the patient disappeared in a sea of blue scrubs and lead aprons. Three people were struggling to be heard at once, including the radiologist, who had ripped off his surgical mask and was shouting orders at someone standing by a phone across the room.

She had seen enough. Her last glimpse of Winfield was from between two nurses as she slipped from the room.

If Monica seemed shocked by Winfield's death, she didn't show it. "It's an occupational hazard of the business we're in," she said. "These risks aren't theoretical. People do stroke out and die."

That, in essence, was what the autopsy showed. The dye had dislodged a huge clot in Winfield's carotid artery that had clogged a smaller vessel, cutting off blood flow to part of his brain. He died quickly, blacking out without pain.

Tracy noticed a change taking place within her during those long days that stretched into weeks. The places that once hurt, the soft spots that had somehow hardened, were now numb. Winfield's death was a blessing of sorts compared with the misery he had waiting for him on the ward or in some nursing home: bedpans, diapers, pureed food, reluctant visits by relatives on holidays, memories of a wife who had died years ago. No, worse for Winfield would be the death of those memories, maybe just the groping around the edges of her memory, trying to feel for the place in his mind where he once stored her image, to find it stolen. If that was his life, then death was better.

It was hard not to blame Monica for Winfield's death, but no one said anything out loud.

Tracy visited Thurgood less and less. The man had lost his hair, most of the spare fat and muscle around his face, and had a bleached yellow complexion. His eyes were surrounded by black penumbras, but the eyes themselves were alive, so alive they seemed almost angry, not at her, but at the disease process that dared to challenge him.

She had stolen four weeks from him—that was the only way to look at it—and as she examined the data on which she based her decision, it seemed flimsier and flimsier. If he didn't develop an opportunistic infection or have his kidneys wiped out by the chemotherapy or just get killed by the cancer anyway, the treatment probably wouldn't have added more than two months to his survival. He was going through four weeks of hell in hopes of eight extra weeks of life. It wasn't much of a trade.

"Your blood counts are low," she told him during the final week of the internal-medicine rotation. "We're going to hold your chemo today and try again tomorrow."

Thurgood nodded. He refused to wear a wig, so the top of his head glinted where the sun came in the window. "I'm going to beat this thing, Doc."

Tracy nodded. "I know you are."

"No, I really mean it. I've bought property on the mountain, and as soon as this treatment is over—just one more course, like you said—I'm going to take the wife and we're going to retire."

Tracy knew that would never happen either; the wife had told her that they had spent all his savings on his treatment, which, since it was experimental, was not covered by Blue Cross Blue Shield. But Mrs. Thurgood couldn't break it to her husband that they had nothing left, that the house had a second mortgage, and soon that would be gone, too.

MAGNETIC
RESONANCE

How long have you had these symptoms?"

Clark found it strange to be on the other side of the white coat. "A few weeks."

"A few *weeks?* What kept you from coming to the clinic then?"

Clark paused. "Internal medicine."

His neurosurgeon didn't laugh; she would have laughed once, but something worried her. Her exam lasted twenty minutes, and when it was over, she seemed less worried. She even smiled. "So was this a medical-school classmate who told you you had papilledema and a field cut?"

Clark nodded.

"Well, tell your classmate he has a vivid imagination. The most likely explanation of your symptoms is a vasovagal event. You're under a terrific amount of stress and probably are eating only irregularly, or maybe not at all." She paused. "Am I right?"

Clark nodded.

"Well, don't abuse yourself. You've got to remember your health. Don't get too hypoglycemic." She paused again. "That's probably all this is. But we should get an imaging study, just to be sure."

It was like a coffin. They slid you in and you stared at a slick white surface only inches from your face, your neck, your chest. There were lights inside, like a tunnel, but it didn't help much. If you tried to move your shoulders, you became only more aware of the narrowness.

Clark closed his eyes and tried to think about something else. He was postcall and should have been tired, but his heart was racing and sleep was the last thing he could think of.

"Take a breath and hold it!" Clark flinched at the voice over the intercom. "Try to stay still. You're doing great."

They said the MRI scanner had a one-hundred-percent sensitivity for claustrophobia and Clark could understand why. Health-care workers were supposed to be the worst, most requiring a little Ativan to calm them before they were eased into the sarcophagus.

There was a clicking sound as something within the giant magnet oriented itself then reoriented itself. It was an awesome tool, a huge doughnut that generated a magnetic field powerful enough to turn a fragment of metal into a deadly missile. But it was also a tremendous boon for medicine, giving a wealth of information without emitting any radiation.

"That's great. Just five more minutes."

"You said that before. At least half an hour ago."

"This time I mean it. We're almost done."

Twenty minutes later Clark heard a thick lead-and-steel door opening and the conveyer belt that eased him into the tube now eased him out. He blinked around the room, stretched his arms, massaged a kink out of his neck.

"Can I at least see the result of all this clicking?"

The nurse led him back to a darkened room that would have made an excellent setting for a spaceship control center in a science-fiction movie. Orange console panels stared up at him. A radiologist in scrubs spotted Clark and rose. "Excuse me, but patients aren't allowed back in this area."

Clark was about to say something when the nurse patted the radiologist's wrist and said, "Leave him alone. He's a medical student."

"Oh, why didn't you say so?" The radiologist smiled at Clark, offered his hand and his name, then looked back at his orange console panel. "I suppose you want to see the pictures of your brain."

"I do."

Clark looked down as a series of gray-and-white images appeared on one screen. The radiologist highlighted an area using a rolling ball on the side of the console, clicked a button, and a section of the image was blown up. "Know where we are, Clark? This is an axial image through right about here." The radiologist tapped on Clark's forehead.

Clark nodded. If there was one thing he knew, it was neuroanatomy. "Those are my frontal lobes; there's my olfactory bulb."

The radiologist grinned. "And do you know what those bright spots are in the center of your head?"

"My pineal glands."

"Excellent. And over here?"

"That's the beginning of my third ventricle. Listen, I've been through all this before. Is there any new lesion? Any mass effect?"

The radiologist scanned the images in silence a moment. "Nothing obvious. You have a clean brain."

"Well, that's good to know."

The radiologist scrolled through the slices of Clark's brain.

Then he froze. Clark saw it, too. The lesion was a

bright white bleb just anterior to Clark's pituitary gland. Clark felt his entire existence focus on that spot, to try to discern its margins, to find out where it began and ended.

"We have a UBO," the radiologist announced.

"An Unidentified Bright Object, huh?"

"That's right."

Clark watched as the radiologist scrolled through the remaining slices. It was like watching some bizarre black-and-white slide show. "It's a recurrence of my tumor, isn't it?"

"It's not a typical location, given your primary. I wouldn't get excited."

"It's not your brain."

The radiologist looked up. "Sorry. Look, it's most likely artifact. We'll have an official reading by this afternoon."

Normally, Clark's mother would have rushed back to the neurologist and demanded that she read the films herself and tell them what it all meant, what the options were. But Clark's mother wasn't here now. He was grateful for that. He hadn't told her anything, hadn't even let her know that he had scheduled an appointment in neurosurgery clinic.

Tracy met him on the way back to the wards. "So what did it show?" Her voice had a teasing quality, as though the idea of the test had been Clark's and he was being a hypochondriac.

"Negative."

"Stone-cold normal?"

"Absolutely."

She giggled and took his arm. "See? I told you Erich isn't half as smart as he thinks he is. Bilateral temporal hemianopsia, my ass!"

Clark smiled back at her and put an arm around her shoulders. "He's presenting today at attending rounds. We'll be in time to catch the show."

It was no secret that Dr. Beinum, Clark's new attending, disliked Erich. Why exactly no one knew, but it probably had something to do with Erich's incessant barrage of questions about almost everything Beinum did. Murdoch loved Erich's presentations; Beinum called them too compulsive, too cluttered, too full of obsessive details. "Just the facts," he'd say. "Just the facts."

Erich couldn't seem to adjust his presentations. He would pare a word here or there, but couldn't resist giving all the details of Mrs. Jones's myocardial infarction in 1989 or the complete results of the tissue pathology on Mr. Smith.

So as Tracy and Clark walked into the conference room, Erich appeared slightly annoyed, even gray. He looked over his typewritten write-up (Dr. Beinum allowed, even encouraged, the use of notes) and made a few additions here and there with a black pen. "How'd it go, Clark?" he asked without looking up.

"Negative."

Erich arched an eyebrow. "Really."

"So you were wrong," Tracy said, poking out her tongue.

Erich grunted. "Either that or they need to recalibrate their MRI."

Jeb strolled into the room and tossed a rolled-up journal onto the table. He looked at his watch, nodded to the students, and sat. "We got everything done we talked about at rounds, right?"

"Yep," Tracy said. "Mr. Thurgood's white blood cell count is normal now."

"Well, that's something, I suppose."

Monica burst into the room at exactly ten o'clock. "You bet it is. We're going to tune up this man, get him out of here, and give him another month or two of life. Maybe cure him."

Jeb smiled at her. "I hope you do." He then picked up his journal and lazily flipped through the pages.

When Dr. Beinum walked in, there was none of the fear and dread that came with the entrance of Murdoch. The man always made it a point to smile at everyone, which Erich only interpreted as further evidence that the attending was sneering at him. "He doesn't take me seriously," he'd whisper to Tracy.

"Of course he doesn't," she'd whisper back. "You're just a medical student."

"How is everyone today?" Beinum asked.

Jeb set down the journal and folded his hands behind his head. "Better than our patients, sir."

Beinum smiled. "Who's presenting?"

Erich's Adam's apple bobbed when he swallowed. "I am."

Beinum swept his small hand before him. "Let's hear it."

To his credit, Erich tried. He really did. But he had only gotten through the first half page of his presentation when the attending became glassy-eyed. By the end of the history of the present illness, the man yawned. When Erich reached the physical, Dr. Beinum had to hold up a hand and say, "Just the positives and any pertinent negatives."

Erich closed his eyes and nodded. "Of course." He then continued to present everything, leaving out nothing.

The attending had to stop him again. "Erich, Erich, Erich. Your attention to detail is superb, but it is too much. I am overwhelmed. Pretend I am a fellow physician and you are describing this patient to me over the phone. You wouldn't give me all this detail, would you?" Before Erich could answer, Dr. Beinum said, "No, no, you probably would. But you shouldn't."

"I shouldn't?"

"No, really, you shouldn't."

Clark didn't eat lunch. His stomach was a tight little knot. He waited until Tracy and Erich were gone from the physicians' workroom, then slid his chair over to the computer. He entered his ID and password, then punched in his name and history number.

The screen filled with the twenty years' worth of imaging studies. He saw the one from today:

MRI, BRAIN   R/O RECURRENCE   FINAL REPORT

His mouth went dry as he highlighted that choice and hit F2 for the official reading.

It was two pages long. He couldn't wait. He had to know. He scrolled through to the end and read the assessment:

Impression: Essentially normal study. No evidence of recurrence. Unidentified high signal lesion probably of no consequence at the level of the pineal gland. Recommend follow-up study in six months.

Clark grinned. He disconnected from the system, slid back his chair, and rose. A nurse and two respiratory therapists frowned at him as he made a little whooping noise and danced around the conference table.

They probably thought he was crazy. He didn't care. All he knew was that he was saved.

He wouldn't have to fall behind his class, after all.

THE END OF
MEDICINE

When the last day of internal medicine finally arrived, Jeb gathered them all for rounds. "Well, this is it, boys and girls. A sentimental moment. Try as you might, you're going to look back and miss this rotation."

Tracy grunted. "I think I'm more likely to miss a case of hemorrhoids."

Mr. Thurgood was the only patient from the original census still on the service. He had survived his chemotherapy, but his hair hadn't.

He was a skeleton, Tracy thought, his eyes dark and sagging somehow. She was sure he would die. She couldn't help crying as she said good-bye to him, and he smiled at her and pulled her into his arms. She could smell the hospital smell of him and wondered if it would be the last time she would ever see him alive. She hoped he would live long enough to get that hospital smell out of his clothes and his skin.

"You know, Doc, we tried, didn't we? Even if I'm dead in two weeks, no one can say we didn't try."

"Yeah, we tried."

Then the rest of the family took turns hugging her. It took her twenty minutes to get out of the room.

As was so often the case in medicine, she might never know if the chemotherapy actually did any good. If she wanted, she could call the hematology oncology clinic every now and then and find out how he was doing.

Or check the obituaries.

But she didn't want to. She wanted to remember him alive, hugging her, telling her a dirty joke as she walked out of the room.

Thurgood was ready for discharge the next day. He almost didn't make it out of the hospital. His potassium had dipped slightly below the lower end of normal and Monica insisted on delaying all discharges until the patients were "euboxic," meaning that their labs were all within the range of normal.

But as they rounded on him for the last time, Tracy reported that all his labs were fine-tuned.

"Excellent," Monica said. "Strong work."

As Jeb said good-bye to Tracy he shook her hand and winked, as though they were in cahoots about something. "You're learning," he told her.

"I don't know what you're talking about."

"The hell you don't. I know you saw his potassium."

Tracy reddened, not knowing if she was in serious trouble. "I might have."

"You did. And the patient's family thanks you. You just spared him a Monica mega-flog." He paused. "Tracy, I think you'll make a great doctor if you don't try so hard."

She scowled. "What the hell does that mean?"

"Think about it. What's your next rotation?"

"Surgery."

Jeb nodded and smiled. "Ah, yes. A chance to cut is a chance to cure."

She winked back at him. "Never let skin stay between you and a diagnosis." And she walked with Clark down the hall and off the ward for the last time.

SURGEONS DON'T ITCH

The administrative hallway of the Mount Rosemont Department of Surgery was lined by the faces of past chief residents and chairmen. They stared down at Clark as he walked toward the conference room. Only one had even a hint of a smile. They were like black-and-white caricatures, clichés of the humorless, brusque surgeon.

He glanced into the oak-paneled offices and met similar humorless, tired-looking faces. Surgeons, nurses, and anesthesiologists hustled by in their sky-blue scrubs under fully buttoned white coats.

Clark felt his sunburn sting under his shirt and coat. The weekend, the only one they hadn't spent in the hospital for the past two months, had been too short. The sunburn was making him regret having starched his white coat. But he had heard about the surgery department's paramilitaristic obsession with pressed uniforms and figured he might as well play along.

Tracy, who walked by his side, looked up at him and

smiled. Her cheeks were also sunburned. They had spent the weekend between the end of internal medicine and the beginning of surgery in an overpriced, pretentious little bed-and-breakfast overlooking Cape Cod.

Clark almost screamed as someone slapped him on the back. The hand felt like a whip lashing him. He spun around to see the Grunt, whose grin faded as he stared down at Clark. "Oh, I'm sorry. Nice sunburn."

"Grunt, don't tell me we're together this rotation."

"This could be fun."

"This could be dangerous."

Clark frowned at his classmate. The Grunt was bulging out of a white oxford. His top button was undone and a few blond chest hairs poked out. "Where's your white coat?"

"Ah, it's at home somewhere."

"They'll crucify you."

The Grunt made a face. His masseters, the muscles on the side of his jaw, rippled. "No, Clark, if they want me to, they'll tell me to wear one."

Clark had made a point of being early, but it turned out he was almost the last medical student to arrive at the surgery conference room. The Grunt attracted everyone's attention—he was the only one not in a white coat.

"I have an extra one in my locker," Erich offered.

"Yeah, pencil neck, and I'm sure it might have fitted me sometime before puberty. I'll be fine."

Clark and Tracy found seats in the back of the room and waited.

It was odd; there was no playful banter as there had been before the beginning of the last rotation. Either the medical students had a better idea of what lay ahead, or surgery had that effect on them. The room was almost silent. Those who communicated with each other did so in a whisper, as though they were in a library or a funeral parlor.

Wrapping around the room above the mahogany wainscoting was a stream of somber faces. Clark recognized them as belonging to all the former department chairmen. All were white. None was female.

Until now.

Three months earlier the former chairman had suffered a heart attack. This every medical student knew, because every medical student had accessed his labs in the computer, following his case closely. What was clear was that the chairman had stepped down; what was uncertain was whether his successor, a woman, was going to survive to become more than just an acting, transitory chairman.

Clark stared at the photograph of the previous chairman, which was larger and more prominent than the others. So that was Dr. Roger Bailey. He really had a most ordinary-looking face. Clark realized he had seen the man a few times walking the halls of the hospital. He could have been any graying old physician, hunching forward a bit at the shoulders as he walked, with gold-rimmed glasses and a tall, narrow forehead.

But Bailey wasn't anyone. His textbook on surgery was the third or fourth most widely read in the world. He was also credited with rocketing the Rosemont surgical program from mediocrity to excellence. Through sheer force of personality, he had managed to woo established faculty members from rival institutions such as Johns Hopkins, Harvard, and Stanford and turn them into loyal, grant-generating Rosemont men (there were only two women in the department).

When Bailey joined the department in 1971, it was ranked thirty-ninth in the nation; after over twenty years at the helm, he had moved it into the top ten. The Department of Surgery was rapidly becoming one of the most prestigious and competitive in the country.

At least that's what half the surgical residents Clark encountered told him.

Now Bailey's regime had ended and a woman had taken over.

A second door from the rear of the room opened and a tall black man, dressed completely in starched white except for his black leather shoes and blue-and-red polka-dot tie, stepped into the room. "Oh, geez," he said, walking up to a podium. "There are a whole lot of you this time." He absentmindedly toyed with the knot of his tie. "My name is John Murray, your teaching resident. You might be asking yourself what a teaching resident is. Well, it's someone whose only responsibility over the next two months is to make sure you guys know enough surgery not to get anyone hurt. Or, more importantly, not to look foolish when you call a surgery consult." He looked around and smiled, but only a few people laughed.

"Oh, you're hurting me. Loosen up, people. All right, let's get to the first slide." He pushed a button and dimmed some lights, but the projector didn't go on. He fiddled with it in the dark for a minute before Erich stepped forward, adjusted a switch somewhere, and got it working. "Aha." John beamed. He tapped Erich on each shoulder with his pointer. "I dub thee teaching resident; you seem to have the main job requirement—the ability to operate a slide projector. First slide."

It was a single word: WORK.

"All right. The Boss—that is the ex-Boss—told me I was to show you all these slides and give you a little song and dance about each of them. Instead, let me tell you this—I'm in the cardiothoracic program here and I love what I do. Now I know I'm not going to turn all you guys into surgeons and I don't intend to, but some of you will see the light over the next eight weeks." He stared at the screen where the word WORK was emblazoned. "To be quite honest, I have no idea what that slide is all about, but I'm sure it's something deep and profound. Next slide."

The next slide was entitled MINIMUM STUDENT EXPECTATIONS. The word MINIMUM was in red and underlined twice. "This is just some gibberish about the do's and don'ts of surgery. Bottom line—use your head and no one will bite it off." His eyes swept the room again and landed on the Grunt. "And by the way, minimum dress code," he said, "is white coat, ironed, preferably starched, and tie for the men. No tennis shoes. This is because, as we all know, no one can operate correctly or hold a retractor if wearing tennis shoes."

He advanced the slides again. A dog, sliced open, came into view. "Ah, yes. Dog lab. Here some of you will inadvertently have the opportunity to see how far blood spurts when you nick an unclamped aorta. A major faux pas. Next slide." He would say this after each slide, although he held the remote for the projector.

A grid of their schedule day by day came up on screen. "As you can see here, your days will be long and busy. You will pull call every third night, which for you guys will consist of tailing an intern and pretending you know what you're doing. If he's nice, he'll probably send you home or to the call room around midnight. Next slide.

"More of your schedule. Nothing important here except for your conferences with the chairman. She"—he adjusted the knot of his tie again—"was the head of orthopedics at Stanford. I met with her a few times and she seems very sharp. For now, she wants everything to continue as it did under the Boss—Dr. Bailey, that is.

"The conferences with her are extremely important in determining your grade. If any of you are interested in becoming surgeons when you grow up, you must make a good impression. About half of you will present a patient formally, from memory, to the chairman. Don't screw up." He grinned. "Not to put you under pressure or anything.

"Every morning you'll meet with me for an hour or so and we'll talk about a basic surgery topic. That will be the most rewarding, exciting part of your day." He flipped through another couple slides. "Nah, you don't need to know any of that. . . . This is crap. . . . Ignore this. . . ." He turned off the slide projector and flipped on the lights.

"Well, that's it from me. Nice meeting you."

He was followed by a pair of scrub nurses, who talked the students through the proper use of sterile technique.

"As far as surgery is concerned," they said, "the universe can be divided into two—the sterile field and everything else."

The idea that an operating room should be sterile had not occurred to anyone until about a century and a half before Clark entered medical school. Sterility had since been refined to a science, an elaborate ritual to be performed during every operation to avoid contamination of the patient's wounds. The nurses demonstrated the proper technique of gloving and gowning, making Clark think of a bizarre dance as one scrub nurse spun around so the other could tie her from behind.

Then the students were issued gloves and gowns and they went through the ritual themselves. It looked simple enough, but could actually be quite confusing, as the Grunt discovered. "No," Clark chastised, "you can't touch there. You have to break scrub now."

"I had an itch."

"It doesn't matter. You have to just let it go."

The Grunt wasn't satisfied with that answer. He held up his hand and a scrub nurse came over to him. "So what do I do if I get an itch?" he asked.

The nurse canted her head and looked at him, somewhat confused. "Surgeons don't itch."

The Grunt began to laugh, but she didn't join him. Apparently, she was quite serious.

THE DOGS

The vivarium was in a separate complex of buildings joined to the Mount Rosemont Hospital by a tunnel twelve stories above the street. Walking across the bridge, which always made Clark a little dizzy, was like walking into another world.

The world of research, Clark surmised, was a world peopled by weirdos. They had pictures of their favorite molecules pinned up next to snapshots of their pets. They were a strange breed, slouching around in jeans and rumpled white coats, the men mostly in beards, the women with hair either down to their backs in ponytails or chopped off in a virtual crew cut. It was almost a uniform. They seemed much happier and more relaxed than the physicians across the walkway.

Clark herded with his classmates into the lab and saw the animals strapped to the tables. He had seen much horror over the past eight weeks, and read about much more over the previous two years, but the sight of the dogs with tubes down their throats and clamps on their paws did something to him.

He looked at Tracy, who also looked a little gray.

The teaching resident ushered them all into a back part of the lab, where they stood with their backs to the dogs. A single animal lay before them on a brightly lit table. The teaching resident stood with his arms behind his back, his face looking much more serious than usual. "Our number-one objective," John said, "is to keep Rover happy. A sleeping Rover is a happy Rover. If your dog starts to kick or make any sort of abnormal movement, then hit him with some more pentobarbital. The last group didn't do that and one of the dogs got loose. Please don't let that happen again. It was a mess."

The teaching resident turned to the animal on the table. "And another thing. Let's not joke about the dogs. Everyone who works in this lab is a dog lover. These animals deserve the same respect you'd give any patient."

He grabbed a handful of gowns and began tossing them to the students. "Put these on; I don't want anyone to get splattered." Tracy began using aseptic technique when Clark tapped her on the shoulder. "Tracy, the dogs are sacrificed after we're done with them."

She frowned. "You mean they're killed?"

"Yep. They won't live long enough to die of infection, so there's no reason for aseptic technique."

When they were all gowned up, John pulled on a pair of gloves and approached the dog. "Now. A word about instruments. There are ways of doing things and ways of not doing things. A major faux pas would be to hold something with your fingers. Use a clamp. Another faux pas would be to kill your dog with too much anesthesia. One third of you will be surgeons today, one third of you will be assistants, and one third of you will be anesthesiologists. Next time you'll rotate. Help your classmate out by keeping the dog alive long enough to remove the spleen, which is today's mission."

The bright light glinted off the blade of the scalpel

John lifted from the table. "This is not a butter knife. It will cut through anything it comes in contact with. That includes your gloves and your fingers. Be careful. Enough said.

"Now, the proper way to make an incision. You'll go in through the abdominal wall—about here. The animals have already been shaved. Hold the skin taught, position the scalpel just above where you want to go, and make a clean, straight incision." A thin, red line formed across the dog's belly as John passed the blade across the animal's skin. The line oozed blood, which John's assistant dabbed away.

"Most bleeding will stop spontaneously, but eventually you'll hit a vessel that will need to be tied off." The surgical resident cut deeper, as though to illustrate his point, and the wound filled with blood, which dripped down the animal's flanks before his assistant could tamponade it with the gauze. John pulled out a needle driver and a suture and drove it into a part of the wound out of Clark's sight. He made a few passes, or "throws," then tied off the suture, and held the free ends for his assistant to clip. He worked fast, naming anatomical structures as he got to them, telling them which vessels they definitely didn't want to nick. Within a few minutes the spleen, an unimpressive little purplish organ, was out, plopped onto a tray by the side of the table. "Then you close and it's all over. Any questions? Good. Now it's your turn."

Clark found that he was assigned a dog with the Grunt and Tracy. Clark was the designated surgeon, Tracy was first assistant, and the Grunt would play anesthesiologist.

He was glad that their dog was a gray-brown mutt that didn't resemble any dog Clark had ever known. He fiddled with his instruments, lining them up one way, then feeling dissatisfied with that, rearranging them and sorting them again. He looked up to see both Tracy and the Grunt staring at him.

"You don't want to do this, do you?" the Grunt asked.

"Of course I do."

"Then why are we the only group that hasn't started?"

"I'll open for you, if you want," Tracy offered.

"Don't be ridiculous."

Clark lifted the scalpel and examined the dog's belly. "Are you sure he's lined up right?"

"Yes, Clark."

"And we got enough pentobarbital on board?"

"I just gave him an infusion a minute ago."

Clark nodded, held the scalpel poised over the belly, then looked at the Grunt again. "You sure?"

"Oh, for God's sake!" the Grunt said. "Would you get started already? The sooner you start, the sooner we finish."

Clark turned back to the glistening pink skin of the dog. He lowered the blade, steadying it with his index finger, and pressed it against the dog's belly. He fought hard to keep himself from shaking, but it was hard, with Tracy and the Grunt following his movements with such intensity. He was convinced the dog would rise and howl when the scalpel pierced his flesh.

The line he made was squiggly and uncertain. He felt ashamed of it immediately after he made it. "You could have pulled the skin tighter," he told Tracy.

The Grunt leaned over from where he stood at the head of the table and squinted down. "Clark, you didn't even break the skin, my friend. We really are going to be here all day."

"Maybe this scalpel blade is dull." He could see from their expressions that they had had enough of him. "All right. Here goes." Angry now at himself and his squeamishness, he looked down at the square of flesh glaring in the harsh light and vowed to get through it to whatever lay beneath it. He applied steady pressure as he retraced his original attempted incision. The skin gave under him and the scalpel sank through the flesh into the animal's abdominal fascia.

There was blood everywhere, a brilliant scarlet pool, that formed within seconds and streamed down the animal's sides. "Oh, shit," Tracy said.

Clark knew his first impulse should have been to panic, but he didn't. Instead, he was seized with a sudden calm, a sense of what needed to be done. He reached over and pressed down hard with a large piece of gauze. Still the blood continued to flow, oozing out of the gauze and around his fingers.

"I nicked a vein," he said, thinking out loud. "I'll have to suture it."

Clark fumbled on the instrument tray for the needle driver. Tracy reached over with her free hand and gave him the right instrument. Then he took a deep breath and pulled back on the gauze.

Clark had practiced suturing on an orange at home, having been told that the orange skin has the same general suturing characteristics as human flesh. Now he buried the semicircular needle into where he thought the center of the bleeding was and twisted the needle driver with his wrist. Then he released the needle, pulled it through and managed to put in another couple throws.

The bleeding stopped.

He puffed out his cheeks as he tied off the vessel. "Thank God," he said. "Do you know how embarrassing that would have been to have my dog exsanguinate from my first incision?"

He joked, but it really was frightening watching an animal bleed like that because of a wound he created.

The Grunt looked over his shoulder and chuckled. "Old pencil neck got the spleen out already."

Clark looked across the lab, and sure enough, it was true: Erich was suturing up his dog's belly; the animal's spleen was plopped down on the instrument tray like some grotesque trophy.

Tracy shook her head. "I can't believe he's closing already." She turned and snipped the sutures Clark presented to her. Clark made another series of cuts, then his scalpel met something hard. There was a little pop and he was through the fascia, the tough lining overlying the abdominal cavity. The dog's guts glistened like giant worms. As he watched they moved. "Check it out," he said. "Peristalsis."

Tracy reached in and moved the intestines out of the way so that Clark could get to the spleen. He clamped off the feeding vessels and began slicing at all the appendages tethering the organ to the abdominal wall.

John came over and peered into the wound. "Nice technique, Clark."

The medical student felt a rush of pride; they would get done early after all. Maybe they'd be only a few minutes behind Erich.

The Grunt wasn't satisfied. "Erich's already washed up and out of here."

Clark looked up, annoyed. "I didn't think this was a race."

"It's not. I'd just like to be done by Christmas."

"Fine." Clark thrust the scalpel handle toward the Grunt. "You take over."

The Grunt stared at the handle a moment, then grinned. "All right. I will." He immediately began cutting, slicing, suturing, and clamping. He was fast, Clark had to admit.

Only one vessel connected the spleen to the dog's body. The Grunt winked—"That wasn't so hard, was it?"—and sank his scalpel into the vessel.

He didn't know why Clark jumped back until he heard the splash of blood against the far wall, at least twenty feet away. Clark watched the scarlet fountain gushing out of the belly and across the room. "Oh, shit." He pressed down with his glove to stop it, but it only diverted the stream, narrowing it and making it carry farther, having the same effect of a thumb on a hose.

Erich, who had triumphantly removed his gown, was hit squarely in the chest. A cascade of tiny red beads splattered on his shirt. He looked like an actor who had been shot in a B movie, his chest covered with a dark stain that grew with each pulse until he jerked himself away.

John rushed toward Clark's dog and slapped a four-by-four-inch gauze pad over Clark's hand, forming a sandwich that managed to hold back the bleeding. "Don't move," he told Clark. "It seems we committed a little faux pas, eh?"

"I'm sorry," the Grunt said.

"Not as sorry as the dog." The teaching resident very calmly directed Tracy to get the biggest clamp from the instrument tray. "My man, it seems you nicked Big Red."

"Big what?"

"Big Red. The aorta. We need to clamp it off and attempt to throw a suture in it."

Clark felt the animal's pulse speed up under his fingers. "I didn't mean to," the Grunt said.

"Tell that to the dog's family." John tentatively freed one hand to allow Tracy to suture. "And the dog's lawyer." He shook his hand. "But don't worry. It happens to the best of us. When I was a medical student, I did the same thing."

"You did?" The Grunt seemed desperate to believe that. His ears burned red as the entire class seemed to stare at him.

Clark gulped as the animal's pulse began to fade. "You got a blood pressure?" he asked the Grunt.

"Sixty over ten and dropping. I think that's bad for a dog."

Enough blood had seeped out of the aorta to fill the abdominal cavity with blood. It was like a bathtub filled with tomato juice. The teaching resident made one last throw with his suture, then relaxed. He leaned back, tossing the needle driver onto the instrument tray. "You don't have to worry about tamponading off the bleed anymore, Clark."

"Why not?" the Grunt asked. "Because you sutured it off?"

"No," Clark answered, relaxing. "Because our dog's dead."

Neither Clark nor Tracy said anything, but the Grunt seemed to sense they were furious. "I'm sorry, guys." He was even more sure of this when they tried to reassure him. "Everyone else except Erich killed their dog." "At least we got to the spleen—Alicia didn't even make it past the abdominal fascia."

Erich, who was furiously scrubbing his tie with Hibiclens soap, looked over at the Grunt. "I hope you're planning on becoming a psychiatrist or something."

The Grunt shot him the finger.

Clark pulled off his blood-soaked gown and peeled off his gloves. "I'm going to stink of dead dog all week." He watched the techs slide the animal off the table into a large black garbage bag.

▲
BELLYACHE
▼

If Clark had felt overwhelmed by his clinical duties while on internal medicine, at least he had a definite role to play on the team, and by the end of the rotation he felt he knew that role well. His clinical duties on surgery, though, consisted of holding a retractor during some operation in the morning, then trailing an intern for the rest of the day. The intern's chief job was to check that all his patients were ready for surgery the next day. He sat at a computer screen, copying lab values into a little blue book.

Clark sat by him, twirling a tourniquet, his chin in his hand. "Is there any way I can help?" he asked for the tenth time.

"No, don't worry about it. I'd just have to copy them again myself."

It was one in the morning and they would round the next morning at seven.

Luke, his intern, had been a literature major at UCLA, and would turn to Clark at various points during the night and pepper their discussion of a patient's gallstones with a quotation from Milton or T. S. Eliot. He stood only five-foot-four, but had intense blue eyes and a way of holding himself that didn't make you think of him as small.

His beeper went off. Luke looked down at it and smiled. He was a strange intern; he seemed to *enjoy* being paged. "The emergency room. Clark, I think we have a new customer."

The intern called the ER, scribbled down some notes, then hung up and turned to Clark. "This is something I'd like you to work up. No matter what specialty you go into, you'd better not miss this." Luke winked. "The name is Battle. James Battle. We'll see him together, then you tell me what we need to do. Take no more than five minutes. If you don't know it by then, you never will."

Clark was wide-awake when they got to the emergency room. Stepping through the automatic doors into the brightly lit bustle of the front lines of the hospital gave him a jolt of adrenaline. "I'm Dr. Devries from general surgery," Luke said to a clerk. "Where's Battle?"

"Room three."

"Thank you." Luke grabbed a clipboard and strode down the hall. Clark caught a whiff of something foul, saw a woman crying through the crack of another door, watched two nurses running with an IV bag. His heart beat faster. The ER always had this effect on him.

They entered Battle's room. "Your patient," Luke whispered.

Clark walked up to the examining table. A young white male, lying flat on his back, moaned. He opened his eyes and fixed them on Clark. The man was covered in a sheen of sweat. "You gotta help me, Doc."

"All right. We'll need some information first."

"It's my gut. It's killing me like nothing's ever killed me before. Right here." He pointed to his right lower abdomen.

"What kind of pain is it?"

"The bad kind. Real bad."

"I mean—does it burn? Is it crushing, is it cramping?"

"All of the above."

"When did it start?"

"Two hours ago. But it wasn't so bad."

"Did it come on suddenly or gradually?"

"Suddenly."

"Did anyone hit you there or did you fall?"

"No."

"Where did the pain start, sir?"

The patient pointed to his belly button. "Right about here."

"Uh-huh. And what was the ride to the hospital like?"

"Like hell."

"Why was that?"

"Because every goddamn pothole made me scream."

Clark continued his interrogation, rattling off a dozen questions about other symptoms, change in bowel habits, and past medical history. Then he picked up the clipboard and looked over the patient's blood pressure, pulse, and temperature. "He's got a fever."

"What are you thinking, Clark?" asked Luke, who had been quietly watching Clark perform.

"I'm thinking appendicitis versus peritonitis. He has an acute abdomen."

"Good. And what lab values would you particularly like to know right now?"

"His white blood cell count."

"So would I. Let's make sure it's ordered. Continue your exam."

Clark laid his stethoscope very gently on the man's belly. Battle's abdominal muscles were still as rigid as a board and his eyes followed Clark's every movement. "Bowel sounds are diminished," Clark answered.

Then came the hard part. Clark had to inflict pain on another human being. "Sir, I'm going to move your leg. Just relax as much as you can."

The patient let Clark flex his hip about five degrees before he howled like a wolf. Clark stopped.

Luke stepped forward and bumped into the table. The man howled again. Clark thought the intern chose a poor time to be clumsy. "That's the best way of eliciting a chandelier sign without really eliciting one," Devries said.

Clark was confused. "A what?"

"A chandelier sign. It's when you press down on their belly and they jump so high they'd hit a chandelier. Jostling the table does the same thing, only it's a lot more gentle. So what are you going to tell the patient?"

Clark turned to Battle. "Well, sir, we think your appendix needs to come out."

"Oh, Christ, do whatever you have to—just get me out of this pain."

"We will," Luke said. "When the sun rises, your pain will be over."

To Clark, this was a welcome change from medicine, where so much of what they did took days or weeks to take effect, if it ever did. There was something almost sexy about the way they could walk into a room and tell this man with reasonable confidence that his agony would end.

Luke quickly duplicated Clark's exam, then led the medical student from the room. "Good job, Clark. I can't think of anything to add to your workup."

"So you agree he's got appendicitis?"

"We'll find out." Luke put an arm around his shoulders and said, "As Ralph Waldo Emerson once said, 'Never let skin stay between you and a diagnosis.'"

Clark thought about that. "Emerson never said that."

"Of course not. But if he knew anything about surgery, he would have. Let's go scrub in for this case."

"It's an amazing thing really," Luke said as they lathered their hands with Betadine. "Just think what we're about to do to Mr. Battle. First, we're going to put him out with just enough drugs to put him into a virtual coma but not enough to kill him. Then we'll fillet his belly, explore his innards, take out what's bad, and leave behind what's good. Finally we'll sew him up. In six weeks the only reminder he'll have that we were there will be his scar." The intern shut off the water and stepped into the operating room, going through the door backward to keep his hands sterile. A nurse handed him a sterile towel, which he used in the ritualistic way Clark had been taught. "We're playing God, Clark. It's that simple."

Clark did exactly as the intern did, pushing his hands into the gown and gloves offered by the scrub nurse. In mask, gloves, and gown, he felt remotely like an astronaut or a coal miner.

The patient was asleep already, his belly shaved and draped in green surgical towels clipped to his skin, which shimmered alabaster in the harsh operating-room lights.

A third-year resident was swabbing the flesh with Betadine, making copper-colored, foamy circles as he worked from in to out. The resident ignored Clark entirely, speaking only to Luke in clipped sentences: "He's coming?"

"Yes. I just paged him again."

"We need him."

"I know."

"Can't open without an attending."

"I know."

"I'll scrub in."

The resident stepped out of the OR. "He needs a sphincterotomy," Luke said.

Clark frowned. "I thought this was going to be an exploratory laparotomy and appendectomy."

"It is. I meant Fremont." He nodded toward the resident beyond the door. "The guy is too anally retentive. A sphincterotomy would help loosen him up."

"Already had one," the resident said, reentering the room. "Didn't help." Clark couldn't tell if the resident was angry or amused; his face was hidden by his surgical mask. Only his eyes showed and those were inscrutable.

Another door opened and a tall, balding man with white, fluffy eyebrows stepped in. "Lap and appy, eh?"

"Yes, sir," Luke said.

"Fine. Any problems, I'm in room six."

Then the attending was gone.

"Let's do it." Fremont stepped up to his side of the patient and Clark stood opposite, next to the intern. He was careful to keep his hands in front of him and away from anything beyond the sterile field.

"You can rest your hands here," Fremont directed, tapping the sterile towels over the patient's body.

"Ready for the first cut?" Fremont asked the anesthesiologist.

"Yep."

Clark's experience in the dog lab had taught him to appreciate a good opening incision. Fremont's was straight and confident, a beauty of a slice. Blood oozed from the wound. The flesh was much thicker than the dog's, much thicker than Clark imagined. Fremont worked his way through the fat and then cut through the fascia. He cauterized with an electric probe that fried everything it touched, stopping small blood vessels from bleeding into the field.

Then the patient's intestines came into view. Fremont grabbed them with both hands, pushing them out of the way. "Gimme a hand, would you, Clark?"

It was a weird, squishy sensation, to be holding this man's guts under his gloved fingers. They felt warm and slippery.

"They're not as fragile as you think," Fremont said. "Push the damn intestines out of the way. Like this." He reached forward and scooped the intestines to the side. He then held them in place with an enormous stainless-steel retractor, the blade of which he handed to Clark.

Fremont felt for the man's gallbladder and liver. He snaked a segment of free intestine through his fingers, squeezing and sliding to ensure that nothing out of the ordinary would escape his attention.

"Now what would we do," Luke asked Clark, "if we found his appendix was stone-cold normal?"

"Take it out, I suppose."

"And why?"

"Might as well while we're in there."

Clark could tell from Luke's eyes that the intern was smiling. "We're going to make a surgeon of you yet, Clark."

But the appendix wasn't normal. It was swollen and angry-looking. It reminded Clark of an enormous pimple. When the resident squeezed, pus came out. "Gross, huh?" Fremont said.

Clark's job during the entire procedure was simple: he was to hold a retractor that held the patient's intestines, muscle, and skin safely out of the operating field. Nevertheless, he was at least doing something.

Luke seemed to read his mind. "As Shakespeare once said, 'This sure beats the shit out of chasing down labs, doesn't it, Clark?'"

"Definitely."

The appendix was removed within minutes, snipped clear, and tossed into a formalin jar that would be sent to pathology. Fremont then took what looked like an enormous eye dropper and filled the man's abdominal cavity with sterile saline. Luke sucked it clear with a vacuum nozzle. He repeated the maneuver five times. "The three most important ways to prevent a peritonitis—irrigation, irrigation, and more irrigation." He then stepped back, peeled off his gloves and mask, and nodded to Luke. "Go ahead and close. Cover him with the antibiotic du jour, something with good anaerobic coverage, then send him up to the floor."

Surgery rounds had been ritualized to an art form. The herd of white coats would meet at the nursing station at exactly 6:00 A.M., then shuffle from door to door. As they stood outside a patient's room the medical student or intern would spout off a twenty-second summary: name, age, diagnosis, procedure, hospital day, ins and outs, and one sentence on how the patient was doing. Just the facts.

To Clark, it was a welcome relief from the compulsivity of medicine, where they could spend three hours at a patient's bedside, going over every aspect of the history and physical in grueling detail.

To Tracy, who was now on a different call cycle than Clark and who therefore only saw him one out of every three evenings, the new ritual was difficult to accept, a dance whose steps she couldn't quite master. She wanted to say more, to give more detail, to talk about her patient's hyponatremia and six things that it could be, but Fremont would hold up his hand and tell her her thirty seconds were up.

They came to Clark's appendicitis. "Mr. Battle is a thirty-two-year-old white male with appendicitis two days status post appendectomy. He took in twenty-two hundred cc yesterday IV and one thousand cc po and put out approximately twenty-five hundred cc of urine. He is afebrile with good pain control." There. He managed to get it all out without taking a breath; if he inhaled, he discovered, he wouldn't make it.

Fremont nodded. "Excellent. Did he have flatus?"

Clark shook his head. "Not as of yesterday evening."

"Well, maybe he did last night."

They filed into the room and turned on the light. Mr. Battle was a different man from the hunched-up ball of pain Clark had confronted the other night in the emergency room. As the patient rolled over toward them, catching his side only slightly as he did, he smiled gratefully. "Can I eat?" he asked, squinting into the light.

"Did you fart?" Fremont returned.

The patient looked around at the twenty or so people crowded around his bed. "Yes, I did."

Passing gas was one of the best and most objective indicators that a postsurgical bowel was working again.

"Then you can eat. Problems or pains?"

"Nope."

It was amazing, Clark realized: one hundred years ago Mr. Battle would almost certainly have died from his appendicitis; today he was asking for a steak.

Fremont smiled. "Excellent. Next patient." He turned and led the group out of the room.

FRONTIER OF IGNORANCE

Clark found himself drifting apart from Tracy. It was more than just the physical separation and the stress. It was because Tracy simply didn't like surgery, whereas Clark was beginning to wonder if he had found his life's calling.

The satisfaction of opening someone up, decisively going for the tissue diagnosis or cure, then sending him home a few days later had a tremendous appeal to Clark. Tracy, on the other hand, found things too rushed, almost cursory. "I never get to know my patients," she complained to Clark one day as they waited for the first chairman's conference.

"You know if they had flatus," said the Grunt, who was sitting opposite. "What more do you want?"

"Very funny." She opened up the latest issue of the *New England Journal of Medicine* and began to read.

"Why do you want to be a flea?" Clark asked her.

"A what?"

"You know—the last thing to leave a dying body. A flea."

"An internist," the Grunt added, when Tracy still didn't get it.

Tracy was about to respond, but something over Clark's shoulder caught her eye. She closed her journal and pulled her chair a little closer to the table. Almost as though on command, the room grew hushed.

The chairman was a trim, medium-height woman who wore her white hair in a tight bun. Dr. Lauren Masterson wore a scarlet, pleated skirt that showed just enough of her calves to remind everyone that despite her age, she was as strong as ever; Clark noticed her gastrocnemius ripple when she walked. She smiled at the students as she entered the conference room, then walked toward the chair that had been set aside for her. "And how is everyone today? Clark, you look tired."

Clark, who had never seen the woman before, had no idea how she knew his name. But when the chairman turned to Erich and said, "That's a nice computer, Erich, but I'd consider moving up to a four-eighty-six at this point; you can upgrade that model, you know," Clark realized she must have memorized their names and faces from the class composite picture.

Erich, whose face glowed blue yellow from the monitor of his notebook computer, looked almost insulted. "How did you know it was a three-eighty-six, ma'am?" he asked.

"I have my sources." She sat at the head of the table, pursed her lips into a more serious expression, and nodded to Alicia, who was sitting in front of a small pile of notes, cards, and lab printouts.

"Alicia, are you presenting today?"

"Yes, ma'am." There was the faintest quiver in the medical student's voice.

"Feel free to begin."

Alicia cleared her throat. "The patient for presentation today is a sixty-two-year-old white female from—"

"Before you go on," the chairman interrupted, "I would prefer that you stood while presenting."

Alicia nodded, her wide eyes blinking furiously at her

notes and around at her classmates. Clark felt sorry for her; she had been sweating about this presentation for a week and the night before she had been on call, so hadn't been able to prepare as much as she hoped to.

"She was in her usual state of good health until one week before admission, when she first noticed that fatty foods made her nauseous."

The chairman frowned. "You mean she inspired nausea in those around her?"

"No, ma'am, I mean she wanted to throw up."

The chairman crinkled her nose. "Then say 'nauseated.' She was nauseated. A pile of vomit is *nauseous*; you, looking at it, feel *nauseated*. Continue."

Alicia blinked wildly around, then referred to one of her note cards.

"I would prefer," the chairman interjected before Alicia had a chance to continue, "that you present from memory."

"From memory?"

"Yes."

"Oh." Clark knew from the expression on Alicia's face that she was sunk now. "Besides feeling nauseated, the patient also experienced occasional sharp pain in her side. Um, that was all, really, until the episode of pain that brought her into the hospital. The pain was so bad it took her breath away. She—um—came to the emergency room, where she was evaluated by internal medicine, then by surgery. Based on her labs and her presentation, they decided to perform a—"

"Hold it." The chairman held up her hand. "You're leaving out the meat of your presentation. What about a complete history of the present illness, followed by past medical history, past surgical history, social history, family history, and review of systems? What about her vital signs, physical exam, and then laboratory values?"

"Well, let's see—her, um, history of the present illness is as above. Her past medical history is—I think she had a heart attack once, but I might be confusing her with some other patient."

The chairman made a face. "Please don't do that."

"I'll try not to. Let's see." Alicia bumbled through the rest of her presentation the best she could. She skipped around from section to section, requiring that she be redirected by the chairman at several points. Finally, the chairman held up her hand.

"That was an excellent job, Alicia. You may sit now." Everyone, especially Alicia, knew it was far from an excellent job. Clark thought she was going to cry as she lowered herself into her chair.

"But there's more," the medical student added.

"I'm sure there is. But I think we get the gist of your patient's problems. And it leads us nicely into a discussion of the gallbladder, cholelithiasis, and the cholecystectomy. First slide, please."

Clark's heart began racing. This was the part he had heard about, the part they had all prepared for. The student presentation was usually just a prelude to a prepackaged interrogation on a given topic. All the students knew the topic beforehand and had been expected to read the pertinent chapters in the former chairman's book. But Clark had gone out drinking with the Grunt last night and had only had time to glance over the chapter.

Nevertheless, there were certain things he did know. The chairman had asked the last class the color of the gallbladder, for example—and the answer, right out of Bailey's textbook, was on the tip of Clark's tongue: robin's-egg blue. Not just blue, or midnight blue, or light blue, but *robin's-egg* blue.

It was one of the few things he knew.

"Clark," he heard her say now, the sound of his name said out loud making him feel suddenly naked and vulnerable in front of his peers. "What is the color of bile?"

This is it! Clark thought triumphantly. He heard the word color and he lunged at it: "Robin's-egg blue!" The enthusiasm in his voice must have been excessive, for every face in the room turned toward him. Then he realized they were smiling. The Grunt slapped his forehead and laughed.

The chairman looked confused. "I'm sorry, Clark, but I thought you said robin's-egg blue."

"I did."

"Well, that is my next question—the color of the gallbladder, but what about bile itself?"

"Oh." Clark felt his ears turn red. "Green, I think."

"Exactly. And Tracy what is the average daily production of bile?"

Clark didn't listen to the answer. He sank a little lower in his seat and prayed the chairman wouldn't call on him again. So that was his first interaction with her and now she thought he was a doofus.

Robin's-egg blue.

The chairman had a definite pattern to her questions, as though she were reading from a script. When a student knew an answer, she would ask another related question. She would not relent until she had reached what Clark heard the teaching resident call a student's frontier of ignorance. "Pushing back the frontiers of ignorance," he would say as they slogged through each day on the wards. "In which direction, I don't know, but they are moving."

Tracy answered four or five questions in quick succession. When she stumbled over a sixth, the chairman asked, "Was that a guess?"

"It could have been."

The chairman turned to stare at her. "Commit. Be precise. Do you or do you not know the answer?"

"I think I do."

"Thinking isn't good enough in surgery. You must know. Or, even more importantly, you must know when you don't know. Guessing will get people killed. Randolph, do you know the answer?"

"That's Randy, ma'am."

"Randy, then. Do you?"

"Not a clue, ma'am."

She nodded, rubbed her eyes, and continued the interrogation. She wanted regurgitation of exact figures: volumes of bile excreted, the components of bile, what percent was reabsorbed in the gastrointestinal tract, and so on. There were enough questions and few enough students to make it painful. Clark wasn't the only one squirming when the session ended. The hour seemed to stretch into two. The students heard the phrase *I don't know* echo repeatedly off the walls of the conference room.

The chairman said nothing when she was finished, just looked around with what seemed an expression of profound disappointment, then said, "I am certain there is some explanation for your lack of preparedness, but I am not interested in hearing it. All I know is that it will not recur." And with that, she got up and left.

Clark let his head slump forward on the table. "This is going to be bloody. Next time I'll read the chapter."

The Grunt turned to him and snickered. "Robin's-egg blue."

Clark flipped him off.

"It doesn't help," Tracy said, slinging her book bag over her shoulder. "I read it and still got slaughtered."

"Au contraire," Randy countered. "By my count, you had a twenty-percent-correct ratio. Which is about twenty percent better than the rest of us."

"She kept going," said Alicia, who stared wide-eyed at the rest of the group. Everyone sat motionless, poised, ready to leave, but not quite ready to, like a movie audience stunned by a horrific film. "She knew we didn't know the answers, but she just kept asking. The worst part was having to say 'I don't know' again and again."

Randy chuckled.

Clark looked up at him. "How can you possibly find this funny?"

"Oh, stop taking it all so seriously. It's a circus. Did anyone get hurt today? Anyone killed or psychologically scarred?"

Clark smiled. "Psychologically scarred maybe. But it's more than that. She knew our names. We let her down."

"This probably will show up on our evaluations," Erich said gloomily.

"Oh, shut up," Randy told him. "You did even better than Tracy. If we all fail, at least you'll get an F-plus."

"So what do we do?" Tracy asked.

Erich shrugged. "It's simple. We have to know everything. We have to study always, every available minute."

Randy frowned at that. "Maybe that's your solution, Erich, but I've got a better one."

Clark studied his classmate. "I don't like when you get that look on your face. What are you thinking?"

Randy had a vacant, far-off stare. "I'm not sure exactly. But did you notice how she seemed to have a definite pattern to her questions?"

"Of course. She's been teaching medical students surgery for years."

Randy waved Clark silent. "But it was more than that. It was almost as though she was reading from a script." He paused.

"And?" Tracy demanded.

"And maybe that script is lying around somewhere."

Clark crumpled up a piece of paper and threw it at Randy. It sailed wide of its target. "Get out of here."

Tracy stood up. "I thought you were serious for a minute there."

"I am."

"Well, good luck finding it," Tracy said, walking out of the room. "I still don't think it would help anyway."

"We'll see," Randy said. "We'll see."

THE CIRCUS

▲

▼

Clark could sense something had changed the moment he walked onto the ward. Everyone was early today and none of the residents or interns were joking around as they usually did. They stood with their coats fully buttoned, without the usual coffee cups or diet Cokes, looking over clipboards and note cards with serious expressions on their faces.

"You're late," Fremont said.

Clark fished his stethoscope and reflex hammer out of his bag. "Actually, I'm ten minutes early," he said.

"No. For the next two weeks we will begin rounds fifteen minutes early. Therefore, by definition, you're late."

"Fine."

Clark trotted out into the mass huddled by the nursing station. The Grunt was standing there, too, and something about him was different. Then Clark realized what it was: he was wearing a white coat, starched and buttoned up.

"So they finally broke even you?" Clark whispered.

The Grunt winked. "I let 'em think that, anyway."

"Listen up," Fremont said, directing the group. "If you don't know already, you should. The chairman is rounding with us next week. That means this week we have to have everything *buffed*. The next seven days will be a dress rehearsal for next week. Need I say more?"

Without pausing, he nodded to the postcall intern, who said, "The first patient is Mrs. Tremont, a forty-seven-year-old white female from Northampton, Massachus—"

"Scratch where she's from."

"What's that?"

"No one cares. Just why she's here. I understand that's what the chairman wants."

"All right. She's a forty-seven-year-old white female with stage-two breast cancer now status post modified radical mastectomy. She is recovering well with good pain control, good ins and outs, and is pending discharge."

Fremont frowned. "Too vague. How many cc's in and out? How much Percocet did she need and when? Reword it, work on it, submit it in writing to me by noon. Also—we need leeches."

"Leeches?"

"Did I stutter? They help minimize venous stasis in the area of the flap. We can order sterile leeches to be placed bid. It will show the chairman that we are thorough, that we have overlooked nothing. Next patient."

And so it went. The interns were coached about where to stand, how to hold their heads, how to avoid distracting gestures. Then the patients' rooms were scanned. "Triple-check your patients' IVs. Make sure what you've ordered is what they're getting and that their IV site has been rotated every seventy-two hours."

The nurses seemed as nervous as the residents. The charge nurse, a middle-aged matriarch who loved nothing more than to double-check something an intern reported at rounds just to prove him wrong to the attending, and who was rounding with the team this morning, scribbled things she noticed into a little book and gave orders to some trailing student nurses.

They came to one room and Fremont stood absolutely still, as though struck by a sudden revelation. He looked the patient up and down, stroking his chin. "What's wrong with this picture?" he asked the intern.

The patient was lying flat on her back, looking up at them, shielding the light with her hand.

"I don't know," the intern said.

"I'll tell you. One word—modified Trendelenburg. I want everyone in that position. It's the chairman's favorite." There were a few snickers at that, but one look from Fremont silenced them.

The patient's legs were cranked up in the air at a forty-five-degree angle and her head was also elevated. In the end, her bed was contorted into a jackknife. "This position will minimize your risk of forming a clot in your deep veins that might get dislodged and end up in your lungs," the intern explained to the patient.

"Don't adjust your bed," Fremont added in a tone of voice that probably could be heard through the walls into the next room; he always addressed patients as though they were hearing impaired and a little slow on the uptake.

"Trendelenburg them all," he said, sweeping his arms in a wide arc before him as they stepped from the room. He reminded Clark for some reason of Napoleon.

Rounds, which usually took from forty-five minutes to an hour, dragged on from 5:45 until eight.

"That's a wrap," Fremont said when they ended. "Tomorrow things will go smoother. Go scrub in on your first cases."

JENSON

They said he was brilliant, a rising star, and he would never let you forget it. Peter Jenson was a rare combination of research-oriented inquisitiveness and think-on-his-feet clinical common sense. Although he was only a third-year resident, most attendings trusted him enough to let him operate with minimal supervision. He was fast and his wounds never dehisced.

He was small, with a round little face and rimless glasses. His pants, which never quite fit him, came up about two inches higher than they probably should have. If you didn't get away quickly, he'd start telling you about the time he was singled out as the Most Promising Young Researcher at Johns Hopkins or how he knew more about managing diabetes than most Rosemont endocrinologists, which wasn't saying much, but still, et cetera, et cetera.

Tracy, who first found him amusing, soon couldn't stand him. "I'm worried," she told Clark one day as they fought to stay awake over their microwave dinners. It was only seven o'clock, yet in an hour or so they would be sound asleep. The 5:45 A.M. rounding schedule kept them from staying up later than eight or nine, since they had to rise at four.

"What are you worried about now?" Clark asked.

"My resident."

Clark considered that. "Oh, Pete? He's a funny-looking guy. How does he worry you?"

"I can't put my finger on it exactly. Maybe it's because he asked me out."

Clark stirred his microwaved mashed potatoes. "I can't blame him for that."

"Clark, he's my resident. He's evaluating me."

"So don't go out with him."

"You don't get it. He never should have asked me in the first place."

Clark shoveled some food into his mouth and gulped it down. The potatoes tasted like the roast beef, which tasted like the corn, which didn't really taste like much at all. "It's not the first time some resident has hit on you."

"I know, but this is different. He won't take no for an answer."

Clark looked up. "He'd better." He touched the back of Tracy's hand. "You want me to talk to him?"

"And tell him what?"

"I don't know. That I'd hike up his pants another foot or so if he ever touched you?"

Tracy giggled at that. "He does wear them awfully high. He has the funniest little body." She waved her hand through the air. "I'm sure he's harmless."

"Did you tell him about me?"

"No. I shouldn't have to give him an explanation. My personal life is none of his business."

"Of course. You're right." Clark ate silently for a few minutes. "You only have to work with him a few more weeks."

"I know, but those are going to be some long weeks. And sometimes I look over at him and catch him staring at me. There's this look in his eyes that bugs me. He just keeps staring, giving me this smile that he seems to think is charming, but that I find repulsive."

"Oh, Tracy, the poor guy is pining over you. Like I said, I can't blame him." He thought about that as he pushed his dinner aside and flipped through the TV channels with his remote control. "But if he's really bothering you, go see the chief resident."

Tracy shook her head. "No. I don't want to get a reputation as a whiner."

Clark didn't want to tell her that among some of his classmates, she already had one. "The guy is a harmless loser. I wouldn't worry about him."

"I hope you're right."

Both jumped when the phone rang, then immediately laughed. "I'll get it," Clark said. He came out of the kitchen a moment later, a frown on his face.

"Must have been a wrong number. The guy hung up."

Tracy smiled. "Either that or it was Peter Jenson, hungry for—"

The phone rang again. They looked at each other.

"Let me get it," Tracy said. Clark could hear her on the phone in the next room. "Hello? Hello? Yes, this is— what? What's that? Who the hell is this?" She slammed down the phone and came back into the dining room.

"What did he say?"

"Nothing you want me to repeat."

"Did it sound like him?"

Tracy rolled her eyes. "Oh, Clark, maybe I should never have said anything. This city is full of perverts; why should we automatically assume it's him?"

Clark thought about that. "Because you're a pretty good judge of character and you just told me he gives you the creeps."

Tracy shuddered. "Still, I can't imagine him saying *that*."

But Clark didn't want to think about it anymore. He pulled Tracy to the couch, draped an arm over her shoulders, and flipped on the television. "Let's do something completely mindless for the next twenty minutes."

Giggling, she tried to resist, but Clark pinned her down. "This might be painful, Dr. Nobel Laureate, but you are going to relax."

"Oh, Clark." She tried to look at her watch, but Clark grabbed her wrist and held it against her ribs. As he did so, the back of his hand brushed against her breasts.

She looked up and it was obvious both thought it at the same time. "I should read," she told him as the sounds of some sitcom about normal people with normal lives reached their ears.

Clark didn't say anything, just leaned forward and kissed her. Her lips felt soft against his. He probed gently with the tip of his tongue and her lips parted. She let out a little moan as he leaned into her, deftly tossing a couch cushion onto the floor.

But as soon as she was horizontal, she began to go limp. When Clark didn't understand why she wasn't kissing him back, he pulled back, only to find that she was sound asleep.

She murmured something unintelligible as he scooped her in his arms and carried her down the narrow hallway to their bedroom. Tracy came awake as he laid her down, kissed her forehead, and tucked her in.

He went out to the living room to watch television alone.

THE DECEPTION

The corridors of the administrative section of the surgery department were dark and empty. Randy found the chairman's office, then worked backward, looking for a room with a light on.

Twenty feet away, in the conference room where they had been slaughtered a few days before, he found exactly what he was looking for. A large man with a square jaw and a paunch was rearranging the chairs, dusting off the tables, and evidently on the verge of using a vacuum cleaner. The man's graying, greasy hair was swept over his sharply angled face. There was a meanness to him, as though he had spent too many years mopping up other people's shit for subsistence-level wages.

"Excuse me, sir," the medical student began. His chest rose and fell and he looked around frantically.

The janitor looked slowly up, working a huge wad of gum or tobacco in his cheek, and studied Randy through half-closed eyes. "Uh-huh?"

"I'm in a terrible bind and thought maybe you could help me."

The face didn't twitch, didn't move. "Uh-huh."

"See, I have this exam tomorrow and I had a conference today with the chairman. In her office. As I was in the library studying it hit me that I was missing half my notes. I'll fail without them. I must have left them in the chairman's office, see?"

The big, broad face moved up and down. "Seems to me you *are* in quite a bind, my friend."

"I am. Can you help me?"

"Maybe." The man canted his head. "What kind of doctor are you?"

Randy thought about that a moment. Didn't need to give any more identifying information than he had to. "A surgeon."

"That right? What kind of surgeon?"

"A good one, I hope." The janitor grinned at that. Then his large dirty hand disappeared into a pocket and reappeared with a set of keys on a ring. "I just done her office, so don't mess it up none."

"I won't. I promise."

The janitor gave Randy a look that might have meant: "I know damn well you didn't leave no notes in there." But he moved out of the room and down the hall anyway, sauntering toward her office. "I'm not supposed to let no one back here."

"I know."

"You got two minutes in there, then I got to fetch you out."

"Deal."

"Get your notes and get out and don't mess nothin' up."

Her door was solid oak. Randy's eyes were drawn to the brass nameplate, much smaller and more modest than her predecessor's, the shadow of which could still be seen on the wall. Hers said:

LAUREN MASTERSON, M.D.
CHAIRMAN, DEPARTMENT OF SURGERY

"Bitch," Randy said under his breath.

"Whas that?" the janitor asked.

"I said I got an itch."

"Uh-huh."

The door swung open and Randy found himself looking into an office much smaller than he had imagined. Or maybe that was just because of the boxes, many of them only half-unpacked, pushed up against the walls. There was barely enough space to get to her desk.

The janitor flipped on a light and Randy was surprised to see the desk cluttered with pictures of family members, arm in arm and grinning like idiots. There was a birthday card propped up with the words TO THE WORLD'S GREATEST GRANDMA. It was odd to think of the chairman as a grandmother. It was odd to think of her as anything except the chairman of the Department of Surgery.

Randy felt a twinge of guilt as he looked at the picture. But the twinge passed when he remembered the slaughter the other day and why he was there now.

"You see 'em?" The janitor's voice made Randy jump. He turned to see the man staring at him, arms akimbo.

"No, she must have put them in a drawer."

"A drawer, huh?"

"Yeah." Randy looked up into the man's face, but he could only discern a certain contempt. It was the same contempt he had seen in the faces of the phlebotomists and nurses and radiology techs and anyone else who came in contact with medical students. Randy reached forward to open a desk drawer, but the drawer was locked. Besides, the janitor was watching everything he did. This would never work. "Look. This is going to be harder than I thought. I need some time, maybe twenty minutes."

The jaw moved, the enormous wad of tobacco pressed against the man's cheek. "I'll give you five."

"Fine."

Randy noted with relief that the janitor disappeared. As soon as he was alone, he pulled open the drawers of the chairman's desk and began rifling through her things. For someone who seemed so regimented and who demanded such attention to detail from others, the chairman was a slob. There were wadded-up bits of paper mixed in with napkins and tissues, as well as yellow stickums covered with unintelligible scrawl.

He thought it would be simple, that all he would have to do was look for a file entitled "Medical-School Lectures." But there was nothing to be found that looked even remotely helpful.

Then he spotted the file cabinet. It looked like an enormous steel casket standing on end. Randy pulled open the first drawer and thumbed through a forest of manila files. There were memoranda and documents on every topic from "Departmental Meetings—Minutes" to "Fraternization Among House Staff and Medical Students." Randy was tempted to read that, but wasn't about to waste a second he didn't have to.

Then he read the labels on the drawer: A-D, E-M, N-R, S-Z, and MEDICAL-STUDENT MISCELLANEOUS. Randy pulled open the last drawer and found a file with his name on it.

This he couldn't resist. He pulled out a photocopy of his transcript with a copy of his evaluation from his last rotation, neurology. *Randolph was a valuable asset to our team, as he never hesitated to remind us,* the evaluation read. Randy grinned at that, then saw his own bio sheet that he had filled out during orientation.

He looked at his watch: three minutes had elapsed since the janitor let him in the room—only two to go. He passed over the files of his classmates, although he was tempted to scan Erich's transcript to see if he really had received honors in every course, and came to a file entitled "Medical-Student Conferences—Topic Outlines and Minimal Expectations."

Randy was disappointed to see that it was a thin,

manila file with only a single sheet inside. It couldn't possibly hold much information.

But then he read the sheet and realized he had struck gold. On it was written:

> See subdirectory "D:\MEDSCHL\CONF*.DAT." Access files via PASSWORD = CHAIRMAN, ID = NUMBER1.

All Randy had to do was figure out where the network was—it must be some common computer net that he probably could find a way to dial into—and retrieve the files via the chairman's password and ID.

"Man, you lookin' *everywhere* for them notes, ain't you?"

Randy spun around to see the janitor standing not one foot away, looking over his shoulder at the slip of paper.

"I thought they might have been in here."

"Uh-huh."

"I did. But I was wrong." Randy replaced the piece of paper into the folder and put it back in the file cabinet.

"You's wrong, all right. About as wrong as you can be."

Randy felt his ears burning. He tried to slide past the janitor to the door and the safety of the hall beyond.

"You never lost your notes at all, did you?"

"I don't have time for this."

"No, fella, you got plenty of time." The janitor reached for Randy's arm, but Randy darted out of reach. That was no small feat given the narrowness of the corridor between the boxes. "I don't want no doctor cutting on me who's some cheat."

"I'm not a cheat. I'm just trying to survive."

Randy was in the hall now, marching away, hoping the janitor wouldn't follow. "You best hope I don't recognize you in the halls, there, fella."

No, I best hope you don't either, thought Randy, breaking into a run. He didn't look back until he had climbed three stairwells and traversed two corridors.

The hallway behind him was empty. He was so grateful for his escape that he was glad to see his intern, glad to be back on the relative safety of the ward.

He had what he needed.

Chairman.

Number 1.

Randy had never been good friends with Erich. Actually, the two couldn't stand each other. What was also no secret was that Randy had little interest in computers. So it was with great surprise that Erich, at work the next day on a write-up on his notebook computer, found Randy looking over his shoulder and firing off a bunch of technical questions between friendly quips and trivialities.

"Does that thing have a modem?"

"Of course."

"So that means you can potentially link with any network, right?"

"Theoretically, yes. But no more so than I can potentially hold a conversation with the president of the United States because I have a phone. With a modem, I have to know the number, the log-on password, and ID."

Randy nodded, pulling up a chair, flipping it around backward, and straddling it with his legs. "Do you know anything about the network the faculty uses?"

Erich frowned. "I'll bet there are several. Why this sudden interest in computers?"

Randy arched an eyebrow and pulled a piece of paper from his pocket. "Let's just say I might have stumbled across a way to make life around here a whole lot easier." He unfolded the paper, on which he had written the information gleaned from the file in the chairman's office. "Does this make any sense to you at all?"

"What is it?"

"Never mind that. Can you access this?"

Erich scrutinized the paper. "Christ, you write like a doctor already. Is that a D-colon or an O-colon?"

"A D-colon."

"Then this is probably some network."

"How do you know that?"

"I don't, but that's a general convention. Usually computer networks that can be accessed by PCs are denoted D-colon, versus hard disks, which are C-colon, and floppies, which are A-colon and—" He cut himself off when he noticed Randy yawn.

Randy patted Erich's shoulder. "Sorry. I got lost in all your A's and B's and PC's. All I want to know is this—can you get to this information?" He rapped his knuckles on the sheet of paper.

"Well, I'm sure I could figure out a way if I had to, but what's this all about?"

"Never mind. Get me there and I'll explain everything."

Erich blinked at the number and the screen. Randy was grateful his classmate seemed to be viewing this as some intellectual exercise rather than inquiring more about what it was all about. "Let's see." He tapped a few keys, exited his word processor, and entered Windows. Then he typed a few more keys and a new screen came up. He hit a series of numbers, then return, and the computer made several high-pitched beeping sounds.

"It sounds like your computer is dialing a phone number."

"It is."

There was a pause, a staticky sound, and three beeps. "We have a connection," Erich announced. A screen flashed up before them in green, white, and blue. There was a prompt to enter an ID and password. "Let's see."

Erich carefully typed in the combination Randy had given him. There was a flashing prompt at the bottom of the screen—PLEASE WAIT—then a new menu popped up before them.

Randy's eyes bulged. It had worked. All they had to do was find the directory now and the information he sought would be there.

Erich was less impressed. "What the hell is this?"

Randy slapped him on the back and grinned. "This, my friend, is our ticket to excellence."

"No, this is our ticket home. Do you know what would happen if they caught us logging into this information? Check out choice seven—Student Evaluation and Profiles. I'm sure this is confidential information that we are not supposed to have access to."

"Well, we do now."

Erich eyed Randy suspiciously. "Where did you get that password from, anyway?"

"That's not important. What's important is that we get into the right directory."

Erich paused. "Randy, you stole it, didn't you?"

"Stole is a strong word. I acquired it."

"This isn't right. It's not right at all." It was clear from the expression on Erich's face that some internal struggle was going on.

"Neither is pimping us to death at that student conference. All we're doing is getting some crucial information. We still have to learn it, don't we?"

Erich thought about that a moment.

"Don't you realize what this could do for your evaluation?"

Erich's eyes, which had expressed deep pain for a moment, now flickered with something else. "My evaluation?"

"Yes. You—we—will shine."

Erich leaned forward like a condemned man, like a general who knows he's leading his men into a hopeless fight. He poised his fingers over the keyboard. "What was that directory again?"

Within two minutes, Erich had called up a directory tree and negotiated his way along its branches until he was in the subdirectory D:\MEDSCHL\CONF. Then he typed: DIR *.DAT.

Randy sank into a chair as he saw the file names parade past him on the screen. "Oh, great. There must be at least a hundred files. This doesn't help us at all."

"One hundred and fifteen files, to be exact." Erich reached across his computer and glanced at his clipboard. "But it might not be as hopeless as it seems."

"No?"

"No. We know who's presenting next, right?"

"Yes. Tracy is."

"And we know the topic, also, right?"

"Of course. Lung cancer."

"Excellent. So let's find all references to lung cancer." Erich's resistance was completely gone now. He was again viewing this as an intellectual puzzle. The keys rattled as he typed a few commands that to Randy seemed cryptic and incomprehensible.

There was a pause and another flashing prompt at the bottom of the screen: PLEASE WAIT.

"What did you just do?"

"A text search. It's going to look through every file in the subdirectory and pull up only those files that have *lung cancer* in the text somewhere."

When the computer stopped blinking, twelve file names were displayed before them. One was called LUNGCA.DAT.

Erich and Randy saw it at the same time. "You mean we went through all that and all we had to do was type in something that simple?" Randy demanded.

Then the door to the conference room they were sitting in flew open and Peter Jenson walked in. He had small hands that he usually seemed to be hiding, when he wasn't pushing his rimless glasses up the bridge of his nose. "What's up, guys?"

"Nothing much," Erich said, pushing a button that made the monitor screen go blank, pulling out his clipboard, and doing his best to look busy.

"Well, Mrs. Murphy is going to need an ABG. Do I have any volunteers?"

Erich smiled. "You know I'd love to, but can you just give me five minutes?"

"No problem. Make sure it gets to the lab within the next fifteen minutes or so."

When the intern was gone, Erich pushed another button and the screen came to life. "We have to be quick," he whispered to Randy.

He typed another command and the contents of the file marched past them on the screen.

Randy scanned them, but they made no sense. There were no recognizable letters or characters. "What the hell is this?"

Erich shook his head. "It must be encrypted."

"You mean for security reasons?"

"Exactly."

Randy swore. "Oh, this is hopeless."

"Not exactly." Erich typed a few more commands, grabbed a floppy diskette, and inserted it into his computer. There was some crunching and grinding and then he exited from the network.

"What are you doing?"

"I downloaded the file to my disk. Later today, when I get a chance, I'll try to break the code."

Randy laughed. "Don't waste your time. If I had known it would be this complicated, I never would have—"

"It's not complicated at all. Most encrypting codes are infantile in their simplicity. I spent most of my undergraduate days cracking them to get at the heart of copy-protected programs. If this is your plain old vanilla binary-based code, I bet I could crack the algorithm in less than an hour."

Randy was impressed, but not nearly as optimistic. "I thought you were hesitant about this whole business."

"I was. But now that we've started, we might as well go all the way." He sighed. "I'll call you when I break it."

"Good luck."

Erich was better than his word. Randy came home from a night of abbreviated barhopping—he needed to get at least four hours of sleep—to find a message on his machine: "I did it. Call me when you get in."

Randy looked at his watch and around the cramped dormitory living area he rented for five hundred bucks a month. He had learned long ago to travel light, but had accumulated a few trinkets from his travels around the world. There was a rug woven for him by some Khmer Rouge women in Cambodia that was now draped over his table. In the centerpiece over his vestigial fireplace (it didn't work, but could be decorated at Christmas) was a photograph of a squatting Tibetan child, playing in the mud, his dimpled broad face beaming up at this Westerner with his strange black box with a glass eye. Finally he had a walking stick, which everyone assumed he had polished through personal use; actually, he had purchased it in a gift shop on Manhattan's West Side, since it epitomized his view of the world: if things get too intense, he'd just walk.

There were a few other odds and ends—a set of copper bells, a laughing Buddha (also purchased in New York), and a small picture of his family, whom he hadn't visited in years—but most of the walls were bare, revealing a dingy yellow-and-brown wallpaper that must have been in vogue sometime in the mid-seventies and hadn't been changed since. He slept on a futon in the corner and studied mostly in the library. If anyone ever cleaned his efficiency, he would be completely lost: small piles of papers, notes, and reprints were scattered in apparently haphazard piles about the place, but they were more or less carefully arranged by organ system, beginning with neurology by the door and ending with renal by the sink. To get to his refrigerator, he had to step around pulmonary and over cardiology, dodging dermatology.

He never actually read most of the articles, but felt that he should have, and had collected them over the years. Every now and then he would go through a pile, sorting them by importance, putting the ones he really thought he should read on top. He thought about tossing them, or at least thinning them, but didn't have the guts to admit to himself that he was abandoning the effort, so the piles grew.

His apartment now resembled a small city of paper skyscrapers.

Randy was drunk enough not to feel the carpet underfoot as he danced from the answering machine to the futon, tossing his clothes into a pile as he did so. "He did it, the son of a bitch! He did it!" Randy's greatest fear—one that was not yet realized—was that he would actually have to work to get through medical school. The hours were long—although he had found countless creative ways of getting out of the hospital to break them up—but it took surprisingly little effort to just get by, if that's what you wanted to do.

And that was exactly what Randy wanted to do. And now that Erich had broken the code, there was little question that he would breeze through surgery, maybe even shine, without much effort whatsoever.

He sat at the edge of his futon in his boxers, too excited to sleep, but too concerned about pissing off Erich to call him. After all, it was Erich who had the information on his disk and Erich who had cracked the code. All Randy's efforts would have been for naught if he were to alienate Erich by calling too late.

But then again, Randy had to know. He had to find out if the files were a gold mine.

He stepped past his gastroenterology pile and picked up the phone. Within seconds, he had dialed Erich's number.

"Hello?" The voice at the other end was groggy with sleep.

"Hey, sorry, Erich, but I had to know. What's in the files?"

There was a moment of hesitation. "Randy, is this you?"

"Of course. What did you find?"

Erich sighed. "I don't know. I didn't have time to read through them after I decrypted them. It's not much information."

"Really?"

"No, just a lot of questions and answers. They're not even very relevant questions. Picky little things, like how many cc's of saliva are produced every day, how many Hertz cilia beat, that sort of thing."

Randy grinned. "Erich, for someone as smart as you are, you're pretty stupid, did you know that?"

"What are you talking about?"

"Erich, those questions are conference pimp sessions, caught on computer diskette. We've got her; we have her script."

Erich thought about that. "You might be right. But we can't be too obvious. She'll know we're on to her."

"Right. Absolutely. Listen, when can we get together and go over the pulmonary file?"

Erich paused again. "I've never known you to be enthusiastic about studying before."

"I'm not. The only studying I get enthusiastic about is the studying I don't have to do. And with these questions and answers, we'll know exactly where to hone our efforts."

Erich giggled. "Who would have thought—you and me study partners?"

"Certainly not me. Good job on the files."

When Randy lay on the sheets and listened to the sounds of the city come up through the window, which was opened just a crack, he realized he was happy. When it came right down to it, medical school was a game, and he had just learned some new rules.

He couldn't wait to apply them.

▲
MOLESTATION
▼

Tracy was trapped. She gripped the retractor with both hands, as though it were her life at stake, and stared into the wound. It was a gaping red liquid cavity that the surgeon across from her had created. Her job was to keep the skin and bowels and fat pulled clear of the operating field.

They were crowded together—at least five people when you counted the scrub nurse standing at her platform handing sterilized instruments one by one to the surgeon, the head surgeon, his large brown eyes staring deep into the wound, Tracy, and the surgery intern, behind her, also holding a retractor, his body so close she could feel the muscles in his thigh contract as he shifted his weight.

"That's it, just a little more. You guys are doing a great job." The surgeon had a soft voice, almost a whisper. Tracy had never heard him raise it in anger. If anyone had shattered her stereotype of the driven, cold, aloof surgeon, it was Dr. Fenstermeyer.

His brown latex gloves were coated in blood and pieces of fat and tissue. The smell of burned flesh smoked out of the wound as he cauterized a small blood vessel. He placed his instruments down for a minute and reached in with both hands, grasping the segment of bowel that he was working on and milking it with his fingers. He closed his eyes as he squeezed, walking his hands up and down the length of gut. "I think we got it all," he said. "We'll see what the frozen path shows."

A nurse walked into the OR with a slip of paper. "Path says you have clean margins, Doctor."

"Excellent. We just might have cured this woman."

Tracy blinked down at the patient's intestine, where a cancerous piece had been cut out, then the healthy ends sewn back together. It was a small miracle really. She had read enough to know that within weeks the gut would work as well as it had before. If the tumor was really gone and hadn't metastasized or spread, what would have been a terminal illness might have been stopped in its tracks.

It was almost enough to make her forget about the fatigue and the heat of the lights and her hunger.

And whatever it was that was pressing against her from behind.

It wasn't a thigh muscle now. It was something definite and hard with its own contour and perhaps a tiny pulse. It was squeezed against her left buttock, and when she shifted her weight, it followed her.

The surgeon looked at her. "Please don't let the retractor slip. We're almost done." He sounded apologetic that she had to stand there and do this.

Tracy wanted to free one hand from the retractor and push the surgical intern away. But that would be unthinkable. She considered turning to him and scowling at him, but that would force the retractor to shift. She tried to scoot ever so slightly to the right, away from him, but was now trapped by the surgical drape.

Fenstermeyer stared at her. "Tracy, are you okay?"

"Yes, sir."

She wasn't. It was still pressed against her, warm and hard. She tried to blink it away, but the knowledge of what was happening made her eyes water over. She wasn't going to cry, wasn't going to shout out, wasn't going to say anything at all.

That was the thing that humiliated her the most.

She was just going to go with the flow. And this seemed part of the flow.

The intern pulled back his hips and then pushed forward again. He began a gentle pumping action, a slow grind, that made Tracy begin to tremble with rage and self-disgust. Why couldn't she say something, do something?

She found her voice. "Stop it."

Dr. Fenstermeyer looked up again. "I'm sorry?"

"Nothing, sir. It's just that—" The intern had pulled back, leaving a shadow of warmth on her left buttock. She swallowed twice. Well, at least he had stopped. "It's nothing, sir."

Dr. Fenstermeyer studied her, looked at the intern, then back at her. "If you feel squeamish, you're welcome to step out."

"No, sir, really, I'm fine." But there were tears trickling down her face and the hands holding the retractor shook. This shouldn't happen, she thought. This shouldn't happen to me, not here, not the one place I thought I could be safe from this. She had been groped once or twice on the subway in New York, but not *here*.

She had never felt so helpless.

"Step back, please," Fenstermeyer commanded. There was a hard edge to his voice now. Tracy hesitated. *"Step back!"* It was only then that she realized two of her tears had dripped into the surgical field.

"Jesus!" She let the retractor go and pulled herself away, taking small pleasure in digging her heels into the intern's toes.

"I'm sorry," she said.

"Please leave the operating room." Fenstermeyer

sounded as angry as he probably ever did. "Let's get some irrigation in that area." He nodded to the spot where her tears fell. "At least a liter of sterile saline. That's it. Suction as you go." Tracy wiped her eyes with the back of her hands, completely breaking sterile technique now. "Sir, I—"

"Please leave, Tracy."

She looked the intern in the eye, who was busying himself with the irrigation of the wound, then marched from the room. As she stepped through the automatic door she tore her bloodied gown and gloves from her body, wadded them up, and tossed them into a disposal bin.

DISSEMINATION

Randy smiled as he waited for conference to begin. Tracy sat to the left of the head of the long, oak table, looking ashen-faced. She had been more irritable and snappy the last few days, which surprised Randy; he hadn't expected the stress of presenting to get to her like this, but that was part of the medical-school experience; you found out new things about your classmates every day. Who, for example, would have thought that the Grunt of all people would have staggered at the sight of a cadaver's chest being sawn open? Who would have believed that Alicia would be the first to anastomose her dog's aorta and the only one whose animal would survive the procedure all the way until her last suture was in place? And who could now believe that Tracy was trembling, literally quaking, as she rose to her feet to greet the chairman?

The woman eyed Tracy with a smile and a nod, and as she made her way to her chair, everyone sat except Tracy.

But Tracy's voice was calm and strong as she launched

into her memorized script. "The patient for presentation today is a seventy-two-year-old black male with a past medical history significant for a one-hundred-and-twenty-pack-a-year smoking history who now presents with hemoptysis, weight loss, and orthostasis. The history of the present illness dates back to . . ."

Randy found his mind drifting off, pondering how to react when the chairman began her interrogation, how he would respond when she asked him questions that she didn't know he already knew she would ask.

There was a silence, and by that silence Randy knew that Tracy had finished her presentation. Randy's eyes met Erich's, but his classmate was poker-faced, absolutely deadpan.

"Randy, you found something in your classmate's presentation amusing?"

Randy didn't realize he was grinning. His smirk disappeared. "No, ma'am. I apologize—I was thinking about something else."

"I see. Well, perhaps you could tell us who was the first surgeon ever to perform a pneumonectomy successfully."

"Well, actually, I could." All faces swiveled toward him as Randy shot her a pensive, concerned glance, as though he had been thinking about the matter a great deal. "It was Graham, who in 1933 performed the first successful one-stage pneumonectomy for carcinoma of the lung."

Randy tried not to grin as he noticed the jaws dropping around him. He could almost hear a dull little plop of the mandibles landing on white coats.

The chairman said nothing a moment, simply studied Randy. "Excellent. It is essential to know the *heritage* of surgery, not just the science and art of it. We must acknowledge the giants on whose shoulders we stand, who help us see far." She paused, staring pensively at a spot over Randy's head.

"An excellent and most apt paraphrasing of Sir Isaac Newton," Randy added.

He almost howled when he felt the toe of someone's

shoe dig into his shin. He looked across the table to see Erich scowling at him, hissing something furiously that Randy couldn't catch.

The chairman didn't either. "What was that, Erich? Usually the mention of Newton does not elicit such a violent reaction in my students."

"Nothing, ma'am."

Now it was Erich's turn. She canted her head and asked, "With all that energy, perhaps you could tell me the top five cancer deaths by site and sex."

Erich gulped. "With percentages?"

"Absolutely. If you cannot quantify what you know, you really don't know it."

"Well, ma'am." Randy was confused as to why Erich sounded so uncertain of himself. He knew that his classmate knew this cold. This was question number three on the text file they had memorized last night.

The chairman was sticking exactly to her script, almost word for word.

"In men," Erich continued, "death occurs most commonly from lung cancer—thirty-five percent—followed by colon and rectum carcinoma—twelve percent—then—um, let me see—prostate cancer—ten percent—and leukemias and lymphomas, which together comprise eight percent of all male cancer deaths."

"Excellent, excellent." The chairman sounded almost disappointed. The students were now batting a thousand. By this time in the last conference, she had punched through easily to their frontier of ignorance. "Tracy, continue where Erich left off, with cancer deaths in women."

Tracy, who again appeared distracted, seemed not to have heard the question. "I'm sorry."

"You must concentrate," the chairman scolded. "Concentration is the hallmark of an excellent surgeon." She repeated the question.

"Oh. Well, the biggest killer in women among cancers is now lung cancer, which surpassed breast cancer as the biggest killer among women only five years ago."

The chairman nodded. "That is correct. Thanks to the Marlboro Man, lung cancer is an equal opportunity killer. Now give us some numbers."

"Numbers?"

"Yes. Percentages. Erich could supply some; so should you. Or should I hold the two of you to different standards?"

Tracy paused. "I believe breast cancer accounts for approximately twenty percent of all female cancer deaths, and lung cancer accounts for twenty-one percent."

"Do you use *believe* synonymously with *guess*?"

Tracy thought about that. "In this case, yes, ma'am."

"As a matter of fact, you are off by three percent total. Does anyone know the correct figures?"

Randy shot up his hand, again causing everyone around him to stare at him. "Ma'am, that would be breast cancer at nineteen percent, lung cancer at twenty-two percent, followed by cancer of the colon and rectum at fifteen percent, and leukemias and lymphomas at nine percent." He sat back and crossed his arms, a triumphant grin on his face.

"That is—correct." The chairman said it almost as if not believing it herself, like a presenter who had just opened the envelope to the Academy Award to find that the least likely contender had won Best Actor.

Erich closed his eyes and pursed his lips, as though so furious he was distracting himself to keep from exploding.

"How does smoking affect the risk of cancer?" the chairman asked, scanning the room. "Clark?"

"Well, it greatly increases the risk of lung carcinoma."

"Greatly." The chairman straightened her lapel as she considered that word. "Greatly. If someone asks you, 'Dr. Wilson, how will this surgery affect my chances of surviving my cancer,' are you going to tell them, 'Greatly'?"

"Well, I suppose, if—"

"The answer, Clark, is no. You will be precise. You will give them exact numbers, figures and statistics, from the most recent longitudinal studies. You will do this because you were trained by the Rosemont Department of Surgery, where it was instilled in you the desire to always be exact. So be exact, Clark, be precise."

"Yes, ma'am." Clark's face was contorted with the effort of thinking. "Ma'am, I don't know the exact figures."

The chairman nodded. "That is apparent. Does anyone know the—"

Randy blurted out before she could finish her sentence: "In nonsmokers, the incidence of lung cancer is three-point-four per one hundred thousand, whereas in those who smoke ten to twenty cigarettes a day, the incidence goes up to fifty-nine-point-three, and among those smoking over forty cigarettes a day, the rate is two hundred and seventeen-point-three new cases of cancer per one hundred thousand every year." He resisted the urge to finish off the sentence with a flourish and pounded fist on the table.

"Those figures are precisely correct." Again, the chairman seemed almost disappointed. "Erich, do you have some gastritis that gives that look of pain?"

"No, ma'am."

"Are you feeling ill?"

"A little. But it will pass."

"And I hope you and your classmates will. Now, Alicia, can you tell me what the most common site of metastasis of lung cancer is?"

She couldn't, and the conference resumed its normal pace, with the students fumbling through their responses and Randy keeping his mouth more or less shut, though he knew all the answers by heart and yearned to fill the void with the carefully rehearsed responses.

The conference ended, and as soon as the chairman was gone, Erich exploded. He stood up and took Randy, who was gloating in the backslapping and stunned praise of his classmates, out of the room and into a side corridor. "You fool! Why didn't you just tell her you had her system figured out? Why didn't you just let her know you broke into her office?"

"Shhh!" Randy put a finger to his lips. "Don't be so paranoid. She'll just think we read all that out of Bailey's textbook. It's all in there."

"Yes, but some percentages have changed. The file is more up-to-date. The only way we could have known all that, and known it so well, is by accessing her file."

Randy looked glumly around. "So we can't make it so obvious?"

"No. We have to get one or two wrong, don't you see?"

"Not really."

"Well, humor me. I refuse to decode any more files until you promise that you will behave."

Randy nodded. "All right. No more Dr. Smart-ass."

"Good. And no bragging about this. You got those answers right because you studied hard, understand?"

"Sure."

"No one else is to know about this."

"Okay."

▲
APPEAL
▼

The deputy chairman of the Department of Surgery was a small man with a paunch. No one had ever seriously considered him for the chairmanship when the Boss stepped down and that suited him just fine. Something about him seemed grandfatherly and friendly. Maybe it was the bifocals, now resting on the end of his nose, now pushed up as he read the memo on his desk, now sliding down again as he tilted his head forward to study the medical student who had come to see him. Maybe it was the gray cardigan sweater he had pulled on, or his tuft of white hair. Or maybe it was his round, smiling face.

He didn't have any diplomas on the walls, just a couple of color photographs taken from the top of some mountain.

He saw her eyes resting on the pictures. "I took those shots in the Austrian Alps last winter. Beautiful, terribly beautiful. I would like to say I climbed one of those slopes, but must admit I took a train ride to the top.

345

Although I daresay, with the condition of the train and the grade, it might have been just as dangerous." He turned to her and his smile broadened. "Do you ski?"

"A little, sir. Although I haven't had much time lately."

"Oh, you must make the time. Give your all on the wards, but carve out a little time for yourself. Somehow." He tapped the memo before him. "But you didn't come here to discuss skiing, I imagine?"

Tracy swallowed. Maybe she was overreacting. This man seemed so nice and what had happened—well, what had happened? Could she have imagined the whole thing?

"Tracy?"

She realized she was staring at her hands. "Yes, sir. The reason I asked to see you—that is, I—" Alone, thinking about this, Tracy had rehearsed in her mind a thousand times the eloquent things she would hurl at the chairman's head, the way Dr. Masterson would bristle and maybe throw the student out of her office. She was prepared to vent. When she was told that the chairman herself didn't have an opening for three months, it had changed everything. Tracy wasn't prepared for this, for this little man's disarming smile and chitchat about skiing in the Alps.

She found her voice. "Sir, I was sexually molested in the operating room the other day."

The deputy chairman yanked off his bifocals with one hand and formed a fist with the other. "In the operating room?" His face was hard and cold and she understood in an instant why this man had risen through the bureaucracy of the department to become at least second in command. "How?"

She explained what had happened the best she could.

"So you are convinced that he pressed against you deliberately?"

"Yes, sir. It was definitely his—penis."

"It couldn't have been that the surgical field was crowded and that he had no choice?"

"No, sir. He had an erection and he pressed it against me. Then he began to—um—grind it back and forth." She closed her eyes at the memory, remembering how she had scrubbed her buttocks in the shower afterward, as though she had to remove the filth of his contact from her. It sounded strange to hear herself talk about it out loud; she hadn't even told Clark yet.

"And it couldn't have been that he misinterpreted something you did or said as sexually inviting?"

Tracy saw the room turn purple at the edges. Her ears burned. "Sir, number one, I made it quite clear to this resident, who had asked me out multiple times and who I had turned down multiple times, that I was not interested in him. Number two, even if I had, he had no right—" She felt her voice quiver, then break. "He had no *right!*"

The deputy chairman raised one hand and nodded. "It's okay, Tracy." He came around from behind his desk and handed her a tissue. "I'm so sorry this had to happen to you. Or to anyone. Nothing so reprehensible has ever been brought to my attention. Never." He gave her another tissue. She was aware of the brown, polished leather tips of his shoes. She looked up into his eyes and it was almost possible to believe him, that she was the first, that in a male-dominated department that paid lip service to the idea of sexual harassment, this sort of thing never happened before.

Almost.

"So what are you going to do, sir?"

He was silent a moment. "Well, the first thing is to make sure you're okay. Do you feel like you need to talk to anyone about this?"

"You're the only person I've told."

He nodded. "It might be best if we kept it that way. Although you might want to see a counselor or something. This sort of thing can be traumatizing for some people." To Tracy, he sounded as though he were reciting something he had read in a popular magazine or overheard on the evening news.

"No, sir, I'm fine."

"Good." He returned to his chair and began scribbling something on a yellow legal pad. His pen made a loud scratching sound. "Now, the first thing we need is the alleged offender's name."

"Sir, there is nothing alleged about it. It happened."

"Oh, I believe you, but you see, this is a very serious charge."

She wiped the tears from her eyes and stared at him. She didn't follow. "Of course."

"I must maintain a policy of innocent until proven guilty. That's only fair, don't you think? Otherwise any of us could be victims of spurious or random allegations."

Tracy wadded her tissue into a damp, warm ball. "But this allegation is neither spurious nor random."

His paunch rose and fell as he let out a deep sigh. "Of course not. Now, the intern's name, please?"

She bit her lip. "Jenson."

The deputy chairman began to write, then stopped. "Peter Jenson?"

Tracy nodded.

"You're quite certain it was him?" The tone of his voice had changed now.

"Yes, sir."

"He's a sharp young man, one of our best. Ph.D. in biomechanical engineering. His work with prostheses is remarkable. He is being groomed for a faculty position even now."

"Sir, I fail to see—"

The deputy chairman looked distracted a moment, then blinked twice. "Of course, of course." He didn't write down the name. "There's no chance it could have been anyone else?"

"No, sir. I checked the OR schedule that morning."

The deputy chairman seemed relieved. "Oh. Well, those things change all the time. Interns switch with each other and don't always—"

"I see him every day. I know it was him." She paused.

The deputy chairman drew his lips into a tight, little line.

"Sir, I don't care if he's brilliant or a wonderful surgeon or a candidate for sainthood, the man had no right to do to me what he did."

The deputy chairman was silent, absolutely silent a moment. "So who else witnessed this incident?"

Tracy paused. She thought of the others in the OR. Focused on the case, of course no one had seen. "I'm not sure anyone did."

"Then it comes down to your word against his."

"I suppose it does. But what reason would I have for making up something like this?"

The deputy chairman spread his hands. "Why, indeed?" He put his bifocals on again, studied what he had written, then tilted back his head and blinked up at his pictures of the Alps. "Is there anything going on in your life that I should know about, Tracy? Any particular stressors?"

She felt her back stiffen, sensing where this was going. "Besides being molested by your house staff, no."

His voice was hard when he spoke next. "The reason I ask is that Dr. Fenstermeyer states that he had to order you from the operating room that day."

"Of course he did. I told you that—"

"He said you were hysterical, that you completely lost any semblance of professional composure, that you jeopardized the patient by violating the sterility of the operating field." He blinked at her, his eyes now somehow gray, steely. There was nothing at all grandfatherly about him then.

Tracy felt a sharp pain in her gut. "I told you that—"

The deputy chairman silenced her by holding up a hand. "You asked me for a reason why someone might make something like this up. Let me give you one. Stress. It can distort things, you know, make them seem other than they are. This is, after all, a stressful rotation. Maybe it *seemed* to you that this resident pressed himself against you."

"You don't believe me."

The deputy chairman made a tent with his fingers, then rested his chin on his fingertips. "I believe you *perceive* you were violated."

"I was."

The deputy chairman nodded, removed his bifocals, and carefully folded them. "So what would you like me to do?"

Tracy leaned forward so that she was sitting almost at the edge of his desk. "I want him stopped, sir. If he did it to me, he's probably done it to others. No one should have to endure that."

Wordlessly, the deputy chairman rose and walked to the window. He stared out at something far away, out of Tracy's sight. "You seem an intelligent woman. You realize what repercussions something like this would have if I even asked the question? It could ruin Jenson's reputation, perhaps forever. People draw their own conclusions." He turned to her, his eyes grandfatherly again, almost sad. "Can you understand why I need more than just your word to go on?"

Tracy rose also, edging back toward the door. She realized that this was a complete waste of time. He would never understand. Her only hope was to get through somehow to the chairman herself, but maybe even that would go nowhere. "Thank you for your time, sir."

Before she had taken two steps, he stopped her. "Tracy."

"Yes, sir?"

"Take this as a suggestion, for all it's worth." He approached her, stood two feet from her. "Seek counseling."

She saw the hallway redden at the edges as it rushed by her.

Tracy's rage simmered throughout the day. She was so distracted by her meeting with the deputy chairman that she almost pulled the surgical staples off the wrong patient. Had she done this, the skin folds of his wound might have popped open like an overstuffed suitcase. Then she wrote orders on the wrong patient's chart, catching herself only as she flagged them for the resident to cosign.

She knew she had to make a decision. Either she could act on this now, perhaps telling her resident that she simply had to go, or she could drop it, push it from her mind, just not think about it for the rest of the day.

She chose Option B. It was something she had become good at, something every physician must learn. People die, relationships end, shit stinks, but you can't ever let it show. You have to be a doctor and doctors are expected never to sweat, never to get angry, never to cry.

Never to be human.

Professionalism was a facade, but it was a facade she could slip into well. And in the end, it was less painful this way.

Going with the flow, they called it. Water off a duck.

While she waited in line at the post office, however, it all came back to her. There was a man staring at her, a man who couldn't pull his coat closed over his gut, a disgusting specimen of a human being whom Tracy summed up with a glance: probably an alcoholic, with adult-onset diabetes, maybe insulin dependent, perhaps with hyperlipidemia. She didn't need an old chart to read to figure that he had smoked two packs a day for the past twenty years. No, thirty. And he would stare at her like that until she left the post office, not knowing she might be his doctor someday.

That would be grand, she thought, imagining the scene: his insolent wisp of a smile would disappear as he rolled in ashen-faced and panting on the gurney, clutching his chest. She could see him cling to her, begging her for something for the pain.

And she could imagine smiling down at him with a little I've-got-you-now-you-bastard look as she leaned close enough for him to recognize her. Maybe she'd ask the nurses if she could put his Foley urinary catheter in herself, snaking it into the urethra of his penis, inflating the balloon a little early maybe, yanking on it to make sure it was in place.

Oh, the cruelties she could inflict on this man if he only had the misfortune of entering her emergency room.

She wouldn't be an object then.

Why am I thinking like this?

You know damn well why.

Peter Jenson.

She hated men, she realized, that day she really, really hated them. She would try to tell herself it was stupid thinking that way, that it didn't do any good, but she couldn't convince herself of it. All she could remember was the way the intern's cock felt pressed against her, the way it made her feel so filthy. And the way the deputy chairman's eyes seemed to turn gray and hard when it became clear that he didn't believe a word she said, that in the end she was a woman and he was a man and she was treading on something no one liked to think a whole lot about.

Just another hysterical bitch, he probably thought.

No, that's not fair. He didn't say that. He might have thought it, but he didn't say it.

She calmed down enough by the time she got her stamps and walked to the parking garage. She looked over her shoulder, but the man hadn't followed her. She hated living like this, a hostage in her workplace, a hostage in the city she was trying to think of as home.

It was true, she realized as she unlocked and started her car, that she had no evidence, no witness to corroborate her claim. It was also true that this allegation, even if some board of inquiry rejected it as untrue, would ruin the intern, stamp him with a question mark that maybe no one could ever remove. That was one hell of a responsibility the deputy chairman had. Perhaps he had heard—how did he word it?—spurious and random allegations before.

Or maybe he was just a man.

No, she couldn't stand to go through life thinking that way. Not all men were sex-starved, perverted creatures.

Just some of them.

She gripped the steering wheel as she drove home. Distrust poisoned her view. Every man under ninety that she cruised by on the dirty, cracked sidewalk was a rapist.

Twenty minutes and three dead bolts later she was ensconced in her favorite chair, a hideous brown sofa that went with absolutely nothing else she or Clark owned, but that she refused to part with. Her mother had been on the verge of throwing it away when Tracy was a freshman in college when she begged her mother to let her move it into her dorm room. Since then, it had been a monument of sorts, a reminder of all that was safe and comfortable. Who would believe that that brown, ugly sofa would one day come to represent childhood?

She found herself jumping at things. The sound of her water coming to a boil in the kettle in the kitchen, although she had put it on for her tea only minutes earlier, made her bolt upright on the sofa and almost drop the remote to the TV. Then the sound of someone or something scratching at the door made her spill the mug of hot water she had just poured. "Who is it?" She moved toward the door.

Then the sound became a familiar one—a key in the lock, the dead bolts turning one by one. "It's me."

It was only when he was in the house that Clark realized how upset she was. "Let me guess—you got a bad evaluation."

"No. If only it were just that."

"Your call schedule is hell."

"No, it's doable."

"Then what?"

He threw his overcoat over the back of a chair, grabbed a handful of cookies, and sprawled himself over a beanbag chair.

"I will only tell you this if you promise not to react in any way, not to do anything rash or stupid."

The cookie froze halfway to Clark's mouth. "The rash part I can avoid; I'm going to have trouble not being stupid. What's going on?"

"My intern molested me."

Clark stared at her.

"In the OR," Tracy added.

"Jesus." His face was blank and expressionless except for a slight downturn of the corners of his mouth. "How?"

Tracy went through her second recounting. Talking about it numbed it a little, gave her some distance. Listening to herself, she could almost imagine it had happened to someone else.

Clark set down his cookies in a neat, little pile on the corner of the coffee table—an overturned crate actually—and turned his whole body toward her. It was clear he didn't know what to say for a minute or two. Finally: "So what are you going to do?"

"Nothing."

Tracy sat on the brown monster and sipped at her tea. She should have waited; it burned the tip of her tongue and her lips, but she didn't care. The pain was a distraction.

Clark was on his feet, zapping off the television and tossing down the remote. "What do you mean nothing?"

"I already spoke to the deputy chairman. He said I lacked witnesses, that he had nothing to go on, that we couldn't do anything."

Clark sat again, then stood up just as quickly. He paced back and forth, trying to absorb what she just said. "You spoke with the *deputy chairman*? Of the Department of *Surgery*?"

She nodded.

The thought seemed to strike him suddenly. "So now you talk to the chairman!"

"No, Clark. It's over. The case is closed."

"But this guy did this thing to you. Don't you want some kind of—I don't know—justice or something?"

Tracy stared into her tea. "To be honest, I'd like to dip his balls into this tea, then bring it to a boil. Maybe watch his face real close as I did." She looked at him. "But that would break a law, and they'd probably believe him, so they'd send me to prison for that."

Clark rolled his eyes. "Don't get paranoid. Let's just think this thing through. I don't think the boiled-balls option is a viable one. What can we do?"

She scowled at him. "I told you—nothing. It's over. It's dropped."

Clark picked up a back issue of the *New England Journal of Medicine* and absentmindedly flipped through it. "Who was it?"

"What difference does it make?"

"It was Jenson, wasn't it? The one you said gave you the creeps."

Tracy ran her hands through her hair. "Yes."

Clark dropped the magazine and gaped at her. "It just doesn't make sense. He seemed an all right kind of guy. And he's smart as shit; remember that lecture he gave us last year on the future of prostheses?"

"Oh, Christ, not you, too." Tracy set down her tea with a bang. "Why is everyone so convinced that someone intelligent can't be a pervert?"

Clark blinked twice. "Well, it is surprising, that's all."

"The truth is sometimes surprising."

"I suppose so."

Clark looked out to where the leaves on the maple in front of the house were turning crimson and gold. The first hint of fall was in the air. Soon they would have to wear coats and sweaters into the hospital.

"So now we just pretend everything is okay and do nothing—is that what you're saying?"

Tracy knew she was not the first woman who had to make such a decision. Either she risked making more noise until something—anything—happened, or she kept her mouth shut and contributed to the Great Lie. Neither option was risk free. If she did nothing, Jenson might become emboldened, might repeat what he did, or maybe even assault her.

Maybe rape her.

She shuddered at that thought.

For now, she had her hands full just surviving the damn rotation. "I have to get ready for rounds tomorrow," she told Clark. "The chairman's going to be there, remember?"

"How can I forget? The chief resident has been hammering that point home all week. If we choke, he looks bad. So we have to know everything about our patients and their diseases. *Everything.*"

Tracy pulled open a textbook of surgery and flipped it open to the section on cancer of the pancreas.

"How can you focus on this rotation after what he did to you?" Clark asked.

"I can't. But I don't have much choice."

Clark sat at her feet and leaned back against the couch. "Is this why you've been so distracted lately?"

"It shows, huh?"

"Tracy, I know you too well to—" His words were broken off by something and she couldn't tell if it was a sob or a spasm of anger. From the way he sat, all she could see was the top of his head.

She stroked his hair. "Hey, it'll be all right. I bet I'm not the first woman in the history of the department to have something like this happen. The worst thing I can do now would be to play into their hands, do something impulsive and foolish that would give them an excuse to fail me or even kick me out of medical school."

Clark hung his head. "Don't talk like that, Tracy. They don't kick people out."

"They do and you know it. It's a privilege to be here. No other school would take me if I was—"

"Just stop it. Let's think about something else. What do we need to know for rounds tomorrow?"

Tracy sighed. "Well, in my case, everything about carcinoma of the pancreas, cholecystitis, coronary artery bypass surgery, and peripheral vascular disease. Those are all my patients' primary conditions. That's only about . . . one hundred and twenty-two pages of this textbook. And that doesn't even include hypertension, peptic ulcer disease, chronic obstructive pulmonary disease, cataracts, prostatitis—need I continue?"

"No." Clark puffed out his cheeks. "We'll never make it. If rounds are anything like those conferences, we'll get crucified. I mean, everyone looked like crap in there."

"Not everyone," Tracy corrected.

Clark turned to her, rising to his feet. "You're right! What about Randy? He was all over that stuff! They couldn't shut him up. It was almost as though—"

"As though he knew exactly what questions were going to be asked."

"It was uncanny."

Clark thought about it. "Let me give him a call. I'm dying to know how he did it."

Tracy clutched Clark's wrist. "Don't get yourself in trouble. I have a bad feeling about this."

Clark blinked at her as he punched the numbers on the phone. "Relax. Randy's a good guy. I'm sure we can trust him."

"Yes, but sometimes he goes too far."

Clark waved his hand at her as he heard his classmate answer the phone. "Hey, Randy, what's up?" He grinned into the phone. "So what do you know that we don't? . . . No, don't play innocent . . . This is like those old biochemistry tests you reconstructed first year . . . Randy, I'm not taking no for an answer . . . How about if I come over and we discuss it over a beer? . . . I'll meet you in half an hour. Now don't let an old friend down, Randy. See you soon."

Clark pulled on his windbreaker and kissed Tracy on the forehead. "You going to be okay?"

"Sure."

"Why not come with me?"

Tracy thought about it a moment. "No, I'd rather just do it the old-fashioned way."

"You mean read through the night?"

"Something like that. Two months from now all you guys will remember is a set of trivia questions. Two months from now I hope to know a little surgery."

Clark giggled. "Two months from now I want to know some surgery also, but I also want to pass the course." He grew serious. "You sure you'll be all right? I'll stay if you want to talk."

"No. No talking. I'd rather not think about *that* right now."

"Okay. Just a feeble attempt on my part to be the kind, sensitive caring man of the nineties."

She chuckled. "It's not completely feeble."

He arched an eyebrow. "Just a little feeble?"

"Go cram your head full of trivia."

He kissed her again and left.

The house felt terribly empty when he was gone. She rose and ensured that all the dead bolts were secure. She looked through the window of her home and saw the sun setting between the dying leaves of her tree.

It didn't feel safe anymore. Nothing did.

As she was to do so often in her career as a medical student and physician, she picked up the textbook and buried herself in her work. She began reading:

Patients with pancreatic cancer present with a variety of symptoms from abdominal pain to obstructive jaundice. Tumor involving the head of the pancreas may lead to a variety of psychiatric symptoms, typically a profound depression that will not respond to conventional antidepressant medications.

She looked up, thought about that, and began reading again. Within minutes, she was lost in the task.

AT WAR

Clark gaped at the twenty or so pages lying before him. "This is unbelievable. I mean, first-class. She has every clinical problem imaginable laid out in detailed questions and answers."

Randy smiled. "You know what she always says about surgery—you do the same thing every time, follow the same procedure with religious exactitude, and you won't screw up. Good surgery, she says, should be boring. Well, I suppose she has the same philosophy toward teaching."

They had copied and decoded all the files from the network. Half were printed out, the other half were humming out of Erich's laser printer.

Erich looked nervously toward his apartment door, as though someone from the administration might charge in at any moment. "Now remember, Clark. This is not to go beyond you. Randy wasn't supposed to share this with even you, but he didn't consult with me before blabbing."

Randy made a face. "Oh, will you stop with this James

Bond secrecy? I think we should let everyone in the class in on this."

"Are you insane?"

"Not last time I checked. Look." He draped an arm over Erich's shoulder. "If you, me, and Clark do really well, we'll stand out, right?"

Erich nodded.

"And that will identify us as the ones who obtained these files, right?"

Erich tried to anticipate where this was going. "That's why I kicked your shins during the conference."

"And they still haven't recovered. Now, if *everyone* was in on this, and we *all* looked good, they would have to punish us *all*. They can't do that."

"Who says?"

"They just can't."

Clark scratched at a spot behind his ear. "I have a bad feeling about this. Something isn't quite right."

"No," Randy said. "What the Department of Surgery expects from us isn't quite right. Look, the chairman doesn't want us to learn—she wants to prove to us repeatedly how stupid we are, and how superior she is. We have at least two hundred pages of proof of that lying around this apartment!" He picked up one sheet at random. "Listen to this. 'Question: At what negative pressure, in millimeters of mercury, does one feel the urge to defecate?' " He looked up. "All the studying in the world won't help us prepare for *this*."

Clark shrugged. "So she wants to feel superior. If that's the way the game is played, so be it. We're not going to be students forever. All we have to do is punch our ticket here, survive a little humiliation, and move on to the next rotation. If that's the price we have to pay to become physicians, so be it."

Randy spread his hands. "But, Clark, why should it be the price we have to pay to become physicians?"

Erich answered for him. "Fine, Randy. Why don't they just make this a correspondence course? Why not just remove any stress and mail our medical degrees to us after four years? No call nights, no unpleasantness, hell, no sick patients coughing or puking on us in the middle of the night."

Randy scowled at him. "All right. Becoming a doctor will always be hard, if for no other reason than that we're surrounded with sick and dying people. But can't we take away some of the bullshit?"

Erich collapsed onto his couch. "I should never have gotten involved with you, Randy." He seemed on the verge of tears. "Look, I always thought the demands placed on us were reasonable and I continue to think that."

Randy thought about that a moment. "You know, Erich, if I were getting honors-plus in every course, I'd support the status quo, too."

Erich jerked his head up at him. "How'd you know my grades?"

The bluff had worked. "I saw it in your file in the chairman's office. It's real easy to say the system is fair when you're not the one getting shit upon. Now, if last year's statistics are any guide, four of our classmates are going to have to sweat through this rotation again."

Erich dropped his eyes. "They should have studied more."

Randy waved the papers in front of him. "Studied what? Defecating pressures and baboon kidney transplants? Our classmates out there are trying to memorize the New York City phonebook. We have the exact phone numbers they need! I say we give it to them."

Erich remained silent.

"If we don't," Randy said, "and it becomes obvious that you and I"—he nodded toward Clark—"and Clark are the only ones in the class who are prepared, she can single us out and screw us."

Erich looked sick. "Fine. Tell everyone. Call the entire class and tell them that you broke into the chairman's office and you'd like to share what you found."

Randy rolled his eyes. "And you tapped into her network using her ID and password."

Clark shot to his feet. "You broke into the chairman's office?"

"No, I didn't break in anywhere. A janitor let me in."

Clark blinked a few times, staring down at the printout before him. "You didn't tell me that."

"You didn't ask." Randy puffed out his cheeks. "Look, you guys are seeing this thing from the administration's point of view. All our lives, we've been good little students, doing what we were told, getting good grades, obtaining letters of evaluation. As a result, we've become compliant, malleable. Yes, sir, I'll memorize that mindlessly. No, sir, it doesn't matter that I won't have a life for the next decade or so. Well, I'm tired of that. This is something we can do for ourselves."

He paced as he grew animated, reminding Clark of a newsreel he had seen of Trotsky exhorting a revolutionary crowd. "This isn't just about surgery, don't you see that? This is about surviving. It's a war out there, and in war, anything goes. We have to fight back or we'll be crushed."

Clark shook his head. "No, Randy, I can't participate in this."

"Why not?"

"I just can't. I'd rather be crushed honestly than shine dishonestly."

Erich rose also. "I'm with Clark. You can count me out too, Randy."

Randy was incredulous. "But we need you. You decoded all this information for us, you tapped into the net, you—"

"Please don't remind me, I feel guilty enough already. Maybe if I bow out now they'll have mercy on me when this half-baked scheme comes to light. I've decoded all the files and printed most of them out. I've copied the rest onto a floppy diskette; you can print it out at the library. But I don't want to hear anything more of this. Wake me up when you want to leave. Good night."

He walked back to his bedroom and closed the door. Clark and Randy heard the squeak of bedsprings.

Clark moved to the door. Randy stared at the printer churning out more information and then back at Clark. "So what are you going to do?"

"I'm going home to sleep."

Randy kicked at a pile of articles, causing them to fan out over the floor. "We could have gotten honors. Guaranteed."

"I know," Clark said. "But that wouldn't have meant anything to me if I cheated to get it. Good night."

Randy stopped him at the door. "Clark."

"Yes?"

"Are you going to turn me in?"

Clark paused. "You know I wouldn't do that." He smiled. "Unless you show up the rest of us too badly."

▲ ROUNDS ▼

The chief resident was nervous, the teaching resident even more so. "Please don't hurt me, you guys. Please don't make me look bad," Murray pleaded. He went from student to student, asking questions that Clark knew were useless. They were favorite questions of the Boss, but the Boss was gone now, the script had changed, and the teaching resident was in the impossible position of trying to teach a new class an old chairman's tricks.

Clark knew that in theory surgery shouldn't change, that what was important about heart transplants one year should be important the next, but he also knew that was bullshit, that so much of looking good in the hospital had to do with anticipating what the attending wanted. He half wished he had stayed up with Randy studying.

"Walk through, people," Fremont said. "Dry run."

It was like some movie set, Clark thought, as the chief resident directed the various actors into position. "Lower the clipboard away from your face. Don't appear to read.

Wait. Get rid of the clipboard altogether. . . . Tom, don't droop. Straighten your shoulders. . . . Don't block the patient's nameplate!"

And so it went as they traversed the halls, moving from room to room. They stepped into each one, flipped on the lights, then Fremont triple-checked everyone's IV and made sure the chairman would have unobstructed access to the bed. "Move that chair. Push back the IV pole."

Clark noticed Tracy. Her lips were pulled tight into an expression she only got when she was having a hell of a time restraining her anger, such as when they fought and she didn't want to say something rash.

Then she looked and saw Peter Jenson not three feet away, looking at her with a half smile on his face.

Clark's first impulse was to step forward and rip the son of a bitch's eyes out. Instead, he just stepped between Jenson and Tracy and put an arm around her. "Don't let the bastard get you down."

Normally she would have shrugged off his arm—they had an unwritten rule about public displays of affection—but today she reciprocated, giving Clark a quick little squeeze around his midsection. "Oh, I won't. Believe me."

Clark looked over at Jenson, but the intern had drifted away to the other side of the herd.

They moved on to the next room and it was then that the disaster happened. "He's dead," someone murmured.

"Shit." The patient was sitting upright in a chair, his head gently canted to one side, as though staring out the window at the pinkening sky. Clark knew the man from rounds; three days ago he had a metastatic tumor resected from his abdomen. No one expected him to do well or even to survive much longer than six months; the surgery was only palliative, to decrease the mass effect in his gut.

Yet here he was, sitting up and dead, and the chairman was to be on the floor in only fifteen minutes.

"When did he expire?" Fremont demanded.

The intern who made the discovery shrugged. "Looks like he's been gone for a couple hours."

The charge nurse stepped forward. "He was complaining of chest pain two hours ago."

"Were you called?" Fremont demanded of the intern.

"No."

"Why not?" Fremont snapped at the charge nurse.

"He always has chest pain. He always has back pain. In fact, there's not a part of his body that didn't hurt in some way." She paused. "Until now."

"This doesn't look good," Fremont said. "He was Do Not Resuscitate, right?"

"Yes."

"But it still doesn't look good. Tell you what." He pulled the blanket from the patient's bed and wrapped it around the deceased man's shoulders. Then he put a pillow between the man's head and his shoulder and pushed the chair up against the window. "He's asleep, see? We won't disturb him because he's resting so peacefully. We will discover him dead after rounds."

Clark looked at Tracy, who made a little gasping sound. Fremont turned to the group. "Does anyone have any problem with that?" Tracy looked like she was about to say something, but instead she just shook her head. "That's what I thought."

When the chairman arrived on the floor, it was as though the Queen of England had stepped into their midst. There was a respectful hush and the chief resident announced, "Dr. Masterson, we are ready to round."

"Excellent. Let's begin."

They came to the first patient's room. Peter Jenson stood carefully six inches to the left of the patient's nameplate, straightened his shoulders, and recited from memory: "This is Lewis Taylor, a forty-nine-year-old white gentleman with severe hepatic cirrhosis now one day status post-portocaval shunt. We are currently ruling him out for an intraoperative myocardial infarction. His ins and outs over the past twenty-four—"

She cut him off. "He is being heparinized, I assume?"

Jenson looked almost offended at being cut off. "Yes, he's receiving twenty-five thousand units in five hundred cc of normal saline at seventeen cc per hour."

"And if you overshot with heparin, what would you use as an antidote?"

Jenson's forehead was definitely furrowed now. "Why, Protamine, of course."

The chairman nodded. "And what is the origin of Protamine?"

Jenson's eyes widened. "I don't know the source."

"How many years have you been using heparin, Dr. Jenson?" It was a convention of hers to address the students by their first names, and the residents by their surnames, preceded by Doctor.

"Two and a half."

"And over that entire period, you never felt compelled to look up the source of Protamine?"

"Why—no."

The chairman nodded. "Hmmm. Well, why doesn't our teaching resident enlighten us?"

Murray gulped. "Because the teaching resident doesn't know."

There were a few scattered giggles among the students, giggles that died as quickly as they were born.

The chairman looked at him, puzzled. "Really? And you are in charge of teaching students?" She scanned the group. "Does anyone know?"

Randy's hand shot up. "Protamine is derived from *salmon sperm*." He drew out the last two words, taking a certain delight in the alliteration.

She looked as though she were going to be ill. "Yes. Yes, it is." Then the chairman eyed the teaching resident. "How did he learn that? You obviously couldn't have taught him."

"Ma'am, I do not know."

The chairman jerked her head toward Jenson and demanded, "Now, tell me, if you would, the average hepatic blood flow, in milliliters per minute."

Jenson looked over his clipboard, as though the answer might be there. "I don't know the exact number."

"Then you don't know. If you know something, you can quantify it." She looked around. "Does anyone?"

Again Randy's hand shot up.

She looked even more mortified than before. "Dr. Murray, you don't know this one either?"

"Ma'am, I believe the blood flow is about one third of the total cardiac output."

"You believe incorrectly and that wasn't the question." She blinked at Randy.

"Hepatic blood flow is roughly fifteen hundred milliliters per minute," he said. "Which represents twenty-five percent of the cardiac output."

"That's exactly right." The chairman frowned at him. "Why don't you tell me what pressure stimulates the development of portal-systemic collateralization?"

"About five to ten millimeters of mercury over the normal pressure."

"And what is the derivation of the word *cirrhosis*?"

"Ma'am, it comes from the Greek word *kirrhos*, which means yellow orange." Randy couldn't suppress a grin.

"And who first described it?"

"Hippocrates, in the fourth century B.C."

"And who first described the histopathological characteristics of cirrhosis?"

"Carswell and Rokitansky, two nineteenth-century English pathologists."

The house staff had turned completely around now, their backs to the chairman, looking at Randy in complete disbelief.

She turned to Jenson. "At Stanford, I was often criticized for holding my students and house staff to impossible standards. But, as Randy demonstrates, my standards are far from impossible. I expect more from you, Dr. Jenson, understand?"

He clenched his jaw, stared hatefully at Randy, and stood almost at attention. "Yes, ma'am."

"Well, let's visit the patient, shall we?"

Clark came up behind Randy. "I'd cool it if I were you."

"Why?"

"You're making it too obvious."

They stepped into the room to find a thin white male with an extremely protuberant belly and severely atrophied arms. His teeth and eyes were yellow. There were pieces of what looked like scrambled eggs in his beard. Clark could almost smell the alcohol. His eyes wandered automatically to the man's antecubital fossa; needle marks ran up and down every available vein. "Hey, Doc."

The chairman nodded to him. "So how are we doing today?"

The patient grinned up at her. "I don't know how *we* is doing, Doc, but I got me some real bad skrosis."

"That's *cirrhosis*."

"Exactly. Hey, listen, think you can get me a dental consult?"

She frowned at him. "Talk to your physician about that."

"Ain't you my physician?"

"No, I'm your physician's boss. How is your belly doing?"

"Oh, it's fine. It's my tooth, though, see?" He peeled back his lip to reveal an enormous, brown-and-yellow canine tooth, the only survivor in his upper gum. "Stinks, too, when you get up real close."

The chairman turned to Jenson. "Anything on physical exam that I should be aware of?"

"No, ma'am. He does have shifting dullness, which might be interesting for the students to see."

"Hmmm." She leaned over the patient, who was now tugging at his tooth. "Do you mind if I tap on your belly?"

"No, go right ahead, everyone else does."

She tapped one finger on another and made a mark on him with her pen.

"You didn't say nothing about *writing* on me!"

She ignored him as she rolled him onto his side and

repeated the movement. "What does shifting dullness indicate, Clark?"

"Ascites."

"Exactly." The chairman turned to the patient. "Any problems or complaints?"

"Just this goddamn uncomfortable position. Can't get no breath, can't get no sleep."

She frowned at him. "What position?"

"You know, all jackknifed, with my feet up in the air and my head up like this. Dr. Jenson told me some idiot said he had to crank up my bed into this position."

Jenson turned red. "I did not use the word *idiot*."

"No, I think it was dumb-ass," the patient said. "And I'd have to agree with you, Dr. Jenson. Ma'am, maybe you could tell this dumb-ass to let me lie flat on my back. I'm in enough pain as it is."

The chairman stared down at the patient silently a moment. "Sir, *I* am that dumb-ass."

The patient looked surprised by that. "Oh."

"And that position is necessary to prevent the formation of deep venous thrombosis, which could lead to a fatal pulmonary embolism."

"A what?"

"Explain it to him later, Dr. Jenson." She nodded toward the door. "Next patient." It might have been Clark's imagination, but the tips of her ears had turned slightly scarlet.

When they came to the dead patient, he was sitting just as he had been a few minutes earlier, staring out the window, the blanket draped around his shoulders. "I'm not sure we should visit him, ma'am," said Jenson.

"And why not? We visited everyone else."

"Yes, but he's not feeling up to it. In fact, he specifically requested that we not come by."

"Is that right?"

"Yes, he's a very cold individual. And very stiff—from his surgery."

The chairman seemed to accept that. She looked in on him, called the patient's name, then turned to Jenson and shrugged. "He's ignoring me," she said. "Well, he must be doing fairly well to be up and out of bed so soon. I'll visit him tomorrow."

No, you won't, Clark thought.

Then they moved down the hall.

When rounds were over, the patient was "discovered" dead. He was in the morgue by rounds the next morning.

▲ PRESSURE ▼

He was waiting for her in the lobby. As Tracy stepped out of the elevator and adjusted the strap of her book bag, she saw him.

He had seen her first and was already on his feet, smiling and walking toward her.

"You know," Peter Jenson said, "you can't keep saying no."

Tracy remained silent, pursed her lips, and tried to ignore him. Her book bag felt heavier than ever as she barreled her way to the automatic sliding doors in front of the hospital.

"Your classmate Randy was pretty sharp on rounds this morning," Jenson added, struggling to keep up with her. "How did he know all that trivia?"

Tracy said nothing, just prayed he would leave her alone.

"Now, neither of us is on call tonight, we all worked very hard for rounds this morning, and I say we deserve a drink. In fact, it'll be my treat. What do you say? It'd be fun."

She spun on him. "Just like rubbing your cock up against me in the operating room was fun, huh?"

"I don't know what you're talking about."

"The hell you don't."

"Tracy, you're being hysterical. Now, why won't you go out with me?"

She rolled her eyes. "What part of no do you not understand?"

He smiled. "The part that falters, ever so slightly, as though you haven't quite made up your mind."

"Don't flatter yourself. You're mistaking hesitancy for repugnance."

"Repugnance?"

"Yes. In case it hasn't hit you, what you're doing to me constitutes sexual harassment. And I don't have to take it."

He laughed, a little chuckle at first, then a deep-bellied laugh that made him almost double over. "Well said, Anita Hill." His smile disappeared as they stepped onto the concrete walkway in front of the hospital. "You know what happened to her, don't you?"

"She won a lot of respect and made all of us think about things that weren't even discussed as much as—"

"No, Tracy. She lost. All women lost on that day, don't you see? You can't win by crying sexual harassment. It doesn't work."

She shot him a sidelong glance and saw that a hard little expression, a meanness she hadn't noticed before, had entered his eyes. "I'm calling security if you don't back off in about thirty seconds."

His eyes widened a little, then his face broke into a broad, warm smile. "You can only hold out on me so long, Tracy."

She closed her eyes and said between gritted teeth, "Fuck off." Then she turned and walked away, as fast as she could, away from him, from that smirk on his face, from the echo of his words.

She had had enough. Tomorrow she was going to get this thing out in the open.

THE CHAIRMAN

They were probably asking for her at rounds. She could imagine Murray and Fremont asking all the students where the hell she was. Even Clark didn't know.

It was 5:30 when Tracy heard the *click click click* of the chairman's heels echoing down the empty corridor. Her bet had been correct: the chairman would visit her office before beginning rounds.

It was the first cool morning of the fall, so the chairman's cheeks were red as she marched to her office, turned the key, and stepped inside. She left the door ajar.

Tracy, who had been sitting at a bench in the corridor was amazed; the chairman had walked past without so much as acknowledging her existence.

Tracy gulped, walked up to the door, and knocked twice.

"Come in, Tracy."

So she had been noticed after all. As Tracy stepped into the room, which was still crowded with half-unpacked boxes, and made her way to the chairman's desk, she began to tremble.

"So what trouble, gripe, or complaint brings you here this morning?" The chairman had not yet made eye contact with her, had not so much as registered the faintest surprise at the fact that a student was waiting outside her door at dawn.

"How did you know I had a complaint?"

"It has been my experience that no one sits outside my door at five-thirty in the morning unless they have some complaint. What is yours?"

Tracy blinked twice. "I am here to complain about sexual harassment."

The chairman nodded. She didn't seem the least surprised. "This department has a policy on sexual harassment. If I remember correctly, you are to report to the equal-opportunity employment office on the ninth floor and file a formal complaint there." She thought about that. "No, wait. Since you're a student, you don't qualify for that. I think you have to see your dean."

Tracy moved closer to the desk. She had not yet been asked to sit, not that there was anywhere to sit. "Aren't you shocked or outraged?"

"Shocked? No. Outraged? Yes. But I have heard your story already."

"Really?"

"Of course. You went to the deputy chairman. He reported it all to me, as he is obligated to. He gave me no names, but I sensed it might be you."

"Why?"

"Because your performance has slipped so remarkably over the past few weeks. There are only so many women taking this rotation."

Tracy almost wanted to cry with relief. "So I don't have to go through telling my story again?"

"No." The chairman pulled on her white coat, straightened her hair in a small mirror on the wall, and jerked her watch up to her face. "We have seventeen minutes until rounds and I'd like to dictate two letters and a memo before then." She sat at her desk and looked expectantly at Tracy.

Tracy was confused. "So what happens now?"

"Nothing." The chairman pulled out a microrecorder, depressed the record button, and began to dictate. "The date is now—" She stopped and looked up at Tracy, who then realized she was expected to leave.

"What do you mean nothing?" she asked.

"I mean, nothing. The deputy chairman informed me that you have no case. I regret your perception of harassment, but there is nothing I can do to help you."

Tracy ran her fingers through her hair. "He accosted me outside the hospital yesterday."

The chairman closed her eyes and lowered her dictaphone, as though asking, "You see how patient I can be?" "He accosted you?"

"Yes."

"Did he strike you?"

"No."

"Did he touch you in any way, in the way you claimed he touched you in the operating room?"

"Well, no, but—"

"Did he use foul or offensive language?"

"No, but he—"

"And did *you* use foul or offensive language?"

Tracy blinked. She saw where this was going. "Yes, I did."

The chairman nodded. "At least you are honest. I received a report yesterday evening that one of the medical students on the rotation was in front of the hospital telling one of my interns to 'fuck off—I believe that is an exact quote."

Tracy balled her hand into a fist and brought it down hard on the chairman's desk. The chairman did not flinch, simply stared up at the medical student standing before her. "Why is it inexcusable for me to react to his continual sexual harassment, but it's okay for him to grope me in the operating room, constantly ask me out, maybe even leave obscene messages on my answering machine?"

The chairman arched an eyebrow. "You didn't tell me about the phone calls."

"Well, I don't know that it was him."

The chairman smiled. "And in a city of millions, it probably wasn't."

Tracy walked to the door. She felt she had exhausted all her options. She had nowhere left to turn. Except: "Ma'am, if nothing is done about this, so help me—I don't want to threaten, but—" She looked down at the floor, a polished hardwood badly scratched by the moving boxes. "I'm fully prepared to get a lawyer and sue this department."

That got the chairman's attention. She quietly directed Tracy to close the door, then pulled out a chair for the medical student to sit in. Then she picked up a phone and paged the chief resident. "I'll be fifteen minutes late. Start rounds without me." Then she hung up and looked at Tracy. When the chairman spoke, her voice was soft and maternal.

"Yes, Tracy, you can bring a suit against the department. You can threaten all sorts of administrative actions. Depending on your financial resources, you can send some lawyer's children through law school churning up fees to harass us, but in the end you know that you are small and the department is big. You will lose."

Tracy could not believe she was hearing this from another woman. "How can you sit there and say that?"

"It is precisely because I am saying this that I am sitting here."

"So you've sold out."

"Tracy, stop the melodramatics."

"There are no melodramatics. When I heard a woman was going to chair this department, I thought all the stories I heard about chauvinism and harassment would become history. But I was wrong."

The chairman bowed her head and studied her hands a moment. They were long and graceful, even at the age of sixty-seven, the hands of a master surgeon. "Tracy, when I began medical school, there were three women in my class. One woman fell in love and married a pediatrician and there was no question of her continuing her medical training. The other was suspected of being a lesbian and was politely asked to leave by the dean. When she hesitated, a mass exodus of students was threatened. I don't think you understand how much times have changed, what pressures we early women had to surmount to secure you the right to attend medical school. We fought for that right, Tracy. We would not even be having this discussion today were it not for what we earlier women went through."

Tracy was now completely confused. "So why don't you support me, then?"

"Because I got to where I am today by keeping my mouth shut and doing what I was told. If I got a dollar for every time someone grabbed a breast, brushed a hand against my ass, or squeezed my thigh, I'd be a wealthy woman. If you could add to that all the times I was pressured to go out, or was the butt of some chauvinist pig's sexual joke, I could buy this hospital. But I did what I had to do, Tracy. I kept my mouth shut and survived, knowing that if I worked hard, one day I'd be in a position like this"—she swept her hands over her office—"and be able to *do* something about it."

Tracy jerked her head back and stared at the ceiling. "Then why don't you?"

"Because it's too early. My position here is tenuous. You may not realize that, but the first few years of a chairman's tenure are extremely vulnerable. I will lose everything if I act too early, if I make too many men who've gotten away with too much for too long start to sweat. I believe I can defeat them, but not all at once, not today.

"The most important decision you make in life is not how to fight, but which battles to fight. Choose them carefully. Your case is too weak. We'd lose, his career might be ruined, and we'd look foolish."

Tracy considered that. "So he has to rape me before you'll do anything?"

The chairman drummed her fingers on her desktop.

"And even then," Tracy added, "if he didn't leave behind some definite evidence, you probably would tell me that we have no case, that—"

"Tracy, that's enough." The chairman blinked at the medical student, and for a moment Tracy was convinced that all was lost, that this woman would never understand, that she was from a different generation with different expectations and that it would never work. She was about to ask if she could at least have another intern, when the chairman asked, "Tracy, are you sure it was Dr. Jenson who molested you?"

"Absolutely, ma'am."

"And you'd be willing to testify to that in court, if need be?"

"Gladly."

"And you are willing to accept the wrath of an entire department of adolescent boys, maybe even scorn and ridicule and outright abuse, if that's what it takes to nail this son of a bitch?"

Tracy grinned. "God, yes."

The chairman winked. "Then let's do it." She picked up the phone. "My secretary usually arrives around now." She spoke into the phone: "Ms. Price, get Dr. Jenson into my office . . . No, he should be rounding now . . . I don't care if he's in surgery, I don't care if he's the patient, I want him in my office in ten minutes. Page him."

Three minutes later there was a knock on the door. Tracy felt an instinctive sense of revulsion as Jenson walked into the room and stood before the chairman's desk. He looked at the chairman, then at Tracy, then back at the chairman. "You wanted to see me, ma'am?" He sounded syrupy polite, almost smug. Tracy wondered if the man had a thinly veiled contempt for all women.

"I most certainly did," the chairman said. "I will cut through all the superficialities. This young woman has a complaint. She states that you took certain liberties with her in the operating room. Is this true?"

"Certain liberties?"

"Yes. Specifically, that you pressed your penis against her. Is this true?"

Jenson sat on a box, looked horrified, began to say something, then stopped. He crossed his legs, then uncrossed them, then crossed them again. "This is a joke, right?"

"Do you think I would call you into my office, pull you out of rounds, and raise this question as a joke?"

"No, I don't suppose you would." The intern looked hatefully at Tracy. "Did she tell you this?"

Tracy nodded. "Damn right I did." She hated her voice for quavering.

Jenson chuckled. "Well, I won't even grace your accusation with a response."

"No, Dr. Jenson, you will," the chairman corrected. "You will because your chairman just asked it."

"I'll take the Fifth. Maybe I should call my lawyer."

"You're welcome to, but the Fifth Amendment only protects you against self-incrimination in a *criminal* proceeding." The chairman paused, letting the word *criminal* sink into the room. "This is a friendly administrative inquiry. At least it is right now. If we clear things up in here, there will be no need to press charges."

Tracy almost smiled. The chairman was good.

Jenson leaned back, crossed his legs and his arms at the same time, and asked, "What proof do you have?"

The chairman shrugged. "This medical student's word."

"Well, she's a liar."

"Someone certainly is." The chairman looked from the intern to Tracy and back.

Tracy turned to Jenson. "Why would I make something like this up?"

Jenson spread his hands. "How do I know? How do I know how any of you women think? First you call me in here for these ludicrous charges, then you project your sexual fantasies onto me." The meanness that Tracy noticed the day before, the hard little ferocity, entered Jenson's eyes as he drilled them into her. "You're a lying little whore and you have no right to try to ruin my career with these ludicrous allegations!" He turned to the chairman. "I'm sorry, but this is outrageous. I ask to excuse myself so I can go back to taking care of patients."

The chairman stared at him for a long hard minute. "I want you to know something, Dr. Jenson. I have no reason to believe this medical student is lying. Therefore, from this day forward, I want you to not so much as look at her, understand? You will be assigned a new medical student, a *male*, while this matter is being investigated."

"Investigated?"

"I'm not finished. Meanwhile I want you to submit in writing your account of what happened in the operating room on the day in question, from the moment you scrubbed in to the moment you left the operating room. Understand?"

Jenson shrugged. "There's nothing to tell."

"Then tell me that. I want it typed and double-spaced and on my desk by five o'clock tomorrow evening so it's ready for the board to review next week."

Jenson frowned. "What board?"

"The board of inquiry that I am about to form to investigate this matter. I also will gather information from all the other witnesses."

"What witnesses?" Jenson didn't sound so cocky now.

"Why, all the others who came forward and said they were willing to testify against you, Dr. Jenson. Such as the scrub nurse, another medical student on the case, and—"

Jenson rose. "They saw?" All the blood had drained from his lips.

"Oh, yes. They were quite graphic in their descriptions. They said it wasn't the first time they had seen you—"

"They're lying!" Jenson shot to his feet. "I never touched Catherine Myers, I can tell you that right now. And Alicia Wright is a scheming bitch who—" He stopped himself, realizing his error too late.

"I never said anything about Catherine Myers or Alicia Wright," the chairman said quietly.

Jenson's lips trembled. He looked like a hunted animal. "Am I excused?"

"You are more than excused, Dr. Jenson."

When the intern was gone, Tracy turned to the chairman and asked, "What was that about witnesses? I thought I was the only one who saw what had happened."

The chairman stood up and buttoned her white coat. "You were."

"But you told him that—" Then she saw the expression on the chairman's face. The woman almost winked.

"Tracy, sometimes you must be somewhat creative with the truth."

Tracy frowned. "And what was all that about a board of inquiry?"

"I'll look into the hospital bylaws and see if I can get one formed. But it will get him flustered enough to do one of two things. Either he will panic and divulge more information, as he did today. Catherine Myers, by the way, rotated through surgery a month ago. And Alicia—"

"I know Alicia," Tracy said. She felt sick, thinking about what he might have done to her.

"Well, I will contact them directly," the chairman said. "If they're willing to testify, we just might have a case."

"And what's the second thing he might do?" Tracy asked.

"Resign."

Tracy shook her head. "That's not good enough. He'll just go somewhere else and do the same thing."

"After the letter of recommendation I write for him, I can assure you he will not be practicing surgery anywhere in the western hemisphere."

Tracy smiled and offered the chairman her hand. "Thank you, ma'am."

The chairman took Tracy's hand and gave it a quick pump. "Thank you, Tracy, for having the moral courage to come forward. We need women like you in surgery."

Tracy grinned as they walked out of the office. "I think I'm partial toward internal medicine, to tell the truth."

"Ah, you're young." She paused as they stepped out of the office and into the hall. "There's still time to see the light."

CONSPIRACY OF SILENCE

She was standing at the end of the hallway, staring out the window. Far below, a man was walking with his two daughters, his hands thrust deep in the pockets of his long trench coat. Every now and then he would look back and say something to his daughters, who were toddling along a few feet behind him. He looked everything the medical students weren't: rich, relaxed, with nothing better to do on a Saturday afternoon than stroll through the streets of the city.

"Alicia."

She didn't turn when Tracy approached, didn't move, just watched the man and his daughters, as though transfixed.

"Alicia, we have to talk."

She stiffened when Tracy touched her lightly on the shoulder and Tracy realized that was a bad move. "What did he do to you?"

Silence.

"I talked to the chairman. She's willing to help us. But we have to come forward or he'll keep on—"

Alicia whirled. "I don't know what you're talking about." There was this glazed-over look in her eyes, as though she were coming out of a deep sleep. Tracy had the urge to shake her classmate, to tell her to snap out of it.

"I'm talking about Peter Jenson," Tracy said. "I know he must have hurt you, too."

"No. No, he didn't. He said he'd protect me. He said he'd keep them from hurting me. And he will."

Tracy didn't have to ask from what Jenson had promised to protect her; the rotation had not been easy on Alicia. The surgical residents had a high-school-football locker-room humor that singled out Alicia as its butt. Forgetful, distracted, usually almost in a trance, Alicia was corrected repeatedly during rounds until they finally gave up on her, ignored her, marginalized her. The other students participated, which was cruelest of all; no one wanted to assist her if she was operating that day on her dog. They called her Almost Alicia, as in Almost There. Alicia smiled and pretended not to care, but Tracy saw her sobbing once after rounds.

Tracy studied her classmate and realized something was lost in those immense brown eyes, something that had been there that summer, before they started on the wards. "Alicia, are you okay?"

"Of course. Tired, but fine." She gave a pert little smile. A condemned man could have done better.

"Listen, Alicia, we can nail this son of a bitch."

"I really don't know what you're talking about."

"C'mon, Alicia. Just tell me what he did."

Alicia stared out the window again. "No."

"Did he touch you?"

Alicia paused.

"Did he press himself against you?"

Alicia hung her head and blinked. Her eyelashes moistened with tears.

"Oh, Christ," Tracy said. "He did the same thing to me.

We don't have to put up with this shit. Maybe twenty years ago we did, but not today. Can you help me?"

Alicia remained silent.

Tracy pulled a pen and paper from her scrub pants and scribbled down her number, folded it up, and handed it to Alicia. "Call me if you change your mind. Or if you just want someone to talk to."

Alicia didn't reach for the paper, so Tracy pressed it into her hand. "We're classmates," Tracy whispered. "We've been through so much together. Let's not abandon each other now, when we need each other most."

She walked away, back to the wards, back to her thousand errands and calls and things she had to check. She looked back and glanced at Alicia, who was smiling now as she stared out the window.

The piece of paper with Tracy's number on it was wadded up and on the floor by her feet.

It was a familiar smell, but Tracy couldn't quite place it. Coppery, moist, recent. It was funny how smells could bring on such a flood of associations, even if you couldn't attach the odor to a name.

Tracy dialed the combination of the padlock attached to her surgery locker and sniffed. By the time she realized what the smell was, she had dialed her combination and was on the verge of swinging her locker door open.

Something stank of blood.

As she recognized it she also heard a rhythmic drip coming from within her locker.

She didn't know whether to be enraged or horrified as she opened the door and looked into the darkness.

Something was swinging from the hook in the center of her locker. As her eyes focused on it she realized it was a rat, hanging by a string, which seemed to emerge from the animal's throat.

Four months ago Tracy might have stepped back and screamed. Since then, she had seen so much gore, had grown so used to the sight of blood, that she only examined it with a remote, almost clinical detachment. She ran her eyes up the length of string to realize the rat had been pierced by a tampon.

There was no note attached. There didn't need to be. She looked down to see the floor of the locker was covered with a pool of blood. It seeped out now and dripped onto the floor.

Tracy slammed her locker shut, but not before two other women in her class saw what was inside.

Jennifer Woo stepped forward. Her eyes disappeared as she crinkled her nose in distaste. "Jesus, what *was* that?"

"A rat." Tracy tried to sound nonchalant. She pulled the padlock off the locker and moved to another one. "We've got to call sanitation STAT. A cockroach or two is one thing, but a *rat* . . ."

No one laughed at the quip. Jennifer stepped forward and opened the locker and soon a small crowd was gathered around. "This is about that Jenson business, isn't it?"

Tracy sat down on the surgical locker-room bench and peeled off her shoe covers. "Look, I just got out of a four-hour colectomy. I'm too tired to think about Peter Jenson. He's not worth the time."

Since coming forward, Tracy had been coolly received by the house staff and most of her male classmates. The only support had come from Jennifer, who quietly told Tracy that she had done the right thing, and, of course, from Clark, who ended up swapping interns with Tracy, and entertained her every night with stories about how stressed-out Jenson was over the impending investigation.

Just as the chairman predicted, the intern's rubbing of his genitals against her became a metaphor for so much more. It was symbolic, she overheard one resident whisper, of the trend in medicine and society: the demise of the red-blooded, American male. It was evidence that a woman, a third-year medical student no less, could make an unsubstantiated allegation and a brilliant house officer could be publicly humiliated, which was what he was when word of the accusation was leaked.

No one had the guts to say anything to her face. It was the deeper things, the unspoken accusations, that poisoned the air whenever clusters of male surgeons grew silent as she approached. And the women surgical residents and medical students were far from thankful; on the contrary, they resented the fact that she had made their positions that much more difficult.

Her only ally in the department was the chairman, but Dr. Masterson was far too professional to allow Tracy the slightest break from her interrogations on rounds and during conferences.

So as she slumped on the surgical bench and rubbed the nape of her neck, still able to smell the dead rat's blood, Tracy was almost angry with Jennifer for not just pretending she hadn't seen anything.

"The man is sick. This doesn't surprise me."

"How can it not surprise you?"

"Jennifer, he molested me, for God's sake! And he hates me because I didn't do what all his other victims did and just take it."

Alicia stood in a corner in her underwear, pulling on her clothes. When Tracy looked over at her, Alicia turned away and continued dressing in silence.

Jennifer stepped away, then reappeared a moment later with a pair of surgical gloves. She reached into Tracy's locker, gently freed the rat from its hook, and dropped it into a nearby trash can. Then she returned to the locker and pulled out Tracy's book bag. "Your clothes are ruined, but your notes look relatively unscathed."

"I can always buy more clothes, I suppose." Tracy smiled.

Her smile disappeared when she unzipped the book bag. "What the hell is this?" She pulled out a jockstrap sutured to something gray and shriveled. The room filled with the scent of formalin.

What the rat hadn't done, the sight of the cadaveric

gonads sewn to the jockstrap did: Tracy dropped the book bag and ran to the nearest sink. She managed to fight the wave of nausea enough to keep down her breakfast, but just barely. She thought she could taste the doughnut she had wolfed down at four in the morning.

"Are you okay?" Jennifer was by her, squeezing her shoulder.

"Yeah. I'll be fine."

"Go home and get some more clothes. Alicia and I will cover for you. Won't we, Alicia?"

"Sure."

"What did the note say?" Tracy asked.

"What note?"

"The note attached to the jockstrap. I don't want to look at it myself, but I want to know what the note says."

"Tracy, I don't think that—"

"Please, Jennifer, read me the note."

Without looking directly at the shriveled meat, Jennifer freed the note from the jockstrap: " 'Since you seemed to want a pair of balls so bad . . .' That's all."

Tracy stared at her reflection in the mirror. "The man is ill."

"Definitely. This is beyond gross."

"He got those testicles from a cadaver, too. Some poor guy donated his body to science and now he's—" Tracy cut herself off. "What am I going to do? I can't keep running to the chairman."

"Report it to the police," Jennifer said.

"The *police*?"

"Sure. I bet tampering with the cadavers breaks some sort of law."

Tracy shook her head. "No. I say we ignore the bastard. He wants us to react, to get hysterical. But if we clean up the mess ourselves and pretend nothing ever happened, that would freak him out more. Since we're the only ones who saw it, no one else has to know." She smiled. "Besides, revenge is a dish best eaten cold."

▲

OPERATION DISIMPACTION

▼

t began innocently enough.
Clark offered to get Peter Jenson a cup of coffee from the
pot by the nursing station before rounds.

The Grunt met him there. "Here." He handed Clark the
white-and-yellow powder.

"You sure this isn't dangerous?" Clark asked.

"As sure as I can be about any two drugs. I looked it
up in the PDR and there are virtually no reported cases of
anaphylaxis." The PDR was the *Physician's Desk Reference*,
a tome containing side effects and indications for any
drug prescribed. Clark stared down at the mixture as he
emptied it into the bottom of the Styrofoam cup. "We
write orders for these all the time, I suppose."

"And they work."

Clark chuckled. "That they do." Black coffee trickled
into the cup. He was grateful that the mixture dissolved
without leaving a trace. Just to be sure, he grabbed a
spoon and stirred it vigorously.

"Did you remove all the toilet paper?" Clark asked.

"Yes. The nurses weren't happy about it, but when I explained what was going on, they seemed to understand. They've got all the toilet paper to the staff rest room locked up in the narcotics closet."

"Excellent."

"Does he take it black?" the Grunt asked.

"Yes."

"Well, I better add some sugar anyway. It'll cover the teste of the Lasix and magnesium citrate." He stirred the concoction with a plastic spoon.

Clark grinned.

"Let's nail the motherfucker."

A voice behind them made them both whirl. Clark almost sloshed the coffee onto his shoes. "What the hell is this—a prerounds kaffeeklatsch?" It was Fremont, his whites immaculate, starched, his hair plastered in place with a dollop of grease.

The Grunt flipped him off. He was the only medical student who could do that and get away with it.

Or at least he seemed to get away with it; he hadn't received his evaluation yet.

"We're coming, we're coming."

Clark was afraid for a minute that the chief wouldn't let him take the coffee to Jenson. It was a quarter to six and the chairman was due on the ward in only fifteen minutes.

But the resident said nothing as Clark took the brew out to the nursing station.

"Here," Clark said, watching Jenson's face for any signs of suspicion. Jenson drank, sipping loudly, then paused. "You screwed up, Clark."

"How so?"

"Sugar. I told you I hate sugar."

Clark's gut tightened. "I can get you another cup."

"No, no, this will do." He sipped at the coffee again as he looked over his patient cards. "I'm so tired of the chairman rounding with us," he said in a low voice. "Fremont almost creams his pants at the idea of looking good in front of the bitch, but I say she doesn't deserve the effort. If you want to know what I heard—and this is just between you and me—I think she's a dyke." Jenson nodded sagely, then sipped some more coffee. The cup was half-empty, Clark noted with delight.

"Perfection, people," the chief resident was saying. "Everything in its place. Everything in its time." He was quoting the chairman. He looked at the students, yawning in the back of the herd. "And if you make us look bad again, it'll be scut city from here to the end of the rotation, understand?"

No one said anything. The chief narrowed his eyes. "Randy, I'm going to find out how you look so good in front of her. It's just a matter of time. I'll fail you if I discover you cheated."

There was absolute silence except for the sound of Jenson sipping at his coffee.

"And you better know some statistics this time," Fremont said, turning to the intern. "Your presentations must be perfect. Speak real quick and she can't cut you off." He turned to the group. "That goes for everyone. Don't pause, don't catch your breath, or she'll jump in and start asking you about defecating pressures and how many cc's of saliva are produced and other such bullshit. Pretend you don't hear her. Barrel through her questions. That seems to work."

"It does, does it?" The voice came from over his shoulder, from the nursing station. Fremont clamped his mouth shut and turned to face the chairman, who must have been on the ward the whole time, observing them.

Fremont said nothing, remained absolutely silent as the chairman walked up to him, a playful smirk on her face. "That's pretty good advice, Dr. Fremont. 'Pretend you don't hear her. Barrel through her questions.' Is that the same approach you take to your patients?"

"Not at all."

"I sincerely hope it isn't." She scanned the group and arched an eyebrow. "Shall we round? Oh, and remember—don't pause, don't catch your breath, or I'll start asking you about—what was it, Dr. Fremont?—defecating pressures?"

When they got to the first room, Jenson, who had been on call the night before and therefore had to present most of the patients, was looking a little gray. Clark exchanged a quick glance with the Grunt, whose expression was inscrutable. All those years in the military gave him an excellent poker face.

"Miss Trumbolt is a forty-seven-year-old white female who presented to the emergency room last night with an expanding, pulsatile abdominal mass. She was found to have—" He leaned forward and grimaced.

"Are you okay, Dr. Jenson?"

"Not really, ma'am."

"Well, you either are or you aren't. What are your symptoms?"

"Just the most intense urge to—"

"Yes?"

"Defecate and urinate. Like I've never known before. Excuse me." He ran from the group to the nursing station, almost flattening a medical student as he did so.

Some house staff looked nervously around, then giggled. It really was quite funny when you thought of it.

"PPPPPP," the chairman said, shaking her head. "Prior Planning Prevents Piss-Poor Performance."

Jenson came hobbling back in a minute, but didn't look the least bit relieved. He walked funny, as though he were trying to keep something from running down his leg. "I must have some sort of viral gastroenteritis."

"Perhaps you have. Can you continue?"

"I think so." But he didn't get three words out when he had to run to the bathroom again. The chairman crossed her arms, impatient. "Dr. Fremont, you supervised the workup of these patients last night; why not present what you know?"

Clark was impressed. From memory, without preparation, the chief resident rattled off the highlights of the woman's history, the exact size of what turned out to be an abdominal aortic aneurysm, and how the decision to operate emergently was made.

The chairman had nothing to add or detract. By the time Jenson came back, they were herding into the woman's room.

The intern followed them in, taking a position two feet from the chairman. He shifted his weight from foot to foot and cast doleful looks toward the door only moments after entering the room, however.

"Oh God, oh God."

The chairman gave him a funny look as he rushed out again. "You need not return to rounds, Dr. Jenson," she called out to him.

He spun around. "But, ma'am, I'm perfectly capable of—"

"No, you're not and I would rather you didn't."

"Yes, ma'am." His voice had genuine shame in it. An unwritten rule stated that there was no greater sin than for a surgeon not to have control of his or her bodily functions. One should be able to go two days without sleep, stand through a six-hour surgery without so much as thinking about defecating or urinating, and never, never call in sick.

The humiliation was evident in Jenson's face. It seemed he didn't need to go to the rest room so badly now.

There was some giggling and whispering among the medical students standing closest to him—the intern had wet his pants.

The Grunt whispered in Clark's ear, "Phase One of Operation Disimpaction is now complete."

Jenson never drank coffee on the wards again. If he had been hostile and suspicious before, he was now twice as vigilant. Clark found him impossible to work with. It was clear the intern figured out that something must have been in his coffee or his breakfast, but couldn't understand how it could have gotten there.

As the days passed and there was no word about any board of inquiry, he grew only more agitated. But that didn't stop him from doing his best to remind everyone around him of his brilliance and his clinical acumen.

"Did I ever tell you about the first abstract I had published in the *Annals of Surgery*?"

About twenty times, Clark thought as he pulled off his shoe covers and waited for Jenson to open his locker. "I think so."

It had been so easy. Clark had simply obtained Jenson's locker combination by watching him dial it— the intern had no reason to hide from Clark. That morning he and the Grunt had planted a little surprise for him.

"Well, I'll tell you, it was quite an honor," Jenson continued in a voice loud enough to be heard by a cluster of attendings standing four feet away on the faculty side of the locker room. Among them was Dr. Fenstermeyer, who never really liked Jenson, but couldn't help overhearing. "My work with fiberglass prostheses in mice was novel, I thought, but I never knew I'd gain the publisher's attention with my little side experiment in grafted bone splints. It was a simple concept anyway . . ."

Fenstermeyer made eye contact and so was more or less included in the conversation as the intern opened his locker. "We re-created a multiple comminuted open fracture in anesthetized rats. Then we resected the entire shattered bone segment and replaced it with—"

He stopped as he spotted what was within his locker.

So, too, did Fenstermeyer, who could see everything over Jenson's shoulder. He noticed the handcuffs first. They were dangling from a central hook in Jenson's locker, not two inches from the cherry-red negligee. It was a gaudy, frilly affair, all lace and bows.

Then they saw the pictures. Clark, who had selected them with the Grunt from a magazine they had purchased in an adult bookstore three blocks from the hospital, now busied himself with his shirt buttons, making sure he didn't let his facial expression show. He couldn't trust himself not to betray his emotions.

But then he had to look, and as he swept his eyes over the locker, he realized the Grunt had done well. Plastered over the sides and walls of Jenson's locker were pictures of men with men, men alone and naked and staring into the camera, even one shot of a man humping a lathered horse.

Jenson reached into the locker and ripped the pictures down, throwing them into a small heap on the floor with the handcuffs and the negligee. "Who the hell did this?" he screamed at Clark.

Fenstermeyer put a hand on his shoulder. "Pete, I'm not going to tell you my politically incorrect views about homosexuals in the Department of Surgery, but can you at least have the decency to keep your private fetishes at home?"

Jenson struggled away. "Sir, I am not gay."

"You don't have to explain anything to me."

"But I'm not!"

"Of course not." The attending patted Jenson on the shoulder, then walked away, shaking his head.

Jenson clutched Clark by his shirt collar. "Who did this?"

Clark blinked into the furious, scarlet face, into the bulging, bloodshot eyes, and shook his head. "You mean you didn't?"

For a minute he thought the intern would hit him, but then Clark remembered what this guy had done to Tracy, and he half hoped that the son of a bitch would. Because if he did, Clark would have the excuse he needed to lay into him.

But Jenson let Clark go, stepped back, and reached for the pile of garbage at his feet, which he dumped into a nearby trash can. The handcuffs made a loud clump as they hit the bottom.

Then the intern, his face red and his eyes watering, walked out of the room.

The Grunt appeared from around the corner. "What happened?" He sounded innocent.

Clark spread his hands. "I think Peter Jenson is gay."

"Really? Peter Jenson gay?" The Grunt leaned forward and whispered in Clark's ear, "Phase Two now complete."

Word of Jenson's homosexuality spread far and fast. There was an effeminate, black nurse the size of a linebacker who worked evening shifts and wore enough cologne to keep the ward scented during half the morning after he left. When Jenson was scribbling orders that night, the man sat next to the intern, pulled up his chair very close, and said, "I'd like a clarification of this insulin sliding-scale order."

"What's there to clarify? If his sugar's between two hundred and two forty-nine, give two units. If two fifty to two ninety-nine, give four, if three hundred to three forty-nine, give six, if over three fifty, give eight and page me. Got it?"

"Sure, Doc. That makes it much clearer now. *Much* clearer."

Jenson stared at the nurse. "You've been acting awfully strange tonight."

"Oh, have I? Well, you know how a girl can be."

Jenson blinked. "Brandon, you're not a girl. We've been through this before. Biologically you're a man."

Brandon waved a large black hand through the air as though to say, "Get out of here." "Biology can be so cruelly out of synch with my emotional reality." He leaned forward. "You know what I mean."

Jenson frowned. "No, I don't."

"Oh, but I think you do."

They were alone except for Clark, who sat three feet away, obviously too busy with the chart in front of him to be paying attention to them. But Clark could feel the tension mount. Jenson seemed on the verge of blowing a gasket.

"I mean," Brandon continued, "I heard you're one of us. Congrats."

The big hand was extended, but Jenson didn't take it. "Get away from me."

"Oh, now, don't get all sore. Sure, it's hard at first. After I came out, my family wouldn't talk to me for *weeks* and I thought I had lost every friend I had in the world. But people get over it. They either accept you or they don't."

"Came out?"

"You know. From the proverbial closet." Brandon reached forward and touched the back of the intern's hand, which was clenched into a fist. Jenson snatched it away. "We all know now."

"You do, do you?" The intern shot to his feet, pushing his chair back.

"Oh, now, don't be sore with a good old girl who's just a little lonely. Here. Think it over. When you feel ready, just give me a call, you hear?" Brandon slid a piece of paper with his name and number on it to Jenson. "First time I do everything. Whatever you want. Next time I'd like a reach around maybe, but I'm not real demanding."

Jenson's lower lip trembled. "You disgust me. Now tell me who else thinks I'm—I'm—"

"Queer? Gay? Different? One of us? Why the whole second-shift nursing staff was buzzing with it. And everyone on third shift knows, too. You're going to get many offers now that you've come out, so I just figured I'd get mine in first."

Jenson slammed shut the chart he was working on, flagged his order, and rammed it into the rack. As he was walking out of the nursing station, Brandon looked at Clark and shrugged. "You said he'd be more receptive."

"Give him time," Clark said. "Give him time."

Phase III of Operation Disimpaction now complete, Clark thought.

◆　　◆　　◆

It wasn't clear if he managed to find a slot in another surgical program or not. One rumor had it that the chairman just let the matter drop after the board of inquiry couldn't even be formed to look into the matter. There were too many bylaws and regulations and technicalities thrust in her path, and in the end she realized she must have been making too many men nervous.

One thing was clear, though: Peter Jenson had resigned. He more or less disappeared one morning, leaving his comrades in the lurch. The worst person for a program to lose was an intern, since an intern had a job that was so grueling, unrewarding, and poorly compensated that no one could be found quickly to fill the position. At the same time the loss of an intern meant the loss of a hell of a lot of revenue for the hospital, since an intern was expected to work over one hundred and twenty hours a week for the wages of another young professional working fewer than forty.

But he was gone, apparently sliding his letter of resignation under the chairman's door one evening around midnight, and disappearing thereafter. Where he went wasn't clear, but one thing was certain: he wasn't at Mount Rosemont Medical Center.

To Clark and the Grunt, the news brought cheers. They high-fived each other and grinned and realized they had managed to do something that the administration couldn't or wouldn't do. It was a small proof that maybe they were something other than work mules in the coal mine of surgery.

Tracy couldn't share in their triumph. She knew that the board of inquiry hadn't gotten off the ground and that the hatred toward her, sometimes hidden, sometimes overt, wouldn't stop. There were men she would operate for who would guide her wrist to position a retractor just so, then stop themselves and say sarcastically, "If I had held your wrist just a second longer, you might have screamed sexual harassment." She noticed how some would stop talking in the corridor when they saw her pass and stare after her coldly. "If you make one fifth the contribution to surgery or medicine that Pete Jenson did," one resident told her, "you'd be one hell of a doctor."

It went on and on like that and Jenson's resignation only intensified things. The next edition of *The Cutting Edge*, the medical-center monthly newspaper, was full of no fewer than ten letters to the editor about what a fine surgeon had been lost in Peter Jenson, including one signed by ten attendings. *If someone as promising and sharp as Dr. Jenson could fall victim to the shrill accusations of some disgruntled female medical student, then no one is safe.*

"I'm tired of it," Tracy told Clark one night as they were studying for the surgery final exam, which consisted of diagnosing a patient cold, as well as a written exam. "No one ever talks about what Jenson did to me, only what I did to him. It's as though he's the victim."

Clark rolled over on the floor of their house and looked at his watch. "Well, just think of it this way—you only have about twenty hours of their wrath to endure."

"But suppose this comes back to haunt me in some way? Suppose I need a surgery letter of recommendation? Who would give me one?"

Clark rubbed his eyes. "We don't need to worry about letters of recommendation for another year. We have to worry about this exam tonight."

She nodded and looked down at the textbook and notes sprawled before her, then immediately jerked her head up. "Suppose they fail me tomorrow?"

"Oh, Tracy, stop being so paranoid. They can't fail you—everyone knows you're one of the brightest students on the rotation. Neurotic maybe, but bright."

Tracy threw a pillow at him. "I hope you're right."

"Besides, Jenson is out there tonight probably looking for some surgery department that hasn't heard of Dr. Lauren Masterson."

Tracy smiled at that. "Fat chance."

FINAL EXAM

Clark realized it was hopeless the moment the patient opened his mouth. For one thing, the man they chose as "Patient X" sounded like he was from the bayous of Mississippi. He spoke with a thick, melodious, southern drawl that was almost impossible to understand. "So's like I's tryin' to 'splain, Doc. I might coulda mashed down heah and heah and done neah keeled mahself."

The story was far from straightforward. The man had a long history of diarrhea and cramping abdominal pain. His past medical history was significant for multiple colonoscopies, hemorrhoids, hernia repair, splenectomy for some unknown reason, cholecystectomy, appendectomy, and three exploratory laparotomies. "And not one of them doctors could tell me nothin' 'bout why I's so sick all the time."

Nor could Clark. He did a careful exam, with one eye on his patient and one eye on the clock—he had only twenty minutes for both the history and the exam. The man's heart and lungs sounded okay, he had multiple scars on his belly, which was diffusely tender, and he had a bulging right abdominal hernia. Clark scribbled all his findings down, thanked the patient for his time, then left the room.

Fremont was waiting for him outside. "So what do you think?"

"I think—well, I think he could have any of a multitude of diseases."

"Such as?"

Clark managed to generate a five-disease differential diagnosis. For each disease, he gave reasons why the man's picture fit the profile and why it didn't. For each, the reasons against were more compelling than the reasons for.

Then Fremont nodded, extended his hand, and gave a curt little smile. "Well, Clark, you were completely wrong, but you had good reasons to be wrong. You *thought*. That was more than some of your classmates, who thought they *knew*. As a physician, it's far more important to know what you don't know than know what you do, know what I mean? I've heard reports that you've got good surgical technique. You can think on your feet and keep your head. I've seen brighter students, but you were one of the hardest working. You get honors. Congratulations."

Clark pumped Fremont's hand and smiled gratefully.

Fremont frowned. "You look surprised."

"I was so baffled by the patient."

"You should have been. He's a hysteric. Managed to talk five different surgeons into opening up his belly for various and sundry symptoms. Nothing. He didn't fool you, though."

Clark felt a twinge of anger—so there was no right answer.

Fremont finished scribbling something on Clark's evaluation and looked up, narrowing his eyes. "You want something?"

"No, I was just wondering—don't you want my opinion of the rotation?"

Fremont looked almost surprised at the question. "No. No, I don't. Good-bye." The chief resident was still scribbling when Clark walked away.

Tracy was the next one out of the room. When she stepped out, Fremont looked up, arched an eyebrow, and asked, "So. What does he have?"

"Nothing. His symptoms fall under no describable pattern and there is some evidence of embellishment, maybe outright malingering. For a while I entertained some smoldering neoplasm or perhaps a parasitosis such as large-intestinal roundworm, but he has no travel history, and if this was a cancer it would have killed him already. Of course, before reaching any definite conclusion, I would insist on reviewing his chart and his lab work, and ensure that—"

Fremont held up his hand. "Stop. You've convinced me."

"Of what?"

"That you know how to think. I also just finished scoring your written exam." He sighed. "Did you obtain a copy of the exam beforehand?"

Tracy looked offended. "Absolutely not."

"Are you certain?"

"Definitely."

Fremont looked her up and down. "Well. You scored fifty out of fifty. A perfect score. I've never seen that before."

Tracy grinned. "I did read a great deal."

"As your classmates obviously didn't. They looked good in rounds, but their exam scores were pitiful." He studied her. "There are many people in this department who wanted to fail you."

Tracy's smile disappeared. "That would be rather difficult to explain, though, wouldn't it, given my exam score?"

Fremont remained stone-faced. "Don't get cocky." He

sighed. "I don't know what happened between you and Jenson and frankly I don't want to. But I must tell you about your performance on the rotation."

Tracy found it difficult to swallow. "Yes?"

"Your attitude needs serious improvement. There is more to being a physician than correct diagnoses and treatments. It's a hard, frequently unforgiving job. If you view yourself as a victim, you will always be one."

Tracy elevated her chin a notch. "I was molested."

Fremont scrutinized her. "Half the department thinks you weren't."

"I didn't think the truth was decided by majority vote."

Fremont stared at her another minute, his eyes narrow, his face inscrutable. "If you were molested, then you're one tough little lady."

"I would prefer to be one tough little *person*, sir."

For the first time that Tracy could remember, Fremont smiled. "Fine. One tough little person then. Congratulations. You get a high pass. Now get out of here."

Tracy knew she deserved better than that, but at this point didn't care. She marched out of the room into the hallway where her classmates were all lined up to see Patient X.

She saw Alicia, looking especially nervous and haggard, and who immediately dropped her eyes. "Alicia," Tracy said. "I understand your not wanting to come forward. It's okay."

Alicia looked up. Her eyes were huge moons. "No, it isn't. You don't know what he did to me."

Tracy looked away. "No, I don't. But he's gone now. He can never do it again."

"Are you sure of that?"

Tracy nodded. "I hope so."

The Grunt grabbed Tracy's arm as she walked away. "How was it?"

Tracy shrugged in a cavalier way. "All I can say is— surgery is over."

THE VOLUNTEERS

The weekend was too short. But it was one they would never forget.

After the exam Saturday morning, Tracy and Clark drove to the Atlantic, found a cozy little bed-and-breakfast, and blew more money in their first three hours out of the hospital than they had spent in the past two months.

It was worth it, though. They stayed out late on Saturday night, something they hadn't done in two months, and slept in late on Sunday morning, something they hadn't done in four. Clark woke up to the sound of seagulls and waves and the smell of brine. He nuzzled against Tracy's sleep-warmed body and they made love before either one was fully awake. Then they slept another hour, ordered a pot of coffee through room service, then made love again. It was noon before they rolled out from under the down comforter, shivering and naked, pulled on some sweats and running shoes, and took off for a run along the beach.

"We'll be on separate rotations next," Tracy said as her shoes slapped down against the wet sand.

Clark looked out over the Atlantic, sun-speckled and blue gray and hazy. "We'll still probably see each other more than we did on surgery. That was crazy, wasn't it?"

"We didn't have much of a life. Out of bed at four in the morning, every morning, for eight weeks."

Clark continued to stare at the ocean as he ran. "I wish I could take a piece of the ocean back with me," he said. "Just to take it out and stare at it every now and then when things get crazy in the hospital."

Tracy moaned and smiled. "That would be nice."

Clark slowed even more, then stopped and fixed his eye on a ship that had just poked its bow over the horizon.

"C'mon, Clark, you're dragging ass."

He looked at the ship, then back at her, and something in his expression made her stop, too. "What is it?"

He studied his hands. "Tracy, you know how they say you get to know your medical-school classmates better than you'll ever know anyone else in your life?"

She thought about it a minute. "I suppose that's true."

"I mean, we see each other at our worst, our best, at all extremes, under incredible duress at times."

Tracy didn't quite know where this was going. "Yes?"

"And I want you to know that the way you put up with everything that happened on the wards—well, it was just so"—he couldn't find the word he wanted—"admirable."

Tracy rolled her eyes. "Did you bring an airsickness bag, or should I just throw up all over the beach?"

"Look, Tracy, there's a point to this. The way I saw you endure, the way I saw you excel, well, it just confirmed what I already believed." He studied her face. "What I had already decided."

Tracy was absolutely silent a moment. A particularly large wave crashed into the shore, the foam creeping up to within inches of her feet. "Clark, what are you saying?"

"I'm saying that you're a quality woman, Tracy, as quality as I'll ever find."

She smiled. "You make me sound like beef."

"You know what I mean. I'm saying I want to spend the rest of my life with you. I'm saying I want to marry you."

Before the words had sunk in, he was down on one knee and the next wave roared in and soaked his sweatpants up to his crotch. He didn't flinch. "Marry me, Tracy."

She tried to pull him to his feet. The water was seeping into her shoes now—she would feel the wetness in a moment, but didn't care—and he was pulling her back, pulling her by the hands down into his arms. His lips tasted salty, his body warm against the late-October wind. She managed to pull away. "When? How?"

"I don't know. After this year maybe."

"And what would we live on? Don't tell me our love of each other."

"The same thing we're living on now."

Tracy was blushing crimson. "I'm one of eight kids, you know, and my father just retired. We might be on our own as far as the wedding expenses are concerned."

Clark was on his feet, running in circles around her. "Does this mean yes?"

She ignored him. "And the honeymoon—well, that will wipe us out for sure if the ceremony doesn't. And do you have any idea how much a dress costs? The cake alone might be a thousand bucks."

Clark squeezed her hands. "Oh, Tracy, you're talking logistics and I'm talking love! Just marry me, for Christ's sake! Just tell me you will!"

She turned to him and the sun peeked out from behind a cloud. Her cheeks were still scarlet and her heart was thudding against her chest wall. "Yes. Yes, Clark, I will."

But her last words were muffled as he pulled her into his arms and off her feet and swung her around and around. "I'll get you a rock," he shouted, setting her down and spreading his arms wide apart. "An enormous rock that will be so heavy you can't lift your arm."

They ran back to the bed-and-breakfast and peeled off their wet sweats and made love in the shower. They ordered a room-service brunch and ate it slowly with a bottle of champagne. They looked at each other over their food and smiled shyly, as though they had just met.

"We're going to be very rich one day," Tracy said.

"Oh, how can you think about money? Besides, they'll socialize medicine and pay us less than schoolteachers."

"At least we'll be comfortable."

"After we pay off our school loans." They clinked glasses.

Tracy smiled. "Do you think our kids will be doctors?"

Clark grinned at that thought. "Kids. Hmmm. So you think we'll have enough time over the next ten years to have kids?"

Tracy's smile disappeared. "I don't know. I hope so."

Clark leaned back on his elbows. "My college roommate now works for Motorola as an electrical engineer making over eighty-five thousand a year, with perks. He just sent me a picture of his second son." He rolled over and faced Tracy. "Can you imagine it? We won't be finished with school for another year and a half, and he's got himself a regular brood."

Tracy blinked. "And after this we have at least three years of residency."

"Probably another year or two of subspecialty training," added Clark.

"Then we'll be just starting out in a new practice."

"If there is such a thing as private practice anymore." Clark stared up at the ceiling. "How old will we be then?"

"I don't want to think about it."

"Neither do I." A dreariness descended on them both as they realized they had to head back. They were silent as they packed.

"I think I'll like obstetrics and gynecology," Clark said.

"And I'm sure I'll like pediatrics." Neither convinced the other.

"Lawyers," Clark said as they were loading the car.

"What's that?" Tracy asked.

"Lawyers. We will raise our kids to be lawyers, then let them make a living suing the hell out of us." He smiled. "Why did we choose this business in the first place?"

Tracy shrugged. "To stamp out illness wherever it might raise its ugly head."

"To help people."

"To show kindness and compassion to those in suffering."

"To accumulate massive debt."

"To work long hours for low pay."

"To work long hours for nothing."

"To work long hours and pay for it."

"To spend our adult lives in the hospital."

"Because we have nothing better to do with the rest of our lives."

They smiled and looked at each other and Clark asked, "So how does it feel to be an engaged medical student?"

"The same way it feels to be a nonengaged medical student, except—" She paused. "Except there are two of us to worry about now."

THE STUDENT INFIRMARY

▲

▼

She didn't smile when Clark entered the room. "Hello, Doctor," she said. Her lips were pulled into a tight blue line and her arms hugged her legs, now wrapped only in a sheet.

Clark blinked at her and knew at a glance that she dreaded this as much as anyone he had ever seen. He thought of explaining for the hundredth time that day that he wasn't really a doctor, but figured she probably didn't need to hear that right now. It was moments like these that made him feel very male, very much the stereotyped, cold, aloof doctor that he desperately didn't want to be.

The student infirmary was located in an older part of the hospital, where the heating system was unreliable and impossible to fine-tune. The temperature in the room was about five degrees below what would have been comfortable for someone in street clothes. For someone half-naked, it must have been a refrigerator.

Clark looked in her chart to get the patient profile, trying to ignore the look she gave him: Lisa Forebush, twenty-four years old, School of Law. It didn't surprise him that she was older and should have been more sophisticated. He had seen enough patients to know that dread of the pelvic exam had nothing to do with age or education; he had seen plenty of poor, inner-city school girls hop up into the stirrups without a moment's hesitation.

Her entire chart consisted of a single sheet of paper, recording her vitals and the reason she had come: *Pain on intercourse.*

Oh, boy.

Hers would be the fiftieth pelvic exam he had performed, plus or minus one or two. Since beginning gynecology, Clark's clinical universe had been restricted to one sex, one organ system. He had probably seen, probed, and examined more vaginas than even the most promiscuous of his friends in college ever had. Ninety percent of the time, it was easy to detach, to drape the sheets over the woman's knees, bring the examining light into the field, put on the latex gloves, and get it over with.

But Clark sensed this would be more difficult. The clinic was a zoo, and he had three other patients waiting to see him. The attending was trying to see four other patients himself. Since the resident normally covering the clinic had been pulled onto an inpatient service for the day, Clark was left alone. "You seem to know what you're doing," the attending told him. "Just tell me if you have any questions."

Clark was terrified at the prospect of overlooking a carcinomatous cervix or an endometrial cancer, but he and the attending had no choice: there were twenty-seven patients to be seen that morning.

Most of them were healthy college students, anyway, Clark reassured himself, out of the age range for most tumors. He had some room for error.

Now he looked at Lisa Forebush and wished he had more time to put her at ease.

She darted a quick look at him. "It's cold in here."

"I'm sorry. Can't control that." Technically, he was supposed to counsel her about contraception and the importance of self-examination of the breast, and several other topics, but his entire history had to come down to six questions:

"When was your last pelvic exam?"

"This is my first."

Clark nodded. It wasn't unusual for some women to wait until their mid- or late twenties to visit their gynecologist. "I see. Are you sexually active?"

She looked straight at him. "Sort of."

"Do you use birth control?"

She nodded quickly, like a bird.

"What kind?"

"Condoms."

Clark nodded and scribbled that down. "Have you ever been pregnant?"

She shook her head.

"And do you have any vaginal discharge, burning on urination, unusually heavy bleeding, or other problems?"

She looked down at her knees, poking out above the sheet. "My boyfriend and I tried to have sex the other day," she said. "We didn't get very far."

Clark waited for her to continue. "What happened?"

"He couldn't—that is, he only—" She looked at Clark again. "He couldn't get his penis inside any more than an inch or so. It hurt like hell."

Clark nodded, relieved; an imperforate hymen was simple to fix. It surprised him she didn't know that already. He was about to say something when she blurted out, "Look, if you're going to tell me it's my hymen or something, it's not. I examined myself down there and know that's not the problem. It's deeper than that."

Clark frowned. "Was this your first sexual encounter?"

"Yes."

It's her hymen, he thought, nodding politely. "Well, why don't I take a look?" He stepped out of the room to get some equipment, and when he came back, a nurse had helped the patient up onto the table. She was lying on her back, her feet in the stirrups.

"So," Clark asked, "have your periods been normal?"

Her hands were folded over her chest as though she were lying in a casket. "I never had a period," she said. "It's why I've never been to a gynecologist before. I was so embarrassed."

"Didn't your mother ever notice?"

"She didn't really ask. We weren't very close."

"I see." Clark focused on the area between her legs. "You're going to have to relax just a little more. There you go. I'm going to touch you first on the inside of your thigh. This is my glove." Clark had been taught that the first place he touched a woman during the pelvic exam should not be her genitalia.

Then he examined her. Everything was normal, although her hair distribution was a little scant, but that didn't necessarily mean anything. He asked the nurse for the clear plastic speculum, touched it to his hand to warm it up, then told her he was going to insert it into her vagina. He wouldn't do anything without first telling her, he promised.

To Clark's surprise, the speculum passed easily past her hymen into her vagina. But he hadn't advanced more than three or four centimeters when he hit something firm.

He looked up and saw she was holding her breath and closing her eyes. The nurse held her hand.

Clark thought it might be his angle, so he withdrew and reinserted. Again, he met resistance.

It was the strangest thing. He tried to visualize it, but as he parted the lips of the speculum, what he saw looked like normal vaginal mucosa—pink and moist and ribbed.

"Do you see anything unusual?" she asked.

Clark began wondering what could possibly be in there. Maybe some horrible tumor that he had read about in pathology, something that now obstructed her vaginal canal.

Or maybe—it struck Clark so hard he almost slipped off his stool.

He looked up and suddenly realized that that's what it must be. They had received a lecture on this just the other day.

"Is something wrong?" she asked.

"No. Not at all. Excuse me."

He had to get the attending for this one.

Dr. Bernstein was scrubbing his hands when Clark came into the room. He looked up and smiled. "Got things under control, Clark?"

"I have a little problem, sir."

"Oh?"

"Yes. I think I have a case of androgen insensitivity syndrome."

Bernstein was a small man with owlish eyes and a pleasant, round face. He now smiled at Clark and nodded. "You do, do you?"

"Yes, sir. She's never had menses, her pubic hair is scant, and her vaginal canal is only about four centimeters long."

Bernstein arched an eyebrow. "Is that so?" The thing about Bernstein that Clark liked was that he never sneered or was condescending. Although it was obvious the attending wasn't convinced, he respected Clark's opinion enough to hear him through.

The attending nodded when Clark was finished. "Let's take a look, shall we?"

"Hello, I'm Dr. Bernstein," he said when he stepped into the room, being careful to approach the patient from the head of the bed, where the examining area was out of sight. It was Bernstein who had taught Clark to be so meticulously attentive to the patients' sensitivities. "Dr. Wilson asked that I do a quick exam. Is that okay?"

Her eyes bulged as she stared at him. "Why? Did he see something wrong? Do I have a cancer or something?"

He patted her hand and smiled. Even Clark was comforted by the gesture. "No one said anything about a cancer. We're just going to take another look."

In a minute Dr. Bernstein repeated Clark's exam, nodded, and straightened up. "Well," he said to the patient, "you can get dressed now. Dr. Wilson and I are going to go out into the hallway to confer."

Although the exam rooms were full of patients waiting to be seen, Bernstein took Clark into a conference room and sat down. "I think you were absolutely right. I haven't seen a case in years, but that is almost definitely what this poor"—he paused—"woman has."

Clark whistled. "Woman?"

"Yes. She was raised as a woman, her whole identity is as a woman; to take that away would be devastating."

Clark was puzzled. "So we aren't going to tell her?"

Dr. Bernstein shrugged. "That genetically she's a man? No."

Androgen insensitivity syndrome occurs in the male fetus, when the part of the body that is to develop into the penis and testicles fails to respond to testosterone. By default, the external genitalia become female. The testes do not descend, but remain in the approximate position of where the ovaries would be. The patient grows into a woman, developing secondary sexual characteristics such as breasts and pubic hair at puberty. Since no uterus or ovaries are present, however, childbirth and menses are impossible. And since the person is externally a usually well-developed female, the problem is not discovered until puberty or later.

"But what about the risk of neoplasm?" Clark asked. "There is a high rate of malignant transformation of her gonads."

"True." Bernstein nodded his head. "So we must tell her that she has to undergo surgery. But we don't need to tell her anything more than that there is an abnormality of her gonads and that we have to take them out."

Clark looked around the room. A transparent plastic model of the female genital tract stood above them, mounted on a pedestal like a statue. "She's a law student. She's intelligent. She'll read about it anyway."

"Perhaps. That's her right."

"But it's also her right to know what she's got."

Bernstein leaned forward and patted Clark's hand. "And it's also her right *not* to know, Clark. *Primum non nocere.*"

"'First do no harm.'" Clark leaned back and stared up at the model uterus. "I wish we didn't have to make decisions like this."

"That's what we get paid for."

"And sued for."

"I'll do what my conscience tells me is right and worry about the lawsuits later. Let's go talk to her."

The chromosomal analysis came back two days later: Lisa Forebush definitely had androgen insensitivity syndrome.

PEDIATRICS

Tracy loved pediatrics. She found herself rediscovering a part of herself that had been lost in the mad scramble to get into and survive medical school. It was fun to be silly and playful with the children, most of whom seemed oblivious to the beeping IVs and to their diseases and prognoses.

Whoever designed the pediatric ward had done a terrific con job: most of the kids thought they were in some bizarre playground. One nursing station had been transformed via the magic of plywood and paint into an enormous train. Another nursing station had been made into a castle; the nurses had almost to duck as they stepped into and out of the sally ports. And the walls of the corridor were plastered with the artwork of generations of the ward's inhabitants.

Tracy didn't like to think that many of those young artists might be dead.

She settled easily into the ward routine. It was a scaled down version of internal medicine—"medicine for little people," her resident once called it. She was instructed not to wear a white coat (it scared the children) and encouraged to put a miniature koala-bear doll on her stethoscope. If they screamed, let the patients play with the stethoscope, show them it was a toy. Make a game out of the physical examination. Ask them to let you see the frog in their ear before sticking in your otoscope and making them scream.

Tracy grew to hate the diseases. It became almost personal. There was an inherent unfairness in the leukemias and osteosarcomas and cystic fibrosis striking before any of the kids had a chance to experience much of life. Tracy could rationalize an eighty-seven-year-old, after a full life, developing a brain tumor and dying; she could not understand why it should have to happen to a two-year-old.

So when she stared down at the chart of her latest admission, Timothy Cole, she found herself tensing up inside. "It's not fair."

Her resident nodded. "Poor kid. That's a shitty disease to have."

Tracy looked up. "What do you think his prognosis is?"

The resident, Monique Antiga, a black woman in a blue-and-white polka-dot dress, narrowed her eyes. "I've only seen one kid with that kind of tumor live past eight. It's a rare bird, though; there's not too much data available."

Then it hit her; Tracy stared at the name of the tumor and realized she had heard it before. "Oh, my God," she said under her breath.

"What is it?"

"Nothing." Tracy wondered if there might be some mistake. Clark had told her his type of brain tumor was exquisitely rare—and virtually curable by surgery and radiation therapy—but here was a kid with his exact same diagnosis.

And the child was definitely not cured. This was his

fifty-second hospital admission. He had undergone three craniotomies and several ventricular-peritoneal shunt repairs, but he continued to worsen. He had been admitted to the intensive-care unit four times over the past four months. His latest CT scan was positive for recurrence of the tumor. And his head circumference was increasing at three times the rate it should have.

Tracy plotted the child's head circumference, measured by the nurse that day in the emergency room, then double-checked it. The little dot she made placed him over the hundredth percentile for age; his head was huge.

"Can I see him first?" Tracy asked.

"Sure. I'll take care of some crosscover stuff while you get your history and physical."

Tracy liked Monique. The resident trusted her more than anyone she had worked with so far. After four months of surgery and internal medicine, Tracy was beginning to acquire some diagnostic skills, skills that were directly applicable.

Even to little people.

Now Tracy appreciated being left alone. She had to know what this child looked like. She knocked gently on the door and entered.

He had a head the size and shape of a bowling ball, but was only two. His eyes were enormous, round, and questioning. They filled with fear when Tracy looked down at him and his face crinkled up as though he were about to cry.

"No needles," his mother said, leaning forward and pulling the child into her lap. "No needles." She looked up at Tracy for confirmation. "Right?"

Tracy nodded. She introduced herself to the mother, who looked remarkably cheerful for someone whose son was obviously dying. Then again, they often seemed like that. Maybe it was ignorance, maybe it was denial, but whatever it was, something kept those parents' spirits buoyed.

Tracy stared at the kid, more in fascination than anything. His head looked as if it were too large for his thin neck to support. His arms and legs were sticks and his clothes sagged around his frame. She had only been on the wards for four months, but she had seen enough preterminal kids to know the end was near.

The light streaming in through a window was caught and reflected in her engagement ring. It wasn't much of a rock, but it was the best Clark could do, and it warmed her insides every time she looked at it. Then she looked at her patient and wondered if Clark might have looked like this.

No, she couldn't think about that. She cleared her throat and began the history. "So what brings you into the hospital?"

"The headaches," the mother answered. "They've been getting worse. He woke up last night screaming, clutching the side of his head, asking me why I couldn't make them stop." The woman's enthusiasm was gone now. Her voice caught and she had to look away. "What could I tell him?"

Tracy looked down at her clipboard, began to scribble. The pain could be broken into discrete, measurable units. When was the first headache, how long did it last, what is its frequency now, when did they first wake him from sleep? Tracy rattled off the questions like an attorney. She didn't want to think about this too much. She didn't want to get to know this woman.

And now she realized that she didn't want to get to know this boy.

But she was committed.

Tracy finished scribbling her notes and approached the child. He was like a bird, he was so small. He began to scream as soon as Tracy got within two feet. "Mama, it hurts," he said.

"It's the headache," the mother explained. "It's not just you—it's the headache now."

"I'll get a nurse." Tracy got up and walked out of the room. She flagged down a nurse by the ward playroom.

"The new patient in fourteen—Cole—needs something for pain."

"Don't we all?" The nurse winked, then smiled down at the boy she was playing with, a little Asian kid hiding behind the ramparts of the nursing-station castle.

Talking to nurses was always a delicate balancing act, since Tracy couldn't be too authoritative—she lacked authority—and she couldn't be too wishy-washy—the nurses would ignore her altogether. "He has an excruciating headache," she insisted.

"Oh, he does, does he?" The nurse continued to play with the boy at her feet, who was giggling at a face she was making. "Well, he won't get anything until his admission orders are written."

"Can't you just give him some Tylenol?"

"Not unless you got an MD after your name, which you don't."

For Tracy, this reminder of her own impotence was the worst part of being a medical student. "Fine." She spun and marched to the nursing station, then paged her resident, who gave the verbal order for some Tylenol.

After the patient swallowed the Kool-Aid-like suspension, Tracy gave him twenty minutes before continuing her physical exam. She listened to his tiny heart, wondering how long it would continue to beat.

It wasn't fair. It wasn't fair at all and she knew it was getting to her, taking away her clinical judgment. She should be detached, professional, but the little boy staring up at her in wide-eyed wonder, drooling over her stethoscope, could have been Clark.

The sunset caught and held in his blue eyes a moment. She wanted to scoop him up and kiss him.

But she didn't. "Well, you know the plan," Tracy said to his mother, straightening up. "We'll consult the neurosurgeons again, then see whether radiation oncology has anything more to offer."

The mother closed her eyes and shook her head. "No. No more radiation. I've decided he's had enough. They told me last time that if he got another five hundred rads, it would interfere with his ability to do well in college."

College. Tracy wondered if this woman's hold on reality was tenuous. If the tumor didn't stop growing, the child would die years before he would even know what the word *college* meant.

Tracy left the room, climbed over a foam-rubber moat to get to the nursing station, and began her write-up.

CONFIDENTIALITY

The music pulsated and bodies swayed in the lurid half-light. The smell of spilled beer filled the air. The medical students were packed in for the first Randy Nor'easter Party of the year.

Outside, ice patches and snow covered the roads. More snow fell each moment. The mayor issued a travel advisory, which the patients seemed to have heard; all scheduled admissions had been canceled and the emergency room was unseasonably quiet. The hospital was running on a skeleton crew and the students were mostly sent home, even those on call.

It was an unofficial vacation. And it was all the excuse the medical students needed to get drunk.

Randy's parties were like this, more statements than social gatherings. He never planned them, they just sort of happened. When the pressures on the wards, in the labs, and in the lecture hall grew too high, when tempers flared and the medical students stared at each other bleary-eyed over lunch, wondering why the hell they hadn't become a lawyer or engineer or something normal and sane, they knew it was time for a party at Randy's.

His apartment was on the eighteenth floor of the building that had been purchased by Mount Rosemont and rented out to students as dormitory efficiencies. The rooms were cramped but cozy and had that indefinable smell of old buildings. The common area had been converted into a dayroom of sorts and now beer sloshed on the floor as the students crowded around the keg and numbed themselves.

Tracy and Clark had no choice about the party; they were snowed in, so decided to sleep out the storm at Randy's.

"So the chief scared me," Randy was now explaining in a low voice. "After he said that about kicking me out for cheating, I went home and destroyed all my files."

"All of them?" Clark asked.

"Every one. Besides, making you guys look like dumb shits wasn't fun anymore. It was too easy." His small eyes flashed when he spoke and he tugged at his little ponytail from time to time.

Clark smiled as Randy handed him a beer. "There's hope for you yet."

Randy rubbed his eyes and yawned. "But I'm so tired now. I've never been so overworked and underloved in my life."

"Don't tell me—you're on internal medicine?"

Randy nodded. "What misery. And to top it off, my resident's insane. I mean really certifiable. He has all these crazy rules about nice guys getting bad diseases and Mr. Death being in the air."

Tracy smiled. "Jeb Morris."

"Yes!"

"He was my resident, too. The man is like fungus; he grows on you."

Randy's face suddenly lit up. "Hey! I just remembered." He reached for Tracy's hand and pulled it up into the light. "I'm sure there's a diamond in there somewhere. They say two months' salary, Clark."

Clark smiled. "Well, two times zero is still zero."

Tracy elbowed him in the ribs. "Clark, it's not that small and you both know it."

Randy grinned at both of them. "Well, congratulations!" He gave Tracy a little hug and slapped Clark on the shoulder. "And speaking of entanglements . . ." He looked over his shoulder, as though searching the crowd. "You guys haven't met my new girlfriend, have you?"

Tracy and Clark exchanged glances. "You mean Rebecca?" Clark asked.

"No, no. We're on to Lisa now. Rebecca was two women ago."

Tracy chuckled. "So what's the half-life of this relationship, do you think, Clark?"

"In hours or minutes?"

"Hey, this one's different." The tired look left Randy's face and he grew animated again. "She's intelligent and witty and kind and—God, she's a looker."

"Always an important asset," Clark said, tipping plastic cups with Randy. "So where is she?"

"Around here somewhere. She might have gone for a potato-chip run."

"Speaking of which," Tracy said, "I could grab something to eat myself. Where is the grub?"

"On yonder table," Randy said. "Help yourself."

"And help yourself for me," Clark said.

"Now there's a little something I wanted to discuss with you," Randy said as soon as Tracy was out of earshot.

"Oh?"

"Yes. Believe it or not, I'm having—well, women trouble."

"Say it isn't so."

"It is." The tone of his voice was serious, almost hushed. This wasn't a joke.

"What kind of women trouble?" Clark asked.

Randy looked around, making sure no one could hear

them. "It's kind of embarrassing to talk about." He spotted something over Clark's shoulder and smiled. "Wait—there she is."

Tracy, who had returned with two plates piled with pizza and potato chips, saw her first. She was a stunning woman, with coal-black hair and eyes the size of marbles, round and azure and glinting. She made her way through the crowd toward Randy. The woman was wearing a baggy Harvard sweatshirt over a pair of tight jeans.

Clark turned toward her and realized he had seen her before.

This wasn't at all unusual. Even in a large city, he frequently ran into people he had seen in the clinic or on the wards.

But then it hit him who she was and he suddenly wanted to run. She hadn't seen him yet, and he might be able to break away and talk to someone else, lose himself in the crowd, maybe find some excuse to sally out into the snowstorm.

"Look, I have to micturate."

"It's your prostate again, isn't it?"

"Very funny." Clark was backing away, almost safe, when she made eye contact.

It was obvious from the moment their eyes met that she recognized him. She walked up to them, her smile frozen on her lips, but her face expressing a mixture of confusion and discomfort.

"Clark," Randy said. "I want you to meet Lisa. Lisa Forebush."

Clark looked from Randy to Lisa and back again. Tracy, who had returned from the food table, frowned at him. "Clark, you're being rude."

Clark had been taught that it was a patient's right to pretend they hadn't met. But here it was so clear from the expression on Lisa's face that they had seen each other in the past that Clark couldn't pretend. He stood there limply, staring at Lisa's hand a moment before taking it.

She rescued him. "We've met."

Randy arched an eyebrow. "Is that right? You make me jealous. Next you're going to tell me that you slept together?" Randy addressed Clark. It was more an accusation than a question.

Clark blinked several times. "No. No, we didn't do that."

Tracy put a hand on her hip and shook her head. "Clark, what is it with you? Is Lisa an old flame or something?"

"No."

"Well, you're acting awfully strange."

Lisa avoided all their eyes. "He saw me in clinic, okay?"

Tracy smiled in a relieved way, as though asking, "Is that all?"

Randy studied Lisa, then Clark, and had a worried expression on his face. "Which clinic?" he asked.

Lisa raised her lovely eyes and looked directly at him. "You know," she said.

"Ah, yes." Randy nodded and looked down. "So Clark here knows—"

Lisa nodded.

"Look, I didn't know you were the boyfriend," Clark said in a whisper in Randy's ear.

Tracy was completely perplexed. "Will someone please tell me what's going on?"

"It's nothing," Randy said. "Nothing at all. Look, I've got this sudden thirst for a Bloody Mary. Anyone else want something from the fridge?"

Clark looked around. "Um, maybe I'll join you."

They hadn't walked twenty feet when Randy said, "Into my office."

The office was a tiny bedroom that seemed to have been partitioned off as an afterthought. "I know what she has," Randy said, closing the door and leaning on it.

Clark puffed out his cheeks. "What do you mean?"

"Oh, cut the confidentiality routine with me, Clark. You don't have to pretend. I know her diagnosis."

Clark stared into his plastic cup. "How did you find out? We didn't tell her."

"I'm not stupid, Clark. Lazy maybe, but not stupid. I knew something was wrong the first time we made love. Or tried to, that is." He stared out his room at an office building far away. It was a black monolith with only a few scattered lights blinking here and there like stars. "I ran the case by a friend of mine who is an ob-gyn resident. I told him I had an interesting patient. Then I did a little reading. It might have been the first time since coming to medical school that I actually entered the library."

Clark couldn't look Randy in the eye. He stared at a pile of laundry in the corner. The sleeve of a crumpled white coat poked out of the bottom of the heap. It was hard knowing so much about the girlfriend of a friend. He had seen her naked.

And he knew she was a he.

"Does she know?" Clark asked.

Randy shook his head. "She asked me many questions, but I wasn't about to tell her." He paused. "Or him. Christ, this is the strangest thing."

Clark managed to lift his eyes from the pile of laundry. "Why?"

"I mean, here I am, head over heels in love with a woman who's really not a woman, but a man who happens to be one of the best-looking women I've ever met. Except that she doesn't know she's a he, but I do." Randy slid down, his back against the door, as though safeguarding it against a sudden intrusion. "Does this make me gay?"

Clark shrugged. "I don't think so. Does it matter?"

"No."

"Do you love Lisa?"

"Yes. I really do."

Clark smiled. "Then that should be enough."

They were silent a moment. Then Randy asked, "Clark, who else knows about Lisa?"

"Just me. And Dr. Bernstein, my attending."

"Can you promise me not to tell anyone?"

Clark nodded. "Absolutely."

"And can you promise not to tell her?"

Clark thought about it a moment. "Of course." He could see the shadow of snowflakes falling against the lights beyond the window. "Do you think you'll ever tell her?"

Randy rose and turned to the door. "Maybe. One day. If she's ready." Then he turned back to Clark. "Let's get those Bloody Marys. I need a drink."

"I'm right behind you."

LABOR AND DELIVERY

The storm was a vicious one. It paralyzed the city and most of the East Coast for three days.

But it couldn't stop the rhythm of human life.

The first thing Clark heard as he stepped onto the obstetrics suite of Mount Rosemont Medical Center was a woman's scream. It was like nothing he had ever heard before, a high-pitched wail that seemed to come from somewhere deep inside her body. There was a rush of two or three people in scrubs who had been lounging around the nursing station. They pulled on gloves and surgical masks on the fly as they ran. "Room three's going. Yes, it's definitely room three." As Clark watched he was reminded of newsreels he had seen of air raids during war.

He was left standing alone. He heard the woman scream again and considered moving toward the room. First, though, he had to ensure he was in the right place. He pulled the memo out of his book bag. This was it all right.

Welcome to the wonderful world of obstetrics, he told himself.

The woman screamed again, and someone was screaming back at her, yelling for her to push. Just like in the movies. Everything except the mysterious request for hot water, the justification for which Clark never could find in any obstetrics textbook.

This was a pattern that was repeating itself repeatedly in medical school: he would read about something, cram for an exam or two, then forget it as he moved on to a new topic. Then, a year or so later, after the remotest traces of what he had once known cold were flushed from his mind, he found himself walking onto a ward where he would have to apply that lost knowledge to a living patient.

Today he expected to deliver his first baby.

He parked his gear and looked up at a chalkboard crisscrossed with rooms and names. Each name had a small graph by it, on which was plotted STATION and DILATATION. He knew those terms had something to do with how far down the baby was descended, but couldn't recall much more.

There was another scream now, this one different from the first, more subdued. Clark listened and realized it was coming from a different direction than the first.

So a second woman was going into labor. Funny thing was, though, no one was reacting to her the way they had reacted to the first patient.

The second woman screamed again. It was more a moan than a scream, a deep-throated groan. Clark paced nervously and stuck his head out the door of the nursing-station lounge. The hallway was empty except for a clutter of crash carts and monitors and various and sundry medical equipment.

He heard the first woman scream a final time, then there was another sound, a tiny cooing, and a baby cried. Clark grinned and looked at his watch. Another human being had entered the world.

He was going to enjoy this part of the course, he told himself. He just wished someone would give him the orientation that was supposed to have begun twelve minutes ago.

Then a man came racing out of the first room. His eyes were saucers, wild, darting, and searching as they scanned up and down the hall, the lounge, then finally came to rest on Clark. "Who are you?"

Clark noticed how red and bloodshot the eyes staring at him were. He couldn't make out any of the other features, hidden by a surgical mask, just the eyes. "I'm Clark Wilson, your new medical student."

"A student, huh?" The eyes blinked three times. They didn't register recognition. Clark got the sudden feeling he wasn't expected. "You ever delivered a baby before?"

"No."

"That's about to change. Room twelve sounds like she's going to go and the nurse and my intern are tied up in room three. Let's go."

Clark followed, his heart in his throat, wondering if this was some terrible mistake. He looked down and noticed that whoever he was following had blood splattered on his shoe covers and scrubs. Then he looked down at his own eighty-two-dollar leather shoes. They had been a Christmas present from his mother.

No one told him there would be so much blood at a delivery.

"I'm sorry," Clark said, struggling to keep up. "But there must be some mistake. This is my first day on obstetrics, and I was told there would be a two-day orientation to the basics of labor and delivery."

"Canceled," the man ahead of him said. "The weather has screwed everything up. Half the staff can't get in. Somehow, though, these mothers managed to." He waved his hands through the air, as though angry at their inconsideration, going into contractions in the middle of the worst blizzard to hit the Atlantic seaboard in decades.

Then the man turned around. He was shorter than

Clark, but with arms as wide as Clark's thighs. His triceps and biceps were clearly visible beneath the short sleeves of his scrub shirt. "By the way, I'm Tom Bakersfield, but everyone calls me Stump."

"Okay, Stump."

"I have been up since sometime Friday, and frankly, Clark, if one of my fellow residents doesn't make it in here to relieve me, I'm going to blow a gasket. You gotta help us."

"I'll try."

"You have to do better than try." Stump canted his head and studied Clark a moment. "You look like a large." He grabbed a scrub shirt and pants and tossed it toward him. "Step behind that cart and slip those on. No time for modesty. Then pull on some shoe covers and meet me in room twelve."

Clark did as he was told and pulled some covers over his leather shoes. Then he trotted down the hall and darted into room 12.

Many years earlier a Rosemont administrator had conducted a survey to find out why so many women chose to have their babies at somewhere other than Rosemont. The hospital's sterile environment was a popular response. So the administrators dreamed up this idea of the birthing room. A professional interior decorator was hired, who made up the rooms to resemble those in a comfortable middle-class home. The lamps and sofas and pictures on the wall and the carefully disguised monitors in the cherrywood entertainment cabinet almost made the women forget they were in a hospital. The only problem was that the interior decorator had never attended a delivery.

So as Clark entered the room, Birthing Room 3 looked like a murder scene. The lamp was tilted precariously up against a wall, pushed out of the way with all the unnecessary furniture. There were deep brown stains in the couch. Clark realized the stains were blood. The linoleum in the hallway gave way to carpet at one point, then linoleum again. The carpet was also deeply stained.

This beautiful birthing room, the dream of some well-intentioned administrator, now looked like some soiled, ransacked motel room.

Clark fixed his eyes on the woman lying in the stirrups, her skin black and glistening, her nostrils flaring each time she inhaled. She groaned, tossed her head from side to side, and arched her back. Her face could have been a mask of pain or of ecstasy; it struck Clark as strange that the facial expressions for the two were indistinguishable.

Her legs were in the stirrups and the sheet was thrown off. There was no modesty in this room. The pain made modesty irrelevant. Clark looked at the woman as the contraction made her writhe, then passed, leaving her to collapse back exhausted.

Stump snapped on a pair of gloves and peered down between her legs and into her birth canal. "Mark—"

"It's Clark."

"Whatever—get on a pair of gloves and get in here. I'm going to show you how to judge a baby's station."

"Its what?"

"How far beyond the pelvic rim it is. This baby is zero station. Confirm that for yourself."

Clark pulled on some gloves on and slid his hand into the woman's vagina. Something hard and slippery met his fingers.

"Feel it?"

Clark nodded.

"That's the baby you're going to deliver."

Clark remained silent.

"Don't worry—I'll talk you through it."

They pulled on sterile gowns and positioned themselves between the woman's legs. "You ever played catcher?" Stump asked.

"No. Shortstop."

"Hmm. Well, did you ever get a handoff in football?"

Clark nodded. "Sure."

"Then you know how to deliver a baby. It's the same thing, really. Just don't fumble."

The woman groaned and thrashed about and Stump

leaned forward and screamed at her. "You gotta push, honey, you gotta push! *Now!* Breathe it out and *push!*"

"I can't."

"No, you can and you will. Push!" Stump turned to Clark when the contraction passed. "Assess the station again."

Clark felt for the baby's head. "It's advanced a few centimeters."

"Good." The resident called to the woman, "You're doing great. Keep it up."

Another wave came, but the baby did not advance. Then another contraction passed, and a third. Stump blinked at Clark. "This may take a while," he said.

Then there was a new sound, a cry Clark didn't recognize. Stump rolled back his eyes and swore. "Oh, no. Sounds like room five. We just don't have the staff." He looked around the room, at the ludicrous sofas and lamps and mock bookshelf, as though expecting to find another resident or intern hiding somewhere.

Clark was curious. "How can you guys identify a room by the sound of someone's crying?"

"It's a talent crucial to obstetrics." He studied the patient, then looked at Clark. "Listen. I think this patient's stable. She's going to have contractions for a while without delivering. I have to check on room five. I've got no choice. Do you feel comfortable with that?"

"I guess." Clark's mouth went dry. "Suppose the baby comes out?"

"Then deliver it, Clark. Just remember—don't fumble." The resident peeled off his sterile gloves and gown and patted Clark on the back. "I'll be back in five minutes."

It was the longest five minutes of Clark's life. He sat staring at this woman's introitus, hoping to God a little baby wouldn't come popping out, and wondering how he would handle it if it did.

"Something wrong?" the woman asked between clenched teeth, taking her breath in sharp little sips of air.

"No, nothing at all." Clark chuckled and tried to sound cavalier.

"You sure now?" She studied him carefully. "You look like a nice doctor."

"Oh, I'm not a—" He stopped himself, thinking this woman probably didn't need to hear that he was only a medical student.

"What's that?"

"Nothing."

"You've done a lot of these, haven't you?"

Clark shrugged, hoped his ears weren't turning red. "I don't count them or anything."

"But this isn't your first?"

"Of course not."

"What was all that about not fumbling and football?"

"Just professional lingo. Technical jargon. I wouldn't worry about it. You're doing fine."

Clark didn't know how many lies he could tell. It looked as though she had plenty more questions. He found deceit painful, for one thing, but tried to tell himself it was for the patient's good.

Primum non nocere.

Lucky for Clark, the next contraction took the woman's breath away; she couldn't probe into his credentials or lack thereof. She stared at the ceiling, then clamped her eyes shut. "Push!" Clark said in his best imitation of Stump. "Push and exhale! Push and exhale!"

He was too good a coach. Clark was about to reach into the birth canal to assess how far the head had descended when he realized he didn't have to—the crown of the head was emerging.

It looked like a melon or a cantaloupe or a wet coconut. There was a scattering of hair matted against the scalp, which now protruded from between the woman's legs. Clark reached down and touched it.

Ohmygodohmygodohmygod.

He jerked his head over his shoulder toward the door, but Stump wasn't in sight. The woman in five was really howling now.

"Is it there?" the woman asked, gripping the sheet with

her hands so hard her knuckles turned white. "I feel it's almost out."

"It is."

The woman arched her back off the table as the next wave of pain swept through her body. Clark watched in horror, fascination, and, for some reason, joy, as the baby's head slid toward him.

All he could do was remember Stump's advice: pretend you're receiving a handoff. As stupid as it sounded, it was all the professional training Clark had on the art of delivery.

And it seemed to work. The football was slippery and heavier than he expected and very warm, but within seconds the whole thing had popped out and Clark realized he was holding a living, breathing human being.

Clark clutched it against his chest, feeling his heart pounding against it. He turned it over carefully and could see the tiny penis and realized it was a he and then the tiny shriveled-up face came into view. Clark smiled as he reached for suction to clear the baby's airway.

He didn't have to. The baby's tiny chest expanded, the infant inhaled deeply, then began to wail.

Clark was grinning underneath his surgical mask, grinning and ecstatic and rocking back and forth, as though he were the father and he had just brought forth the child into the world.

He almost forgot about the mother, her neck muscles flaring as she struggled to look down at her child. "Is he—"

"A boy. And he's fine."

The mother grinned and reached out her arms. She was trembling from fatigue and pain, but she wanted to hold her child.

There was just one problem. The baby was tethered to the mother by an umbilical cord and Clark had no idea what to do about that little fact.

He looked over his shoulder, but no one was in sight. Then he looked back to the patient and her face was strained again.

Clark thought there must be some mistake. Maybe she was having twins. What would he do then?

Ohgodohgodohgod.

He reached out for a table on which was laid a series of instruments. Very carefully, he covered the table with a sterile towel, felt it to make sure nothing sharp protruded, and set the baby onto the tray. The little boy still hadn't opened his eyes but began wailing all the harder as soon as Clark let him go.

"Is something wrong?" the woman asked again between breaths.

"No, nothing at all."

"They usually don't put the baby up there."

"Well, this is a new procedure."

"Oh."

As the contraction gripped her again the umbilical cord advanced. It was a slippery, gray rope that kept coming and coming and coming. Not knowing what in God's name he was to do with it, Clark gave it a gentle tug.

It came quicker, and before Clark completely realized what had happened, the afterbirth was complete and he was holding a huge, slippery, wet bag. "The placenta," he whispered, realizing there was nothing else.

Clark didn't know what to do with it. There was a sound like water falling and he felt warm moisture on the tops of his feet. He looked down to a see a tiny waterfall of blood flow from between the woman's legs. It formed a puddle at his feet.

Then the waterfall became a trickle, then stopped. Clark never remembered seeing so much blood, even in the surgery of a man who had been shot eighteen times outside a convenience store.

Clark decided to set the placenta on another tray and pulled the baby into his arms, wrapping him in the sterile towel. The crying stopped and the mother was watching them both, grinning. "Can I hold my son?"

Clark nodded. Just as soon as I figure out what to do with this damn umbilical cord, he thought.

"Aren't you going to cut the cord?" she asked.

"Not quite yet." He looked at the door—no one. "It's—um—a new technique, where we let the infant stay in contact with the placenta for a little longer to—um—improve his vital fluids." *Improve his vital fluids? Jesus, Clark, you can do better than that.*

A voice behind Clark made him jump. "So, are we any closer to delivering?"

Clark turned around with the baby in his arms.

Stump's jaw dropped. He stared from the baby to Clark to the woman. Then he rushed to the baby, checked its airway, color, movements, and a few other things, and smiled. "Well done, Clark, but you're not going to send this child home with his placenta attached, are you?"

"Of course not, it's just that—well, I don't know how to cut it."

The resident chuckled, ratcheted a plastic clamp in place over the placenta, and snipped it with a pair of scissors. Then he took the baby from Clark's arms and handed the infant to the mother.

Clark didn't want to let him go.

The resident slapped Clark on the back. "So how does it feel?"

Clark grinned. "It's pretty wild."

"It's birth, Clark. After dealing with all that death up on the medical wards, it's nice to be on the other end of the spectrum, isn't it?"

"Definitely."

The resident asked some details about the delivery, then showed Clark how to check the woman's vagina and uterus for any evidence of trauma or bleeding.

After the woman was cleaned, dried, and moved onto a gurney with fresh sheets, Clark asked her, "So what are you going to name him?"

She smiled. "Anthony. But he needs a middle name."

Clark looked at the boy, who was sleeping against his mother's chest, and realized what an awesome privilege it had been to be present to witness all this. "You have to consult with your—the father of the boy."

"Last I heard, he was in Texas somewhere." She looked up and Clark realized how pretty she was. "What's your name?" she asked.

"Mine? Dr. Wilson."

"No, what's your first name?"

"Clark."

"Clark." She tried that out and looked at her baby. "That's it. Anthony Clark Parker."

Clark beamed. He hadn't felt so proud since coming to medical school. This was better than getting honors in surgery. By God, this was a living, breathing legacy. "I'm honored."

"You should be." The woman turned to him and smiled. "Anthony is going to grow up to be a great man."

Clark had no time to linger. Another woman had begun to howl. "Room six," Stump said authoritatively, and they were off to another delivery.

Two days later Clark drove home, still wearing his scrubs and bloodstained, ruined leather shoes. The roads had been cleared now and enormous piles of ice-coated snow glistened everywhere. As he drove out of the city the snow became more pure and white, the salt and grime less evident.

He hadn't slept in forty-eight hours. He lost count of the number of babies he delivered, assisted and unassisted. He had never received a formal orientation, but probably learned more about labor and delivery over the past two days than he would have by spending two months in the classroom. He had helped or performed breech births, forceps deliveries, twins, triplets, and two stillbirths. He had cut a half-dozen episiotomies to widen the vaginal opening, and sewed them up again. He had taken two women to cesarean section and had completely lost any sense of time as he ran from room to room with Stump, who wasn't relieved until Tuesday evening, when the roads were finally cleared.

Clark watched the sun set as he drove, negotiating his car over ice patches and through piles of snow. Abandoned, snow-covered cars lined the side of the road.

He was completely oblivious to all that. All he kept thinking about was a little black boy out there who carried his name: Anthony Clark Parker.

"I am a father," he told Tracy as he walked through the door. She was sitting at the dining-room table, notes and open textbooks sprawled everywhere.

She looked up at him as it registered what he had said. "What's that?"

"I'm a father. A woman on obstetrics whose kid I delivered named him after me."

She smiled, but wasn't nearly as enthusiastic as he had hoped her to be. "That's touching."

"Touching? It was the greatest high I've experienced since starting this grind. Do you realize what this means?"

"Not really."

"Then I'll tell you. If I am crushed by a truck tomorrow—"

"Don't say that."

"—then I have a legacy that will bear my name after I'm gone." He pulled Tracy onto her feet and into his arms. "Tracy, let's have a dozen kids."

"A dozen? Shouldn't I have a say in this?"

"Okay. We'll negotiate. A half dozen."

Tracy pulled out of his arms and studied him. "What's gotten into you?"

"Obstetrics, that's what. You don't know what it's like to pull that wet bundle of flesh and amniotic fluid and blood out of a woman's body, towel it off, and hear it cry. It does something to you."

Tracy smiled. "Apparently."

He clasped both her arms and pulled her toward him. "Oh, Tracy, I want to be a father. I want us to fill this house with screaming, toddling, fighting rug rats. I want it so badly without ever realizing it."

"Clark, you're covered in blood."

"I don't care."

"Well, I do." She disappeared into the bedroom and reappeared with a robe and some slippers. "Get out of those things and slip into these. Toss the scrubs in the washing machine and those shoes—well, looks like they're a lost cause."

Clark gripped her shoulders. "Tracy, to hell with my shoes! Don't you hear what I'm saying? I want to make a family with you. Doesn't that idea excite you?"

"Of course it does, Clark." She turned away and sat back down at the dining-room table. "It's just that—well, there are some practicalities you might not have considered."

"Such as?"

"Such as, when are we going to have time to do all this child raising? Who is going to take care of our kids when we're both in the hospital?"

"There's day care."

"Twenty-four-hour day care? And who is going to pay for it?"

"We can borrow the money."

"Okay. And get even deeper into debt. And what about me? Pregnancy takes a lot out of a woman; I'll fall behind in my training."

Clark nodded as he peeled off his scrubs and pulled on the robe. "I hadn't thought it through, I guess."

"Clark, I don't want to disappoint you, but we are medical students. After med school, we'll be residents. We'll work over one hundred hours a week for the next five years at least. I don't see much room in there for a baby."

Clark lowered himself onto a couch and rested his chin on his hand. "Unless one of us drops out for a year or two and takes care of the kids full-time."

Tracy slapped her hand on the table. "I *knew* it would come to this! I just *knew* it! Why is it always the woman who is expected to quit what she's doing in order to start popping out babies while the man—"

Clark got up and placed a hand on her shoulder. "Who said anything about you dropping out?"

She looked up at him. "Oh, Clark, you couldn't do that. Medical school means so much to you."

"And so does having a family. If that's what it takes, then that's what it takes."

She smiled up at him and kissed the back of his hand. "You'd really do that?"

"Of course. I am a sensitive, politically correct man of the nineties." He pulled away and giggled. "And I want rug rats!" He swept his arms over the room. "A whole houseful of them!"

Tracy canted her head. "Get some sleep, Clark. We'll talk about it when you're less manic."

He smiled down at her. "So how's pediatrics?"

She looked away. "Fine."

He studied her profile. "You sound as though something's bothering you."

She sighed. "It's just that—I don't know. I'm tired of watching kids die."

Clark walked up to her and put an arm around her shoulder. "That must be hard."

She turned around and wrapped her arms around him. "Clark, Tim isn't doing well, not well at all. His electrolytes are all out of whack and he's getting neutropenic. The neurosurgeons won't touch him; they say he's inoperable."

Clark stroked her hair and was grateful he was dealing with the land of the living.

Mostly. He closed his eyes and remembered the two babies who came out dead, doing CPR with two fingers on their tiny chests, knowing that the bodies were far too blue, almost gray, ever to have much chance to live.

"And that makes you worried about me, right?" Clark asked.

"Maybe. He does have your diagnosis."

Clark sighed. "But that's where the similarity ends. My tumor is gone, Tracy. Remember that."

"I want to. I want to so badly. But every day I walk into his room, I'm reminded of what—of what could have happened to you."

"But it didn't." Clark lifted her chin and saw that tears streaked her face. She sniffled and wiped them away. "Tracy, maybe you should swap patients with another medical student. You don't have to follow this one if it's too painful."

Tracy shook her head. "No. Absolutely out of the question. If I did that, then people would think—"

"What?"

"That I'm weak."

"You mean that you're human?"

"In Rosemont Medical Center, it's the same thing."

Clark cocked his head back and laughed. "Tracy, we are being brainwashed, do you realize that? First we are told we should suppress our natural desire and need for sleep. Then we are told we shouldn't care if we don't have a life, if we spend every waking moment of every day and many nights in the hospital. And somehow it seeps into our conscience that if we have any emotions about our patients, it's 'unprofessional.' Well, being human isn't unprofessional."

She remained silent.

He pulled her away from the table. "Let's get the hell away from here."

"But I have to read about hypokalemia. Otherwise—"

"No buts. You'll go crazy if you don't take care of yourself. Let's go out on the town, have a nice romantic dinner, maybe dance in the moonlight."

She was about to say something, but Clark put his hand gently over her mouth. "We owe it to our patients."

She frowned. "How's that?"

"If we don't take care of ourselves, we can't take care of them."

She crossed her arms and grinned at him. "That's pretty convoluted logic."

"Maybe, but it might keep you from feeling guilty."

"It might. But what about you? When's the last time you slept?"

Clark thought about that. "Sunday night, I guess. Though I don't feel tired. I'm wired with caffeine and adrenaline and the desire for you." He held her in his arms and began to sway his hips, dancing with her in the living room as orange sunlight streamed in.

She laughed. "Clark, you make it sound so easy."

"It is easy. Just leave all that shit behind for one night and come dance with me and be my love."

She looked at him. "And we can all the pleasures prove."

"Exactly."

"All right. But we're going to regret this tomorrow when we have to roll out of bed at the crack of dawn, hung over and tired."

"I don't care about tomorrow. All I care about is tonight, and tonight I want to be with you and forget about anything medical." He smiled. "Except for a little boy named Anthony Clark Parker."

I'LL BE HOME FOR CHRISTMAS

▼

■t was too cruel. Thanksgiving had come and gone and now the castle nursing station was sprinkled with fake snow and icicles. An attending from pediatric hematology oncology, a small man who didn't look the part at all, went around ho-hoeing the children, who stared up at him, more terrified than amused, bald and tethered to IV poles. No matter how much they tried to get around the fact, Tracy thought as she wound down her final weeks of pediatrics, the hospital was a lousy place to spend Christmas.

She looked at the kids and tallied the ones that probably wouldn't be alive when she got back from her Christmas break. Six months earlier she might have been horrified even to think this way, but as she walked down the hallway mentally ticking off things she had to do, she tried to lay odds on how many cancer patients would survive the holidays.

It was almost comforting, this ability to detach.

Somewhere along the way she had picked it up. Somewhere along the way she had become numb.

She smiled at herself as she leafed through the pages of her clipboard. It was much better this way. She recalled the days when she had agonized over the fate of Thurgood's lung cancer. Now she had no idea where the man was, whether the chemotherapy had done any good at all. She had been too busy to devote a conscious thought to anything except surviving her rotations. She liked it better this way.

Someone was playing Christmas music. She recognized "Joy to the World" coming from the room of a child who had AIDS cerebritis. The virus had attacked his brain and made it difficult for him to do much more than drool. He was comfortable, though; Tracy and her resident made sure the morphine took care of that.

As the song ended and another one began—"I'll Be Home for Christmas"—she heard the loudspeaker crackle to life and a nurse's voice came on: "ALL PERSONNEL PLEASE WALK TO ROOM EIGHTEEN. PLEASE WALK TO ROOM EIGHTEEN."

Tracy froze for a second, before spinning and racing down the hall to Timothy Cole's room.

The signal to "walk to" a given room was a system dreamed up by the pediatrics department to stave off parental panic; it was a euphemism for a code 5, hospital speak for a cardiac or pulmonary arrest. The residents, medical students, and nurses rushing toward room 18 were doing anything but walking.

It reminded her of a scene from M*A*S*H, where the crew rushes toward helicopters laden with wounded from the front. Except the boy lying in the bed panting up at them was two decades too young to be a soldier and was dying not from a pointless conflict but from a pointless disease.

There were too many people in the room to be of much use. She bit her lip as the family was ushered out into the hallway. The child's clothes were ripped from his body and his groin was coated with Betadine as someone prepared to snake a central line into his body. Someone else hooked up the monitor from the crash cart and a third person was plunging a needle deep into his tiny wrist.

There was little shouting. Tracy was always amazed at how much the house staff and nurses managed to keep their cool. Codes brought them together, elicited a sense of teamwork that wasn't always evident in the day-to-day grind of running a pediatric ward.

"Let's get the oxygen flowing."

"Do we have an airway?"

"Yes, yes. He's intubated already. One hundred percent please. How are we doing on the femoral line?"

"He's got little arteries. Let me try the other side."

"What kind of rhythm we got?"

"V tach at about one fifty."

"Shit. Let's get the paddles ready."

"I got a blood gas."

"Who's going to run it to the lab?"

"Give it to the stud."

A *stud* was shorthand for student. Tracy was surprised; she didn't even realize she had been noticed, standing at the periphery of the crowd.

She took the tube of blood and it was only then that she realized how much this was affecting her.

It came out of the blue, this feeling, this reminder that she wasn't so detached after all. She looked down to see her hands shake, so badly that some ice from the cup in which the syringe had been plunged sloshed onto the floor.

"You okay, Tracy?" her resident asked.

"I'm fine." Tracy was angry at her body for betraying her. She was surprised she could even walk. She watched the tinkling lights overhead sway and swoon and she had to grab the wall for support as it hit her.

Timothy Cole was dying. The cute little boy with Clark's diagnosis would be in the morgue.

She was furious with herself, but it was all she could do to stand upright. She tottered down the hall, away from Bing Crosby's "I'll Be Home for Christmas," away from the snow-covered nursing station, toward the lab around the corner and down a flight of stairs.

She was almost there when she realized she couldn't go back. Not that afternoon, maybe never. The thought struck her as absurd, as ridiculous, as completely ludicrous—she still had ten phone calls to make and a dozen labs to check, for one thing—but it stuck in her head and wouldn't go.

She just had to run. She wasn't even sure why, but she just had to get away. They didn't need her at the code. Someone else would call with the lab results.

Now.

She dropped the sample off at the lab. "Code blood gas!" she called out.

A tech appeared from behind his machine and grabbed the sample from her. He whistled when he saw it. "Please don't tell me this is arterial."

"It is."

"It's dark."

"No shit. Can you run it, please?"

The tech frowned at her as he hit a few buttons and let what looked like a huge metal straw suck the sample up into the machine. There was a whirring and a rumbling, then some more beeping.

The tech whistled again as he watched the printout: "pH seven-point-two, pO-two sixty-one, pCO-two fifty-two, bicarb fifteen, met hemo-"

"Forget all that. What's his O-two sat?"

"Seventy-eight percent."

"Shit." Tracy scribbled down the numbers and ran back up to the code. She would give them the results, then run. She didn't want to see this, didn't want to bear witness to another pointless death.

She didn't need another reminder that the universe was a pointless, random place.

Someone from the crowd in Timothy's room snatched the blood gas from her and that was it.

"An amp of bicarb STAT!" someone called out.

"Let's get that femoral in—do we have a central line or not?"

"Continue CPR."

As far as she was concerned, Tracy had just performed her last duty as a medical student. She felt a million miles away from the group huddled over the little boy in the room.

No one noticed as she stepped away and slipped down the hall.

No one, that is, save the family, who stood huddled and bleary-eyed in the waiting area just off the ward. They searched her face for news, but Tracy had nothing to say to them.

She broke eye contact and rushed off.

▲ RESIGNATION ▼

"**A**re you sure you don't want to think this over?"

"Yes."

"The door will be open."

"That's okay. I'm never coming back."

The dean blinked at Tracy. The expression on her face reflected a strange mixture of sadness and seriousness. Tracy couldn't look this woman in the eye, the same woman who only two months earlier had congratulated her on winning a prestigious Rosemont Emerging Clinicians scholarship.

Tracy had expected a harangue, a diatribe on the virtues of commitment and the dangers of acting on impulse. But the dean offered no argument, made no attempt to change Tracy's mind. All she asked was: "Why are you leaving?"

"Because I want a life. I want to go to work where people don't die on you if you make a mistake, where you don't get spit on and bled on and"—Tracy hesitated—

"and shit on. I want to go somewhere where I'm not reminded every day of the terrible, unspeakable things that can happen to a human body."

The dean nodded, as though she had heard all this before. She probably had, Tracy realized.

The medical student leaned forward. "And I don't mind working hard—you know that—but this, this is abusive. It's too much. I can't go all the time, seven days a week, thirty-six hours at a stretch. I look around at the people who are supposed to be my role models, and I don't want to be like them—cynical and burned out and embittered."

The dean nodded again. "I have to ask this, Tracy, because it would be a tragedy if I didn't."

Tracy paused. "What's that?"

"Are you sure you're not depressed? When people are depressed, they can distort things. I mean, is it really that bad?"

Tracy remained silent.

The dean removed a piece of paper from the file in front of her. "Tracy, this is your transcript from Harvard. Not a single B. Did you know that I argued against your admission here on the grounds of this transcript?"

Tracy blinked at the dean. Why was she bringing this up now? "You did?"

"Yes. You see, my experience has taught me that perfection exacts a terrible price. I knew before meeting you that you were driven, a perfectionist, and harder on yourself than anyone else would ever be on you."

Tracy struggled to follow. "Ma'am, a little boy just died. I had nothing to do with his death, but—"

"But in some way I wonder if you don't blame yourself."

Tracy chortled. "That's ludicrous."

The dean was silent a moment. She wasn't angry, just considering Tracy's point of view. "Perhaps. Listen. Maybe you need six months off."

"No, maybe I need my whole life off." Tracy had had

enough of this psychobabble. She rose, pulled a folded sheet of paper from her purse, and handed it to the dean. "Good-bye. I'd like you to distribute this farewell letter to my classmates." She found it hard to swallow suddenly. "Or ex-classmates. And I'll be at this address. I want no one to disturb me; no one will pressure me into coming back, understand?"

The dean canted her head. "Sounds as though you're not terribly confident in your decision."

Tracy found herself wavering a moment. She stared at the dean through a film of tears as she thought of Clark and the Grunt and Randy and Alicia and all the others she had struggled so long with.

For what?

She couldn't think about that now. "Please. Tell them good-bye for me. Promise me you won't tell them where I am."

The dean sighed. "On one condition. If you promise to call me in six months, no matter what decision you make."

Tracy thought about that. "I'll consider it. But I really don't know. I really, really don't know."

She tried to remember what Timothy Cole looked like before he died, but all she could think of was Clark.

If she didn't do this now, she would never have the strength.

She lowered her head as though charging a battering ram and marched out of the dean's office. She saw a cluster of her classmates standing by a candy jar set up outside of financial aid. They waved to her and she felt stabbed by a deep sense of betrayal.

She waved to them, then walked quickly away.

▲
DEATH
▼

Clark pulled his overcoat over his scrubs and barreled down the hall. He had seen enough.

He tried to pretend it hadn't happened, or that if it had, he hadn't seen it. Every time he blinked, though, he saw her as she was, the moment they stopped the code, the moment they all sagged at the side of the mother who had become a patient who had become a body.

As a student, his curse was to have time to think. The intern was busy with the death certificate. The nurses were busy with the shroud kit. The family was busy with the first waves of shock and grief, having just been told.

"Clark, where you off to?"

It was his chief resident, scribbling something in the woman's chart at the nursing station.

"Don't know exactly," Clark said, buttoning his coat. He really didn't.

The chief resident eyed him a moment, then nodded, as though understanding, and continued writing in the chart. Maybe he had seen this before. Maybe he had walked out himself, years ago.

Maybe he wanted to now.

As he marched down the corridor Clark found himself reviewing the case, looking for clues. Who was she? A twenty-three-year-old mother, no previous medical history. Did she have any warning? No. None whatsoever. Did she know about her baby before she died? Yes. She asked them to show it to her and they wouldn't and she must have known then. Everyone in the room must have known. The father, standing not ten feet away, his eyes blank behind a surgical mask, the grandparents waiting in the hall as the pediatricians sucked the secretions from the baby's mouth and slapped it and rubbed it and turned it over and tried to get it to breathe.

Him. It was a him, not an it. Clark remembered the little blue penis, like a miscolored green bean.

So how did she die? Massive hemorrhage. They could have stopped it; this was a major medical center. But they didn't. They tanked her up with unit after unit of blood, with normal saline wide-open, they rushed her to the OR, but she never made it.

There was a hum and a whir and the automatic doors to the maternity entrance of the hospital slid open. The blast of November air hit Clark like a wall, enveloped him, reached down into the space between his collar and his skin, chilling him. He pulled the coat tight, but it was too large and the scrubs were too thin. He felt a wetness on his legs that he hadn't been aware of before, an icy wetness now, and looked down and saw her blood.

It was just a splatter or two, not enough to make him turn back and change. He pulled off his shoe covers, though, and tossed them into a trash can. They were saturated with blood, damp in his hand.

His fingers felt naked. He thought of all the bad things he could get from direct contact with the woman's fluids: HIV. Hepatitis B. He let the shoe covers drop and walked on, against the wind that ricocheted against the hospital wall and slapped him in the face.

He had no idea where he was going. He didn't want to know. He just wanted to get away, to put the hospital behind him, to forget.

In another block he would come to the burned-out neighborhood that used to be a working-class section of town, centered on an old brick textile mill. He tried to imagine men treading home, slapping each other on the back, making plans: bowling, a bar, a night with the family.

They were all gone. The mill was shut, condemned, surrounded by a perimeter of barbed wire and Cyclone fencing. Now there were just blackened buildings, the glassless windows like gaping spaces where teeth used to be, and lawless row houses with paint stripped off by years of rain and sleet. A female medical student had been raped here last year while jogging. A memo had been circulated that the neighborhood was off limits to students.

Clark didn't care.

The block was empty. There would be no rapes today. It was too damn cold.

He clamped his eyes shut against the cold and there she was again, staring up, her lips parted, looking a little surprised, a little tired, a little peaceful, as though they had told her she would have to stay an extra day or two before taking her baby home.

Her baby. Clark remembered the way they packaged him—it was the only way to describe it—the way they took him away and he was the wrong color, all blue and not moving and dead maybe for hours inside her, his cord twisted wrong, a question of not enough blood, not enough oxygen, death in the dark of her.

He tried not to think of the grandparents in the hallway, of what they must be going through, of the plans they must have made. He remembered seeing a gift as he walked past, a mobile of toy bears.

He knew on any other day he could have handled this,

it wouldn't have gotten to him. But what he discovered the night before sucked away all his emotional reserves.

Tracy was gone. Her note was short, cryptic, almost intentionally mysterious. She loved him, she needed time, she didn't know when she would come back. Maybe she never would, maybe that's just the way things had to be. She couldn't face him after leaving because she would have stayed for him alone and she thought both deserved better than that.

Frankly, he had no idea what she was talking about. All he knew for sure was that she was gone and that he didn't have the time or energy to make any more phone calls.

No one claimed to know where she was.

Well, the block wasn't entirely empty. A black man sauntered toward him, appearing around the corner in an oversized parka. Clark wasn't scared, just cold. He nodded toward the man as he approached, breaking rule number one, making eye contact.

The man nodded back, smiled. "Whassup?"

"My blood pressure."

Clark was going deeper and deeper into this city he hardly knew. It was a city he had only driven through. For him it was a large black box, a grid of streets and buildings and housing projects that provided a steady flow of patients into the emergency room and wards.

The worst thing was that the baby had a name. Clark forgot it, but the mother had discussed it with the father, arguing about it, teasing him with the sound of it, hours before she died. He was glad he couldn't remember it.

There was a whole block of rubble. Unbelievable. An entire building had collapsed, leaving nothing except a hole in the ground, piles of stone and mortar and glass. A fence topped with concertina wire encircled the site, but there were holes in the fence.

Clark had seen pictures of bombed-out European cities after World War II. Billions had been spent and the damage was gone, but there had been no war in the United States.

Not an overt one, none that was ever declared. No Marshall Plan for this town.

Clark wasn't cold anymore. He was angry and tired and disoriented and a little scared. Where the hell was he? There was a fire burning in a trash can. Three men huddled around it, their palms held outward.

He remembered the way she blew the hair from in front of her face when the contractions began, the way her husband gripped her hand and said to push, the way she told him to go push himself, the way she began to question his parentage when the pain became too intense.

The way her hair was plastered with sweat against her forehead six hours later when the contractions wouldn't stop and something wasn't quite right.

The buildings were better now, intact, with windows. Clark passed the lobby of an apartment complex. A concierge in a ridiculous maroon uniform, cap and tassels and all, stared out at him. Clark waved. The man ignored him.

He walked on, then came to a central plaza area, all brick, with a sunken fountain and a flock of pigeons. The birds huddled together, picking at the ground.

There was a long row of stores on either side of an open area, just beyond the plaza. Clark walked into the first one, not realizing how cold he was until the sauna-like heat hit him.

"What'll it be?" The woman behind the counter looked him up and down, not at all pleased, and he realized he must have made a strange sight. There was more blood on his scrubs than he originally thought, and some had rubbed off onto his coat. His hair was plastered against his head, and a surgical mask still dangled from his neck. He caught a glimpse of himself in a mirror behind the counter: a wide-eyed, confused medical student stared back at him.

"Two-dollar minimum purchase to eat in here," the woman said. "Otherwise you gotta take it out there." She stabbed a fat finger toward the cold beyond the storefront glass.

He had stumbled into a bakery.

"I'll take three of those, one of those, and a coffee." He was hungry, voraciously hungry, and the éclairs and pastries were calling to him, little Sirens of dough and sugar.

Then he reached back for his wallet, and realized he had left it in the delivery-room locker room. The only money in his possession was a collection of quarters he had stashed in his coat for the laundromat. He counted them: five.

"Look. I only got a dollar twenty-five."

"That'll take care of the coffee. I suppose I should put these back."

Clark nodded. "Sure." He felt sick, a little humiliated. Christ, he wanted to eat. He just wanted to sit, sip at his coffee, and eat.

The woman hesitated before putting back the final éclair. "Here, kid. You look like you had a rough night."

"I don't have enough."

"Don't make me offer it twice. Now go sit and don't tell my boss." She took four of his quarters and slid him back the last one. "You might need that for a phone call or something."

Clark left it on the counter, backed away, dug into the éclair before he was seated. His faith in humanity had just risen a notch.

Half the éclair disappeared in his mouth before he had even sat down. He tried to remember the last time he had eaten: maybe lunch the night before. Three deliveries in a row had made him miss dinner.

The coffee was too hot; it burned his tongue as he sipped at it. The pain didn't bother him as much as the fear that he might not be able to taste the other half of the éclair.

He had no ice water, so grabbed two napkins and pressed them to his tongue. It was like that, with his tongue half stuck out, wrapped in paper, that he saw her.

She was sitting at the next table, holding a Styrofoam cup with two mittened hands. She had been blowing on it to cool it, but as Clark made eye contact with her she began to laugh. Her eyes crinkled up and almost disappeared. "Do those napkins taste good, Doctor?"

Clark frowned at her, tried to pull the napkins away, but they ripped apart in his mouth, part of the paper clinging to his tongue. He spat it out. "Where do I know you from?" Clark tried to sound dignified.

"You mean you don't remember?" Without being asked, she rose, walked toward him, and sat down across the table.

"No, I don't. And I'm not a doctor."

"Oh, I know that, but you're close enough for government work." She winked at him and brushed her black hair behind her ear.

Clark looked around the bakery; they were alone except for a man in a pinstripe suit reading the *Wall Street Journal*. "Who are you?"

"I still think you can remember, if you try hard enough."

Clark rubbed his temples. "Give me a hint." He bit into his éclair.

"All right." She leaned back and cocked her head. "Try imagining me naked."

It was only with supreme effort that Clark kept his mouthful of éclair from shooting across the table at her. "Look, I think you have me confused with someone else."

"No. No, I don't. You're Dr. Wilson, right? Clark Wilson, if I might be so bold."

Clark examined her cockeyed. "You were a patient of mine?"

"Yep."

"What service?"

"Gynecology." She looked around, then leaned forward. "You did a pelvic on me, then put me on the pill. Remember? It was only three weeks ago. The student infirmary?"

Clark felt his ears redden. Was there anyone on his gyn service that he *hadn't* run into? If she had met him in the safety of the hospital, it would have been different, but this was not his turf. And something about her threatened him. "I think I remember now." He didn't. He saw so many patients on that service, doing pelvic exams assembly-line fashion, until he thought he never wanted to see a set of female genitalia again.

Well, that was a lie.

"I'm Julie," she said, extending a hand. "Julie Bradshaw. I'm a law student."

Clark shook her hand. It felt soft and warm against his. "Well, I'm glad to meet you—again, I suppose."

She arched an eyebrow, leaned forward, and put both elbows on the table. "You look beat. Long night?"

Clark nodded. "Long morning, too."

Julie looked at her watch. "It's only eight-thirty."

"Exactly."

She smiled at him. Her teeth were crowded together and her nose was peppered with freckles, but there was something about the way she held herself that made Clark smile back.

"So how many lives did you save last night?" she asked.

Clark wadded his napkin up and lobbed it into a trash can. "I guess I was three and two for the night."

Julie frowned, but Clark didn't explain.

"I'd rather not talk about it. That's why I came here."

She looked around. "To get away for a while?"

"No. To get away forever. I quit." He liked hearing himself say it out loud. The thought had been echoing, bouncing off the inside of his mind, brewing inside him all the long walk over.

"Wow. It really was a rough night."

"Like you wouldn't believe."

She nodded. "So you're playing hooky?"

"No, I'm done. Finished. It's over."

He was half-disappointed when she didn't argue with him. Instead, she reached for her handbag, a black square number Clark hadn't noticed, and asked, "So what do you want to do?"

Clark grinned at her. "With you?"

She pulled out a map of the city and spread it on the table before them. "Now. We could hit the Arts Festival—it's winding down, but should be good, even on the last day. My roommate loved it. Another option is the Woody Allen marathon session over in Bakersfield. Of course, we could always—" She stopped when she saw the way Clark stared at her.

"You're quite serious?"

"As a heart attack. Or maybe I shouldn't say that around you."

"I don't know you."

"No, you do. You've seen more of me than most guys I've gone out with the past year would probably have liked to."

Clark didn't know what she was talking about, then remembered: the stirrups. It was at that point that he recalled her, the way she yawned her way through the exam, laughing at his nervousness. "Don't you feel weird about this?"

"No, I feel—I don't know—invigorated."

"But what about your classes?"

"Maybe I'll quit, too." She winked at him. "For today at least."

He looked at his watch, or at the spot on his wrist where it should have been, then back at her. "The only thing I've got that's mine is my underwear, socks, shoes, and coat."

"That's a start."

"I'm tired."

"Then I'll get you another coffee." Before he could stop her, she was at the counter, pointing, ordering, directing. She flashed a twenty, then turned around with an armful of pastries, swaddled in napkins like a plump baby.

Baby. Jesus, there she was again, lips slightly parted, staring up, eyes not quite dead looking yet, a grayness creeping into her. The sound of the shroud kit being zipped up. They were tagging her toes and her fingers and her hair with identification labels before sending her down to the morgue.

"You okay?"

Clark blinked twice and he was staring across the table at Julie, who had pushed three éclairs over at him.

"I'm fine."

"Sure?"

"Yeah. I can't eat these." It was true. His appetite had disappeared somewhere in the time it took her to get up and get to the counter.

She canted her head and shot him a maternal look. "Now, now. I saw the way you scarfed down the first one."

"That was enough."

"Eat just one. I'll take the rest home in a box."

He chewed on it, feeling the goo coat his throat, washing it down with his coffee. "Are you going to sue me if I don't?"

"One day maybe."

The wind hit him without mercy. There was a pitiful excuse for a sun, a pale, bleached orb hanging half-mast in the November sky. It did nothing to warm him.

"Here's my bomb," she announced, with a flourish of her mitten.

They stopped at a gray-blue ship of a car, not at all what Clark expected. "It's not a BMW."

"Are you disappointed or impressed?"

"Impressed."

"It's the family tank. Gets two miles to the gallon, but could absorb a broadside by a truck and you wouldn't notice."

The vinyl felt cold against his legs and back. He tried to bury himself deeper into his coat.

The engine coughed to life. He looked across the wide expanse of space separating them. Her profile was quite pretty, especially when she tried to brush back her hair with her mitten. "I remember you now," he said.

She smiled, darted a look at him, then put the car in gear. "I knew you would."

"I'm really not supposed to be doing this, you know."

"Doing what?"

"Going out with patients, or former patients."

She shrugged. "But you quit, remember?"

"That's right."

He sank back as the engine warmed up and the first blast of heat filled the car. The sun felt warmer through the windshield glass. His eyelids were heavy. It was as though every pothole, every bump in the road, were jolting them closed.

He was floating through the hospital now, everything in a haze, all warm and out of focus. He was in her room and they were taking off her arms, unscrewing them at the shoulders and putting them in garbage bags. Yet she didn't seem to mind, just stared up, her lips parted.

"I'm sorry," Clark said.

She was almost completely disassembled now, just a torso and a head. A mannequin.

"I'm sorry," he said again, but was jostled by a workman pulling her apart. A sound in the next room made him start.

It was the cry of a baby, the wet trill of new life. He ran into the room and saw the infant on its back in a patch of sunlight, moving all four limbs at once as though trying to swim through the air.

Clark turned back to the mother, but her head was gone. She was now just a torso. When he tried to grab the workman holding her head, he pushed him back and pinned him to the seat.

It was cold again.

He woke up looking into Julie's face. There was a whole constellation of freckles, he noticed, galaxies of tiny brown stars spread across her pale nose, cheeks, and neck. "We're there," she said.

He got out of the car and staggered into the cold again, over a sidewalk, and into a plain, red-brick building with only a few windows breaking up the facade. She unfastened three dead bolts and pushed him ahead of her into the apartment.

"It's not much," she said, "but for the money, it's a real find."

They stood in a three-story-high vestibule. Clark stared at the hardwood floor, then overhead at a domed skylight, dirty at the edges with a small collection of leaves.

"It used to be a warehouse," she said. "Let me take your coat."

The walls were bare red brick. They were adorned with the staple middle-class prints: a Monet, a Matisse, and a black-and-white photograph of a man and woman embracing in a train station. Farther on, toward the interior, hung a watercolor Clark didn't recognize.

"Who painted that?" he asked.

"Me."

"You paint?"

"I try." Julie disappeared with their coats and called from the other room, "What can I get you to drink?"

"Nothing."

Nothing in her place looked expensive or lavish, but everything seemed handpicked, carefully chosen: a cedar bowl here, a vase there with a collection of dry flowers, an antique sign for some nineteenth-century skin lotion: IT PRESERVES, IT BEAUTIFIES, IT HOLDS THE PROMISE OF YOUTH.

He remembered her skin again, the way it seemed to gray at the edges, the way her lips turned blue after several minutes of lying there.

"You okay?" She was back with a short, fat glass of something.

"Just tired." He took the glass and sniffed at it. It brought back memories of his mother, of nights she entertained, the glasses she left out that he sniffed as he took them back to the kitchen: sherry.

"It'll warm your insides. Drink."

She was right. Within a minute of emptying his glass, he felt the cold leave his body.

"Do you live here alone?"

"Now I do."

Clark thought of pursuing that, but didn't. He simply didn't have the energy. He glanced at her white leather couch and was more aware than ever of the blood on his scrubs. He felt filthy, permeated by an ambience of death. He didn't want to touch anything.

She seemed to sense his discomfort. "Let me get you out of those."

"Do you have any normal clothes?"

"Tim left a few things behind. He was about your size." She ran up what was more a ladder than a flight of stairs to a loft overhead. Clark could hear her up there, moving around, opening drawers.

"Who's Tim?" he called up to her.

"My ex."

"Boyfriend?"

"No. Husband." She trotted back down and handed him a towel and a bar of soap. "Does that bother you?"

"I don't know yet." Clark was beginning to feel uncomfortable standing in this strange place with a strange woman away from the hospital. Maybe he should return.

But there was no harm in just taking a shower, rinsing off the smell of the hospital.

"The bathroom is the third door on the right," she said.

It was a tiny room, done in peach, seeming to glow as he flipped on the light. Even the towels matched the shower curtain and walls. The onslaught of water made something inside Clark relax. His eyelids grew heavy as a thick mist enshrouded him.

It was when he was almost asleep, leaning against the tiled wall of her shower, that he began to think of Tracy.

He hadn't thought of her for hours, had tried not to, had hoped that maybe if he just blotted her out of his mind and focused on what was in front of him, this nightmare would end and he would return home to find she'd come back.

But she was gone and he had to face that.

He ran the bar of soap over his body and realized what a ridiculous position this was. Here he was, in the apartment of a strange woman, just to avoid the prospect of going home alone. Clark was terrified of loneliness.

He had seen too much of it in the hospital, the ultimate loneliness, the loneliness of death. His patients might be surrounded by a hundred family members, but when they died, they died alone. He could see it in their eyes and he realized that's what it was.

And it hit him just as he was shutting off the water that that's what it must be.

Timothy Cole.

Tracy couldn't stop thinking about him at the beginning of the rotation. They would go out to dinner and she would take him with her. He would ask her what she was thinking about as she gazed off at something across the restaurant and she would smile and say nothing, but he knew. He knew that she couldn't forget the boy who had Clark's tumor.

"That's it!" he called out, toweling himself so vigorously he almost gave himself a friction burn.

"What's that?" Julie called.

"The reason Tracy left. Something must have happened to—" He cut himself off. "Do you have a computer?"

She appeared from around the corner with two steaming mugs. Handing one to Clark, she answered, "Yes, I do. Who's Tracy?"

"My fiancée."

She arched an eyebrow. "Oh."

"Look. I shouldn't be here, shouldn't be here at all."

"Do you want to go back to the hospital?" She sounded disappointed.

"Eventually. Maybe. Look, does your computer have a modem?"

"Yes."

"Do you mind if I access the computer's patient database?"

Julie frowned. "Not at all. If you know how. It's the

second door on the right. I haven't powered it up since my parents gave it to me as a graduation gift from William and Mary."

Clark sipped at the hot chocolate and burned the tip of his tongue. He didn't care.

The scalding liquid sloshed around as he trotted down the hall and stepped into the room. Within a minute he had turned on the computer and worked his way through a maze of screens to access the initial database screen. "Erich taught me how to do this once. Aha! Now let me type in the patient's name and—"

There was a blinking WAIT . . . prompt at the bottom of the screen. After twenty seconds, the prompt disappeared and the screen filled with a long string of Coles. Clark scrolled through them, holding his breath: if Cole was dead or discharged, his name would not appear.

Cole, Robert James	38 y/o	BPH
Cole, Samuel Williams	78 y/o	CHF
Cole, Timothy Anderson	2 y/o	glioblastoma

Clark grinned. "Well, he's alive at least."

Julie was behind him now, her hands on his shoulders. "Who?"

"Tracy's favorite patient. I bet that's why she left."

"Left where?"

"Medical school. I came home yesterday to discover she had gone."

"She quit?"

"That's right. Out of the blue. I'll bet twenty bucks that it's because of this little boy. She was obsessed with him."

It was then that Julie must have noticed the scar on the back of Clark's head. A sixth sense always told him when people discovered it, when they found out he was different. She was quiet a moment.

He didn't really care. He would be out of this apartment in a few minutes. "Let me access his labs," he said to himself.

He worked his way through a list of lab values sorted by date. He noticed the ordering physician's name had changed sometime the morning of the day before yesterday. He looked at the entry under PATIENT LOCATION and understood what must have happened. He checked a few arterial-blood-gas values just to confirm it. He whistled. "This kid almost died." He stood up and turned to Julie. "But he didn't. Can you drive me back to the hospital?"

"What happened to the playing-hooky plan?"

"Oh, I'm not going back to work. I just need to get a few facts before I go hunting for Tracy."

Clark always envied Tracy for having parents that lived only three hours away. When things got tough during the first years of medical school, or when money got tight, they would drive north to the small Massachusetts town and crash. It was a sanctuary and Tracy's parents had the good sense to leave them alone. Above all, they respected an unspoken rule: they never talked about medical school unless the students brought it up.

It was a small home, set back from its neighbors on the elm-lined street. The walkway leading to her door was cracked and covered with dead leaves. Clark ran up to the front and rang three times.

No one answered. There was no car in the drive.

Clark rang a final time, pounded on the door, and called out, *"Tracy!"*

No answer. He ran out to the mailbox leaning into the road, felt underneath for the key held in place by a small magnet, and pulled it free.

They told him he was welcome whenever he wanted to come up, that he had the same freedom of access to their home as their daughter. They made him feel as relaxed as he could in the home of his future in-laws, but now he didn't know if he was overstepping some boundary. He had always been with Tracy before.

The smell of some Italian dish, maybe a pizza, lingered in the air as he opened the door. A cat fixed its eyes on him then darted from the room. "Tracy?"

It could have been his imagination, but he thought he heard a creak overhead. Clark looked up and smiled. "Tracy, I just want to talk to you."

From above came the sound of moving feet, then she appeared at the top of the stairs. "I thought I told you I didn't want you to follow me." She was wearing a set of baggy, oversized sweats and her hair was pulled back into a ponytail. To Clark, she looked exquisite.

"Tracy, I know why you left."

"No, Clark, you don't. You never will and I don't want to hear what you have to say if you're trying to talk me out of it. I'm not going back."

Clark moved toward her. As he reached the base of the stairs she pulled back into the upstairs hallway so that her face was hidden in shadow. He spoke to her silhouette: "He's not dead, Tracy."

"I don't know what you're talking about."

"Timothy Cole. The boy they coded the morning you walked off the ward. He survived the code. They had coded him for forty minutes, but he pulled around and they managed to get enough oxygen to his brain to keep him from getting gorked."

Tracy moved toward him and eyed him suspiciously. "How do you know all this?"

"I read his goddamn chart. And I eyeballed him myself, only three hours ago, just to be sure. He was playing in his room, bouncing up and down on his bed and giggling."

Tracy sat on the top step and rested her chin in her hands. "I'm so burned out, Clark. It's only been six months on the wards and I'm just numb." She looked at him. "Or at least I thought I was until I saw Timothy in there being coded. It sort of shocked me that I still had any feelings left."

Clark climbed the stairs and sat beside her. Outside,

the wind howled against the window pane. "That scared you, didn't it?"

Tracy gave him half a smile. "I guess so. It's easier to be numb. When I first started out, I thought guys like Jeb were assholes. Now I realize they're right; it's the only way to survive."

Clark shook his head. "That's one way of dealing with things. Some people do get better, though, Tracy. They do." He lifted her chin and peered into her eyes. "I did."

She threw her arms around him and he knew she was sobbing. "Oh, Clark, I'm so tired."

"You don't have to be. Come back to us, Tracy. Please come back." She cried for a minute, then straightened up and wiped her eyes. Clark noticed a picture of her as a teenager over her shoulder. She was with some guy Clark had never met, who looked stiff and formal and hopelessly young in his tux.

"You weren't really going to stay away, were you, Tracy?"

"I don't know. God, how I wanted to." She studied Clark's face. "So he's really not dead?"

"No."

Tracy smiled. "I think I'd like to see him again."

▲
EPILOGUE
▼

Clark stared at the back of the Grunt's sunburned neck. His classmate was sitting one pew ahead of him. The chapel was too hot, and Clark had trouble focusing his mind on the dean's farewell remarks. Words about service and obligation and not harming your patients drifted through to his consciousness. All Clark really wanted was to get this ceremony over with.

Then he could begin his four weeks of vacation before internship started in July.

It was the last act of medical school, the final rite of passage. It all came down to this: a fifty-foot walk from his pew down the aisle, then onto a platform in front of his classmates. There the dean would pump his hand, whisper a few words, and give him what he had worked so hard to obtain: a rolled-up, stamped piece of paper with the words *Doctor of Medicine* beneath his name in Gothic lettering.

The two letters trailing his name would follow him for

the rest of his life. In a society that couldn't quite make up its mind if it hated or loved its doctors, Clark knew he should expect a little of both.

His mouth was dry and his robe was hot. Underneath all he wore was a tank top and shorts with flip-flop shoes. No one wore much else. The Grunt bragged about being naked, and Clark believed he probably was.

The tone of the dean's voice changed and it was obvious she was coming to the end of her remarks. "You don't need me to remind you that the career you have chosen is not an easy one. But I will. In your career, a work week of one hundred and twenty hours is not considered excessive. Internship and residency will be grueling. In the midst of it, if you can remember one thing, just one piece of advice, then I think I have served my purpose as your dean." She looked out over the audience.

"Try not to lose your naïveté. Your sense of innocence is a perishable, precious thing. It compelled you to choose a career in medicine. It sounds mawkish to say it out loud, but my sense is that each of you has that desire to help other human beings who are suffering, who are near death, who often have nowhere else to go. Please do not bury it under layers of cynicism. Without any humor, sometimes black, you will not survive; with only black humor, you will soon find yourselves bitter and burned out.

"When all the labs are drawn, when all the high-tech wizardry at your disposal is used up, it still comes down to you and your patient. Medicine ultimately consists of one human being laying hands on another and offering solace in a time of bewilderment and pain. Please, never forget that."

Clark felt an elbow in the ribs and turned to see Randy give him a thumbs-up. He had been out drinking all night the night before and Clark figured he'd probably do the same thing again that night. And then . . .

Clark didn't like to think about that. He was off to Chicago to begin a residency training program in internal medicine; Randy was going to San Francisco, where he would do a transitional year, then begin his life as a radiologist. The Grunt, to everyone's surprise, had decided to become a psychiatrist at Johns Hopkins, in Maryland.

They were together now for perhaps the last night of their lives. Never again would they all be assembled under one roof. As Clark looked around he saw faces he knew he might not see again, and something inside him tightened.

Then he saw Tracy. She was sitting beside him, her hair tightly braided, her face brown from a month of swimming and lounging in the sun. She had had enough credits to finish a month early, and Clark convinced her to take time off and do absolutely nothing.

She followed his advice.

Their wedding, like everything in their medical-school career, had felt rushed. Somehow they had wedged a honeymoon into their medical-student schedules. Somehow they had managed to pay for the ceremony, rings, dress, and flowers and countless other expenses that a wedding entailed.

And somehow Tracy had managed to get pregnant.

She was entering her second trimester and was beginning to show. Clark reached over and patted her belly and Tracy giggled, draping her hand over his knuckles and pulling it into her side. Clark thought he could hear the growing infant's pulse as Tracy held his hand and they listened to the dean's final words.

"The world of medicine you are entering today is one vastly different from the one I entered twenty-seven years ago. Most of you will be sued at least once for medical malpractice, something that was almost unheard of when I began training. You will spend one fifth of your time completing insurance forms and trying to justify the subtleties of your medical decisions to some clerk or administrator who has never taken care of a patient. The number of tests, procedures, and medications you have at your disposal is exponentially higher than anything I ever would have dreamed of as an intern. To succeed in medicine, you must master them all, and keep up with the ones that are just being developed. It is a daunting task, but one I am confident you can accomplish.

"Medicine will never be a forty-hour-a-week job. At the same time you must learn to carve out a space for yourself and your families. If you do not, you will become a statistic, a grim reminder that physicians' suicide, divorce, and substance-abuse rates are so much higher than that of the general population."

Clark's hand froze on Tracy's belly. He felt a spasm of fear and couldn't identify exactly why. She stroked his hand.

"It's not an easy job you've chosen," the dean continued. "You will be comfortably reimbursed, but few of you will be wealthy, despite the popular stereotype of the rich doctor. You will often be misunderstood and frequently misjudged. As you walk up here tonight you will become physicians. May you be good ones. Now would you please rise for the Hippocratic oath."

Randy leaned toward Clark and whispered, "Cheery talk, eh?"

"I knew I should have become a lawyer."

"Or a chiropractor."

Tracy placed a finger to her lips and frowned at them. "Shhh!"

The dean waited until the entire class was on its feet. Of the one hundred and forty-two queasy recent college graduates who had filed into the gross-anatomy lab four years earlier, one hundred and twenty-four now stood and recited:

> I do solemnly swear by whatever I hold most sacred, that I will be loyal to the profession of medicine and just and generous to its members.
>
> That I will lead my life and practice my Art in uprightness and honor.
>
> That into whatsoever home I shall enter it shall

be for the good of the sick and the well to the utmost of my power and that I will hold myself aloof from wrong and from corruption and from the tempting of others to vice.

That I will exercise my Art, solely for the cure of my patients and the prevention of disease and will give no drugs and perform no operation for a criminal purpose and far less suggest such thing.

That whatsoever I shall see or hear of the lives of men which is not fitting to be spoken, I will keep inviolably secret.

These things I do promise and in proportion as I am faithful to this oath, may happiness and good repute be ever mine, the opposite if I shall be forsworn.

Then Clark sat again and waited for his name to be called. First they graduated the top-ten ranking students, then the rest of the class in alphabetical order. That meant Clark had a long wait.

He felt a terrible sense of foreboding, as though something terrible would happen just now, just as he had reached this point that he had worked so hard to attain. It would be too cruel, but it would be his luck.

So when he heard his name echoing off the walls of the chapel, it caught him almost by surprise. He rose, feeling his bare legs brush against the billowing, velvety robe, nudging Tracy's knee as he squeezed past her, making his way down the aisle and up the three steps to where his dean stood, holding a white tube that contained his medical degree.

"Congratulations, Dr. Wilson."

He had been through so many graduations before that he didn't think this one would affect him as much as it did. There had been college and high school and before that some junior-high-school celebration that was only a fuzzy memory. Each ending was a beginning, and each beginning was an ending.

Tracy gave him a bear hug when he reached his seat. Then it was over and a new class of physicians was released into the world.

They poured out of the stifling chapel to the sound of Wagner piped over the chapel's organ. Clark knew this was only the beginning, that the real work began in July, that all this was only preparation for the real trial of internship, but he didn't care. He just wanted to bask in this moment as his mother searched for his face and flash-bulbs blinded him. It was intoxicating and tacky and hot and he just wanted to go out with Randy and the Grunt, maybe for the last time in their lives.

And as they spilled onto the street Clark could see it out of the corner of his eye, two blocks down and on the right: the alabaster phalanx of Rosemont Medical Center. The blue-and-white strobe light blinked at them from the helipad on the top of the building. And even from where they stood, they could hear the scream of the Life Flight helicopter's turbine engines coming to life and the *wop-wop* of its blades. Farther in the distance an ambulance wailed.

Randy put an arm around Clark's shoulders. "You know what I think when I hear that sound? More business."

Clark turned to him. "It's funny. Whenever I used to hear an ambulance, my first thought was for the patient. Was it some guy with a heart attack or a little old lady pulled out of a wrecked car? Now the sound of an ambulance makes me think of the intern on call, of that sinking feeling you get when you're about to get another admission."

The Grunt shrugged. "We've all been a little desensitized. It's natural and inevitable."

Randy rolled his eyes. "Grunt, ever since you decided to become a shrink, you've got a buzzword for everything."

"Which, of course," Tracy added, "is 'natural and inevitable.'"

The Grunt glared at them. "That's *Doctor* Grunt now."

The wailing of the ambulance grew louder and the red-and-white lights appeared from around a corner. The siren drowned out all thought of conversation. As the ambulance whooshed by, Clark caught a glimpse through a small window of a paramedic in the back of the vehicle hanging an IV.

The ambulance turned toward Rosemont Medical Center and disappeared.

They were silent a moment, staring after it like children. Then Clark took Tracy's hand, Randy muttered a joke to the Grunt that no one else heard, and they moved toward their waiting families.

Mark Vakkur attended Duke University School of Medicine and is currently completing a residency in psychiatry while working on his next novel. He graduated from West Point, which was the setting for his earlier novel, *A Matter of Trust*. He lives in Durham, North Carolina, with his wife, Susan, who is also a physician.

MORE THAN FRIENDS
Barbara Delinsky
The Maxwells and the Popes are two families whose lives are interwoven like the threads of a beautiful, yet ultimately delicate, tapestry. When their idyllic lives are unexpectedly shattered by one event, their faith in each other — and in themselves — is put to the supreme test.

"Intriguing women's fiction." — *Publishers Weekly*

CITY OF GOLD
Len Deighton
Amid the turmoil of World War II, Rommel's forces in Egypt relentlessly advance across the Sahara aided by ready access to Allied intelligence. Sent to Cairo on special assignment, Captain Bert Cutler's mission is formidable: whatever the risk, whatever the cost, he must catch Rommel's spy.

"Wonderful." — *Seattle Times/Post-Intelligencer*

DEATH PENALTY
William J. Coughlin
Former hot-shot attorney Charley Sloan gets a chance to resurrect his career with the case of a lifetime — an extortion scam that implicates his life-long mentor, a respected judge. Battling against inner demons and corrupt associates, Sloan's quest for the truth climaxes in one dramatic showdown of justice.

"Superb!"
— *The Detroit News*